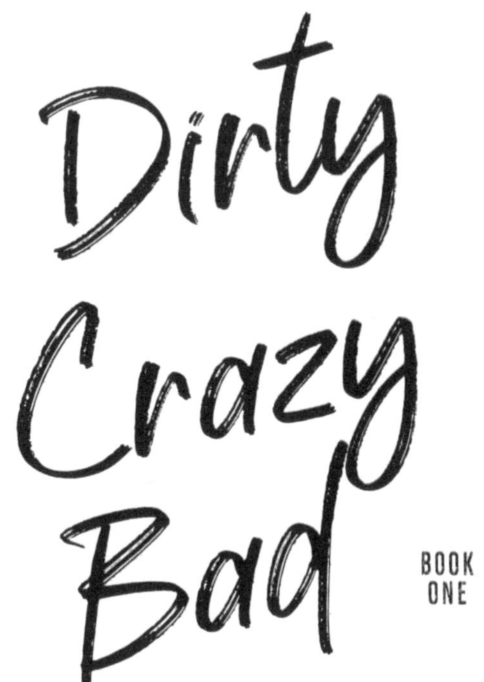

BOOK ONE

USA TODAY & WSJ BESTSELLING AUTHOR

SIOBHAN DAVIS

ISBN-13: 978-1-959194-28-6

Edited by Kelly Hartigan (XterraWeb) editing.xterraweb.com

Proofread by Amanda (Drafthouse Editorial Services), Aundi Marie, Nicki SG, and Carolyne Belso

Cover design and luminary symbol design by Shannon Passmore of Shanoff Designs

Licensed interior imagery – © depositphotos.com

Licensed cover imagery - background © adobe.com and © bigstockphoto.com

Licensed cover imagery - skull image © shutterstock.com

Formatted by Ciara Turley using Vellum

In the secret society of The Luminaries, no sin will go unpunished...

Sleeping with my boyfriend's best friend, behind his girlfriend's back, probably wasn't my smartest idea.

But Jase is *mine,* and it's about time Julia knew it.

Attending Lowell University was supposed to be a fresh start. A chance to end all the sneaking around and make our relationship official.

I couldn't have been more wrong.

Julia is digging her claws into Jase.

My boyfriend, Chad, is getting in deeper with a local gang.

And my loathsome new stepbrother, Ares, has just moved in.

Ares despises Chad and Jase, and the feeling is mutual. As their rivalry escalates, Ares seems determined to use me as a pawn, and I'm trapped in the middle. It doesn't help that he's hot AF, knows exactly how to push my buttons, and my body hasn't gotten the memo he's off-limits.

I wish that were the least of my worries.

Pride. Wrath. Lust. Envy. Greed. Gluttony. Sloth.

My life turns upside down the moment the dark secret society of The Luminaries is revealed to me.

Everything I thought I knew was a lie.

Now, I have lost all control over my future, and a heart-breaking new reality emerges.

One where lovers become enemies, enemies become allies, and corrupting sinners to sin is my only way to survive.

Note from the Author

This is a dark college reverse harem romance with bullying/enemies-to-lovers themes and mature content. It is not recommended for readers under the age of eighteen. Contains graphic language and sexual content including some non-con/dub-con scenes. Some scenes may be triggering for readers. I cannot be specific without ruining the story. If you are concerned about a particular trigger, please email me. For a list of triggers, refer to my website.

This is a duet, and that means you will get some answers to the plot in this book, but you will have to wait for the rest of the answers in book two. The same statement applies to the romance. This *IS* a reverse harem romance, meaning Ashley will end up in a consensual, loving relationship with three men or more by the time the duet concludes. The relationships all develop differently and at different times and will not be finalized until book two.

Thank you for reading and enjoy!

Siobhán.

siobhan@siobhandavis.com

Prologue
Ashley

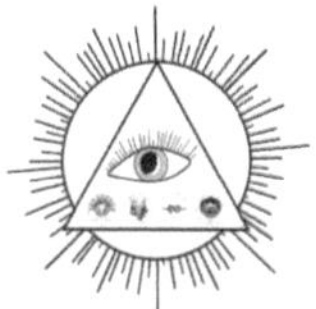

The door slams against the wall as I stumble into my bedroom on shaky legs. Reaching behind me, I shove it closed, instantly muting the sounds of the party raging downstairs in the lower level of the townhome I share with my boyfriend, Chad, and my loathsome stepbrother, Ares. The place is packed with coeds, jocks, members of frats and sororities, and our personal friends from Lowell University. Along with the degenerates Ares is hanging out with tonight.

The room spins, and I sway a little as I hold on to the wall while removing my heels and kicking them away. I'm not feeling so hot as I flop down on my king-sized bed, staring up at the stark white ceiling, wondering why I thought it was a good idea to drink so much.

Usually, I am pretty smart when it comes to alcohol. Drinking enough to generate a nice buzz without losing control of myself.

Tonight is different.

Tonight, I am trying to forget my broken heart.

Seeing him walk through the door with *her* draped all over him sent me over the edge. I knew I would never survive the party unless I blotted it all out and numbed myself to the harsh reality of my current existence.

Pain slices across my chest as intense as if someone has plunged a knife into my flesh.

A lone sob travels up my throat, surging for freedom, and it's an anguished, strangled, desolate sound as it rips from my lips.

Fuck, it hurts.

It's not getting any easier.

Turning on my side, I pull my knees up to my chest and wrap my arms around myself as if that will keep me together.

Everything is turning to shit, and I seem powerless to stop it.

The more I learn about the secret world of The Luminaries, the more I lose control of my life. Sometimes, I wish I had a time machine so I could go back to senior year of high school and warn myself of the danger lying in wait for me when I started college.

To think my biggest worry coming here was extracting Chad from the deal he made with The Sainthood.

Gang warfare is a normal way of life in this part of California, but The Luminaries make The Sainthood and The Bulls look like kindergarteners.

What a fucking joke.

It's not true what they say—ignorance *isn't* bliss.

Most everyone in my life was hiding huge secrets from me, and I was walking around, living a lie, like the biggest fool.

I have been ignorant my entire life, largely thanks to my mom and her misguided sense of protection. Blood boils under my skin as Pamela's image surfaces in my mind's eye. I dig my nails into my knees, enraged as I think of all the ways she has fucked up my life. Some mother she turned out to be.

Music blares, hurting my ears, and a burst of light from the hallway has me squinting in the darkened room as the door swings open. I glance over, scrubbing my eyes as a tall, muscular form kicks the door shut with a booted foot before stalking toward me. His familiar hulking frame is a shadowy blur as he strides across the room.

"I want to be alone, Chad," I say, my words slurring slightly. I angle my face away without looking at him. Things have been increasingly strained between me and my boyfriend since arriving at Lowell University a few months ago.

Especially these past few weeks.

I'm not the only one who has lost Jase. I met Jase through Chad, and it was my boyfriend who proposed I take his best friend as my lover too. They have been best friends and teammates on the football team for years. This is the first time they have stopped talking to one another, and I'm not sure if the damage to their relationship can ever be repaired.

The bed dips as Chad climbs up behind me, ignoring my wishes, as per usual. Warmth coats my back as he presses his long, hard, ripped body up against me. Firm fingers land on my hip as he thrusts his hard-on against my ass. Lust stirs low in my belly despite my frustration and melancholy. Pushing my hair aside, he plants a slew of drugging kisses along my neck, and my skin tingles from his addictive touch. I close my eyes, and my drunken brain conjures my dreams to life. I imagine it's Jase touching me, eliciting little moans and whimpers, and dampening my panties as Chad's hands begin to wander.

Shoving those images aside, I am immediately remorseful and shamefaced. Chad doesn't deserve to have me check out on him, no matter how fragile our relationship is right now. We haven't had sex in weeks, and I need to feel closer to my boyfriend.

I can't lose him too.

Notes of citrus, spice, and sandalwood tickle my nostrils as he moves, and the heady scent of his cologne hits me like a direct stab to the heart.

I would know that scent anywhere.

My eyes pop wide in realization, and I attempt to turn around, but firm hands stop me. My heart is thrashing against my rib cage, pounding in excitement as adrenaline charges through my veins and lust elevates my arousal to dizzy heights.

He came looking for me.

Jase is here.

Touching me. Kissing me. Holding me. Comforting me.

Does he miss me as much as I miss him? Does he walk around with a constant pain in his heart and an ache in his soul?

I need to see him. To peer into his gorgeous emerald-green eyes as I reclaim his lips. I attempt to turn around again, but he stops me once more, and my newfound hope stutters to a halt.

He won't face me because nothing has changed.

He can never be mine.

This is as much as he can offer me.

But it's not enough.

It never will be.

That horrific night replays in my mind, like it often has these past couple of weeks, and my heart ruptures again in my chest as the pain of his betrayal slays me anew. His arms tighten around me in the dark, holding me steady as I thrash around, desperate to get away from him before my treacherous body gives me away.

No matter how much I want this, want *him*, I can't give in.

But it's not that simple.

Every nerve ending on my body craves his touch, and I'm like an addict chasing a high I know isn't good for me, but I'm struggling to resist.

I'm waging an inner battle as much as I'm fighting him.

How can I still want him after everything he has done?

My body so needs to get with the program. Determined to be stronger than my base desires, I continue fighting him, trying to escape his embrace, but it's a weak effort, at best. My head is at war with my body and my heart, and my inebriated limbs can't muster the appropriate strength to get away from him because my man is ripped. Tall, strong, muscular, and a force to be reckoned with.

No longer *your* man, my snide inner voice reminds me. *He never truly was*, the voice adds, driving the knife in deeper.

No matter how futile it is, I continue to fight, thrashing around in his solid hold. "Fuck off, Jase," I hiss. "I don't need you. Don't want you," I lie. "Go back to that bitch." I grip his arms, ready to drag my nails through his flesh if it's the only way I can break free, but my fingers meet material. My brows knit together as I look down at the long sleeves of the dress shirt he's wearing. Jase doesn't dress like this. Anger churns in my gut. This is *her* influence. She's already turning him into something he's not.

I hate her.

As much as I hate The Luminaries and their stupid rules and traditions.

And I have a hate-love thing going on with the man currently holding me to him. I hate Jase for what he did to me, yet I can't stop loving him. I wish there was an off switch in my heart and my head so I could bury those feelings and forget I ever loved Jason Stewart.

"Let me go," I snap, digging my nails into his clothed arms and lashing out with my legs.

One beefy leg clamps down on mine, restricting my movement, as I sense, rather than see, him shaking his head. His lips go on the offensive, planting addictive kisses along my neck and my jawline, his teeth tugging on my earlobe before his mouth suctions on that sensitive spot just under my ear.

He isn't playing fair.

Fuck him to the high heavens.

I am losing the battle and I know it.

If he's so determined this is happening, maybe I'll let it. A good hate fuck might be just what I need to sever the lingering ties to my ex. It might be good to remind him of what he has destroyed. And if it gets back to *her*, it'll be the cherry on top.

Let her know she'll never have him the way I did.

The intense chemistry and connection we share will never be broken.

Jase will never love her the way I know he loves me.

He chose me in a way he never chose her.

What good is having a man if he's forced to be with you?

She might think she's won, but she's lost. She will always know he's unfaithful and that he's still in love with me. She will always know he's incapable of loving her.

It doesn't sound like much fun.

He may no longer be mine, but at least I know what we had was real.

So, I stop fighting, going placid in his arms.

If this is the last time I get to be with him like this, I am not going to deny myself what I need right now.

I will fuck him one last time, and then I'm moving on and shutting him out completely.

His fingers trail up my leg, and he moves my thighs apart while keeping me on my side, rocking his erection against my ass through our clothes. Closing my eyes, I succumb to the myriad of sensations rioting in my body. A whimper escapes my lips when his hand continues its upward trajectory. Brushing his fingers against my lace-covered pussy, he rubs me aggressively through the flimsy material for a couple minutes, rocketing my arousal into the stratosphere.

Cool air wafts over the bare cheeks of my ass when he lifts my dress from behind and pulls my panties down. Shoving them to my knees, he leaves them there, like a restraint, as he repositions my legs so he has access to my weeping cunt. The arm around my waist moves lower, joining his other hand as he parts my pussy lips with his thumbs before driving two fingers inside me.

I can't see his wicked smile, but I know it's there as his fingers glide easily through my slick channel. Wrapping my long hair around his fist, he tugs my head back slightly, enough to grant him greater access to my neck. I keep my eyes closed as he peppers kisses along my neck, my collarbone, and the swells of my ample breasts.

If he insists on doing this without looking at me, I'm going to do the same—we can pretend together.

A grunt tumbles free from my lips when he tweaks my nipples through my dress, sending darts of desire shooting to my core. He tugs roughly on the hardened peaks and a pleasurable painful sensation ricochets across my sensitive skin. I'm not even aware I'm rotating my hips and riding his hand until he adds another digit and increases his pace. My climax is already building because Jase is just that good. Releasing my hair, he continues pumping his fingers in and out of me as his thumb makes circles on my swollen clit, swirling my juices around my tightening bud as I chase a familiar high.

I shriek in surprise when his free hand lands on my bare ass with a sharp slap. My pussy throbs with need, pulsing and gushing as he lands a succession of hard slaps on my ass. I'm not in the least bit surprised when his thumb presses against my puckered hole because Jase is a big fan of anal.

Memories of better times flip through my mind on a loop. Happy times spent with both my guys in bed as we explored and fucked for hours, none of us ever getting enough. Our insatiable fucking never satisfying us for long.

I come apart at the seams, shattering completely the instant he plunges two fingers all the way into my ass. My pussy clenches around his fingers in my cunt while I tighten and pulse around the digits in my ass. I'm a writhing mess of hormones and incoherent mumbles as he works my body like a pro.

I don't even hear his zipper lowering in my blissed-out drunken state. A scream rips from my mouth when he thrusts his cock in me in one claiming stroke, pushing so far inside it feels like he's nudging my womb. He's half draped over my back as he fucks into me, pushing my body farther into the bed with my face mushed against the comforter. The angle is a little awkward, but the constriction of my legs makes him seem fuller and bigger inside me, his thrusting tighter, hotter, and so much more.

"Yes," I hiss, rocking my ass back against him as he drives his big dick into my cunt in a feverish pace, rutting in and out like a wild savage, brutalizing me in a way that speaks volumes.

This is an elevated form of hate fucking. And. I. Am. Here. For. It.

He slams in and out of me over and over, and I'm moaning and whimpering like this is the first time I've had sex. Sex is always phenomenal with my guys, but this is next level.

Why does his dick feel so much bigger at this angle? And is that...?

A primitive groan filters from my mouth as I feel the additional friction sliding against my inner walls, and it clicks into place. "You got your dick pierced," I rasp, reaching back to grab hold of his ass because I need to be touching him. "I never thought you'd do it." I squeeze his ass as I pivot my hips, as best as I can from this angle, working in sync with his rough thrusts. I feel impossibly full, and the sensations his magical cock is evoking in me is out of this world.

In the past, I have suggested the guys get some metal in their cocks, but neither Chad nor Jase seemed interested, so I hadn't pushed my agenda. Now, I wish I had pushed harder, because ho-lee fucking shit, nothing feels better than this. "Oh my god, Jase," I pant when stars burst behind my closed eyes. "That feels incredible."

A dark chuckle ripples through the air, raising goose bumps all over my arms. My pulse picks up, and my heart beats faster against my rib cage as an ominous sense of dread sweeps over me.

I stop moving.

Stop breathing.

His hand wraps firmly around my throat as he presses his mouth to my ear. "Wrong dick. Try again." His warm breath fans across my earlobe while his fingers grip my neck painfully.

This cannot be happening.

"No!" I croak, pushing past my restricted airway as he continues fucking me. "No! Stop!"

This time, his chuckle is downright menacing as he rams his dick inside me like he's trying to stab me with the damn thing. "Don't pretend you don't love my dick inside you, slutty little sis. You're so wet I'm practically drowning. Your hungry cunt is hugging my cock so hard it's almost suffocating it."

"I thought you were Jase!" I scream, clawing at Ares's arm as his fingers squeeze my neck.

"No, you didn't. Deep down, you knew it was me."

I don't dignify that with a response because I'm terrified he speaks the truth. "Get off!" I yell, my voice raspy and strained. "Get the fuck away from me!" I try to pull off his dick, but it's impossible at this angle. His hand locks on to my hip, holding me in place as he continues driving his monster cock into my slick channel. Angry tears prick my eyes, but I refuse to let them fall. I won't give my despicable stepbrother the satisfaction. Not when he's already reveling in my bodily reactions. I hate how I'm still reacting to him, and I bite the inside of my cheek to stop myself from crying out in pleasure.

"Stop lying to yourself. You're fucking loving this, and Jase doesn't want you. He used you up and tossed you aside when you passed your sell-by date," Ares cruelly replies. "I saw him in the hallway on my way to your room. He was balls deep in his fiancée, and she was screaming his name as she exploded all over his dick."

His words dig deep, carving new scars in my heart. "I hate you," I rasp, the words squeezing out of my narrowed airway.

"Now, now, dollface, let's stop with all the lies."

He thrusts deep inside me, and I almost come again. Biting down hard on my lip, I trap my moans because I'd rather choke on my tongue than let him know how much I'm enjoying this.

"You might think you hate me, but your greedy cunt says otherwise," he taunts.

"My body is responding the way it would to any dick inside me," I lie. "But I don't want this. I don't want you. I want you to stop. If you don't, I'll scream."

"Go for it." He bites my ear, and a choked scream tears from my throat. "There's no one up here to rescue you, and no one downstairs will hear over the music."

In a lightning-fast move, I'm flipped onto my back as he straddles my thighs. The instant his hand releases my throat, I suck in greedy lungsful of air, and then I lunge for him, reaching to slap him, but he's quick, restraining my wrists in one of his meaty hands. He tut-tuts. "Always so eager for violence."

"Only when it comes to you," I bark.

It's embarrassing how easily he restrains me with his powerful thighs and one firm hand. His free hand reaches behind him to his jeans, which are pooled halfway down his legs, and he yanks his belt free. I buck and writhe underneath him, but it's pointless because he's got at least eighty pounds on me, and he's fueled by months of pent-up aggression when it comes to me. Hooking his belt around the top of my bedframe, he loops it around my wrists, securing it tightly.

My back arches off the bed as my arms stretch over my head, and I try to buck him off, but it's useless. My legs are still restrained at the knees by my panties, and he's too heavy. He barely even moves as I work up a sweat trying to get him away from me.

"Chad!" I roar, ignoring the soreness in my neck as I scream for my boyfriend, hoping he'll miraculously show up and save me.

Ares chuckles as he slides down my body and climbs off the bed. "Are you sure you want your boyfriend to come up here? I doubt he'll be sympathetic when he hears what we've been up to and how incredible you think my dick is." He puts his smug face all up in mine as I wrestle with the belt securing my wrists to the headboard.

"You're going to pay for this, asshole," I snap before I resume screaming for help.

In an unexpected move, Ares rips my panties from my legs and stuffs them in my mouth, grinning like the maniac he is as my muffled shouts go nowhere. Anger churns in my gut, and I react on instinct. Swinging my leg to the side, I shove my foot into his upper thigh, narrowly missing my intended target. Ares falls back a little, chuckling with amusement as a scowl spreads across my face. A growl forms at the back of my throat as I wriggle on the bed, pleased when my movements cause my dress to lower, hiding my bare pussy. I'm sweating from all the exertion involved in trying to get free, and strands of my hair are plastered to my face.

Adrenaline courses through my veins as I watch Ares kick off his boots, jeans, and boxers before whipping his shirt over his head in a typical one-armed guy move. He is completely naked, standing before me like a resurrected Greek god, teasingly stroking his dick and licking his lips. He hovers over me like a looming dark threat, a salacious smug grin curling the corners of his lush mouth.

Desire coils low in my belly, and my pussy throbs with raw need. Heat flares in my cheeks as my body reacts to the jerk, and I fucking hate it.

I hate I'm so attracted to him.

Why isn't there a pill I can pop to cure this disease?

Purposely, I jerk my head to the side, not wanting him to see me ogling his naked body.

Ares has spent months parading around the house naked and semi-naked, in a deliberate move to piss me and Chad off, and I know what I'll see if I let my eyes linger—a body carved straight from my fantasies. Powerful thighs. Chiseled abs. Broad chest. Rippling biceps. V-shaped indents at his hips. A monster cock with impressive piercings laddering the underside of his shaft.

Ares is not shy about whipping his dick out any chance he gets. It's where my new obsession with metal has come from. He's not shy about any part of his body, and who could blame him? He's all sharp lines, hard edges, and rock-solid muscle—a testament to hours of daily dedication in the gym.

But it doesn't matter how hot his body is. He's a crazy

motherfucker with a giant chip on his shoulder. Chad hates him, for obvious reasons, and the feeling is mutual.

"Fuck the hell off," I shout when he climbs back on the bed, aiming for me. My words are muffled behind my gag, but he doesn't need to hear it to know what I've said.

"Nah," he replies, stroking his monster dick. "I'm just getting started." His grin is downright evil as he pushes my dress up to my waist, parts my thighs, and spreads them wide. I fight him, trying to close my legs, but he tightens his grip on my inner thighs and forces them wider.

Dipping his head, he blows across my exposed pussy, chuckling when my hips buck of their own volition. Angry tears prick my eyes as I resume an internal battle. My entire body jolts when he slides his hot tongue up and down my slit, and I let my tears fall as my body responds positively to his touch. Frustration comingles with anger, fear, and lust as he thrusts his tongue inside me and buries his face in my pussy.

I close my eyes, unable to bear witness to this.

Ares knows what he's doing.

This is his payback. He waited until the most opportune moment to catch me vulnerable and drive the knife in all the way.

He knows this will be my utter ruination.

Like I know nothing short of a miracle can stop this from happening.

"Salty and sweet," he says in a voice that's gruff and deep. "My favorite flavor." Plunging three fingers inside me, he drives them in and out in rough strokes. "I could eat you all night, but you don't deserve it."

Air trickles over my chest when he shoves my dress up higher and removes my bra. My eyes pop open as pain shoots through my body when he bites down on my nipple, tugging on it with his teeth as he continues shoving his fingers inside me. Angry tears leak from my eyes as he plucks my body like a damn guitar. He alternates his attention from one breast to another, sucking, biting, and licking, and I'm so fucked because I like it.

I really like it.

But he will never know that.

Narrowing my eyes, I glare at him because it's the only power I have.

Except my fucked-up stepbrother likes it.

"Keep pretending if you like, but we both know you don't want me to stop."

I glare harder at him, trying to deny the mountain my body is ascending in a rush to reach the peak. Just as I'm there, ready to fall off the cliff, Ares yanks his fingers out of me with a smirk, denying my body its release.

More frustrated tears cling to the corners of my lashes, and I scream behind the panties in my mouth. In my head, I toss obscenities at him and plot creative ways to murder the fucker.

Lifting my legs, he forces them back until my knees are pressed up against my stomach and I'm spread wide before him. "Look at you," he says in a voice thick with need. His eyes are glued to my exposed pussy and ass as he pumps his dick hard in his free hand while licking his lips. "You're dripping," he adds, gathering my pussy juices on his fingers before smearing them around my puckered hole. Panic mixes with molten desire when he pushes his thumb into my ass. "I would fuck you here, but you'd like it too much." His eyes are dark pools of wicked intent when he lifts them to meet mine as he removes his thumb. "This isn't a reward. It's a punishment."

His body covers mine as he presses me down into the mattress. "I meant what I said that first day I was at your house with my mom. I won't stop until I've ruined you, dollface." His fingers sweep over my cheeks as his erection presses against my raised leg. "It's what you all deserve." He grips my chin painfully, tilting my face up. "You should make wiser choices in the future."

Pressing my raised legs back farther against my upper body, he stretches my limbs almost painfully as he brings his thick cock to my entrance. His engorged head is leaking precum as he rubs it against my folds. Fear spikes in my blood as he slams inside me without a condom. This cannot be happening. I'm not on birth control right now, so pregnancy and STDs are a concern. Who knows where his giant dick has been?

I glare at him as he fucks into me, helpless to stop him. His devilish grin expands as he nips at my breasts with his teeth, tugging my sore hard nipples as he pummels my pussy with manic energy. Lifting up on his knees, he keeps one arm across my bent legs to hold me in place while raising my hips and shoving into me deeper.

He fucks me raw, pounding and thrusting into me like a demented man. Sweat glistens on his ink-covered chest as he screws me into the bed and tightens his grip on me in a way I know will leave bruises.

But that's the least of my worries now because he's edging me, and I'm close to the brink of insanity. Every time my orgasm rises and I'm ready to fall apart, he stops, stilling his cock and halting his fingers.

And every time, I cry inside in sheer frustration.

He will pay for this. The gloves are off this time, and it's all-out fucking war now.

Beyond frustrated, I shout against the gag in my mouth and move what parts of my body I can even though I know there is no way I can break free. I refuse to lie here docile and just take it.

His dark chuckle is quickly becoming my least favorite sound as he smirks at me with amusement. "You can try to deny this all you want, but your body gives you away every time. Your cunt can't get enough of my cock," he says, sliding it in and out in a more leisurely fashion. "It doesn't matter what you say; Chad will never believe I forced you into this. Not when he sees the evidence."

Pressure sits on my chest as alarm bells screech in my ears at his words. It's how he's able to untie his belt from my headboard and flip me around until I'm on my stomach. My wrists are still restrained at my back when he lifts me up on my knees and slams back inside me. We are both kneeling on the bed with my back to his sweat-slickened chest and his cock buried deep inside my cunt when he grips my chin and angles my head toward my bedside table. His cell is propped up against my lamp, and I see the flashing red light, confirming he's recording this.

Silent tears spill down my cheeks as he pivots his hips and fucks into me from behind.

His thrusts are rough, aggressive, possessive, celebratory, and all the fight seeps out of me.

One muscular arm traps me across my middle while his free hand covers my gagged mouth as he picks up his pace and screws the shit out of me. "Come, slutty little sis. Come all over my cock like you've been dying to." His fingers creep down my stomach, reaching my clit and rubbing aggressively. The second he pinches my oversensitive bud, I explode, detonating into a thousand tiny pieces, hating how much pleasure he has given me while simultaneously destroying me.

Ares continues fucking me after my climax has abated before pulling out and pushing me flat on my back. Kneeling over me, his winning smirk pins me in place as he fucks his hand in a fast skillful manner. A loud roar bounces off the walls, and his dick jerks as he starts to come. Ropes of hot cum stream over my bare breasts and across my face as he unleashes his release all over me, completing the ruination.

I know what he's done.

I know what happens next.

I just lost Chad too.

Chapter One
Ashley

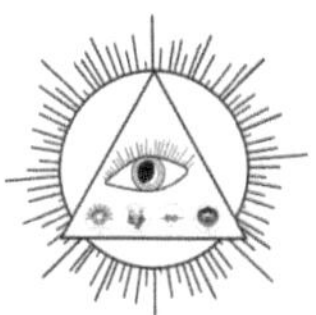

3 months earlier - Start of Freshman Year of College

"This is the start of a wonderful new adventure," Hera—my stepmom—says, bundling me into her arms. "College is such an amazing experience, and I want you to enjoy every moment."

"I'll try." I grin as I pass the last suitcase to my boyfriend Chad. He pecks my lips briefly while throwing a glare at Hera before stalking off with my bag to load it in the back of his truck.

Pain flits over Hera's face for a second, like it always does when she's in Chad's company.

We ignore that interaction, like usual. There isn't much more to be said on the subject.

"I hope you like your new home." She brushes strands of

long, wavy midnight-black hair away from her face. "Your mom and I tried to design it with your style in mind."

Mom and Dad bought a townhome close to Lowell University as a surprise for me. Mom visited from Switzerland with her new husband, Richard, and their cute four-month-old baby daughter, Emilie, in tow for a couple of weeks to work with Hera on the interior design. I knew nothing about it until three nights ago, believing I was moving into an apartment on campus with my boyfriend.

"I'll believe that when I see it," I murmur under my breath. It's not like Mom has ever done much for me or done anything my way. I'm betting when I get there it's all minimalistic and cold with stark white walls and little color. Although, if Hera had any say, I might be in luck.

My stepmom is the complete opposite of my mother. It's almost like my dad purposely set out to find a woman who was the antithesis of Pamela Stewart.

My dad is head over heels in love for the first time in his life, and it wasn't difficult to warm to Hera. We jelled fast after I met her last October despite initial reservations. I was shocked at how sudden and unexpected it all was. Plus, there was the Chad situation. I naturally sided with my boyfriend at first. Until she explained and I got to know her better and realized she's not responsible for what happened.

Chad doesn't believe it, and that's his prerogative. It has made things super awkward though. He refuses to hang out at my house if Hera or Ares is there.

Now, Hera's obnoxious son is an entirely different matter. I'm fully with Chad in that regard. Ares and Chad have already come to blows several times, and mention of his name instantly puts me in a bad mood. However, I refuse to let that crazy motherfucker occupy any of my headspace today. Today is a good day, and I won't let Ares Haynes ruin it for me.

My dad, Douglas Shaw, married Hera five months ago, and she has been more of a mother to me this past year than my own mother has been in my eighteen, almost nineteen, years on this planet.

I expect Mom wants a pat on the back because she sacrificed time with her new family to work with Hera on furnishing and decorating the place I will call home for the next four years.

I'm not ungrateful, but she all but abandoned me last year, and she wasn't around the previous couple of years either. I have pretty much been on my own since I was sixteen, so it will take a lot more for me to find forgiveness in my heart.

Dad is trying, and I'm giving him the benefit of the doubt. For now at least.

"Ready, babe?" Chad asks, interrupting my inner monologue as he comes up behind me, wrapping his arm around my waist and nuzzling his nose into my hair to avoid looking at my stepmom.

Hera wets her lips in an anxious tell and steps back. She glances at her cell. "Your dad wanted to see you off. He should be here any minute now. He left the conference early on purpose."

Chad radiates anger as his arm tightens around my waist, and I know we need to get out of here before things escalate.

"I'm not sure why Dad felt it was necessary. We spoke on Tuesday before he flew to Seattle," I say.

Hera runs a hand through her hair. "He wanted to speak to you about, uh, a new development."

A frown creases my brow. "What new development?"

"I really think it's best if we tell you together."

"Can we please go?" Chad whispers in my ear. "You know how I feel about that woman."

I exhale heavily, hating that Chad despises Hera so thoroughly. His hatred for Ares I understand and share. But I trust Hera when she says there is more to the situation. It would help if she explained, but she says it's complicated and she can't go into details because it's likely to upset Chad even more.

I really don't see how whatever Hera is hiding could make it worse, but I don't push her.

It's not like Chad would listen to a word she says anyway.

"Sorry, but we've got to hit the road." I lean in and kiss her cheek as Chad walks toward his truck. "Tell Dad to call me." It's not like we're going far away. The private university is only a forty-minute drive to the northern tip of my hometown of Lowell. If it's urgent, he can always come visit.

She chews on her lower lip, opening and closing her mouth, looking conflicted for a few seconds. "Okay, love. I'll get him to call you."

I climb into Chad's truck, waving at Hera as my boyfriend peels out of my driveway.

Tense silence fills the cabin as Chad turns out onto the road, and I hate it. Going to college together is supposed to be a new beginning, and I don't want to start off on the wrong foot. Reaching across, I rest my hand on Chad's thigh while I lean over and kiss his cheek. "I don't want to fight, babe. Not today."

A heavy sigh pitches from his lips. "I don't want to either, sweetheart." He takes his eyes off the road for a split second to look at me. "I love you, and I'm excited to be moving in together. It's just every time I see that woman, or that fucking asshole she spawned, it puts me in an instant bad mood."

"Ares does the same to me," I admit, rubbing my hand up and down his leg in what I hope is a soothing gesture. "But Hera is different. If you got to know her, you'd see."

"She fucked my family over, Ash!" he bellows, grinding his teeth and gripping the steering wheel tight.

No, your father did. I think it but I don't say it, silently berating myself for saying anything.

"I know you think she's great because she lavishes attention on you and your mother is seriously lacking on the maternal skills front, but that doesn't mean she's a good person. She's not."

I whip my hand back, glaring at my boyfriend. "Fuck you, Chad. Don't make out like I'm some needy little girl begging for any scraps my stepmom throws my way. It's not like that with us." If anything, Hera is the best friend I never had.

"She screwed my dad behind my mom's back, breaking up their marriage and destroying our family. She was the catalyst that started everything," he says, his voice rising as his emotions go into overdrive. "My dad is dead because of that woman."

I can't let that go. Swiveling on my seat, I turn to face my boyfriend as he takes the entrance for the highway. I work hard to keep my tone quiet and calm. "Your dad is dead because he was involved in trafficking little kids to sick perverts, and when he got caught, he took the easy way out rather than face the truth at his trial."

Chad's breath oozes out in exaggerated spurts as he white-knuckles the wheel. He doesn't retaliate though because you can't circumvent the truth, and he knows it.

"I'm not saying that to hurt you, babe," I softly add. "Blame Hera for having an affair with a married man, but you can't blame her for anything else." I don't condone it, and I'm not excusing her actions, but Hera was single when she met Jasper Baldwin. Jasper was the one cheating on his wife of over twenty years, and I'm betting it wasn't the first time. If he could hide his involvement in sex trafficking for a reputed eight years, he could surely disguise his adultery.

Chad's chest heaves, and pain glimmers across his face. "I

know I'm projecting," he admits in a cracked tone. "But I can't look at that woman without seeing how it all started." He pins troubled eyes on me. "I still don't believe Dad committed suicide. I still contend it's shady as fuck."

Jasper was found hanging in his cell one week before his trial. It's been almost seven months since he died, and Chad still can't accept it's the truth.

Perhaps he's right and there is more to it. It's not inconceivable. With all the scandals that have come out in the past year involving corrupt elements within governments, secret elite groups who think they're above the law, and local gangs involved in drugs, guns, and sex trafficking, it's not outside the realm of possibility.

My good friend Harlow Westbrook was involved in taking a lot of key players down last year. Her four husbands made up the junior chapter leadership of The Sainthood gang, and they were all pivotal in forcing that organization to its knees. Now the guys have cut all ties with the drastically downsized gang and moved to Rhode Island with their wife to attend school.

I miss her and wish she was attending LU with us. I could use a friend.

Anyway, it just proves that Chad's suspicions could be correct. I imagine there are plenty of people involved in the sex trafficking ring Jasper controlled who would want to ensure his silence. Who knows how high up it goes? But I don't articulate those thoughts or do anything to encourage that line of thinking. Chad is struggling enough and already up to his neck in shit he shouldn't be involved in. I'm really worried about him.

Cupping his handsome face, I lightly sweep my fingers over the dark-blond stubble on his chin and cheeks. "I hate that you're suffering for your father's sins. It's not right."

He shrugs while leaning into my touch. "It's not like I can abandon Mom and Tessa. I'm all they've got."

I know discovering the truth about her husband devastated Carole, and I'm not unsympathetic, but she needs to get her act together. She's a grown-ass woman with a fourteen-year-old daughter to take care of. She needs to dust herself off and go get a fucking job instead of relying on her only son to provide for her. It's putting way too much pressure on Chad's shoulders, and he's digging a bigger hole for himself.

"My offer still stands. I—"

He slams his hands down on the wheel. "Do *not* offer me money again! I'm sick of having this same argument with you and Jase. It's getting old. I'm not some charity case, Ash. Neither is my mom." A muscle clenches in his jaw, and I wish I could rewind time and start this conversation all over again. "I swallowed a lot of pride agreeing to move in with you as it is."

Hurt bursts forth on my face before I can stop it. I have been on a countdown to the day we officially live together, yet he makes it sound like a chore.

The truck jerks to the left as Chad pulls it over to the shoulder and kills the engine. "Sweetheart." He clasps my face in his large palms and his gaze ensnares me. Sincerity radiates from his gorgeous big blue eyes. "You know I didn't mean it like that. I love that I get to wake up beside you every morning and go to sleep with you every night. But you're still paying for everything, and that doesn't sit right with me."

Technically, my parents are paying. They won't let me touch my inheritance, stating it's for my post-college life. Which is why this is hard on me. I have millions sitting in the bank, and I want to give Chad and his family some to ease their burden, but he stubbornly refuses every time I broach the subject.

"You're covering the rent on your mom's apartment, paying her utilities and groceries, and putting Tessa through high school. You've got enough financial responsibilities," I gently remind him.

The authorities swooped in after Jasper's arrest and seized all his assets. Chad and his family had to move out of the only home they've ever known, and they were virtually penniless overnight. When you have led an affluent lifestyle and wanted for nothing your entire life, that is a massive adjustment.

"You moving in with me won't cost any more than it would if I was living by myself in a three-story townhome," I add, purposely omitting mention of how I'll probably be spending three times as much on food with the amount he and Jase consume on a daily basis. "I want to help. Please let me."

Tipping his head down, he kisses me, infusing his kiss with adoration and desperation and I cling to him, pouring everything I'm feeling into every sweep of my lips, hoping he can feel how much I love him.

"You help me more than you know, Siren." His voice thickens with lust as we break our kiss. His fingers tangle in my hair as I run my hand over his newly cropped, newly dyed white-blond hair. "I could not have gotten through this last year without you. You're my rock, Ash. You're my everything."

"As you are mine," I say, closing the distance between us and kissing him again.

He rests his forehead against mine. "I love you so fucking much."

Circling my arms more tightly around his neck, I mirror the sentiment. "I love you too."

"I know you are only trying to help, but this is something I have to do by myself. I'm the man of the family now. Taking care of Mom and Tessa is my responsibility. I won't fail them like Dad did. They are relying on me to look after them. *Me*." He lifts his head, thumping a hand over his impressive chest.

"Not you or Jase." He arches a brow, his expression silently imploring me to understand.

And I do, to a point.

But selling your soul to The Sainthood and risking your scholarship and future NFL career is not the answer.

I just don't know how to get him to see that.

Chapter Two

Chad

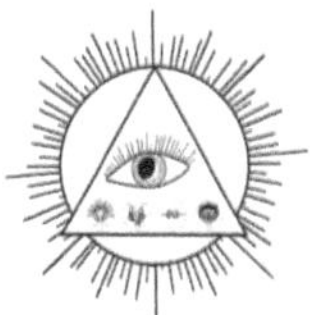

"Wow," I say, pulling into one of four empty parking spaces in front of Ash's townhome. "This place is something else."

"It's not at all what I imagined," my beautiful girlfriend says, twisting her head from side to side as she inspects the small, gated community of modern townhomes through the windows of my truck. I only managed to hold on to it because Dad had the foresight to put it in my name.

What a pity he hadn't applied that foresight to other aspects of his life. We might not be in the mess we are now if he had been better prepared.

I still can't believe the man I knew, the man I looked up to, was a sick predator and a serial cheater. I feel sick to my stomach every time I think about the things he has done. He was trafficking girls the same age as my sister, and my blood boils thinking of the risk she was in by his actions and associations. I'd have murdered the fucker in cold blood if anything had happened to Tessa.

Forcing thoughts of Jasper Baldwin from my mind, because

my mood is already too black, I concentrate on the here and now. Ash is right. This is a new beginning, and I need to set my dark thoughts aside. I owe Ash that much at least. I owe her much more, but we can start there.

This place is nice. Secure, private, and peaceful. I think living here could be good for us—if Ash can get past the bombshell Jase will be dropping in her lap when he arrives.

There are four houses on either side of the road between a small park. Heavily wooded grounds enclose all eight townhomes at the rear, and high wrought-iron gates at the entrance ensure complete privacy.

We hop out of the truck at the same time, and I move to the back to start unloading our bags. Ash's dad organized movers earlier in the week, and they took heavier items and personal belongings. Setting our suitcases down on the sidewalk, I watch Ash as she twirls around, taking everything in with a slight frown on her gorgeous face.

I don't spot any other vehicles, and I'm glad the parking spaces at the adjacent townhome are empty. I still haven't worked out how to break that news to her. Not that it's my responsibility, but she deserves to know. I would have updated her immediately last night when I found out if Jase hadn't begged me not to breathe a word. It's only been foisted on him at the last minute I suspect so he can't say no. Yet my best friend and fellow jock rarely accepts no for an answer, and that's why he headed off this morning to present a last-minute case to his father and his brother.

I wouldn't bet on either of them doing him any favors.

His dad is a cold fish, and his brother is cut from the same cloth. It's like they don't feel human emotions. Or if they do, they have learned how to hide them. I doubt they will have an ounce of sympathy for Jase's predicament.

I care because I know how much this will hurt our girl.

For the first time, I question my decision to bring Jase into our relationship.

Leaving the bags, I walk to Ash's side and reel her into my arms, needing to hold her, wanting to comfort her. "Why the frown?" I ask, smoothing my thumb across her forehead.

"It's not quite what I had in mind for college," she admits, and I love that she's such an open book with me. "I don't want to appear ungrateful, but I wouldn't have minded living in a typical student apartment or even a dorm." Her nose scrunches up in that adorable way it does anytime she's thinking deeply.

"We wouldn't get to live together if we were in the dorms."

"True." Her brow evens out, and a wide smile graces her delectable mouth. "And we couldn't continue our party tradition if we didn't have the space to host it."

For the past couple years, Ashley's house was party central on Friday nights. Everyone at Lowell Academy—the private high school I attended with my girl and my best friend—knew Ash's parents traveled a lot for business and were rarely home. Parties at her house on Friday nights were the norm, and we made the most of it.

Those were good times.

"Exactly." I sling my arm around her shoulders, and we head toward the sidewalk. "Let's check out your new place."

"*Our* new place," she corrects, fixing me with a challenging look.

I know how to pick my battles, and this isn't one I need to win. I playfully swat her ass. "Yep. Let's get our shit inside and explore."

"We need to pick bedrooms," she says, grabbing a couple of bags. "I mean you'll sleep with me in the master, but you need to choose your own room for nights when Jase and I want to be alone. I told him the same thing." Ash's parents don't know she invited Jase to move in with us too. She would rather her parents didn't know she's fucking her so-called best friend's boyfriend.

"Leave those to me." I swipe the bags from her hands as she puts her foot on the first step, deliberately not touching the Jase topic. I told my friend I would give him until today to talk to her, and I'm giving him another couple of hours. If he doesn't show soon, I'm updating Ash. I don't want her blindsided and knowledge is power. Especially when it comes to that bitch Julia Manford. I have never trusted that girl, and I'm convinced there is a lot more going on than she'd have us believe.

Ash rolls her eyes. "I'm not an invalid, Chad." Her tiny fingers attempt to wrap around one of my biceps. "I might not have your big, brawny muscles, but I'm no weakling. I can carry some bags up a few steps."

Dropping the bags, I scoop her up into my arms, grinning at her like a loon as I change the plans.

"What the hell are you doing?" she shrieks, flinging her arms around my neck and beaming at me as I bound up the steps.

"Carrying my ladylove over the threshold," I say, plucking the key from her fingers when we reach the door.

"Oh, be still my heart." She pats her chest, before leaning in to press a kiss to my jaw. "I love sweet Chad," she purrs, licking the side of my neck. Fiery tingles shoot down my chest and arms, and I love how she still turns me on so much. It's how I know she's the one. The only woman for me. The one I will navigate through life by my side and draw my last breath with. "Almost as much as I love *bad* Chad," she adds, waggling her brows suggestively.

Losing our virginity to one another at fifteen had many advantages. We got to explore sex together, and she didn't bat an eye when I revealed a few kinks. Ash is game to try everything and anything, and she loves my naughty side. She truly is the perfect woman.

Cradling her in my arms, I maneuver the door open, whistling when I step inside. The circular entryway has a high ceiling with industrial lighting and distressed wooden floors. An enclosed coat closet is tucked sleekly under an impressive wooden staircase that has a glass railing and strip lighting under each step. A long table holds a lamp made of stained glass, a bowl for keys, and a vase filled with colorful flowers.

Not that Ash has noticed. She's too fixated on me.

My inner Neanderthal man growls in satisfaction as she pins me with lust-drenched eyes and wicked intent. I like where this is heading.

"I say to hell with unpacking," she purrs in that unintentional sultry tone she reverts to when she's aroused. "Let's start as we mean to go on." A naughty glint flickers in her eyes and I'm instantly sucked in. Ashley has this way of hypnotizing me with one molten look or one wicked word.

She's my sexy siren, and I'm a fucking lucky bastard I get to call her mine. I know half the guys on my old football team had a major hard-on for her. Especially when some of them discovered I was sharing her with Jase. I had more than a few additional offers, but I'm not into sharing my girl with just any Tom, *Dick*, or Harry.

It works with Jase because I trust him to treat my girl the way she deserves to be treated. It was clear there was an attraction between them, and I knew what Ashley needed before she could voice her desire. It's not like I don't get anything out of it. Watching my best bud fuck my forever girl is so hot. I'm not into dudes, and Jase and I have never, nor will we ever, cross swords, but damn if it doesn't turn me on watching him drive his cock inside my woman in every way imaginable.

"Babe." She snaps her fingers in my face. "Where'd you go?"

"The same place you did." I lick my lips as I reposition her so she's plastered to my front with her legs wrapped around my waist.

"I want to christen the hall first," she says, grinding her pussy against the growing bulge in my jeans.

"I love the way your mind works, Siren." I crash my lips against hers as I spin us around and walk over to the wall just inside the open doorway. Shoving her spine against the exposed brickwork, I pivot my hips and thrust against her, already leaking precum behind my boxers.

"Chad," she moans into my mouth. "Take me here, right now, with the door open."

My brows climb to my hairline as a grin tugs up the corners of my mouth. "Taking a page out of Jase's book now?"

"He doesn't own the monopoly on exhibitionism or public fucking," she says, sucking my lower lip into her mouth. "I need to ride your dick, and I want it now." She slides a hand between our bodies, and her confident sass turns me the fuck on.

Reclaiming her mouth in a searing-hot kiss, I groan as she grips my straining dick through my jeans, tracing the outline of it with her fingers. I grind against her as she pops the button on my jeans, her hand diving into my boxers to stroke my hard length, while our lips lock in a slew of mind-blowing, earth-shattering kisses. Shoving my hand up under her shirt, I yank her bra down and grope her tit.

"That's it, sweetheart," I rasp as she pumps me in her hand while I pluck and tweak her nipple. "Work me good." We're thrusting against one another as I hold her up against the wall and fondle her gorgeous tits, both of us panting and craving more. I'm so lost in my woman I barely register the sound of a motorcycle parking, the thud of footsteps approaching, or the barely discernible intake of breath as someone steps into the hall.

"Smile for the camera," a man with a gruff, unfortunately familiar voice says after a few beats.

Fixing her bra into place, I remove my hand from under Ash's shirt and whip my head around as I help her to her feet, an instant irritated scowl firmly planted on my face. "What the fuck are you doing here?" I bark, glaring at Ares Haynes as Ash extracts her hands from my boxers and secures my jeans into place. My hands automatically clench into fists, like every time I'm around that son of a bitch.

I hated him on sight because of who his mother is, but now I hate him for so much more.

"Give me that," Ash snarls, reaching for her stepbrother's cell. He's holding it up like he was taking pics, and I swear I will knock him the fuck out if he caught anything on camera.

Dude has lightning-fast reflexes, and he steps back before she can grab it.

"You better not have taken any photos or videos," I warn, tucking Ash into my side.

"Or what?" the degenerate snarls. "What is *bad Chad* going to do to me?" he mocks over a chuckle. I hate that the asshole has a couple of inches in height on me, but I outmatch him in sheer physical size. He might work out religiously, but I train more, and I'm a god on the football field.

Ash grinds her teeth and flexes her jaw. "Get the fuck out!" she hisses, dipping out from under my arm. She storms toward him, jabbing her finger in his chest. "This is my place and you're not welcome. Like ever. At any time."

Folding his arms across his chest, he props himself up against the doorjamb and smirks at us. "Seems like someone didn't get the memo." He flashes a perfect set of straight white teeth and I really want to smash them down his throat. "So, I'll clear it up for you, *roomie*."

Ash almost chokes on her breath. "Hell to the no," she pants, glaring at him.

"Hell to the yes." He winks, raking his gaze up and down her body in a way that makes me want to remove his eyeballs from their sockets.

I would say something, do something, only I have learned this is how he pushes my buttons. I won't give him the satisfaction even though I want to murder the motherfucker for daring to look at my woman like he wants to devour her from her head to her toes.

"This is not happening." Ash extracts her cell from the pocket of her jeans. She punches a couple of buttons, glaring at Ares as she puts the call on speaker, and we listen as the line rings out. "Call me now, Dad. It's urgent!" She barks a message into the phone before hanging up and repocketing her cell.

I don't want to believe this is the development that bitch Hera spoke about, but her assface son showing up here can't be a coincidence.

"You don't even go to college. You're too old." I narrow my eyes at him as I wrap my arm around Ash's waist.

"Twenty-two is hardly old."

"It is when you're pretending to be a senior in high school," Ash says, reminding him of his shady ways.

We still don't know why he was enrolled at Fenton High public school last year. Or why Hera originally kept up the charade he was a teenager. Hera gave Doug and Ash some bullshit excuse I don't buy for a second. I know Ash thinks Hera is sweet and loving, but I'm not believing it. It's all an act. Those two have an agenda. I'd bet my scholarship on it. They are both as shady as one another, and I will do everything in my power to protect Ashley from whatever they are up to.

Ares has done his best to make her life miserable these past ten months. It got way worse when he and Hera moved in with Doug and Ash after her dad married his mom last April. Jase has a theory. He thinks Ares is using Ash to get back at me. But it makes no sense. I haven't done anything that would warrant revenge. I'm the only one with the right to vengeance. His mom shit all over my family. He has no reason to come after me, so I think his hatred of Ash stems from something different—like lust.

He wouldn't be the first bad boy from the wrong side of the tracks to lust after the popular, pretty, rich girl who seems to have everything and to hate himself for it.

"Your predictability knows no bounds, dollface. Get over it already." Reaching forward, he twirls a lock of her long, wavy silver-purple hair around his finger. "You do this for me, baby?"

Anger is like a charging bull pummeling through my veins and coating my retinas in a layer of red. How fucking dare he put his hands anywhere near my woman! I shove his chest hard, forcing him to step back and release her hair. "Touch her again, and I'll remove your fingers, one at a time, with a hacksaw."

His amused chuckle cranks my anger to another level. "I'd like to see you try, pup. I eat pussies like you for breakfast."

He's so full of shit, and he knows it.

"Don't." Ash steps in front of me, preempting my move as she peers deep in my eyes. "He's not worth it." Her face pleads with me to drop it as she whispers in my ear. "Think of football and your family."

Ares and I have had a few bust ups with neither of us gaining the upper hand and both giving as good as it gets. He has the height. I have the physical edge. Our raging anger is evenly matched, so there is never a clear winner.

My high school coach benched me for an important game

when I turned up with a black eye, a split lip, and obvious bruising on my neck after a particularly vicious fight with Ares. At college level, I cannot afford to show up like that. My entire future is at stake, and I'm risking enough as it is.

Those are the only words my girl could say to get me to back down.

"Why are you really here?" I grit out, done with this bull crap.

"I live here." He waggles his brows before sauntering through the door into the next room.

Ash races past me to chase after him, and I follow suit.

"Nice try, shit for brains, but I'm not buying it," she snaps, trailing him into a large, airy open-plan kitchen-slash-dining room. "You don't go to college. Your job, your pervy friends, and your pitiful gang are all in Fenton, more than an hour away. Why the fuck would you move in here?"

I can't even enjoy the sleek modern kitchen because I'm too busy seething and worrying. I can't stay here now. I can't live with that douche because I'll end up on a murder charge before the week is out. I don't doubt he's telling the truth. He's Doug's new stepson. I'm betting he offered to keep a brotherly eye on Ash, and Ash's dad fell for it because he seems to think the suns shines out of his ass. I thought Doug was smarter than that, but he seems to have been completely taken in by Hera and her son.

"Because I got a new job in a garage three miles away and The Bulls need me to take care of some shit on campus."

He levels me with a malicious grin, and I'm immediately suspicious.

"I love fucking with your head," he adds, flashing her a savage grin before he opens the refrigerator, peering inside at the fully stocked shelves. "And I haven't even begun to ruin you," he replies, like it's totally normal to spout that shit at anyone. He grabs a beer and a container of leftover Chinese takeout. "Your father agrees you need a chaperone." He closes the refrigerator with one hip, popping the top off his beer. "And maybe my mom worries about you shacking up with talentless jocks with fluff between their ears." He shrugs, not losing the obnoxious grin. "Take your pick."

He puts his beer and the takeout carton down on the counter. Whipping his shirt over his head, he mops the back of his neck before tossing the clothing on top of the island unit. Beads of sweat glisten on his inked chest and abs, confirming he's already found a new gym to work out at.

"This isn't happening," Ash repeats, glowering at him.

Walking around the counter with a purposeful swagger, he flicks her nose, and I lunge for him. Ash steps in between us before I can reach the dickhead. He smirks at me, and I'm ten seconds away from smashing the dude's skull in, consequences be damned.

"It's already happened. It's a done deal. There's nothing you can do or say to change it." Bending his head down, he puts his face all up in hers, and I see red again. Ash reaches behind to grab my hand in warning. "*Roomie.*" Ares rubs his hands in glee as his gaze bounces between me and my girlfriend. "We're going to have so much fun."

Snatching his cold takeout and beer, he walks away. Ares's dark chuckle follows him out of the room as Ash and I stare at one another, all hint of good humor long gone from both our expressions.

Chapter Three

Jase

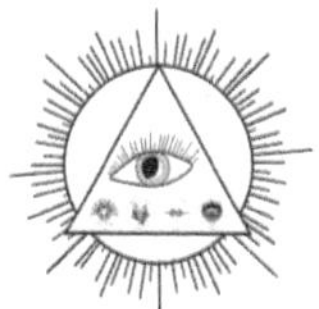

I stop my Range Rover in front of my house rather than parking it in the garage because this will be a short visit. Chad and Ash are already en route to the townhome, and there is no time to waste. Hopping out, I stride past the ornate stone water feature in the direction of the front door, my feet crunching on gravel as my long strides eat up the short distance.

Glorious August sunshine beats down on the two-story fifty-thousand-square-foot beige and brown modern-day castle as I approach. My late grandfather built it in the nineteen thirties, replicating the European home some of our ancestors had lived in, back in the Middle Ages. The turrets, towers, stained glass panels, and curved windows are an exact copy of the first property, if the large, framed painting of the original castle hanging on the wall as you go up the main staircase is a true representation.

"Favorite brother," Jocelyn says, smiling expansively as she stands in the open doorway. "I thought you were moving today?" She leans in to hug me.

"I am." I bundle my youngest sister in my arms, inhaling

the smell of peaches from her hair, which always reminds me of carefree summers spent in France at our maternal grandparent's vast country estate. "I need to talk to Father first."

"Ah, that's why he's been peering out his office window with a constipated look on his face. Mom and I were taking bets on whether it was you or Bree who ruffled his feathers this time."

It's not difficult to predict it was myself or my twenty-year-old sister as we're what Mom affectionately calls her "problem children." Balthazar was born the perfect son and heir; instantly enamored by the world we live in and champing at the bit to immerse himself fully in every aspect of the Luminary lifestyle. He's my father's mini-me in every regard.

Breanna hates everyone and everything, and she's like an out-of-control tsunami every time she sets foot in a room. My hatred of the rules and traditions, which govern us and every Luminary family, fades into the background when compared with my older sister's outright loathing of our secret elite society. If it wasn't against our laws to kill a member of a Luminary family, I'm sure my father would have had her dealt with by now. Instead, he happily let her head off to Peru to find herself eighteen months ago, rather than enrolling in Lowell U like the rest of us.

Out of sight, out of mind is definitely the motto in Dad's case. At least for the moment. Bree knows her so-called freedom has an expiration date. Dad may be letting her rebel now, but she will be forced to toe the line at some point in the next couple years.

I'm less easy to push aside, and he'd never let me get away with the same shit. As a second son, there is a lot riding on me. Father has several expectations for me. Expectations I will most likely fail to live up to, but that doesn't mean I can escape them.

I chuckle as I ruffle Jocelyn's dark hair. "Bree's over a thousand miles away, so I hope you put your money on me."

"You're usually the safe bet, but you clearly haven't heard the news."

That stops me in my tracks. "What news?"

"Bree is coming home. She's going to be a freshman like you."

I blink at her like she just announced my sister was a born-again virgin dedicated to a vow of chastity and a lifelong commitment to God. I couldn't be any more surprised if that was the reveal. "Yeah, right. Sure." Sarcasm drips from my tone as I nudge her aside and step foot in my family home.

"I'm not lying." Jocelyn loops her arm in mine. "She's in the air right now."

"Why?" I question. "The last time I spoke to Bree she was shacking up with some hot South African photographer and his girlfriend, and she had zero intention of coming home any time soon."

Jocelyn shrugs as we walk through the hallway toward the rear of the house. "Shit went down with the photographer. He didn't like how much Bree and his girl were into one another. Felt threatened by strong pussy." She rolls her eyes. "Such masculine bullshit."

That doesn't explain why my headstrong sister is returning home. But I'm guessing I'll have to wait until she lands on US soil to discover the real reason.

Jocelyn swings left, pushing open the door to my mother's art studio, and I trail her inside.

"PC2. My handsome boy," Mom says, setting her paintbrush down and beaming at me. She wipes paint-smudged fingers down the front of her shirt before walking toward me. Her thick dark hair is tied in a messy bun with strands wisping around her unlined face.

While Dad appears to age every year, Mom almost seems to get younger. It's not thanks to a surgeon's knife either. Mom is considered something of a hippy in our social circles. She does yoga, paints, and loves gardening and cooking family meals from scratch instead of relying on the hired help. She has taken a ton of online courses in nutrition, alternative therapies, photography, calligraphy, and a bunch of others I can't remember. She is heavily involved in charity work, and she's happiest dressed down, surrounded by her family, drinking wine, and dancing like she doesn't have a care in the world.

Keeping busy and denying reality seem to be her two main coping mechanisms.

I have no complaints. She's an awesome mom. While my relationship with my father is fractured in the extreme, I'm super close to my mother.

"You get even more handsome every time I see you," she adds, clutching my cheeks in her small hands.

"You're my mom. You're biased." I lean down and kiss her cheek when her hands fall away from my face.

"Pfft. There is nothing wrong with my eyesight. No bias involved."

Jocelyn snorts out a laugh. "Don't start acting all humble now, Jase. It really doesn't suit you."

I toss a smirk over my shoulder at my sister. "Can't help how I look, pipsqueak. It's all in the genes."

"We have hardly seen you this summer." Mom cocks her head to one side. "You must come for dinner on Sunday."

"I'll try," I promise. "My schedule is pretty packed between football and classes and the demands Dad is making on me."

Her face softens as she grips my hand briefly. "I take it you're here to meet with your father?" she says as she moves over to her painting.

I nod before standing behind her, admiring the vibrant

burst of color on the canvas. I don't want to talk about Dad. I know what Mom will say, and it will only end up in an argument. "That's stunning, Mom," I admit, glancing out the window. "It's like looking at a photo of our garden."

"This is my fourth attempt," she explains. "I think it's finally coming together." Mom is way too self-critical, and she always downplays her talent. If she hadn't been forced to marry Dad after she graduated LU with a fine arts degree, I think she would have made a career out of it. Now, it's just a hobby. An outlet when Father and the restrictions of our world get too much for her.

"It's good, Mom." I press a kiss to the top of her head. "I better go. Can't keep His Highness waiting."

Jocelyn snorts out a laugh, and Mom frowns. "Things are a bit intense right now. You should tread carefully with him."

A muscle clenches in my jaw. "You know what he's forcing on me."

Sympathy splays across her face. "I know this is hard for you, but he's given you as much leeway as he can. Despite what you think of your father, he has tried his best to soften the blow. He only has your best interests at heart, Jase. You'd do well to remember that."

"Sit down," my father demands in that unemotional tone he is famous for.

"Thanks, but I'll stand." Folding my arms across my chest, I level him with a dark look.

"It wasn't a request." He gestures at the empty chair in front of his desk before he walks to his liquor cabinet. He glances over his shoulder at me. "If you expect me to treat you with respect, you'll show the same to me in my own home." He points at the chair. "Sit, or this meeting is over before it's begun."

Begrudgingly, I sit my ass down. I know to pick my battles carefully with my father, but I'm struggling to find my voice of reason today. Thanks to his bombshell call last night, I'm all riled up and ready to hit something.

Preferably his annoyingly calm face.

He hands me a glass of expensive bourbon from a twenty-year-old rare bottle of Old Rip Van Winkle—nothing but the best for the Lust & Envy Luminary. "It's only eleven a.m.," I remind him, swirling the amber-colored liquid in my glass. "That's early, even for you."

"Don't try my patience, boy. You looked like you needed it. It would serve you well to get control over your emotions. You give too much away, and I didn't raise you to be this kind of man. I'm humoring you by granting this meeting. Remember that."

He reclaims his seat behind the ornate mahogany desk with the dark-green leather trim. It's been in the Stewart family for years, passed down between each successive heir. "I can just as easily have your brother haul your disobedient ass to HQ to beat some manners into you."

The HQ he's referring to isn't the impressive Stewart Freight head office in downtown Lowell. He means Luminary HQ. A secret facility, hidden deep in a valley in the middle of the remotest part of California, surrounded by dense forest, and protected by impenetrable security, where all manner of illegal operations go down.

I'd like to say I'm not familiar with the underground levels —where informers, rulebreakers, criminals who operate outside our laws and traditions, and wayward siblings of luminaries and masters are taken to be taught a lesson—but that would be a lie. I think I came out of my mother's womb rebelling against the world I was born into. Not that it's done me any good. The only way I'm getting out is in a body bag, and I value breathing more than rebellion.

"Training has already started, and classes commence next week. I'm sure my absence would be noted."

"That is your only saving grace," he says before sipping his drink.

I take a healthy mouthful, welcoming the burn as it glides down my throat. I decide to cut to the chase. "You know why I'm here," I say through gritted teeth, working hard to rein my anger and frustration in. "I'm not moving in with Julia and that's final."

A dry laugh tumbles from my father's chest as he sets his glass down and flicks a piece of imaginary lint off the sleeve of his pinstripe tailored suit. "You don't get a choice," he drawls, eyeballing me with piercing green eyes I share. "I have been far too lenient with you as it is. You're a freshman in college now, and it's time for you to play your part. You have responsibilities to this family and the organization as a whole. You cannot shirk your duties."

"I'm not your heir, so you can cut me some slack. I have four years of college to fulfil my familial duties."

He leans forward, resting his elbows on the desk as he stares at me. "You act like you are the only one who has to step up when you know that isn't the case. Your peers, their heirs and siblings, and siblings of masters are all in the same position. You have graduated high school and ascended to the next level. Your college years are pivotal in your development, and you need to start as you mean to go on. No son of mine will undermine my status and reputation by denying his duties and responsibilities."

I drain the rest of my drink and place my empty glass down on the desk, working hard to leash my anger. "I'm not denying them, Father. I know what I must do. I'm just questioning why now. At least give me this first semester to settle in and adjust to college life." I need to buy more time to find a permanent solution.

"Don't lie to me, boy, or you'll be sorry." A glimpse of anger flashes on his face before disappearing behind the cold indifferent expression he usually wears. "I know this is about that Shaw girl."

I mask my surprise before it shows on my face. I'm not surprised he knows because there is nothing that goes on The Luminaries don't know about. I am surprised he has articulated it though. This is a first. "It is," I truthfully reply.

"She can never be yours, and I never should have allowed it to continue."

I scoff out a laugh. "As if you could stop me."

"Come now, son. Don't pretend to be naïve. We both know I could have easily stopped you. I still can."

Cold dread tiptoes up my spine and I sit straighter in my chair. "Are you threatening Ashley?"

He arches a brow. "I don't know? Am I?" He throws the ball back in my court, watching me with shrewd eyes as he takes another sip of his drink.

Chapter Four

Jase

I grip the armrests of my chair, digging my nails into the taut leather, as I glare at him. "If you lay one finger on Ash, I will kill you," I hiss.

He's around the table in a flash, yanking me up by my shirt and shoving me sideways until my back hits the wall.

I could get him off me in a nanosecond.

Flick him away like an annoying insect because I have height, weight, strength, and youth on my side.

But my father is not to be underestimated.

He is skilled in all forms of combat, and he keeps himself fit.

He's killed and tortured more men than I've had hot dinners and outmaneuvered men arguably more intelligent. He may not be as lethally devious as the Pride & Wrath Luminary, as excessively compulsive as the Greed & Gluttony Luminary, or as cunningly sharp as the Sloth Luminary, but he is skillfully persuasive, and he has talked his way out of more situations than anyone I know.

My father's real talent is hiding and waiting and manipulating and I can't ever forget it. My actions and reactions will feed into his planning, meaning Ash's welfare is in my hands. I won't do anything to risk her life, so I don't push him away as he holds me against the wall, close to losing his legendary control.

"You don't get to threaten a Luminary and live to tell the tale. Our shared blood won't protect you." He releases my shirt and grips my face in a painful hold. "This is why I need to act now. You've always been a loose cannon, Jason, but it ends here." He gives me one last shove before stalking back to his chair.

Reluctantly, I follow, reclaiming my seat.

Draining his drink in one go, he slams the glass down on his precious desk. Ordinarily, I would take pleasure in seeing the unflappable Eric Stewart with ruffled feathers. But I get no enjoyment seeing him like this, knowing I may have placed Ashley in danger.

There is only one thing, well, two things, I can do to protect her.

"I love her." I admit something I haven't even told Ashley. How could I when I will still have to walk away? I admit it now to my father in the hope it's enough to keep her safe.

He barks out a cynical laugh. "You know nothing of love. Love is for the weak and foolish. Why else have we valued arranged marriages and familial partnerships for hundreds of generations? Because joint loyalties and bonded ties are what keep people focused, loyal, and smart. Not love."

He throws out the word like it's poison, and I have even more pity for my mother.

"You believing you love her makes you weak, and it's blinded you to your reality." He leans back in his chair, looking contemplative as his tongue darts out, wetting his lips.

"Me loving her makes me strong," I contend, "and you

should be happy because she is the only thing that could ever make me toe the line."

He taps his fingers on the table in a steady beat. "You would sacrifice her, sacrifice the so-called freedom you have fought me for over the past few years, all to protect her?" he asks, sounding incredulous as he connects the dots.

"I would do anything to protect her including"—I pause for a breath, drawing bravery from some hidden place to force these words from my mouth—"letting her go if that's the only way to keep her safe."

"Hmm." He inspects my face with the intensity of a magnifying glass. "You truly mean that."

"I do."

He clasps his hands on the desk in front of him as I swallow over the massive lump in my throat. I drag a hand through my hair, sending waves of dark locks tumbling across my brow. I haven't cut my hair all summer because Ash loves when it's longer on top. More for her to tug on when I have my face buried between her thighs and my tongue thrust so far inside her pussy I see stars.

"If I promise to leave the girl alone, you—"

"And to protect her," I add, risking his wrath by cutting across him. "You won't harm her, and you'll ensure no one else does either."

"I didn't raise an idiot. You understand I can't promise that. I give you my word no harm will befall the girl at the hands of our family. I cannot be responsible if she falls prey to any other family."

"You mean the Sloth Luminary." It doesn't take a genius to guess who he means, but he shakes his head.

"I believe the girl is safe with James Manford."

I crank out a laugh. "Now you're treating me like a fool. I know he knows I've been fucking around on his daughter with

Ash. I know their two families are close. You can't tell me he isn't pissed."

I was seventeen when Chad approached me about joining him and Ash in the bedroom. I had been lusting after her for a long time, and it was becoming harder and harder to disguise my attraction from my best friend. So, it was a no-brainer. The words had barely left his mouth when I agreed, and we've been in this three-way ever since.

It might have started out as sex, but it's so much more now.

If it wasn't for this shit hanging over my head, this past year and a half would have been the best time of my life. Rebelliously stupid, I hadn't given much thought to how this might impact Ash at first. As we quickly grew closer, I thought she could be my ticket out of this nightmare with Julia.

I knew The Luminaries were aware of our relationship because they are all-seeing and all-knowing. I thought the billionaire owner of Manford Media, the most publicly recognizable of the four luminaries, might eschew the arrangement made with my father in light of the insult.

But James Manford has taken no action, continuing to welcome me warmly at the quarterly meetings at HQ and at family dinners.

"No man in his position would ever hold that against you. Men have needs, and there is no required exclusivity until after college graduation. Then you will be expected to remain loyal to your intended, outside of your responsibilities of course." He lets loose a feral grin. "You may not be my heir, but you are still a second son. That comes with great responsibility, and the time has come to step up to the plate." A sleazy grin spreads across his mouth as acid churns in my gut. "You can hardly fulfil your duties as part of the Lust & Envy Luminary family by sticking your dick in one pussy." A hearty guffaw slips from his mouth in a moment of uncharacteristic humanity. "You need to start thinking like your brother. Balthazar sees the benefits of the responsibility under our control. You could be stuck weeding out addicts or narcissists like some of your peers. Count your blessings you get to fuck and manipulate for a living. There are far worse things in this life."

He disgusts me. The whole situation does. But there is no point waging a pointless war. This is my future. My reality. My responsibility. My burden. My death sentence.

"Can we get this over and done with," I snap, needing to be out of here before I wring his neck. "Do you give me your word Ashley Shaw will be protected to the best of your ability?"

"I do—as long as you commit to Julia and your role in all the ways we have discussed."

I would rather stick pins in my dick than share a bed, let alone a home and a life, with that insipid, vain, weak, whiny bitch. But she's the Manford heir, a first daughter who was highly sought after. Dad considered it a coup when he won her hand on my behalf. We were chosen for one another at age eight when we were formally inducted and our training commenced.

I have known this day was coming.

Been dreading it from the moment I found out.

I'm still not prepared to lose Ash. Lose Chad.

I doubt I ever could be.

Unless I can find a solution, I know the only way this will work is by cutting all ties and making it irreversible. They will both need to hate me.

"I will commit to Julia as is my duty. I will move in with her as you wish, but I want two months before the engagement announcement is made."

"No," he quickly and calmly replies. "This isn't a negotiation."

"Give me some time to come to terms with it and to say

goodbye to Ash in my own way. I know what I need to do to make this happen, and I will do it, but let me make peace with it first."

"That's not an unreasonable demand," my older brother Balthazar says, entering the room from the hidden stairs behind the shelving unit. I wonder how long he was standing there and how much he heard.

"You would go easy on your brother?" Father asks, eyeing my eldest sibling with something akin to mild curiosity.

"His mopey ass won't be able to perform his role to the required standard, and as much as I like pussy, there are only so many hours in the day." His lips twitch as he leans against the wall, flashing me a knowing grin.

Baz is loving this.

It's what he's wanted for years—to fully immerse himself in his responsibilities as the renowned player heir. His manwhore ways are even more legendary than his predecessors, and that thrills him.

Getting to lord his superiority and power over me is an added bonus.

He knows how I feel about Ash. He knows how hard I have resisted my Luminary responsibility and how much I will loathe screwing around with others in the name of duty. This isn't some grand charitable gesture on my brother's behalf. He knows this will prolong my agony, and he's going to twist the knife as deep as he can.

"Very well." Father concedes because it seems like his heir can do no wrong in his eyes. "You have two months to satiate your lust for the Shaw girl, and then you must end things permanently and commit to Julia and your duties. But you move in with her today. Is that clear?"

"Crystal," I spit out as I rise, wondering how I can soften the blow with Ash. This will devastate her, and I'm not sure how I can explain it when I'm forbidden from telling her the truth.

"You're excused," Dad says, not even looking at me as I storm across the room toward the door.

"Little brother." Balthazar calls out after me, and I stall with my hand curled around the door handle. I throw a glance at him over my shoulder. "There can be no going back. She must understand with no ambiguity."

Pain stabs me through the heart as I contemplate what I will need to do. It will kill me as much as it will kill her, and I know I will lose Chad too. But I'm running out of time and plays. "I understand what I need to do."

"Which is?" The amusement dancing across my brother's face sends me into a silent rage, but I conceal it.

I won't give either of them the satisfaction of knowing how much this will break me. "Rip her heart out and stomp all over it."

Chapter Five

Ashley

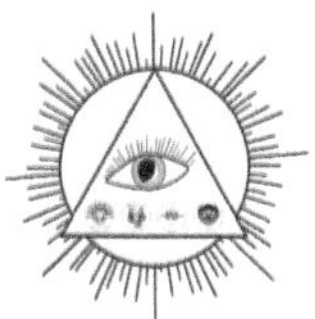

"I know this sucks, but you can't just walk off!" I yell at Chad as he paces the sidewalk in front of the townhome that is supposed to be a new start. I don't point out he literally has nowhere else to go unless he wants to commute to LU every day from his mom's poky apartment. I won't add insult to injury. "He is fucking loving this!" I add in a quieter tone, angling my head and shooting daggers with my eyes at the asshole lounging in the open doorway above, watching our argument with an expanding smile. "You reacting like this is playing straight into Ares's hands, babe." I grip Chad's shoulders, forcing him to stop walking and look at me. I clasp his face, fixing his gaze on mine. "I will find some way to get rid of him. I promise. But for now, you need to calm down and come back inside."

"How?" my boyfriend asks, placing his hands on my waist and pulling me in close to his body. "How will you get him out when he always seems two steps ahead of us?"

It's frustratingly true. "We need to up our game. To turn the tables and gain the upper hand." Running my hands over the velvety-soft cropped bleach-blond hair on his skull, I stretch up on tiptoes and plant a slow, lingering kiss on his lips. "You don't need to worry about it. Focus on football and your family, and leave my stepbrother to me." I know who I can turn to for advice, and I make a mental note to call Lo later.

He opens his mouth to speak just as a familiar Range Rover pulls into the parking spot alongside Chad's truck. Dad is having my Lexus SUV delivered tomorrow. He insisted on hauling it into the garage for a quick checkup, which seemed overkill to me because it was only serviced three months ago.

"What the fuck is that motherfucker doing here?" Jase asks as he climbs out of his car and slams the door shut. His gaze narrows on Ares as my stepbrother flips him the bird.

"He lives here," I say, my sigh heavy with resignation. I had a blazing argument with Dad over the phone, but he won't back down. Not until I give him some reason to, and I'm determined to find one sooner than later.

"And I thought this day couldn't get any worse," Jase mumbles, exchanging a loaded look with Chad.

All the fine hairs on the back of my neck prickle in awareness. "What's happened?" My gaze bounces between my two guys as I arch a brow.

"Let's talk inside," Jase says. He quickly looks around before bending down to brush his lips across my mouth.

While we go to great lengths to hide our relationship—for obvious reasons—Ares knew about it from the get-go. He refuses to explain how he gleaned that knowledge, which only makes us more suspicious of his motives. Apart from us, only Lo and her husbands, Jase's older brother, and a few of the guys' close friends from Lowell know. Creed and Nix are attending LU with us, but the rest of the gang accepted scholarships to USC. So, it should be easy to continue as we are until we find a way to extract Jase from his fake relationship with Julia.

"I'm not going in there," Chad says, pouting and throwing a tantrum like a toddler.

It's starting to seriously piss me off.

"Grow up, for fuck's sake," I snap, glowering at my boyfriend. "Every second you spend sulking is a victory for the asshat. Don't give him that power."

"Ash is right, and you need to be there for her. You can't leave her to deal with him alone." Jase slings his arm around my shoulders and gives them a little squeeze. My brows knit together as I process his statement, confusion immediately setting in. Before I can question him, he says, "Ignore the prick. Pretend like he doesn't exist. That'll piss him off."

"I'll fucking throttle him before the night is out," Chad says through clenched teeth. His knuckles are blanched white he's fisting them so tightly, and the vein in his neck visibly throbs as his entire body literally radiates anger and aggression.

"Channel that anger into training," Jase suggests. "I know that's what I'm going to do."

Tilting my head back, I peer up at my other lover, noticing the strain tightening his face for the first time. "What don't I know?" I have a superbad feeling, and I'm hoping I'm wrong about it.

Jase opens his mouth to reply when a high-pitched annoyingly familiar whiny voice cuts across our conversation. "There you are, my love." Jase drops his arm from around my shoulders and discreetly steps to one side as Julia comes toward us wearing a super-short, tight-fitting summer dress, teetering on ridiculously high heels. Expensive black sunglasses dwarf her heavily made-up face, hiding the look in her eyes. She's clutching an oversized designer bag in one hand and carrying her cute designer dog tucked under her other arm.

She's the walking definition of a dumb, pretty, filthy-rich, self-obsessed socialite. Except I'm no longer buying the act she's peddling. No one could be that brainless or clueless.

Julia tosses her long dark hair over her shoulders as she draws up alongside us. Snuggling into Jase's side, she smiles at us like she hasn't a care in the world.

Trapping the snarl building at the back of my throat, I subtly dig my nails into the side of my jeans as Chad slings a supportive arm around my waist. Julia pets her dog and clings to Jase as she pins me with a megawatt smile through her surgically enhanced lips.

I long to smash my fist in her smug face, drag her away from Jase, and berate her for daring to touch what's mine.

But I don't.

Because I can't.

And it's killing me inside.

This is what I've been dealing with the entire time I've been with Jase, so why has it suddenly become excruciatingly unbearable?

Jase creates a little distance between them as he looks down at his girlfriend. "I need to speak with Ash and Chad in private. I'll talk to you later."

She pouts for a few seconds before the fake smile is back on her face. "Okay, baby." She rubs his arm and licks her lips. "But don't be long. I thought we'd christen the master suite first." She leans into him and giggles, her head turned in my direction, waiting for my reaction.

All the blood drains from my face with her words, but I hold it together, refusing to let her see how she's just cut me down to size. I know for a fact Jase hasn't had any sexual involvement with Julia. He has no interest in her like that. Their parents are forcing them to be together, and their relationship is as fake as they come. They pretend in public and in front of their parents, but it's a totally different matter behind closed doors. Julia knows Chad and I are aware of the true status of their relationship, but that doesn't stop her pawing at Jase any time she is in our company.

Which is why I now suspect she knows I'm fucking him.

"Julia." Jase's harsh tone barks a warning.

"What?" She feigns innocence. "Didn't you tell your friends you're moving in with me?"

Pain glides across my chest, making breathing difficult.

"Why do you think I wanted to speak to them?" he says through gritted teeth, leveling her with a "butt out" expression.

"Oh, I thought you wanted to tell them about our engagement."

Chad tightens his arm around me in warning as her revelation hits me as hard as a physical punch to the face.

"Fuck off, Julia!" Jase snaps, scrubbing his hands down his face. "Get inside the house, and I'll deal with you later." Grabbing her arm, he hauls her toward the house directly beside ours.

Oh, joy.

"Did you know about this?" I ask Chad in a choked tone as we watch Jase escort Julia up the steps.

"I knew the moving-in shit was a possibility though his dad only dropped it on him last night. I had no clue about the engagement." Chad wraps his arms around me as he tucks me into his side. "What's with that? They're not even nineteen yet and only starting college."

Jase bounds down the steps and runs toward us.

"I can explain," he says as he comes up to us. "But not here. Let's go inside."

"Is it true?" I blurt, clinging to Chad's arm as I slant emotional eyes at Jase. "Are you moving in with her, and are you two engaged now?" I didn't see any ring on her finger, so maybe Julia just threw that out there to hurt me.

"I'm not discussing this here," Jase insists, reaching for my hand.

Ducking out from under Chad's arms, I purposely avoid Jase's touch as I stand back from both my guys. "Fine. Let's talk inside," I supply before turning on my heel and stalking up the steps.

Ares stands in the doorway, chuckling and grinning as he stares at me stomping up the steps with a face like thunder. Beyond enraged, I punch him in the nuts, catching him completely off guard for once.

"Fucking bitch," he snarls, hunching over as he cups his crotch.

"Insult my girl again, and I'll cut your tongue out," Chad retorts, shoving his broad shoulder into Ares's chest as he comes up behind me.

"Try it, pussy. I dare you," Ares snaps back, straightening up and squaring off with my boyfriend.

"Ignore him," Jase says, nudging us both forward. "He's inconsequential."

I toss a grin at Ares over my shoulder.

"That's what *he* is to you now, dollface." Ares smirks right back at me. "How does it feel to lose again?"

"Why don't you tell me? You've spent a lifetime as a loser. You're so much more experienced than me."

Jase grips me by the waist and lifts me up, carrying me into the house before Ares and I get into it.

"Put me down," I demand the instant we're inside the house.

"Temptress," Jase says in a pleading tone. "Don't shut me out. At least let me explain."

I head for the door to the left of the main stairs, wanting to have this conversation away from prying ears.

I took a quick tour of the house while Chad was outside pacing the sidewalk, and I'm pleasantly surprised. It's warm and homey with all the comforts and luxuries we need. Though not everything is to my taste, I like that it has color and character. I don't know how Hera managed to convince Mom, but I owe her one.

Flicking the switch on the wall, I trudge down the stairs into the basement level. The two moms did good with this space. There's a small gym to the left and a game room with pool table, large wall-mounted TV, and a fully stocked bar on the right. An L-shaped blue velvet couch takes center stage, surrounded by several high-backed black leather gaming chairs. A couple of gaming consoles will ensure this becomes Chad's favorite room in the whole house.

The guys come up behind me as I slide onto one of the barstools and spin around, fixing them with a dark glare. Chad's on my shit list too because he knew some of it and didn't tell me. "Start talking, Jase."

"There's no easy way to say this, so I'll just lay it on you." He pins me with earnest eyes. "It's true. I'm moving in with her, and we are getting engaged. The official announcement will be made in two months."

"What the actual fuck, man?" Chad's brow furrows. "Why the hell are you agreeing to marry someone you cannot stand?"

"The same reason I've been dating her for the past two years. It's what's expected of me."

I snort out a laugh. "You need to grow a pair and tell your dad to fuck off."

"I have tried that. Where do you think I was this morning?"

"I don't know, Jase, because you seem to be keeping secrets." I slide off the stool and walk right up to him. "This doesn't make any sense. It never has." I have questioned him in the past about it, and he's always given me bullshit answers. I have seen how the Manfords are about him and Julia. Unfortunately, my parents are great friends with the Manford Media billionaire CEO-slash-owner, and I've spent an intolerable amount of time with Julia and her family.

Our dads formed a friendship when they attended LU, and it's lasted to this day. When Julia's mom died in a skiing accident, a few days after her eleventh birthday, my mom stepped up to support James. I have had Julia's friendship forced on me. I was guilted into hanging out with her in high school, so I can kind of understand a certain level of parental pressure.

But forcing a guy to marry a woman he doesn't even like is cranking the implausibility factor to the max.

Why does it feel like I'm missing a puzzle piece?

"I know it's hard to understand," Jase says, fisting handfuls of his dark hair. "It's all tied up with business deals our fathers have made." Averting his eyes, he lowers them to the ground, and I know he's lying to us.

"He can't make you marry her," I say. "It's the twenty-first century. We're not living in the Middle Ages."

"He will cut me off, Ash. I'm not on a scholarship like Chad. If I don't do this, he'll withdraw my trust fund and stop paying for college."

"Pfft," I scoff. "Let him." I stare him straight in the face. "I have my inheritance. We don't need the Stewart money."

A pained look shimmers in his eyes. "It's not cut-and-dried. The consequences are far-reaching. He'll ostracize me from the family and drive me out of town. You know he's a powerful man with important connections. He will ruin me if I disgrace the family name. Believe me, if there were any way to get out of this, I would. But there isn't. My hands are tied."

Hurt comingles with frustration and disbelief as I peer into his piercing green eyes. "So, what? That's it? What we have means nothing to you? You're going to marry Julia? You're really going to do it?"

"Baby." He reaches for me, but I step back, avoiding Chad's touch as he reaches for me too. I'm pissed with both of them today. "What we have means everything to me. You know that," he pleads, beseeching me with his eyes. "I am so sorry about this and the way you found out. That bitch did it on purpose." He exhales heavily, his eyes still imploring me to understand. "It's not what I want, Ash. It's the very last thing I want, but I can't get out of it."

"This is such bullshit." Chad rubs a hand along the back of his neck. "All the plans we had for college have gone up in flames."

"We still have two months," Jase says, hope flaring in his eyes. "The engagement won't be official until then. After that, we'll have to fully end things. I can't risk disrespecting my fiancée."

I suck in a sharp gasp as the words leave his mouth. The pain is like nothing I have ever felt before.

"Baby." Jase is on top of me before I've processed the motion, sweeping me into his arms. "I'm so sorry. I don't care about her. At all. You're the only woman I want."

"Then fight for me!" I shout, tipping my head back to plead with him. "You are giving in too easily."

"I have spent a lifetime fighting my destiny," he cryptically replies, peppering kisses into my hair as he holds me tight. "If I could fight for you, Ash, believe me, I would. You are worth everything and more."

"Clearly not." I shuck out of his hold, walking straight into Chad's comforting arms.

"Temptress, please." Jase's anguished voice sounds at my

back, but I can't look at him anymore. "Let's not waste the time we have left."

"Fuck you!" I roar, spinning around in Chad's arms. Venom seeps from my pores as I lash out at him. "If you think I'm going to fuck around with you so you can get your rocks off before you commit to her, you have another think coming, asshole."

Does he seriously think I would be okay with that?

I'm super close to nut-punching him like I just did with Ares.

"That's not what I meant, Ash. You know how much you mean to me."

"This changes everything, Jase." Tears prick the backs of my eyes, and I work hard not to let them fall. "I want you to leave. I can't even look at you right now." Snuggling into Chad's chest, I am barely holding it together.

I stare at Jase—a man I'm deeply in love with—wondering why I ever thought it was a good idea to get mixed up in this shit. I should have resisted him from the start. I should have pushed my feelings down and pretended like I wasn't lusting after him too. If I had, I might not feel like he's just taken a machete to my heart.

Jase opens his mouth to interject, but Chad shakes his head. "Just go, man."

Jase's Adam's apple bobs in his throat as he stares at me. "Ashley, I—" His voice cracks with heady emotion, but I get no joy from his pain. What good was any of it if it's left all of us hurting?

"Leave me alone, Jase," I whisper, struggling to keep my composure. "Go to her." My voice cracks as tension bleeds into the air. "We might as well get all the breaking done now."

Chapter Six

Chad

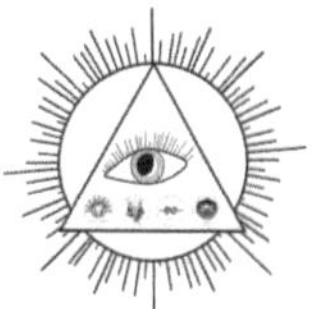

Ashley is holding it together after Jase leaves, but only just. Her pain is palpable, massively outweighing my own. "I don't understand him," I say, steering the love of my life over to the couch. "There is definitely more to this."

"I know," she agrees, flopping down on the couch with a strained sigh. "None of it ever made sense, but we pushed our questions and concerns aside because we were having too much fun."

I crouch in front of her. "It's going to be okay. You're going to be all right."

Tears pool in her eyes, and I hate seeing them there.

"It hurts, Chad," she croaks, circling her arms around my neck and hugging me. "It hurts so much."

"I know, sweetheart. I'm not happy about this at all. I like our dynamic."

"Me too." Sadness reverberates in her tone.

"I hadn't given much thought to the future, to what might happen after we leave college, so maybe it was naïve to think we could continue like this forever. It's not exactly conventional, and we both know Eric Stewart is a traditionalist. Appearances matter to Jase's family."

"Was I wrong?" she asks, pulling me up to sit alongside her. "Should I have been so quick to deny us our last couple of months together?"

I shrug. "You can only go by how you feel, Ash." I slide my arm around her shoulders and pull her into my side, kissing her temple. "You might feel differently tomorrow or in a few days." I tip her chin up, staring at a face I have loved from the second I laid eyes on it. Her big brown eyes look so sad, and I will do everything in my power to eradicate her sorrow. "You are in control like you always have been. You decide what happens next." Jase and I agreed that from the outset, and it hasn't changed. Dipping my head, I kiss her voluptuous lips, needing her to feel my love.

"Is this too much for you?" she inquires when we break our kiss, and I tilt my head back.

"What?" I ask, winding my fingers through her gorgeous hair. I loved Ash as a natural blonde but I'm really digging this silver-purple look she is owning right now. I didn't think it was possible for her to be any more beautiful, but she is fucking stunning. She's my dream woman in every single respect, and no matter what happens with Jase, I'm determined to hold on to her.

"Me heartbroken over your best friend."

I smile softly at her. "I never want you to be anything but real with me, sweetheart. I am secure in our love. I wouldn't have suggested sharing you with my best friend if I couldn't handle it." Tilting her head back, I kiss her lush mouth, pouring everything I'm feeling into the kiss so she knows I'm telling her the truth. When we break our lip-lock this time, I lift her onto my lap and band my arms around her. "I know you love him too, Ash. I would probably be more pissed if you weren't upset. It'd be like admitting our feelings weren't genuine."

"God, Chad," she whispers, dotting kisses all over my face. "I couldn't love you any more than I do right now. You're one in a million." She peers at me through glassy eyes. "Not many guys would be so accommodating. You put my needs first all the time, and I'm not sure I ever told you how much I appreciate it."

"I have always known, Ash, and trust me, it isn't entirely selfless." Grabbing hold of her ass, I reposition her so she's straddling me and feeling the semi growing in my pants. I nip at her lower lip, gently sucking it in my mouth. "You know I get off seeing him fuck you. You know I like to watch."

"Fuck," she rasps, grinding on my now rock-hard dick. "You make me so horny."

"Do you know what I think we should do?" I waggle my brows as I slide my hands underneath her shirt.

"Please say screw like rabbits?" she pants, helping me to remove her shirt as her pupils darken with desire.

My low chuckle rings out in the air. "That's a given, Siren." I still my hands on her stomach as I look into her pretty, warm-chocolate-brown eyes. "We have suffered a few setbacks today, and we should let the dust settle. Then we'll see how we're feeling and work out a plan together." Taking her hand, I lift her fingers to my mouth and kiss each one of them.

She bobs her head. "Okay."

"I love you, and that won't ever change," I say before slanting my lips against hers in a feather-soft single kiss.

"I love you too," she says, unclasping her bra and flinging it on the floor.

My hands creep up her tempting body to cup her heavy tits in my palms. "I guess we're christening this room first, huh?" I ask, thrusting my crotch into her hand as she pops the button on my jeans.

"I need you." Desperation is clear in her tone as she tugs on my jeans.

"I know what you need, and I will always take care of you." I kiss her again. "Let's fuck, unpack, and then go out for pizza, ice cream, and a movie."

"Sounds like a plan."

I'm happy to see a smile on her face as I set her feet on the ground. We make quick work of shedding the rest of our clothes, kissing and groping as we remove layers. Sitting down, I pull her back onto my lap. Our lips are frantic as we devour one another, getting lost in heated kisses and sinful touches as we temporarily forget our problems.

When we are together like this, nothing else exists.

Precum leaks from my cock when Ash takes my hard length in her hand and rubs the crown back and forth across her folds. She moans when the tip presses inside her hot pussy, and my dick jerks with the need to fill her.

"Fuck," I groan as my dick throbs with desire. "Ride me, Siren. Claim what is yours."

"Gladly, babe." Her tongue darts out, swiping a path along the seam of my lips as she slowly inches down on my erection.

We both sigh in relief when she's fully situated, neither of us moving as we take a moment to savor how we are connected. I have never had sex with any other girl, nor do I have any desire to, because I know nothing will ever top this.

Ash is all I have ever wanted and needed and that won't change.

My hands explore her sexy curves as she begins to rock on top of me. Slowly at first before she lifts her hips, moving her body in a rotating motion as she fucks me in measured strokes. I fondle her tits and caress her silky-smooth skin as she gradually drives me insane with lust. Grabbing her hips, I slam her up and down on me, setting a more punishing pace.

The sounds tumbling from her lips are enough to set me off. I fucking love how vocal my woman is during sex. It only serves to heighten my arousal. "Fuck me harder, Siren. Destroy my cock until I'm swollen and spilling my seed inside you. I want to fill you full of my cum."

"Shit, Chad." Her boobs bounce as she glides up and down on my dick, and it's fucking heaven. Grabbing handfuls of her tits, I lean forward, sucking and biting her nipples as I plunge into her, meeting her thrust for thrust, while I manhandle her soft flesh. I roughly fondle her perfect tits as my teeth tug on her hard nipples. Ash's moans and whimpers are growing louder, and when her pussy clamps down on my dick and her writhing grows more intense, I know she's close.

Burying my head in her chest, I slide one hand down between our bodies to rub her clit. My balls are heavy, and a familiar tingle shoots up my spine as my orgasm crests. I pinch her clit, and she screams out my name as she convulses on top of me, her warm pussy squeezing the cum from my dick as I explode inside her.

We rock against one another, hugging and kissing, until we are both sated. Then I hold her sweat-slickened body against mine, promising myself I will do everything I can to protect her broken heart from further pain.

Using my shirt, I clean us both up, and then we get dressed and head upstairs.

Shit for brains is walking out of the master suite when we reach the door.

Ash narrows her eyes at her stepbrother. "What were you doing in our room?"

"Moving my shit out."

His ever-perpetual arrogant grin is plastered on his face,

and as usual, my fists itch with a craving to wipe it away. It's not surprising he'd taken the master suite. His apparent amicable vacating of it is much less so.

My girlfriend shares my suspicions when she says, "And you're just giving it up with no reservations, huh?" She pushes into his face. "I don't trust you."

"Fuck if I care." He shrugs. "Daddy wants his precious princess to have the master suite, and I need to keep the old man on my side. There's no big conspiracy theory behind my actions, but if you want to create one, knock yourself out, dollface."

Deciding to take Jase's advice, I snatch Ashley's hand and brush past Ares, ignoring him as I guide my girlfriend into the bedroom.

"You should probably change the sheets," he hollers, and I hear the grin in his tone. "Unless you don't mind questionable stains and a few wet patches."

"You're disgusting," Ashley says, her face contorting into a grimace as she turns to face him. I wrap my arms around her from behind, glaring at the asshole.

"Well, *someone* is loud when they come, and I'm a guy with a high sex drive." He presses up against her, and I'm seconds away from making good on my murder threat. "If you don't want me jerking off to your moans and screams, maybe tone it down next time, dollface," he adds just before I shove him backward and slam the door in his face.

Chapter Seven

Chad

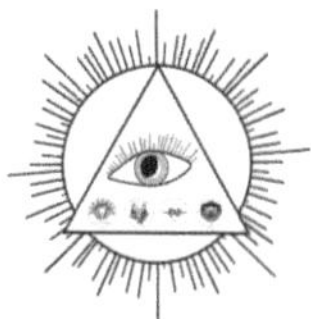

"I'm going to end up on a murder charge," I mumble, flipping the lock on the bedroom door after Ash steps inside. I toss my soiled shirt in the laundry basket by the door as I rake an approving look around the spacious room.

"Not if I beat you to it first," Ash quips, scrunching her nose as she stares at the messy sheets on the king-sized bed.

Removing my cell, I swipe my finger across the screen and scroll through my apps. "Can you close the curtains, Siren?"

"It's the middle of the day." Ash tilts her head to one side and frowns.

"I downloaded this app you can use to check for cameras and bugs," I explain, opening it up. "You have to darken the room for it to work."

Ash's eyes pop wide. "You think the asshole installed a camera?"

"Why else would he give up the master so easily? I don't trust the dickhead."

"Valid point." My girl pulls the heavy drapes over, plunging the room into almost complete darkness.

Ash leans against the door to the en suite bathroom, watching me as I scan every inch of our bedroom.

"Fucking prick," I hiss when a light flares as I scan my cell across the socket just inside the door. "Did you come across a toolbox on your tour earlier?"

"There was a box of basic supplies in a cupboard in the laundry room," she says, striding toward me. "I'll grab a screwdriver."

I turn the light on after she's left, cursing that asshole every which way to Sunday. I like filming my girl but always with her permission. How dare that fuckface try to pull this shit. We owe him major payback for it.

Ash returns a couple of minutes later, and I unscrew the socket and remove the small, thin, cylindrical recording device. I smash it to smithereens under my foot before picking up the ruined remains and tossing it in the trash. That'll teach the prick to try to get one over on us.

"I can't believe he did that," Ash says, shaking her head as she relocks our bedroom door.

"I can. The guy's a complete jerk, and he's obsessed with you," I reply, toeing my sneakers off before I pad toward the bathroom.

"Not in the way you're implying." She follows me into the bathroom, shedding her clothes on the way.

"He wants you, Siren." I shuck out of my jeans and boxers before reaching in to turn the shower on.

"He wants to fuck with all our heads. Leering at me pisses you and Jase off. That's why he's doing it."

She's delusional if she thinks he doesn't want her, but I'm done with this convo. Ares has no place in this moment with me and my girl. "Be careful around him."

"I always am," she says, removing the last of her clothes.

My eyes drink my fill as she steps toward me. Ashley Shaw has a rocking body to match her perfect personality, and she's the full package. "Fuck, you're sexy."

"Right back at ya." Stretching up, she kisses me before stepping under the flow of water.

I close the door behind me as I come up behind her, my hands gravitating to her body like a missile.

We indulge in round two in the shower. This time, I fuck her from behind, pressing Ash up against the tiled wall with my hand over her mouth to stifle her moans and screams when she comes.

After we dry and get dressed, we unpack and change the bed linen before leaving the house hand in hand. I take her for pizza and ice cream, and then we watch the latest blockbuster at the state-of-the-art campus movie theater. We make out in the back row like we're fifteen again, and I lavish her with affection, hoping it might help to distract her.

"This was fun," she says, taking my arm and wrapping it around her back when we leave the theater.

"It was." I tweak her nose as I lead us toward the parking lot. My cell pings with an incoming call as we approach my truck. I glance at the number flashing on the screen and my stomach dips. "Get in the truck, sweetheart." I hand her the keys. "I need to take this call." She sends me a withering look as she plucks the keys from my fingers. "Don't, Ash." I peck her lips. "Trust me to handle things."

She closes her eyes for a few short beats before nodding. I swat her ass as she walks off, laughing when she flips me the bird over her shoulder.

I walk off to the side as I press the answer button, accepting Jose's call before he hangs up. Angering the new VP of the Sainthood would not be a smart move. "Hey, what's up?" I ask.

"We need to meet. Usual place. Thirty minutes. Don't be late."

He hangs up before I can barter for more time. Fuck! I kick a couple of lose stones across the parking lot. After a few beats, I compose myself and walk to my truck.

"What is it?" Ash asks the second I climb behind the wheel.

"Nothing for you to worry about."

"But I do worry. It's eleven o'clock at night, Chad. No good comes from calls received that late."

Turning in my seat, I clasp her beautiful face in my hands, hating to see the troubled look in her eyes. I had only just put a smile back on her face, and one call has extinguished it. "I don't want to fight with you, Ash. We've been through this before. We've both already said what we need to say."

"This is dangerous, Chad!" She wraps her fingers around my wrist. "You could get hurt or killed. Saint Lennox warned you to back away. He is the son of the last Sainthood president. The one rotting in a shallow grave for his sins. Saint almost lost his life that night. He knows what he's talking about. If he says steer clear, then you should steer clear."

"I'll be careful." I repeat what I've said to her countless times when this argument has arisen.

"That's an oxymoron when it comes to gangs and drugs, Chad, and you fucking know it." Her body language is rigid as she sits stiffly in her seat and turns her head away from me.

Sighing, I start the engine and reverse out of the spot. "It's late. We're both tired, and it's already been a trying day. Let's not end it arguing."

She says nothing, silently steaming as I drive us home.

I don't kill the engine when I pull up to the curb at our new house. I'm already going to be late because it's a good thirty-minute drive to the meeting point on the far side of Lowell from here.

We sit in silence for a couple of minutes until Ash turns to me. "You know I'm only arguing with you because I worry."

I nod. "I know, but you should trust me to handle myself."

"It's not you I don't trust. This is so risky, Chad." She reaches over the console for my hands. "What good will you be to your mom and Tessa if you're dead or behind bars for drug offenses?"

"It won't come to that," I say through clenched teeth.

"You don't know that."

"A little faith would be nice, Ash," I snap, fucking done with this same pointless argument. She doesn't understand. No one does unless they are in my shoes.

"You are putting your life and your future at risk for stupid fucking money!" she shouts, yanking her hands back and throwing them in the air. "It's ridiculous and unnecessary when I have more than enough to support all of us!"

"For the last time, I am not a fucking charity case!" I roar, slamming my hands down on the wheel.

"I never said you were," she shouts back. "What difference does it make whose money it is as long as we have enough?"

"I will not be beholden to my girlfriend. It's my job to support myself and my family. Not fucking yours!"

"Actually, it's your mom's job to support the family. Not yours," she says, holding her chin up defiantly, and I see red.

Ash hasn't tried to keep her crumbling family together since that bitch Hera ripped into her life and tore it to shreds. Ash wasn't the one holding her sobbing mother in her arms when she fell apart. She wasn't the one watching helplessly from the sidelines while her mother sank deeper and deeper into a black hole. Ash has never had to stay awake at night, fighting sleep from a chair in her mother's room, terrified to nod off while on suicide watch.

I love my girl to bits, but she doesn't get to throw shade at my mom.

"Get the fuck out of the car, Ash!" I yell, needing her to go before I say something I can't take back. Stretching across her, I fling her door open. "I did not want to do this tonight." I try to leash my anger, but she has me fully wound up now. "You want to keep me safe, sweetheart?" I snarl at her. "Then don't fucking rile me up before I'm going to meet my contact. It pisses me off and distracts me."

"Fine." She hops out. "Go meet your contact, you fucking idiot! Ugh." She slams the door shut with more force than necessary, before thumping her fist on the hood of my truck. Ash sends me one final glare before she stomps off.

"Fuck, fuck, fuck!!" I smash my head back against the headrest, beyond aggravated. Remembering the time and the dangerous asshole I'm scheduled to meet, I put the pedal to the metal and peel out of there.

The entire drive to the meeting point, I'm trying to calm down because I need my wits about me when meeting Jose, but I'm too fucking pissed. At myself as much as Ash.

I'm trying to put myself in her shoes. It's natural Ash would point the finger at my mom. She doesn't know how bad it got—how bad it still is—because I sheltered her from the worst of it. I know my girl feels caught in the middle. As much as I hate Hera Shaw, and I really, really do, she is Ash's new stepmom, and she's been there for her in a way her own mother hasn't.

I don't want to come between them any more than I have.

So, I hid a lot of the stuff going down at home to spare Ash having to pick sides. Perhaps I should have told her everything. God knows, I could have used her advice and support when things were really bad. But I made my decision, and I can't exactly backtrack now.

The truth is, Ash cares about me. I know her words are

coming from a place of concern and love, and I need that in my life. If shit blows up with Jase, as I suspect it's going to, Ash is all I have. I don't want to fight with her and risk what we have. I couldn't bear to lose her. She's my reason for living.

I regret the things I said to her and vow to call her the minute I'm out of the meeting to make things right.

But she beats me to it.

My cell rings when I'm five minutes away from the rendezvous, and I contemplate blowing Ash off. If she's calling to drive her point home, I don't need the extra irritation. Yet, I want to make things right, and I don't like ignoring my girl. I'm conscious she's home alone with that shit-for-brains step-brother. If she needs me, I want to be there for her. So, I answer. "What?" I ask in a gruff tone, hackles raised and on edge.

"I'm not going to say sorry for worrying about your welfare, Chad, but I am sorry for angering you just before a meet." There's a brief pause. "I just love you so much, and the thought of anything happening to you terrifies me, babe."

A huge chunk slices off my anger as I turn the corner, spotting headlights in the distance. "I'll be super careful, I promise. And I have my gun."

The other piece of advice Saint and the guys gave me was to get armed and to learn how to use it. So, I did. Ash is already skilled with firearms, thanks to her dad. He's been taking Ash hunting and to the gun range for years. My girl spent hours with me at the range over the summer, teaching me what she knows. Add that to a few lessons I had with a pro trainer, and I'm confident now with a gun in my hand.

"I can't lose you too, Chad," she quietly says. "Come home to me safely."

"I will. Love you."

"I'll be waiting," she says before hanging up.

Pulling up to the side of the warehouse, I cut the engine and kill the lights. Removing my Glock from its hiding place underneath my seat, I tuck it into my jeans. Feeling eyes on me, I look out the side window.

An unfamiliar guy wearing a Sainthood leather cut sits behind the wheel of the beat-up Chevy parked alongside me, eyeballing me like I'm his next meal. I get out, and he flicks his head in the direction of the warehouse. Lifting my head, I project confidence as I walk toward the wooden structure with a swagger in my step. A lot of the time, confidence is all in the way you hold yourself and how adept you are at faking it.

The instant I step inside the door, the cool head of a gun is pressed into my temple from the side. I work hard not to panic. The Sainthood needs me, so they're not going to put a bullet in my skull. At least, not yet.

"You're late," Jose snarls, reprimand evident in his pissy tone.

"I was in North Lowell when I got your call. Got here as fast as I could."

"Sit your ass down," he barks, pushing me toward a small cluster of wooden chairs residing against the side of the warehouse.

"I'd rather stand."

"There's a time to follow the rules and a time to deliberately break 'em," the older man says, shoving me down into a chair. "Word to the wise. This ain't the time to break 'em." Jose props his foot up on the chair beside me, leans his elbow on his knee, and points his gun in my face. "Wanted to introduce you to Deke here," he says, jerking his head sideways at his younger companion.

I'd put him at mid-twenties, but it's hard to tell with the facial tattoos and the ugly-ass scar running along one cheek. Dude is ripped too and heavily armed. It's obvious he's a veteran of this life, and I'm in way over my head. Yet there is no turning back, even if I wanted to find a way out. "He'll be your contact point from now on. Midnight Sunday is the regular drop-off and pickup time. For security reasons, we'll vary the location."

Deke slaps a cell in my hand. "That's a burner and the only cell you call me from, understood?"

His accent isn't Californian and I wonder if he's transferred here from a different Sainthood chapter.

"Understood." I will gladly use the untraceable phone. I know Ash is right to be concerned. What I'm doing could seriously fuck up my future, so I'll do what I can to cover my tracks and hide this part of my life.

"Our guy is loading up your truck as we speak," Jose confirms. "Ensure the product is sold before the next meet. Our new supplier has their fingers in lots of different pies. You get requests for other product, just let me know."

"Okay." I doubt I'll have issue offloading supplies on a campus the size of LU. In previous years, a local gang controlled the drug market on campus, but the new leader of The Sainthood got rid of that problem over the summer. Now, Jose and his boss are eager to stamp their mark on this turf. They have ambitious plans to rebuild The Sainthood to even greater heights, so owning the monopoly at LU is a big coup.

"We have recruited a few other distributors," Jose explains. "For obvious reasons, we will keep things separate. We won't divulge their details to you and vice versa." He hands me a distinctive brown leather bracelet stamped with a fire emblem.

"You spot anyone selling on campus wearing one of these, he's our guy and not a threat," Deke says. "You spot anyone else selling shit, you take his pic, get his name, and send the deets to me." He flashes me a devilish grin. "We'll take care of the problem."

I really don't like the fucking sound of that, but I mount no protest. "Understood," I say.

"Get the fuck out of here, pissant," Jose says, tapping his gun against my cheek. "And don't be fucking late to a meet again."

Chapter Eight

Ares

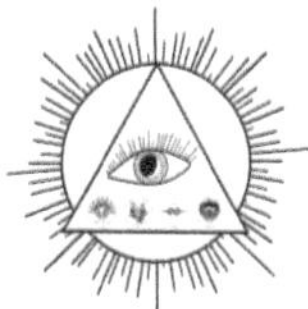

Standing under the warm spray in my en suite shower, I jerk my dick faster when I feel the familiar tingle start in my spine. With all the new metal in my cock, I had to learn different masturbation techniques, which I've put to good use since Ash and that pussy Chad moved in on Friday.

My stepsister is a total slut.

She lets him bang her whenever he wants, however he wants, and she's *very* loud when having sex. It's been a strange weekend locked in a pleasure-pain constantly aroused cycle as I jerk off non-stop while listening to and watching them fuck.

I hate the sleazy prick, even more so now. He doesn't deserve a woman like Ash.

Which is one of the reasons I intend to steal her from him and break them up.

It's already so fun toying with my little sister, but the best is yet to come—pun intended.

"Damn," I hiss, tugging my dick harder when my balls lift and tighten, and my release is imminent.

Closing my eyes, I visualize us together, like I have been

doing these past six months. In this particular fantasy, I have Ashley's silver-purple hair wrapped tight around my fist and her naked body pressed flush against a window as I roughly fuck her from behind, slamming in and out of her with my pierced dick as she screams and moans and pleads for more. All while pussy one and pussy two look on from outside with mournful expressions that quickly morph into anger.

My arousal spikes, equally spurred on by visions of nailing Ash and her fuckboys' obvious rage. I explode all over the tiled wall, grunting as my elongated cock spurts ropes of cum in a seemingly endless arc.

Thank fuck, my last piercing is healed, and I can resume sexual activity. I have had the worst blue balls for weeks. I have wanted a Jacob's ladder piercing for a long time, but I never had the patience to deny myself sex. Until I moved into my new home and began sharing living space with my smoking hot new stepsister. No other woman existed after that. That bitch is all I see.

Ash is a cunt in more ways than one, but I love that about her. From my stalking, I knew she was beautiful, but she still stole my breath when I came face to face with her for the first time. Her instant dislike of me was the cherry on top. Nothing gets my juices flowing more than when she's mouthing off at me. Her involvement with those two idiots only added to the attraction. After all, they were who led me to her. Though it would have happened anyway when Mom fell in love with her dad.

It just confirms I am on the right path.

The sexual tension between us is growing by the day, and I can't wait until she gives in. I actually hope she doesn't at first. Forcing her to confront her attraction to me will be all the sweeter.

Turning off the shower, I get out and grab a towel, drying

off quickly before wrapping it around my hips. I head into my bedroom, making a beeline for my closet. I'm reaching for a clean pair of jeans when an idea comes to me. Chuckling to myself, I forget about clothes and dump my towel on the ground, walking downstairs stark naked. I know the others are up because it's their first day of classes and I heard them moving around before I jumped in the shower.

Whistling under my breath, I stroll into the kitchen with a smirk on my face. "Sup, assholes?" I say, waggling my brows when Chad turns to look at me, his mouth hanging open in shock.

"Oh my fucking god!" Ash shrieks, dropping the dish in her hand the instant she spots me. The glazed plate cracks apart when it hits the floor, sending ceramic shards and eggs and bacon scattering across the white porcelain tiles. "What the hell are you doing?" Her eyes are glued to my dick as I step around the debris and open the refrigerator.

"Getting breakfast," I say, removing a bowl of chopped fruit and natural yogurt from the shelf.

"Put some goddamned clothes on!" Chad hisses, finally finding his voice.

I work hard to smother my laughter. "Why?" Spinning around to face him, I set the yogurt and fruit on the island unit. "Does the naked body offend you?" I arch a brow, conscious of Ash's heated gaze laser-focused on me as I stretch up and remove a box of granola from the overhead cupboard. I purposely flex my ass cheeks, and her sharp little inhale is music to my ears. Grinning, I turn around, deliberately swinging my dick from side to side.

Ash's cheeks are flushed red, and she's struggling to keep her eyes on my face. My dick swells under her attention, and I know it won't take long to achieve full mast. I haven't had sex in months, and I'm starved for pussy.

"*Your* naked body offends me," Chad retorts, getting up and moving around in front of me, blocking the view from his girlfriend.

Placing the box of cereal on the counter, I turn to face him, putting myself all up in his personal space. I like that I'm a little taller than him, and the pathetic ink he added to his chest and one arm over the summer isn't a patch on the one-of-a-kind artwork covering my body. His eyes flit briefly to my nipple piercings, and I smirk. Yeah, he knows he's fucked. He knows there is no way his girl will be able to resist me forever. I make a silent no-clothes-in-the-house vow. Teasing Ash with my naked body will deliver my goals that much sooner.

"Intimidated much?" I taunt, grabbing my cock and slowly rubbing the side of my shaft. "Jealous?" My grin threatens to split my face in two as he backs up, valiantly trying to shield Ash from my nakedness. Ignoring the wimp, I turn my attention to my newest obsession. "What about you, slutty little sis?" I fix her with a heated stare full of wicked intent. "Does my nakedness offend you?"

"You're being an ass." She lifts her chin, piercing me with beautiful big brown eyes. "If this is an attempt to mess with us, it won't work." She shrugs, like she's not creaming her panties at the sight of my ripped, tatted-up body and pierced dick.

I crank out a laugh. "Tell that to your boyfriend. He's so insecure he has to shield you from my dick." I smirk at the asshole. "He knows he won't ever measure up to me."

"You're full of shit." Chad puffs out his chest before pulling Ash in under his arm. "I keep my woman very satisfied. I'm not threatened by you."

"You should be," I say, grinning manically. "Your girlfriend hasn't taken her eyes off my cock since I stepped foot in the kitchen. Isn't that right, dollface?" I turn to Ash, catching her lowered gaze before she conceals it. Her heated glare feels like a win, and I chuckle as I slowly undress her with my eyes while pumping my rock-hard dick. "It's okay, babe, *he* likes you too. Look how hard you made him. In record time as well." I waggle my dick in her direction, enjoying the look of frustrated anger mixed with reluctant arousal on her face.

She can deny it until she's blue in the face, but I know she wants me. Chicks always do when they get a look at what I'm packing in my pants and hiding underneath my clothes.

"Fuck off, you degenerate." Chad shoves me, and I narrow my eyes at him.

"Touch me again, and I'll flatten you," I warn.

"Hit on my girl again, and I'll kill you."

Brave words for such a pussy. "Not my fault my dick likes her attentive gaze. Seems to me your woman has an issue with commitment," I add, twisting the knife. "Or maybe it's just *your* dick that can't satisfy her." I purposely twist my hand, arching my cock to give her a proper look. The bright overhead lights glimmer off the side of one piercing, glinting and bouncing against the cupboards.

A smug grin spreads over my mouth as Ash's eyes pop wide. Shoving my breakfast to one side, I jump up on the counter and stand with my legs slightly spread, gripping my dick at the base and holding it up for her inspection. "You can see better from this angle, dollface." I lick my lips as I let her drink her fill of all the metal on the underside of my shaft. "Don't be shy. Get up close and personal." I thrust my hips as I slowly stroke my hard-on. "You know you want to."

She audibly gulps as Chad looks like he's two seconds from grabbing a knife and stabbing me with it. "The last piercing only just healed. Haven't had a chance to test-drive the experience with the full ladder. Just say the word, and I'll bend you over this counter and drive this beast into your wet cunt. I guarantee you haven't ever been properly fucked until I've fucked you."

I cast my eyes briefly in Chad's direction before refocusing on Ash. It's time to move the stakes up and take this to the next level. "Whenever you're ready to trade up, dollface, just say the word. I've been fantasizing about fucking you every which way to Sunday from the second I met you. I fuck my hand every night and every morning to visions of you." It's no lie.

Ash's face pales, and she reacts a split second too late, not reaching Chad in time before he lunges at me. "You crazy motherfucker!" he roars, making a grab for my leg just before I pivot off the counter, jumping onto the floor in one skillful move. "She's not yours, you delusional prick. She's *mine*, and if you don't quit with this shit, I'll fucking kill you right now!" he adds, racing around the counter toward me.

"I thought you liked sharing your woman," I reply, ducking down as his fist comes at me. "I hear there's a vacancy. I want to apply," I add, swinging around and landing a solid punch in his gut.

"Knock it off!" Ash shouts. "You're acting like idiots."

We both ignore her. Chad stumbles back but recovers fast, thrusting his arm out, and I don't move fast enough this time. His fist glances along the side of my jaw, and it's fucking on. "The way I see it, you owe me. Your dad screwed with my mom. Now it's my turn to return the favor."

My words throw gasoline on the flames, and we really get into it then, throwing fists and spewing angry words as Ash screams at us to stop.

Chad and I enter into the spirit of it, channeling weeks of pent-up aggression into every punch and jab. It's been too long since our last fistfight, and this was inevitable.

Chad is so predictable. Too volatile, and so easy to wind up, but I respect him for giving it his all. Dude is a melting pot of violent repressed rage, and I like coaxing it to the surface. If he knew it was playing directly into my hands, he might act smarter, but he won't figure it out until it's too late.

Blotting my surroundings out, I focus solely on him as we beat the shit out of one another.

"What in the actual fuck?" someone says, and I peek over Chad's shoulder, spotting Jase Stewart charging toward us. Behind him, his fiancée clings to the doorway, her eyes bugging out of her head as she surveys the scene in front of her.

"Do something," Ash implores Jase, walking alongside him. I'm guessing she swallowed her pride and went to ask him for help.

Chad swings at me, and I duck to the side, bringing my leg up and kicking him in the stomach.

"Enough," Jase shouts in a firm tone. "Chad, dude, you need to stop."

Julia giggles, eyeing my dick like it's the finest filet as she comes up behind her fiancé. "This would be infinitely more exciting if you were naked too, Chad," she drawls, her eyes glued to my dick much like Ash's previously. Jase wrestles Chad back, and Ash stands in front of him, whispering in hushed tones.

I straighten up, knowing when to call it quits. I'll expunge the rest of my frustration at the gym after work.

"Fuck, your piercings are hot," Julia says, licking her lips and blatantly eye fucking me.

"Yeah?" I wipe sweat from my brow as I return her eye fuck, even if she's not my type. I'm not one to turn down an opportunity when I see it. "Want to see how hot they are thrusting inside your pussy?" Grabbing her by the waist, I reel her into my naked body and grind my dick against her. "Bend over the counter, and I'll fuck you until you see stars."

Julia shrieks as she's suddenly yanked away from me, and

it's an awful high-pitched, keening sound. "Go home, Julia," Ash snaps, flexing her jaw as she glares at her former friend. "We have this under control now."

Julia barks out a laugh. "Sure, you do, Ash." She turns to me with a wolfish grin. "Raincheck, sexy?"

"You betcha, beautiful." I play along purely to see how Ash reacts, and she doesn't let me down.

"Don't you have class?" she snaps, moving in front of Julia to block her view of me much like Chad did earlier.

Interesting.

I hadn't factored Julia into my planning. Now I'm thinking it was an oversight. This could work out very advantageously.

"Don't *you*?" Julia snaps back, shoving Ash's hand off her arm. "You don't get to push me around, Ash. This isn't high school, and you're a fucking nobody. I'm the Manford heir, and I won't be talked down to by anyone, least of all you."

Seems like somebody has grown a pair of balls over the summer.

"I see the gloves are finally off," Ash says, holding her back straight.

I lean against the counter, deriving enormous enjoyment from this morning's entertainment.

"Took you long enough," Ash adds, whipping her head in Jase's direction and smirking. Her fuck buddy, ex-fuck buddy, or whatever the hell he is, stares at her with abject longing while Chad glares at me, dabbing at a trickle of blood leaking from his nose.

"Don't flatter yourself, *Temptress*. I have always known." Julia levels her with a withering stare.

"Bullshit," Ash retaliates.

Julia's haughty laugh rings out around the room. "I wanted to give you enough rope to hang yourself. I knew you'd fall in love with him, like I knew he would never be yours." Walking over to Jase, she cups his cock through his jeans. "It doesn't matter whether I want him or he wants me," she adds, not casting a glance at her fiancé when he forcibly removes her hand from his dick and curses at her. "I'll ride his dick anyway, and he'll let me because he has no choice. I don't even care if he imagines it's you when he's fucking me." She walks right up to Ash, tipping her chin up to gloat at her.

I am loving this interesting development and salivating at all the additional prospects it presents.

"Because it'll be *me* he's fucking not you." She shoves her finger in Ash's chest, and Ash automatically bats it away. "Every time he drives his big cock inside me, I will be driving the knife deeper in your heart, so I'll keep doing it, and I'll rub your face in it every chance I get."

In an unexpected move, Ash's arm juts out, and she punches Julia in the nose. I lean against the island unit and chuckle. Ash's violent, possessive streak only adds to her appeal. "You talk a big game, Julia, but everyone in this room knows you're full of vapid air," Ash says.

Julia doesn't go down screaming and crying like I'd expect her to. Eyes burning with hate, she lunges at Ash, and they tumble to the ground in a tangle of limbs.

"Girl fight. Oh goodie." I grin as I settle in to watch the show. My dick instantly hardens watching the two chicks wrestle on the floor. "I didn't think this day could get any better, but it's already surprising the heck out of me," I add, talking to myself.

Julia wraps her hands around Ash's neck and squeezes hard. Ash's face turns a pale shade of blue, and that snaps pussy one and two out of it. They swing into action the instant Ash brings her knee up into the other woman's groin and simultaneously lifts her chin and headbutts Julia. It works to loosen Julia's hold on her. Ash grabs Julia's tits through her flimsy dress, squeezing hard and digging her long nails in.

Julia howls in a mix of pain and rage, and I crack up laughing. It's magnificently dirty, and I'm here for it. My cock is painfully hard now, and I need to rub another one out.

This time Julia doesn't disappoint as a strangled, frustrated, high-pitched scream leaves her lips when Jase lifts her off a snarling Ash. Chad helps his girlfriend to her feet while I curse the spoilsports for ruining my fun.

The girls glare at one another, and I'm hard as steel.

Might as well throw another jab. "A good hard dicking is just what you ladies need to channel all that aggression in the right way." I push off the counter and straighten up with my cock in my hand. "Lucky for you, threesomes are my specialty, and I volunteer as tribute." I wink and lick my lips as I let my gaze roam from one woman to the other, disappointed when neither of them looks at me. The beef between them has clearly been years in the making if my magnificent dick and the promise of a fucking good time doesn't break their stare off.

Ash's mouth curls in distaste, but she doesn't look at me as she says, "Fuck off, Ares. No one is buying what you're selling." Ashley peers down her nose at the much shorter woman. "Tell yourself whatever you must to feel better about yourself, but know this, bitch. Jase will never care about you. I will always have his heart, and you'll always have his contempt and indifference."

"Whore, you're as dumb as a bag of rocks if you truly believe that."

Chad bands his arm around Ash to restrain her before she can reignite the fight. Nail marks are evident on her slender throat and a nice colorful bruise is already mushrooming on Julia's forehead and another one on her nose.

Jase hauls Julia back, stabbing her with a warning look

before his gaze darts to Ash. His Adam's apple jumps in his throat as he stares longingly at her.

I do believe the pussy actually loves my slutty little sister.

Boo-fucking-hoo.

"Yes, let's go." Julia spins around in his arms, pressing herself up against him. "Let's continue what we were in the middle of before we were so rudely interrupted."

Jase removes Julia from his person, looking like he's ready to dig a hole in the backyard and bury her in it. His gaze darts to Ash. "It's not what she's insinuating. I haven't touched her."

"Yet," Julia purrs, turning around to face Ash again. "But it's only a matter of time." She straightens up, and the ditzy, dumb, bored socialite expression she prefers a lot of the time drops off her face. "I'm the daughter and heir of one of the most powerful billionaires on the planet. You can never compete with me. We're on different levels." Her face contorts into a nasty grimace as she rakes her gaze up and down Ash's body. "You won't be clueless for much longer, and then you'll realize I was always the winner, and you are nothing but a pawn in a game you were always destined to lose."

Chapter Nine

Ares

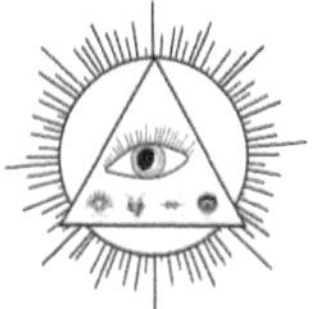

"This was wildly entertaining," I say, pushing off the counter after Jase and Julia are gone. "We should definitely do it again sometime soon." Smirking, I trail my fingers along Ash's arm as I pass by. "My offer still stands, dollface. Anytime you want to test-drive a real man, you know where to find me."

"Eat shit and die," Ash deadpans, gripping Chad's arm tight in warning.

Flashing them a smug grin, I make a lewd gesture with my fingers and my hand. "Peace out, assholes," I say before exiting the kitchen and making my way up to my bedroom.

Dropping down on my unmade bed, I blare some heavy metal as I spread my thighs and wrap my hand around my junk, jerking off in record time as I imagine bending Ash over the island unit and destroying her cunt with my cock.

After I'm dressed, I move to the window when I hear the front door slamming downstairs. My good mood elevates watching Ash and Chad sharing heated words as they bound down the steps toward their cars.

Ash's brand-spanking-new LX 570 is parked beside my Triumph Bonneville. Doug dropped it off sometime on Saturday when I was out. I heard Ash talking about it on a call later that night, complaining she didn't need a new SUV and her dad was going completely overboard.

Spoiled, ungrateful little bitch.

I agree it seems unnecessary, but it's done now, so why is she whining?

When you have grown up with the bare minimum, like I did, and money was always tight, you learn to appreciate the things you are given.

That car is wasted on my slutty little sis.

It seems old Dougie boy is determined to win the Most Protective Dad award. I get he's nervous his little girl is at college and out in the big bad world, but I think he's taking it a bit far with his expensive gift. That SUV is usually used by heads of state and their security teams. Gifting one to a college freshman is ridiculous. If Dougie wanted to earn brownie points, why not buy her a flashy sports car? Or if he's that worried about safety, there are plenty of conventional choices. What does Ash need with an armored SUV that has a shatter-protection floor, battery and tank armor, hand grenade and side blast protection, a fire extinguishing system, and state-of-the-art tracking system?

I can't help wondering if there is some ulterior motive. Like does he have a legit reason to be this concerned about her safety? It doesn't make sense. Doug is only a glorified accountant, albeit a successfully wealthy one, and I know wealth can bring the crazies out. I make a mental note to ask Xavier—my friend and go-to tech guy—to dig further into Doug's background. The background check I had performed on him when Mom first started dating him came back clean. I'm probably being paranoid, but it can't hurt to take another look.

I chuckle to myself when Jase and Julia emerge from their townhome, also arguing. Rubbing my hands with glee, I give myself a proverbial pat on the back for a job well done.

Waiting until the warring kids have left, I exit the house and power up my motorcycle.

The ride to work is disappointingly short. The owner of the garage is there to greet me on my first day, and he personally introduces me to the rest of his employees before leaving me in the capable hands of his manager. I spend my day underneath a first model Dodge Hellcat, chatting with the other guys as Led Zeppelin plays in the background.

I hit the open road when my shift ends, avoiding the highway as I head to South Lowell to visit Mom and collect the tech from my stepfather. I stop by the gym first for a quick workout before heading home.

"How did your first day go?" Mom asks when I step into the kitchen of the home she now shares with Douglas Shaw.

"Good." I lean in and kiss her on the cheek. "I'm going to hit the shower."

"Don't take too long," she calls out after me. "Doug is on his way home, and dinner will be ready in ten."

Heading up to my room, I dump my dirty clothes in the laundry and hop in the shower. I am coming downstairs in a clean shirt and jeans, in my bare feet, when Doug enters the house.

"Ares, my man." Doug grabs me into a hug and slaps me on the back. I roll my eyes, even if he's not the worst in the world. He makes Mom happy, and that's all that matters. "Good first day?" he inquires, depositing his leather briefcase on the hall table.

"Yep." I cut straight to the reason for my visit. "Do you have the equipment?"

Doug's eyes flash in warning as he glances toward the door

to the kitchen. "Not in front of your mother. We'll talk after dinner."

Nodding, I follow him into the kitchen, glad we are eating here and not in the stuffy dining room.

Mom sets heaping plates of moussaka in front of Doug before leaving bowls of ratatouille, rice, and salad in the middle of the table.

"There's enough here to feed an army, Ma." I scoop up a forkful of the minced lamb, eggplant, and potato mix, pleased she cooked my favorite dish.

It's important to Mom we remember our Greek heritage, so she generally cooks a traditional meal at least once a week.

"I thought Ashley and Chad might join us for dinner," she explains, sitting beside her new husband. "But they were both busy." Her shoulders slump a little.

Doug chuckles. "She only just moved out, honey. You need to give her space to spread her wings."

I smother a laugh. That's a bit rich coming from the man who bought his only child an armored vehicle.

"I just miss her."

I know Mom means that, which is problematic. When I destroy Ash, Mom is going to lose her shit with me. The thought makes me uncomfortable but not enough to change my plans. I don't have that luxury. Every day that passes with no progress or new leads, that kernel of hope I'm nurturing fades a little.

Shoveling moussaka in my mouth, I force the food down over the painful lump in my throat.

"I'll ask her to drop by on Sunday for dinner," Doug supplies, circling his arm around Mom and squeezing.

"I'll tell her," I offer, purely so I can exclude pussy one from the invite. Seeing his girl leaving with me will seriously piss him off, and I live for that shit.

We chat casually the rest of the meal, and I help Mom with the cleanup while Doug goes upstairs to change out of his suit.

"How are things working out with you and Chad living in the same house?" Mom asks as I'm rinsing plates at the sink.

"Peachy." It's no lie. I'm perfectly happy with how things are going with the pussy. Doubt he'd make the same statement if you asked him though.

Mom sighs while stacking plates in the dishwasher. "It's not Chad's fault, Ares. You need to let that animosity go."

Gripping the edge of the sink, I turn my head to look at my mother. "Give me proof he wasn't involved, and maybe I'll consider it."

Glancing at the open door, she lowers her voice. "Give me proof he *was*, and maybe I'll agree you have a right to your vendetta."

"Until we know either way, he's on my shit list, and there's nothing you can say that'll change my mind." I resume rinsing the dinnerware, finishing the last few items and stacking them in the dishwasher while Mom stands there looking troubled and lost in thought.

"Maybe it's time we accepted the facts," she whispers, staring at me through blurry eyes. "Maybe it's time to admit defeat and let it go."

"What?" Shock ripples through me. "No," I bark, glaring at her. "How can you even say that?"

"It's dangerous, Ares, and it's changing you." She clutches my hand. "You are all I have left. I will die if anything happens to you."

My anger ebbs as quickly as it arrived. "Nothing is going to happen to me, Ma. I'm being smart. I'm biding my time even when I want to do the opposite."

"What about The Bulls?" She casts a wary glance at the door.

"I'm beginning to think it's a waste of my time." I rub the back of my neck. "I still can't get near Ruben."

"I've been thinking about that. What if we asked Doug to help? I bet he could get you into the prison to see him."

I stare at her like her brain just dropped out of her skull. "Doug is an *accountant*, Mom. How the fuck could he help to get me into a maximum-security prison to see the ex-president of The Bulls?"

She bites on the corner of her mouth in an obvious tell.

I cross my arms and level her with a sharp look. "What haven't you told me?"

Her features smooth out too fast and I just know she's going to lie to me. "Nothing, except he's far better connected than you think. He might have qualified as an accountant, but he co-owns and manages a multimillion-dollar business. You don't get to do that without rubbing shoulders with powerful men."

Before I question her on the blatant lie, Doug reappears in the kitchen ending our conversation. Mom hastily hurries out of the house to meet with her friend for their weekly salsa dancing class, conveniently leaving me alone with my stepfather.

"Let's talk in my office," he says, and I trail him through the plush mansion to his large home office.

I stand against the wall by the door as he rounds his desk and unlocks the top drawer. Removing a large brown envelope, he dumps it on the desk and straightens up, eyeballing me. "Before I give this to you, I want to make one thing abundantly clear." I arch a brow, eager to hear his little speech. "This is for Ashley's *protection*."

"I know," I deadpan, schooling my features into a neutral line.

"I put a list of locations in with the devices. You plant the cameras in those places only." He narrows his eyes at me in warning. "My daughter is entitled to her privacy."

I shoot him an incredulous look. "If that's the case, why are you asking me to install cameras in the house? And why didn't you do it when the place was being done up? I would've been none the wiser."

"It wasn't deemed necessary then." A muscle pops in his tense jaw as he stares at me.

"And it is now?" My spidey senses are tingling. There is definitely more to this than meets the eye.

"You agreed to help keep Ashley safe. The reasons behind my motivation don't matter. You are either with me or not. Which is it?"

"No need to get your panties in a bunch, old man. I said I'd help, and I'm a man of my word."

"No cameras in her bedroom or bathroom, Ares. The same goes for Chad."

"I wouldn't dream of such a thing," I lie.

"I'm trusting you with my daughter. Don't let me down."

"Wouldn't dream of it, *Dad*."

A tired sigh slips from his lips, and strain is evident on his face as he drops down in his chair. "I know we didn't exactly get off on the right foot, but I'm trying to make it right. I love your mother, and you're her world. I thought we'd come to an understanding."

I claim the seat in front of his desk. "We have. You'll keep my mother safe, and I'll do the same for your daughter."

He nods slowly before sliding the package across the desk to me.

As I reach for it, he slams his hand down on top of mine over the envelope. Drilling me with a dark look, he peers directly into my eyes. "You're not to touch her."

I hold his stare as tension bleeds into the air. "Who said I was going to?"

"I see the way you look at her, and I know you hate Chad. I also know the reasons why. They're good kids. Don't fuck with them, or this understanding we have will become something else."

Grabbing his shirt with my free hand, I yank him toward me, getting all up in his face. "Are you threatening my mother, Doug? Cause I got to say, that won't end well for you. Just look at what we did to the last guy who hurt her."

Forcibly removing my hand from his shirt, with more strength than I thought he possessed, he glowers at me. "Of course, I'm not threatening your mother. I love her. I wouldn't harm a hair on her head. But I won't hesitate to hurt *you* if you do anything to hurt Ashley, even knowing how much it would hurt Hera." He shoves my shoulders, pushing me back before he rises. "You'd be wise not to underestimate me, son."

"Understood." I shove the envelope down the front of my jeans and stand.

"She's your sister, Ares," he adds as I turn to leave. "That means she's off-limits to you."

I walk to the door in silence before deliberately turning to face him. "She's my *step*sister, we're not blood related, and if she wants me to fuck her, I will and there isn't a damn thing you can say or do to stop it."

Chapter Ten
Ashley

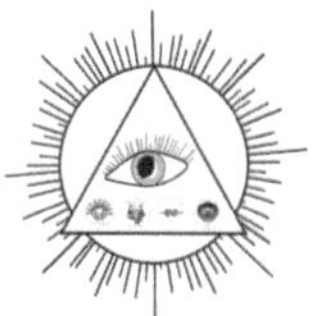

"Psst," a girl whispers in my ear, attempting to drag me from sleep at the same time she tugs on my elbow. "Wake up. Class is over," the unfamiliar woman adds, and I reluctantly force my eyes to open.

"Ugh." Rubbing the back of my sore neck, I straighten up. Tilting my head from side to side to loosen out the kinks, I ignore the amused looks of my classmates as they file out of the auditorium. Up on the podium, the gray-haired man with the potbelly shakes his head as he stares at me, and it's fair to say I haven't made the best first impression with my History of Psychology prof. "I cannot believe I slept through the entire class," I admit over a yawn as I look at the girl sitting beside me.

She grins, yanking the tie out of her bright-blue hair, letting it fall in straight lines down her back. "You were in a deep sleep too." Her brows climb to her hairline in amusement. "Had to nudge you in the ribs a couple times when you let out a snore."

"Oh shit." I bark out a laugh as I stifle another yawn and begin stuffing my things in my book bag.

"I was told the first couple of weeks are rough, and it's the fucking truth." She stands, slinging her bag over one shoulder.

"You're a freshman too?" I ask, noticing her strange eyes for the first time. One eye is a silvery-blue, and the other is a vibrant green. I have heard about heterochromia before but never met a person with the trait. It's really cool.

"Yep, for my sins." Cocking her head to one side, she winks, and there's something so familiar about the gesture.

"Have we met before?"

She shakes her head. "I don't think so."

I thrust my hand out. "I'm Ash."

She pumps my hand in a firm grasp. "I'm Bree."

"What other classes are you taking?" I ask as we exit the lecture hall together.

"Why don't we share schedules," she suggests, extracting her cell from the back pocket of her jeans. "Digits too," she adds, smiling warmly at me, and just like that, I've made my first new friend at school.

Jase comes charging out of the locker room first, making a beeline for me. I reinforce the walls around my heart like I have been doing these past two weeks. I'm determined to cut Jase out of my life, and he's determined to get me to change my mind.

"Can we talk?" he asks.

"I have nothing to say to you." Turning around, I give him my back because it's too hard to look at him and not want to throw myself into his arms.

"Please, Ash. I'm dying without you."

At any other time, I'd roll my eyes at such blatant melodrama. But the truth is, I feel like I'm dying without him too, so

I know he's not being dramatic on purpose. I haven't managed to snatch more than three or four hours of sleep each night since the revelation. Hence why I'm snoozing in class.

College life is not off to an auspicious start.

"Perhaps you should've thought about that before getting engaged to that bitch." I am still incredibly angry over the whole situation.

"I'm not engaged to her. It hasn't happened yet."

Spinning around, I glare at him, spotting other members of the football team exiting the locker room. "That's just semantics, Jase, and you know it."

"I miss you." He fixes puppy-dog eyes on me and leans in closer. The spicy, citrusy scent of his cologne wraps around me like a comforting blanket, and I feel like crying. "I miss you so fucking much. You're the only thing on my mind, every second of every day." He threads his fingers through my hair, moving in even closer.

At this proximity, it's hard to remain strong.

Piercing green eyes trap me in place as his lips curve up in a soft, seductive smile. "You're the other half of my heart and soul, Temptress," he says in that deep sexy tone I love. His warm breath fans across my face as he brushes his thumb along my lower lip, dragging it slowly from one side of my mouth to the other while his gaze devours me. He still hasn't cut his dark hair, and it tumbles in sexy tousled strands across his strong brow, the ends slightly damp from his shower. Heat rolls off him in hypnotic waves as his eyes dip to my mouth, and he grasps my hips, pulling me in flush with his body. "I'm barely existing without you, Ash. I can't eat, can't sleep, can't concentrate for shit. I'm fucking up at training." His arms band around my back as he moves our faces closer, and it's like I'm spellbound, caged in his magnetic attention, incapable of breaking free. "Not that I care about any of that. I only care about you."

His eyes probe mine as his mouth descends. His lips glide against mine in a featherlight touch, and everything inside me turns to a puddle of goo. As if on autopilot, I grip his hips and crush his body to mine as our mouths meet in a marriage of frantic lust. Slanting his head, Jase takes control of the kiss, ravishing my mouth like he never thought he'd get to do it again.

His mouth is warm and demanding as he kisses me deeply and passionately, and I'm clinging to him with a desperation I know I'll regret, but right now, need trumps everything else. When he prods at the seam of my lips, demanding entry, I readily give in, unable to deny either of us what we need. His tongue plunges inside my mouth, and we dance a tango, battling for supremacy, as liquid lust sweeps through me at his familiar touch.

Jase's hands roam my body, molding to my curves through my clothes, and I grab his ass through his jeans, wishing I could snap my fingers and our clothes would be gone so I could climb his body and impale myself on his giant dick.

"I know you like being risqué in public, and I'm into watching, but dry-fucking right outside the locker room is probably taking things too far." Chad's words are like a bucket of ice water over my head, and I rip out of Jase's arms, panting and inwardly berating myself for being so fucking weak.

What the hell was I thinking making out with him like that in front of their teammates?

"Shit," I hiss, noticing our actions are drawing a crowd. Members of the team who were heading down the tunnel toward the parking lot are doing U-turns and coming this way.

My boyfriend snakes his arm around my waist before shouting over his shoulder. "Nothing to see here, folks. Be on your way."

I look up at my boyfriend. "Chad, I'm so sorry. I don't know what the hell came over me." Whirling around, I narrow my eyes at Jase as I point my finger in his direction. "Actually, I do. You fucking bamboozled me."

Jase's mouth tugs up at the corners. "Pretty sure I don't have any magical powers, baby. We just can't resist one another. We never could."

"No." I vigorously shake my head as I link my fingers in Chad's. "No, you fucking seduced me! Asshole. And you did it in public too!" Jase has always been a flirty guy, and I have seen him lay the charm on thick in certain social situations. I have never met his older brother, Balthazar, as he's been at LU the past three years, but I have heard all the stories. He's a known charmer and a big manwhore to boot. Their father too, if the rumors of his repeated infidelity are true. I guess it runs in their genes, but this is the first time Jase has deliberately seduced me, and I don't like it.

It feels dishonest. Fake. Manufactured.

"Julia knows about us. We don't have to sneak around anymore." Jase stares at me with pained, pleading eyes. Bruising dark circles paint the skin under his eyes, and there's at least a week's worth of growth on his chin and cheeks.

Jase is beautiful.

He truly is.

And I'm so attracted to him, but it doesn't excuse what he's done or change anything.

He's watching emotions flit across my face as Chad holds on to me. "I know things are messed up right now, but it doesn't change how I feel about you. How I have always felt about you. Please don't push me away. Please give me a chance to fix this."

I lean back into my boyfriend, needing his strength to stick to my resolve.

Jase's shoulders hunch as he shoves his hands deep in his

pockets. "Tell me what to do. I'm begging you, Ash," he says in a quiet, desolate tone.

"Move out of her house and tell your dad to stick his engagement where the sun doesn't shine." I repeat what I told him yesterday when he accosted me, the day before that, and the day before that.

"I wish I could. I really do." Sadness shrouds him in a heavy veil, and it feels like I have rocks pressing down on my heart.

"You *can* do it. You just refuse to."

Strands of dark hair fall into his eyes when he shakes his head. "It's not up to me. It's not my choice."

"Then explain it to me, and don't say it's about money because we both know that's bull."

Chad nuzzles his nose in my hair and holds me tighter.

"I wish I could, but I can't."

A harsh laugh erupts from my throat. "You're like a broken record, Jase, and I'm sick of hearing it. Until you grow a pair and fight for me, I know one thing you can do." I glare at him. "Leave. Me. The. Fuck. Alone!" Grabbing Chad's hand, I turn my back to Jase once more. "We need to go, or we'll be late."

Chad looks over my shoulder, silently communicating with his best friend in that way of theirs. I don't look. I don't want to know what's being exchanged.

Things have been tense between them lately, but I'm encouraging Chad not to let what happened between Jase and me impact their friendship. They train and play on the same team. Our personal shit can't get in the way of Chad's NFL ambitions.

Chad slides his arm around my shoulders and steers me toward the tunnel.

"Ashley!" Jase roars after me, and a few seconds later, the thud, thud of approaching footsteps echoes behind us.

I rub a tense spot between my brows. He needs to let this go. To let *me* go. I won't play second fiddle to Julia. It's all or nothing now.

Jase runs in front, forcing us to stop or slam into him. "Ash, baby, please." Tortured green eyes meet my heartbroken brown ones. "I meant everything I said. I care about you so deeply. You're my world. I...I..." His mouth opens and closes a couple of times and it's like he wants to say more but the words won't come out.

"If you've got something to say, say it." Chad encourages his buddy to fess up.

I arch a brow at Jase as I watch him wage some inner war. Losing my patience, I throw my hands in the air. "Oh, whatever, Jase. Just fuck off." I nudge Chad and walk around his prone best friend. We have only taken a few steps when he calls out after us again.

"I'm not the only one who can fight," he yells. "If you care for me like you say you do, then fight for *me*!"

Twirling around, I walk back up to him. "I am fighting for you, Jase." I prod his chest with the tip of my index finger.

He shakes his head. "No, you're not. You've given up. You have shut me out and just rolled over and let her win. You're not hearing me, and you're not even willing to try. Maybe the next time you're busy pushing me away, you'll think about that."

Chapter Eleven
Ashley

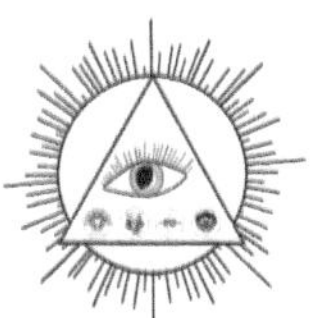

"Are you sure this is the right place?" Chad asks, slotting his truck into an empty parking space in front of the single-story redbrick building. It's tucked right at the back of a large industrial estate on the outskirts of the bustling town of Grenlow. His brow puckers as he peers out the windshield at the chunky red lettering on the side of the structure. GRENLOW VINTAGE TOYS doesn't seem like the right location, but I triple-checked the coordinates Theo Westbrook sent to my cell, and this is correct.

"This is it," I confirm.

"Now what?"

I shrug. "I guess we wait? We *are* a little early."

"I don't know, Ash." Chad looks anxiously around. "I'm not liking this one little bit."

"I trust Lo and the guys. I thought you did too?"

"It's not that I don't trust them. This just seems shady as fuck."

I quirk a brow at him. "Really? That's what you're going with?" I slant him a knowing look.

He mumbles something under his breath, and it irritates me.

"I'm doing this for you!" I snap. "If you insist on putting your life on the line, then the least you can do is learn how to defend yourself. Between you and Jase, I am barely getting any sleep because I'm all torn up and fucking worried. I don't think this is too much to ask."

"You're right." He unknots my fisted hands, rubbing my tense fingers. "I'm sorry. Forgive me?" Leaning across the console, he puckers his lips and cocks his head to one side.

I can't help but soften. "Just promise you'll keep an open mind and try your hardest." I cup his handsome face. "I need you to be safe, Chad."

"I promise, sweetheart." He kisses me deeply before lacing his fingers in my hair. "I know I've been an insufferable ass these past couple of months, and Ares's antics aren't helping."

"I know." I heave out an annoyed sigh. "He's deliberately trying to push our buttons, and we're letting him. We need to start retaliating."

"I'm all for that plan," he agrees, dusting kisses across my face. "Do you have something in mind?"

"I have a few ideas." My lips twitch. "We can talk later."

He straightens up, leveling me with a solemn look. "So, are we going to talk about what just happened back there?"

"I had a momentary loss of sanity. It won't happen again."

"Siren." He tilts my face up. "Talk to me."

"Are you mad?"

Shock splays across his gorgeous face and his blue eyes pop wide. "Why would I be mad? I told you you're in control, and I meant it. I will do whatever you want to do when it comes to Jase."

"I made out with him in front of your teammates."

"That's what you're worried about?"

"Aren't you?"

He vigorously shakes his head. "Nope. With everything else we've got going on, that is the least of my worries. If assholes want to give me shit, that's on them. What we do in our relationship is no one's business but ours."

"What if it gets back to the coaching staff? I don't want to cause trouble for you when you're new and you need to make a name for yourself."

"Sweetheart." He sweeps his fingers up and down my cheek. "This is college. All kinds of shit goes down. I'm sure we'll get some comments and teasing, but I doubt it'll last long, and I really don't think Coach will care. As long as I perform on the field, he won't give a shit."

"Good." I breathe a sigh of relief. Chad has a lot on his shoulders already. I never want to add to his load.

"What are you going to do about Jase?" he asks.

"Nothing, because nothing has changed."

He waits me out, softly touching my face and my neck, his gentle caresses helping to comfort me.

"He used my feelings for him, my attraction to him, against me back there in a way he never has before."

Chad chuckles, leaning in to peck my lips. "He's in love with you, Ash, and he's desperate. You can't blame a guy for trying every trick in the book."

"That's not what we do, and he's never told me he loves me."

Chad's face registers shock. "He hasn't?"

"Nope."

"Well, I know he does. He doesn't need to say the words to you or me for it to be true. I've known that guy most of my life, and I have never seen him look at any girl the way he looks at you. I would never have broached the subject of sharing you with him if I didn't think he was serious about you."

"What?" I bolt upright. "Why is this the first time I'm hearing this?"

"I thought it was assumed." He kisses me firmly on the lips. "I'm crazy about you, Ash. I would never bring any guy into our relationship if he couldn't show you the same love and adoration."

"I don't understand," I truthfully admit. "I thought it'd be the opposite. That you'd want the other guy to be casual so there was no competition."

"Bringing a third party into our relationship was a serious matter for me, Ash. It took me ages to reach that decision, and that was before you and I properly discussed it. I needed to ensure I was okay with it first. I'm upset about this as well, and not just for you because I know how hurt you are. It's hurt me too because the decision to bring Jase in wasn't taken flippantly, and I didn't see it ending like this."

I have been super pissed with Chad recently over The Sainthood drugs nightmare, but it's times like this when I realize how deeply he cares about me, and I'm reminded of all we have been through. I don't support what he's doing, and I'm scared of it backfiring on him, but I won't walk away from him because we have a difference of opinion. We have been together for years, and he was my rock at times when it felt like I was falling apart. I can set aside our differences to be here for him now and hope that together we can navigate these choppy waters and come out stronger on the other side.

"Do you think he's right?" I ask, refocusing on the man in front of me. "Should I be fighting for him? Should I set aside my hurt feelings and make the most of the time we have left together?"

"I can't answer that, Ash. I can't tell you what to do. You've got to reach that decision yourself because I won't sway you either way."

"What do *you* want?" I whisper-ask.

"I want things to return to the way they were, but that's an impossibility."

"Yeah." I rest my head on his shoulder. "Me too. It feels weird for Jase not to be around, but how can we go back to the way things were when I know he'll be getting engaged to her in a few months and eventually sleeping with her? I don't think I can get past that."

"If you can't, you can't." He presses kisses into my hair while checking the time on his watch.

"It must be nearly time."

He nods. "I expect someone will come for us soon."

"Should I message Lo to see if there's been any change with the plan?" I lift my head, staring at the dark building in front of us.

"Let's sit tight for now."

"Okay."

"I'm glad you're doing this with me, Ash. It helps to know you'll be able to defend yourself too. I couldn't bear it if anything happened to you because I'm tangled up with The Sainthood."

"Nothing is going to happen to either of us cause this guy is the best in the country, according to Lo."

His eyes sparkle with mischief as he clasps the nape of my neck and pulls my face to his. "Imagine how flexible we're going to be. Think of all the additional benefits." His eyes glimmer suggestively.

Desire coils low in my belly. "I can't wait to test it out."

His mouth collides with mine in a passionate kiss, and I run my fingers over the short velvety hairs on his neck as we devour one another.

A loud slap on the window breaks us both apart with a jolt. A stern-looking guy wearing a fitted, black, short-sleeved shirt and black cargo pants stands outside our window, crooking his finger at us. A gun holster is strapped to his waist, the outline of a gun visible.

"He looks a little scary," I murmur, hoping he can't read lips.

"We trust Lo and the guys, right?" Chad brings our conjoined hands to his lips, pressing a light kiss on my knuckles.

"Right. We'll keep the faith."

We climb out of the truck, and the guy jerks his head, signaling for us to follow him. Chad clasps my hand in his, and we trade excited looks as we follow the tall, built, broad-shouldered man to a side door of the building.

He stands in front of a wall-mounted pad, and it quickly scans his face. Chad and I exchange "what the fuck" expressions as the door mechanism clicks and it slides open. The nameless man steps aside to let us enter first.

Row upon row of shelving, housing boxes of all shapes and sizes, greets us when we are inside. In one corner, a bunch of forklift trucks, pallet trucks, and overhead cranes lie idle. Lighting is low, and there isn't a soul in sight.

"Through here," the man says, shepherding us into a small office. Another man, dressed in the same attire as our guide, is standing in front of the only desk in the room with his arms folded and his legs a little spread. He looks suitably badass, and adrenaline courses through my veins. I grip Chad's hand tighter as unease ramps up in my veins.

"We have a standard security protocol for all visitors," the new man says. "This won't take long, but I need your full cooperation."

Gulping back nerves, I nod my agreement the same time Chad does.

The guy processes us one at a time while the other dude stands guard at the door. We are both checked for concealed weapons, and then he takes some personal details from us. After, he conducts a full range of biometric scans including fingerprint mapping, a retinal scan, and full facial recognition.

It seems intense for a session with a kick-ass trainer, and I'm wondering what the fuck Lo has gotten us into.

"You're all set up on the system now," the new man confirms. "Any time you have an appointment, you will enter by the side door. Every door within the facility has a biometric scanner you will need to pass through."

"Thank you," I say before we follow the first man back out the way we came.

They are not big on introductions or names around here.

The man leads us through the dimly lit room to a cargo elevator at the back. Chad stands in front of the biometric scanner as it scans his face. The elevator doors ping open, and we step inside. Standing behind the strange, mostly silent man, we hold hands as the elevator descends underground. We get out on the lowest basement level, entering a long, wide, brightly lit hallway.

"What the fuck is this place?" Chad whispers.

I shrug because I don't have the answers. We pass by a number of concealed doors, and a few men and women, dressed in the same black uniform, walk past without paying us any attention.

The silent one stops at the last door, gesturing for me to stand in front of the scanner this time. It scans my eye, and the door slides open. Chad and I enter the large room that is outfitted with a multitude of different training equipment, a ton of mats, a boxing ring, and a wall of knives at the end.

The door glides shut behind us, leaving our tour guide on the outside. Weird and rude.

"This is sick." Chad's eyes are out on stalks as he examines the large empty space.

"I'm glad you think so," a man with a deep voice says, startling us. The man appears from a small office to our left, walking toward us. "We have a shooting range on the level above, and we'll train up there some days." His commanding presence stops in front of us. "You must be Ashley," he says, extending his long arm.

I shake his hand in a bit of a daze. This dude is freaking hot, for an old guy. I'm pretty shit at guessing ages, but he looks like he's in his thirties, maybe? He's like the new-age classification of tall, dark, and handsome with a side of imposing. He's as tall as Chad and equally as broad and ripped. Muscular biceps strain the material of his black shirt, and the black combat pants he's wearing cling to his powerful thighs. His dark hair is cropped close to his head, not too different from the way Chad is wearing his hair these days.

Intense ice-blue eyes lock on mine with amusement, and I realize I'm staring.

Chad clears his throat, and I snap out of it.

"Sorry, yes, I'm Ashley. It's nice to meet you."

"I'm Chad." The guys shake hands. "Thank you for agreeing to do this."

"Harlow and I go way back," he cryptically explains. "I'll be honest, this isn't something I do anymore, but our friend can be mighty persuasive when she needs to be." His lips twitch, and warmth fills his face.

I smile, instantly feeling at ease with this man. Which is strange, cause he's pretty fucking intimidating. "Lo is awesome. I miss her."

"The feeling is mutual. But she's happy and safe, and that is all I have ever wanted for her."

There is obvious affection in his tone and his expression, and now I'm all kinds of curious about who this man is to Harlow Westbrook.

"We're not big into names for security reasons," he explains, adopting a professional face again. "We will also not divulge anything about our facility, who we are, or what we do. You won't ask questions. You come here to be trained in combat and weaponry, and you never speak of it. *Ever*. You take this to the grave." His eyes probe mine and then Chad's.

My heart is thumping against my rib cage with all he isn't saying.

This dude is someone important, and what we have stepped in is something high level, top-secret, and most definitely classified.

"We understand," I say, and Chad nods.

Lo's friend drills us with a look, and it takes effort to hold his gaze and not back down when he just stares at us in silence for a couple minutes. It's a test of sorts, I assume, and I don't want to let Lo down. She obviously went out on a limb to arrange this, and I'm ever so grateful. I just know the skills we will learn here will be invaluable.

"Lo assures me you can be trusted, and I trust her judgment, but this needs to be said before we go any further. You cannot tell anyone about this. It has got to remain a secret. You can't tell siblings, friends, parents, teachers, *anyone*. Especially not law enforcement or government bodies or representatives."

"We hear you, and we can be trusted to keep it confidential," Chad says.

"We can sign NDAs if it would help," I suggest because I know that's usually the done thing.

A grim smile stretches his lips. "We don't ask visitors to sign NDAs because it's a waste of time and effort. If anyone talks, we don't take them to court to seek redress." All the tiny hairs lift on the back of my neck as his intense gaze bores a hole in our skulls. "We just eliminate the threat."

Chapter Twelve

Ashley

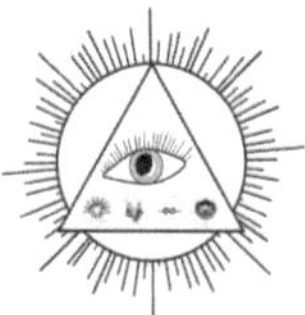

The screeching ringtone of the alarm shakes me from a blissful sleep. Blinking my eyes open, I roll onto my side as Chad snatches his phone from the bedside table and turns it off. "I ache in places I didn't realize could ache," I moan as my strained limbs protest the rolling motion.

"I work out daily and train most every day with the team, and even I'm sore. That dude really put us through our paces."

"He did, but it was good. I'm glad I asked Lo now."

"Speaking of Lo, did you call her last night when I was in the shower?"

I shake my head as I move closer to my man, draping my arm over his toned waist. "We were told not to ask questions. Those guys strike me as the type who could easily get into our phones and tap into our messages. I don't want to risk it."

"Good call, sweetheart." Chad idly toys with my hair. "I wouldn't be surprised if they're watching us for a while to ensure we can be trusted."

A chill skitters up my spine at the thought, but if that's the price to pay for becoming a badass ninja, I'll pay it. "Nor me," I reply. "Besides, it would be a waste of time. I know Lo. She clearly got the same memo we did, so she won't tell me a thing. I don't want to risk our friendship or ruin the arrangement we have. Sore as I am, I like that I'm learning how to defend myself in all manner of ways, and it comforts me to know you are upskilling too."

Chad threads his fingers through my messy hair, pressing his lips to my brow. "Please stop worrying, beautiful. I promise nothing is going to happen to me."

"I'll try." I snuggle into his warmth, trailing my finger over my name inked in a love heart over his chest.

My boyfriend went through a bit of a metamorphosis this summer. Cutting and dying his hair, adding piercings in his brow and nose, and inking parts of his chest and one arm. I know he wants to get more tattoos when he has the money. I would pay for them, but I know he'd reject my offer, and it'll only cause another argument, which I want to avoid. I want to firmly get my relationship with Chad back on track.

"I've got to go. Coach arranged an early-morning workout. Team bonding, apparently." Chad dots kisses all over my face. "You should go back to sleep." He peels back the covers and climbs out of bed, stretching his arms up over his head.

The muscles in his abs flex and roll with the motion, and his sleep pants slip a little lower, offering me a tantalizing glimpse of the V-indents on each hip and the trail of dark-blond hair snaking underneath his waistband. I'm licking my lips and squirming on the bed as I eye the considerable bulge at his crotch, wondering if I'd get away with tackling him and handcuffing him to the bedpost so he can't leave.

Chad spots the direction of my thoughts, chuckling. "I want to, Siren, but it'll have to wait." He adjusts his morning wood, piercing me with a look loaded with devilish promise. "I'll make it up to you tonight."

"You'd better." I waggle my brows and grin. "I think I'll get up and go to that DIY place. Might as well start putting our plan into action." Last night, after we hobbled out of the secret training facility, we stopped by a local diner to discuss retaliation plans against Ares. Now, I'm itching to execute it.

Chad kneels on the bed, pressing an all too brief kiss on my lips. "Don't do anything without me and be careful. I'll pick up a sturdy padlock after training later today like we discussed."

"Okay, babe." I fling my arms around his neck, yanking his body down over mine. "Are you sure you can't be late?" I bat my eyelashes as I grab hold of his muscular butt cheeks.

"You don't play fair." He pouts before nuzzling his head in my neck.

"I never pretended to be an angel." I nip at his earlobe, and delicious tremors rip up and down my body as he growls sexily against the throbbing pulse point at my neck.

"Jase had the right idea calling you Temptress," he says before letting a couple of expletives loose. He lifts his head, and his eyes find mine. "Sorry, babe. I wasn't thinking."

Pain spears me through the heart, like always, when I think of my ex-lover. "It's okay. I know you didn't say it intentionally." Mention of Jase has effectively quashed my ardor, so I release him and swing my legs over my side of the bed.

"I love you." Chad comes up behind me and kisses me on the shoulder.

"Love you too." I angle my head back, and he drops a soft kiss on my lips.

A light goes off in his eyes. "I have something that'll cheer you up. Stay put." He races into our closet, emerging a minute later carrying a large, wrapped box.

"What's that?"

He hands it to me. "A gift for you."

My brows knit in confusion. "It's not my birthday until next month."

"Who said it's a birthday gift?" He arches a brow, nudging the edge of the box. "Open it, sweetheart."

I tear into the wrapping, gasping when I see what's inside. "Chad!" My gaze flips from the expensive Nikon to my boyfriend. "This is too much."

A muscle clenches in his jaw, and I swallow back bile. "You're my woman. I love you, and I can afford to treat you again. Please don't make this into something. Just accept the fucking camera, Ash. Photography makes you happy, and I want you to be happy."

We are treading on eggshells when it comes to anything money related these days, and I'm sick of it. I want to tell him he shouldn't be spending this much money on me when he's carrying the entire financial burden for his family. I also want to tell him I don't want something bought with ill-gotten gains, but I can't. If I voice those sentiments, it'll turn into World War Three, and I don't want to fight with Chad anymore. I will just have to find a way to make peace with all of this. Which is easier said than done. But I'll try.

"Thanks, babe. I love it." I set it down on the bed before throwing my arms around my boyfriend. "And I love you." I hold him tight, relieved when he hugs me back and I feel his tense muscles relaxing against me. "For the record," I add, tipping my chin up so I'm peering directly into his eyes. "*You* make me happy. Don't ever doubt that."

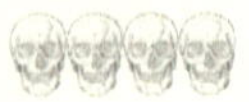

"Morning, slutty little sis," Ares says, sauntering into the kitchen as naked as the day he was born. I spray coffee all over the island unit as I quickly divert my eyes. If he intends to do this every morning at breakfast, Chad is going to lose his shit.

"Seriously, asshole?" I say when I have composed myself. I climb off my stool to grab some paper towels. "Have you suddenly developed an allergy to clothes?"

"Nothing sudden about it. I grew up in Europe with a hippy mother who liked to drag her kids to nudist beaches. I'm used to nudity in the home." Grabbing his semi, he points it at me like it's a weapon. "I suggest you and that pussy you call a boyfriend get an attitude adjustment and fast."

I stop with my hand on the roll of paper towels. "You grew up in Europe?" This is the first time I have heard this. I know Hera is of Greek descent, but I got the impression they have always lived in the US. Hera sure sounds fully American, but now I think of it, Ares does have a peculiar drawl to his accent.

Ares scowls, like he's annoyed at himself for revealing something important.

Then it clicks with me. "Kids? You have other siblings?"

"No," he snaps. "It's just Mom and me."

"Then why did you say—"

He's in front of me in a flash, his large hand wrapped around my throat as he shoves me back against the cupboards. "Slip of the tongue, now drop it." Barely concealed rage burns behind his eyes as he glares at me, and I have clearly struck a nerve.

Intriguing. I tuck that away in a mental drawer, deciding I'll ask Hera about it the next time I see her.

"Get your hands off me, and I will."

My words remind both of us he is naked and currently pressed all up against me.

The change in Ares is as fast as flicking a switch. His rage recedes, replaced with something way more dangerous. Lust dilates his pupils as he stares at me with a familiar smug expression. His hand drops from my neck, lowering down my body until he clasps my wrist. My chest swells as we share intimate breathing space.

At this proximity, I see the alluring gold specks in his hazel eyes. They're an intriguing sage-green color today and truly stunning. His angular jawline, strong nose, broad brow, high cheekbones, and full lips are perfectly symmetrical, and I hate how he steals all the breath from my lungs. Today, his hair is styled in a perfect faux hawk, the tips of his ink-black hair spray-painted a green that almost matches his eyes.

"Yeah, dollface. Just like that." His words and the lust-fueled look on his face snap me out of my reverie.

I look down in horror to where he has my hand clasped around his hard dick as we both stroke his erection.

How the hell did that happen without me noticing? It seems Jase isn't the only one capable of bamboozling me.

"I know you want me," he purrs, moving my hand faster around his pierced dick. Leaning into my ear, he whispers, "I know you dream of my cock in your cunt." His words send shivers cascading down my spine, and I visibly shudder. I can almost hear the smile in his voice as he says, "I know you finger yourself at night imagining me thrusting inside your tight, wet pussy, ruining you for all others."

Lifting my leg, I knee him firmly in the balls, pushing him away when he shouts out a roar and bends over. "You know nothing, and if you touch me again without permission, I'll slice your dick off and shove it so far down your throat you'll be shitting it out for a week."

Appetite vanquished, I flee the kitchen for the safe confines of my bedroom, only emerging when I think the coast is clear.

I'm cutting it close to reach campus in time for my first class, so when I hit the sidewalk and discover my brand-spanking-new Lexus has a flat tire, I instantly know he's responsible. I turn around, ready to stomp back up the stairs to give him a piece of my mind when I crash into a hard body. Strong arms band around me as I sway on my feet, and I would most surely have fallen if Ares hadn't caught me.

"You." My nostrils flare as I stab my finger in his chest. "What the fuck did you do to my car?"

He peeks over my head at my SUV before rolling his eyes as if I'm being overly dramatic. "Don't be ridiculous. It's not my fault you got a flat."

Attempting to wriggle out of his iron hold, I glare at him. "Bullshit! It's a new car, and I haven't driven it enough to get a flat. I know you did this."

"You flatter me, but contrary to what you seem to think, you're barely a blip on my radar. Why the fuck would I go to such trouble?"

"Because you're a deranged lunatic," I snap, squirming in his arms. "Let me go!" His wolfish grin irritates me to no end, and I yell in frustration as I beat my fists on his chest. The sooner I am fully trained, the better. I cannot wait to kick the shit out of my annoying stepbrother.

"Not until you calm down. Whatever would Mom and Dad say if they saw you throwing a temper tantrum like a toddler?"

I lift my leg to knee him again, but he clearly learned that lesson.

"Now, now, dollface. That's not very ladylike."

"I don't fucking care," I say, arching my neck before I head-butt him.

Pain rattles across my skull, and I have an instant headache. Fuck. The jerk has a real hard head, and that probably wasn't the smartest idea, but it worked. His arms automatically release me, and I'm free.

Removing my cell, I pull up the Uber app, peering at the

screen through blurry eyes. I rub my sore head and curse under my breath when I see there's no car in the area for at least fifteen minutes.

A dark chuckle rings out, lifting all the fine airs on my arms. I jerk my head up. "Your violent streak seriously turns me the fuck on," Ares says, rubbing his junk through his jeans.

"Why are you doing this?" I ask, tired of dealing with his annoying ass all the time. "Why can't you just leave us alone?"

"Because it's fun." He thrusts a helmet at me before unlocking his bike. "Get on. I'll give you a ride to school."

"Hell to the no." I pointedly fold my arms. "I bet that was your plan all along."

"Believe what you want, but I didn't touch your car." He swings his leg over his motorcycle and turns the engine on. "Are you coming or not? It's no skin off my back if you're late to class."

I'm on the verge of telling him to shove it, preferring to be late than get on Ares's motorcycle when the door opens next door and Jase appears. "What's wrong?" he asks, a scowl instantly appearing on his face when he spots the hostile expression on my face and the direction its facing. He takes the steps two at a time until he's standing right in front of me.

"Mind your own business, dipshit," Ares says, patting the space behind him. "Hop on, little slutster."

"Fuck no." Jase grabs my arm and pulls me back. "You're not going with him. You can ride to campus with me."

Ares just arches a brow.

I am caught between a rock and a hard place. Torn over what to do until Julia emerges from her house, and my decision is made. I don't see her car anywhere, which means she must be riding to campus with Jase. I'd rather take my chances with my loathsome stepbrother than hitch a ride with those two.

Wrenching my arm from Jase's grip, I level him with a scathing look as I climb on behind Ares.

"Baby, no." He claws a hand through his hair, looking like he wants to hit something.

"I'm not your baby, and you don't tell me what to do."

Ares fixes my helmet on my head, tucking my hair up while I stare at my ex.

"Forget about the whore," Julia says, latching on to Jase's arm. He instantly shoves her hand away. "Perhaps Ares will do us all a favor and crash."

Before I can retaliate, Ares grabs my hands and locks them securely around his waist. Then he revs the engine and takes off, leaving the others in the dust.

Chapter Thirteen

Jase

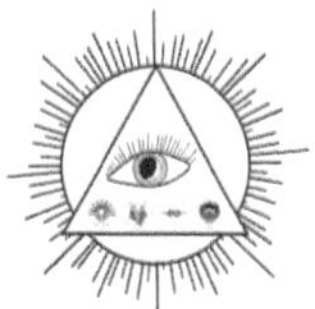

"What the hell are you doing?" I snap at Julia, enraged she ruined my plan. "I didn't think you were home." She wasn't home when I went to bed, and her car is missing, so I assumed she stayed somewhere else last night. I purposely planned it for a time when Julia wasn't here, and I knew Chad was occupied, so I could get Ash alone. She won't talk to me, and I'm getting desperate. So desperate I lied to Coach, feigning illness so I could be excused from the early-morning fitness session and sneak out to let the air out of Ash's front tire.

"Aw, were you worried about me?" Julia bats her eyelashes as she presses her big tits up against me.

"Nope. You could fall off a cliff, plunge to a violent death, and I'd throw a celebratory party," I say because I owe her payback for that nasty comment she just made to Ash.

She scowls before folding her arms across her chest, pushing her tits up with the motion. I'm betting that's on purpose. She seems to be hellbent on seducing me, which is fucking hysterical when you think about which Luminary family I come from. And the fact I'm in love with the woman she seems determined to make her enemy.

"You appear to be laboring under an illusion, my love." Her tone drips with condescension. "I'm an heir, and you're just a second son. You don't get to speak to me like this. My father expects you to treat me like a queen, and I won't accept anything less. Continue to push me, and you won't like what I do next."

Circling my hands around her neck, I push her up against my Range Rover, letting her see the darkness I work hard to hide. I hold nothing back, letting years of frustration and pent-up rage shine through. "I don't take well to threats, especially veiled ones. Be very careful how much you push me, Julia. I will push back three times as hard and not give a fuck who you are."

I figure at this point I have nothing more to lose. It's not like her dad or mine can kill me for disobedience. Sure, they can torture me and make my life miserable, but I fail to see how that would be any worse. If I can't force my dad or my brother into doing something to negate this marriage contract, maybe I can piss Julia off enough that she'll request it.

I know it's not that simple. The Board of Luminaries is ultimately who decides who marries who. They are careful to keep the power balance between all four families.

While many men applied to marry the Sloth heir, she was chosen for me. Not because my father sealed the deal, but he would like to believe that. No, it was the most fortuitous match, one that would keep their system of checks and balances in place. There are other male members in our extended family who could step up to marry Julia Manford. But no one else is a second son, and therein lies the problem.

Even if I cause trouble. Even if I succeed in angering Julia enough, there is no guarantee it will change anything.

But I have to try because I can't live without Ashley Shaw. In my heart, I know she is the only woman for me, and I am going to fight for her.

It's a delicate juggling act though. Piss Julia off too much, and I could show my hand. She won't give in if she thinks I still want Ash, so I've got to convince her I don't. Otherwise, she will dig her heels in purely to deny my temptress.

My PDA with Ash yesterday was ill thought out and stupid. I hope Julia doesn't hear about it.

I need my intended to believe my abhorrence of this marriage is because I cannot stand her and refuse to bow to her command. Which is the truth. Even if Ash didn't exist for me, I still wouldn't want to marry the Sloth heir.

Julia needs to know I won't be pushed around. To understand if I become the rightful heir by marriage, I will make her life a living hell. She has to want to not marry me enough to convince her dad to extract her from the deal.

I have less than six weeks to make it happen, so it's a tall order, but I'm determined to give it my all.

"Get your hands off me." She seethes, showing more tenacity than I expect. I am beginning to realize Julia has been playing her own long game, and she is not the sum of how she comes across. Not by a long shot.

Digging my fingers into her neck, I squeeze harder, pleased to see a glimmer of fear rise in her eyes. "Don't give me orders and expect me to obey. I want to make one thing perfectly clear." I tighten my grip on her throat, and her eyes pop wide. Grabbing my wrists, she tries to pry my hands away. Panic is etched across her face, and I'm a prick because I like it. "This isn't about Ash. That time has passed. This is about you and I."

Her translucent skin is turning a delicate shade of blue, and it works quite well with her midnight-black hair and pale coloring. "I will never love you. I hate you and barely tolerate you. I will never treat you with anything but disdain. I am marrying you for what this contract gives me. When I am Luminary, your role will be diminished to the lowest level, and I will be in control."

Reluctantly, I let her go. As much as I'd love to throttle her and solve the problem that way, killing a Luminary, his heir, or any member of his extended family is punishable by death, and this bitch isn't worth dying over. "I will own you," I add in a cold tone, matching it to my expression. "You will be mine to do with as I please, and there is nothing you or your father can do to stop me." Interfering in the relationships between a Luminary and his wife or children is another no-no.

As much as The Luminaries love their checks and balances and their rules and traditions, they don't personally abide by many of them. All of them have regular extramarital affairs though it's frowned upon for others. They are discreet, in an attempt to at least look respectful to their wives, but everyone knows. Including the women they are married to. I have seen what it's done to my mother, and it's another reason I hate my father. The phrase "a law unto themselves" was coined after The Luminaries.

Julia sucks in huge lungsful of air, panting as she glares at me. She rubs her neck as she straightens up, collecting herself. "You can try to break me," she rasps in a hoarse voice. "But you won't succeed." Grabbing her bag, she brushes past me, rounding the hood of my car. "You're not the only one hiding things." She yanks the passenger door open. "Underestimate me at your peril."

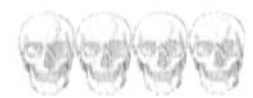

The short journey to campus is silent, both of us stewing and plotting. I park in my reserved slot, frowning when I see a familiar person standing on the sidewalk, apparently waiting on us. "What does *she* want?" I ask in a neutral tone, channeling nonchalance.

"My friends are none of your business," Julia retorts, applying a layer of gloss to her lips before she gets out.

I climb out my side, staring at Anita Hoare, trying to figure out the angle. Julia walks up to her and pulls her into a hug as if they are the best of friends.

Back in high school, Anita was on the cheer squad with Julia and Ash. Like most of the cheerleaders, she sucked up to Julia while bitching about her behind her back. No one liked Julia, but they tolerated her because her father is a bigshot, billionaire, media mogul with a lot of power and influence. None of it is real though. And they don't even know the half of it.

The four luminaries are all successful, rich businessmen, but their legit businesses are a front for the real work they do behind the scenes. If anyone really knew who they were and the ultimate power they wield, they would have run the other way screaming.

Anita shoots me a flirty smile over Julia's shoulder. Or what she perceives to be a flirty smile. Hard to pull that look off when your face resembles the result of a crossbreed between a human and a pug. Her personality is even uglier than her face, and I have no time for the nasty bitch.

Ash was friendly with Anita for a time until she discovered she was a manipulative narcissist with a massive chip on her shoulder and a malicious secret agenda.

These two striking a friendship can only be self-serving. If Anita is sucking up to Julia to target Ash again, I will bury the ugly bitch. I mean that literally. There are no rules or laws that prohibit me from killing a plebeian.

Julia has her fake smile and faux persona firmly in place as she chats with her new friend.

The roar of an engine distracts all of us, and I turn around in time to see the degenerate pull up to the curb with Ash on the back of his motorcycle.

They should have arrived way before us. I'm guessing the dickhead took an extended route on purpose so Ash would be late to class. Judging from the deep scowl on her face as she yanks the helmet off her head, my girl knows it too.

"You're an asshole." Ash fumes, lifting her helmet like she's seriously considering smashing it into his head. Silently, I encourage her to do it.

"You're cute when you're angry." Ares snatches the helmet from her hands before she can wield it like a weapon. He knows he has a captive audience, so of course, he hams it up for them. "You loved being pressed all up against me," he says, sliding the helmet on one of the handlebars. "Your hands were so low on my stomach you were practically touching my dick. Didn't want to deprive you, dollface." He flicks her nose, and Ash's face turns puce with anger.

I grind my teeth to the molars. It's excruciatingly painful to maintain a nonplussed expression, but I need to execute my role perfectly. I sense Julia is keeping me in her peripheral vision while she watches it go down with Ash and Ares.

"I wanted to ensure you had enough time to grope me." He leans in close to her face. "You're welcome." Sarcasm drips from his tone as his eyes lower to her lips.

That's nothing new.

Chad and I have seen the way he looks at her.

We know he wants her, but he can't fucking have her.

I will murder that motherfucker before I let him touch what's *ours*.

Mine.

Shoving my hands in the front pockets of my jeans, I dig my nails into my thighs, needing some physical outlet before I explode and give the game away.

"Bet if I shoved my fingers inside you you'd be dripping," he adds.

My initial fury is quickly replaced when Ash punches him in the nose, drawing blood, and I disguise my snort of laughter as a cough.

That's my girl.

Not your girl, my nasty inner voice whispers, but I punt that asshole to one side.

Ash moves to walk away but not before Ares slaps her on the ass, and I'm back to instant rage. "Keep Sunday free, doll-face. The rents are expecting us for dinner."

She ignores him, stepping up on the sidewalk, holding her shoulders back and lifting her chin.

"It's a date!" he shouts before revving his engine, like the giant dick he is, and tearing out of the parking lot. He flips me the bird as he passes, and I return the gesture.

I hang back as Ash approaches Julia and Anita, pulling out my cell, ready to message Chad, should they start any shit with her, because I can't intervene.

"Look what we have here," Ash says, stopping in front of Anita and Julia. "Cunt face one and cunt face two pretending to be friends while planning to stab each other in the back."

Julia's shrill laugh stabs me through the ears. "You'd know all about that. You did write the playbook after all."

Anita convulses with laughter, like it's the funniest thing she's ever heard.

Ash just rolls her eyes.

"Unlike you, Julia knows what it means to be a true friend," Anita says, getting over that fit of laughter in record time. "I like

Julia, which is more than I can say about you." Anita plants her hands on her hips and smirks at Ash.

"I'm wounded," Ash deadpans, rolling her eyes again. "And you're an even bigger fool than I thought." Ash returns the smirk and then some. "Couldn't happen to a nicer bitch." She turns to Julia. "Funny how you've changed your tune." She taps a slim finger on her chin. "What was it you used to call her? Ah, yes, now I remember." She levels Anita with an amused look. "A-kneetta-face-transplant. Get it?"

It's clear Anita *doesn't* get it because she's lacking any form of self-awareness. Narcissists tend to have a high opinion of themselves and an inflated sense of self-worth. Julia opens her mouth to deny it, no doubt, but Ash clamps her hand over her lips, shutting her up. Julia slaps her hand away, ready to physically retaliate, before she seems to come to her senses.

As an heir, she is constantly under a spotlight, and getting into a public brawl with a girl whose parents are best friends with her dad would not be a wise move. Julia realizes it in time, and I'm guessing it's killing her to have to sit this one out. She glowers at Ash, and Ash pokes her tongue out the side of her cheek.

This is fucking priceless. I should have recorded it for Chad. He'd get a real kick out of it after the stunt the whore tried to pull last year. I wonder what Julia would make of her new friend if she knew that truth. I tuck it away to use when the right opportunity presents itself.

"Wow, you really are dumb." Ash pats her on the head like she's a simpleton. "I'll let you ponder that puzzle, a-kneetta-whore."

Ash walks off, leaving both girls fuming with steam practically billowing from their ears.

And I'm not even angry my plan failed this morning because I wouldn't have missed that for anything.

Chapter Fourteen

Jase

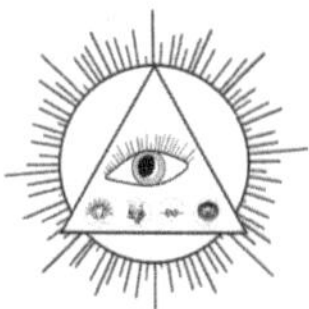

During my midmorning free period, I call my sister after arranging for a guy to go fix Ash's tire. I need to find out what's going on with Bree, and there's no time like the present. Bree doesn't have classes until the afternoon, so she's at home. Which isn't convenient. However, I haven't managed to speak with her for more than five minutes since she returned from South America, so I decide to drive out to my parents' place to catch up with her. I can skip my Introduction to Business Analytics class if I don't make it back to the campus in time.

I rap three times on my sister's bedroom door and wait. Bree opens it a few seconds later with a flourish and a big smile. "Little brother, it's good to see you." She flings herself at me, and I pull her into a bear hug.

I have missed my partner in crime.

"Can't breathe," she jokes, her words muffled against my chest before I release her.

Bopping her on the head, I smirk as I push past her into her room. "PC 1. How the fuck are you?"

"That's a loaded question," my eldest sister says, slamming the door shut behind her.

"I thought you voluntarily came home." I flop down on the couch positioned in front of the window which offers stunning views of the gardens surrounding my parents' lavish home.

"I did. Doesn't mean I'm happy to be back living here." She throws me a soda from the mini refrigerator before sitting beside me. Bree rests her head on my shoulder. "Missed your ugly face."

I bark out a laugh. "Missed you too. It's good to have you home." I pop the lid on my can and take a swig. "Why are you back? I thought you were enjoying traveling."

She lifts her head and sips from her own drink. A comfortable silence settles in the air. "I was, but I can't deny reality forever," she admits after swallowing a few mouthfuls of soda.

My eyes pop wide as I stare at my sister. "I thought that was your motto in life. That and causing as much trouble as possible."

"I've grown up," she says, staring off into space, looking contemplative. I can tell there is more to this, but I won't pry. Breanna will tell me in her own time. She turns on the couch, swinging her legs up and placing them over my lap. "I might have accepted my reality but that doesn't mean I'm ready to hang up my PC1 moniker entirely." Mischief dances in her eyes, and I'm all ears.

"I like what I'm hearing. Tell me more."

"I saw a lot while I traveled around South America. Extreme poverty. Overcrowded cities. People living with next to nothing, Jase. And I met people who had fled their home countries with only the clothes on their back. People who had experienced the worst atrocities and lived through the worst experiences. I volunteered in a homeless soup kitchen in Bogota, a rape support center in Guatemala, and a domestic violence shelter in Bolivia. I worked with this group of environmentalists in the rainforests of Brazil. I was also a part of a sea turtle conservation project in Chile, and I did a bunch of other stuff. It really opened my eyes. The decisions our father and the other luminaries make impact the world on a global scale."

She swings her legs to the floor before resting her elbows on her knees and putting her head in her hands. "It's not right, Jase. The world we live in is responsible for so much of the bad shit that goes on, and I can't stand by and do nothing anymore. We are the next generation, and we can do something about it."

I sit up straighter. "What are you planning?"

Bree lifts her head and turns to face me. "I want to change things, little brother, and the best way for me to do that is from within. I know it will take time and the kind of change I want won't happen in my lifetime, but we have to start somewhere. I may not succeed, but I've got to try. I can't ignore my destiny forever anyway. That dickface Toby is a sophomore this year, and I knew his father would start pressuring Dad to make me return. I willingly chose to return, to play their stupid game, so I'm back in the fold and in a position to do something."

"That sounds very noble and extremely dangerous. I'm not knocking your logic, but it's a lofty goal. How much change can one person achieve?"

She leans back against the couch. "I don't plan to do it alone. I want to build a team of supporters who share my goals. I'll start small. Take the wins where I can and work to convince the next generation of leaders that things can be done differently." Hope sparks in her eyes as she sits up straighter and clutches my arm. "Imagine how much good we could do with the power in our control if we did the right thing? The collective wealth of all the Luminary families alone could resolve the poverty issue across the entire US."

"That will never happen, sis. Can you imagine Baz, when

he is Luminary, handing over a massive chunk of our wealth for a good cause? I sure as hell can't. And you can forget about Toby Salinger. It doesn't matter if you're married to him. That guy is as big of an ass as his father. No amount of great sex will convince that prick to do anything he doesn't want to do. Knight Carter is a decent guy, but Rhett Carter won't be handing the mantle to his eighteen-year-old heir for some time, and he's the biggest prick of all."

"I'm not naïve, Jase. I know they won't hand over everything. But even a fraction of money set aside for different charities and causes would go a long way. It's not just about money though. I'm talking about changing the way things are run. To stop doing the inhuman things they do—the killing, violence, drugs, guns, spying, and manipulation. Their blatant lack of regard for climate change and environmental issues. The abuse of power. The excessive wealth and luxurious lifestyles. Human trafficking and servitude. I could go on. It makes me so fucking sick. They could do so much good with their power and influence." Sighing, she scrubs a hand down her face.

My sister might think she's not naïve, but that's how she is coming across. I think it's honorable she wants to effect change, and I love how she has found her passion in life. Her face is alive in a way I haven't seen for a long time. Being away was good for her. But there is only so much one person can do to change a society as deeply entrenched as ours and an organization built on archaic rules and traditions that are revered and never scrutinized.

"I think you are extremely passionate, you have a good heart, and I admire you so much for what you want to do. But what you seek is the impossible."

"I won't know until I try," she says.

"This could get you killed."

She eyeballs me with steely resolve. "It's a risk I'm willing to take. I can't return to this corrupt world unless I do it my way."

"I won't tell you not to do it. Just be really fucking careful."

"What about you?" She stares me in the eyes as she drains the last of her soda. "You'll be the Sloth heir when you marry Julia. Can I count on you?"

"You can always count on me." I move closer and sling my arm around her shoulders. "But you should know I'm planning my own rebellion, and I may need your help."

"Ooh, now I'm intrigued." She waggles her brows. "Tell me more."

So, I do.

"I'm going to grab that table over by the wall before someone else does." Bree points across the large cafeteria to a table beside a massive potted plant.

"Cool. I'll pay for our lunch and join you in a few." Usually, I hang out with Chad or some of the guys from the team at lunch, depending on who is around. Today, I want to eat with my sister and discuss more of our plans.

When I make my way over to our table, ten minutes later, Bree is no longer alone. A slow smile spreads across my face as I make my approach.

"Oh, here he is." Bree looks up at me from her seat with a smile. "Jase, I'd like you to meet my friend Ash."

"Hello, gorgeous." I grin at her as I set the tray down on the table.

"You have got to be shitting me," Ash mumbles, giving me the evil eye.

"Wait!" Bree's gaze dances between us as a light bulb goes off in her head. "Holy shit! This is the girl you were telling me about." Her eyes focus on the love of my life. "You're Ashley Shaw."

"I knew you looked familiar," Ash replies. "I should have made the connection."

Ash doesn't know either of my sisters, and she only knows Baz by reputation. "You look beautiful, baby," I say, claiming the vacant seat on the other side of Ash. "I'm glad you're here. Maybe now we can have that talk."

"Don't fucking *baby* me, and you have nothing to say I want to hear." Ash's venom hasn't faded in the least. She faces my sister. "I like you, Bree, and this isn't personal. But I can't eat lunch with you if your brother is staying."

Ouch. "It's only lunch, Temptress. It's not like we're making any big statement sitting beside one another in the cafeteria."

She spins around to face me. "Don't play dumb, Jase. It doesn't suit you. As long as you are continuing this ridiculous charade with Julia, I want nothing to do with you. I thought I made that perfectly clear."

"I'm working on it," I calmly reply.

"Great," she says, sounding like it's anything but. She starts gathering up her stuff, getting ready to leave. "When you have it figured out, hit me up. I *might* forgive you."

Bree fixes me with a "make it right" look, and I subtly nod. "Don't go." I curl my fingers around Ash's slender wrist. "I'll leave. I don't want to ruin your lunch date."

"If you're expecting a thank you, you'll be waiting." She levels me with a biting look, and I want to smash my lips to hers and show her sassy ass how much I adore her.

Bree grins, and I already know these two will become the

best of friends. I like that for them. They need one another. It also means I have another way of staying close to my girl.

Taking my sandwich from the tray, I shove it and my bottle of water into my backpack before removing the tickets from the inside pocket. I was hoping to give these to Ash after practice, but now works better. It's not advisable to give the team another show so soon after the last one.

"I got these for you," I say, offering them to Ash. "I know how badly you wanted to go to that photography expo. I was hoping we could go together."

Ash audibly gulps as she stares at the tickets in my hand. "How did you get these? That expo has been sold out for months."

"I have my ways." Grinning, I unfold her hand and place the tickets on her palm. Her fingers brush against my arm, sending a flurry of tremors cascading over my skin, and I visibly shiver.

Bree smirks, and I'd flip her the bird if I wasn't so laser-focused on Ash.

"So, will you go with me?" I ask, closing her hand over the tickets and keeping it there.

Her chest heaves, and I see the conflict raging in her eyes when she tips her chin up to look at me. "No." She places the tickets down on top of my bag. "It was a thoughtful gesture, but it won't sway my mind." Pain glimmers in her eyes as she stares at me. "I can't go on a date with you when you're planning to marry her."

Rejection slams into me, but I don't know why I'm surprised. I knew this would be her answer.

"Please stop trying, Jase," she adds in a whisper. I spot the tears welling in her eyes before she lowers her gaze to the floor. "You're hurting me and only making it worse."

Sympathy splays across Bree's face, but she doesn't interfere. I like that she's not picking sides or forcing anything.

"I'm sorry," I say in a quiet voice. "That is the last thing I want." Plucking the tickets up, I put them back in her hand. "Take the tickets, Ash. Go with Chad. Maybe you'll be inspired to use that new camera he got you."

I don't wait to hear her reply, walking off and leaving the girls to their lunch.

Chapter Fifteen

Jase

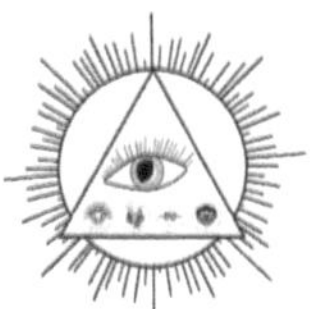

"Fuck, I ache in places I didn't even know existed," Chad complains after we exit the showers in our bare feet with towels wrapped around our waists. Coach put us through our paces today, and it was an especially rigorous training session.

"What's the matter, Cap? Can't hack the pace anymore?" I tease him, using his old nickname, with a heavy heart. I've been singing the blues all afternoon since my conversation with Ash at lunchtime. I think I have seriously blown it with her, and if I don't fix things soon, I will lose her forever.

"As if." He elbows me in the ribs, and I laugh as I pad to my locker to grab my clothes.

"Ash told me about the tickets," he says, opening his locker alongside me. "You did a good thing."

He wouldn't say that if he knew I let the air out of her tire this morning. The guy I sent over to fix it said it was already pumped up when he arrived. Ash must have arranged for someone to do it. I doubt Chad even knows she had a flat, and there's no way that dick Ares would have done something nice for her.

"Fat lot of use it's done me." Dumping my bag on the ground, I sit down on the bench. "I think I've lost her for good, and I can't even blame her."

"You should tell her you love her." He drops down beside me.

I shake my head as I dry off and pull on my boxers. "I'll only admit that truth when I can offer her my whole heart and my dedicated commitment. It wouldn't be fair to either of us otherwise."

"Maybe you're right." He pulls his boxers on before tugging his shirt down over his head while I shimmy my jeans up my legs.

I stand to fasten the button as O'Sullivan and Wentworth approach.

"Sup, dudes?" O'Sullivan asks, injecting himself into our conversation.

I jerk my head at the newcomers as I continue getting dressed. I have zero desire to talk to the douche.

"Is something up?" Chad asks in a cool tone while stepping into his jeans.

"What's the score with you and that Shaw chick?" Wentworth asks.

"Thought she was your girl," O' Sullivan adds. "Until we saw Stewart chewing her face off yesterday."

"I don't see how it's got anything to do with you," I reply, shoving my feet into my sneakers. We got a bit of teasing when we were getting changed before practice, but it was all good-humored. I'm not liking the vibes I'm getting off these two one little bit.

"We're just wondering how we get in on the action." O'Sullivan waggles his brows and licks his lips. "She's one hot piece of ass. I'm game to pound her tight cunt."

"Ass too, if she's used to taking two at a time," Wentworth adds, winking at me like he knows something.

"Fuck you." I work hard to leash my anger. "Mind your own business, and stay the fuck away from her."

"Nah." O'Sullivan rubs his unshaven jawline. "That slut needs a good dicking, and we're just the men for the job. You rookies wouldn't know how to show a woman a good time without an instruction manual and a compass."

O'Sullivan is the stereotypical jerk jock. An obnoxious, spiteful asshole with a sense of entitlement almost as large as his ego. He's been picking on a couple of the other freshmen recruits, thinking he's the big man when he's nothing but a bully. Unfortunately, he's one of our star players and Coach can't seem to find any fault with the jackass. At least we won't have to deal with him for long. Like Wentworth, he's a senior who is one of our wide receivers. Unlike Wentworth, O'Sullivan is hotly tipped to be a first-round draft pick next April.

Unless he doesn't shut his fat mouth before it gets him in serious trouble—the life-changing, career-ending type of trouble.

Wentworth cracks up laughing, and Chad, predictably, goes nuclear. He throws a punch at Wentworth, knocking him off balance and sending him tumbling to the floor. I grab a handful of O'Sullivan's shirt, hauling him back before he can land one on my buddy in retaliation.

Chad turns around and slams O'Sullivan against the lockers, shoving his arm up under his chin and snarling at him. "Ashley is my girlfriend, and you won't talk about her like that. Show some goddamned respect."

I clamp my hand on Chad's shoulder, drilling him with a

look when he glances back at me. Reluctantly, he steps away from the douche, seething and clenching his fists at his sides.

"Or what, rookie?" O'Sullivan shoves Chad's shoulders, forcing him back a few steps.

A few of the other guys approach, shooting various looks in our direction. One of them leans down, helping Wentworth to his feet before restraining him. I nod, cautioning him to hold him back.

Throwing punches in the locker room never ends well, and Chad needs to learn some self-control. There are smarter ways to handle this than a fistfight that could end up with him being suspended or kicked off the team. The last thing he needs is a rep as a troublemaker.

Our captain, Danny Dwyer, steps in between them. "Quit this shit, unless neither of you values your place on this team." He glares at Chad and O'Sullivan.

Chad flexes his knuckles and glares back at our team captain. "He was insulting my girlfriend and making threats against her. I don't take that lightly."

"Starting fights is not the way to resolve things, rookie," Dwyer replies before stabbing his finger in O'Sullivan's direction. "I heard what you said, and you're way out of line. The two of you came over here to stir shit, and I won't tolerate that on my team. Unless you want to kiss your career goodbye, you'll say nothing about this."

He looks around the room at our remaining teammates, those who were here to witness this go down. "This didn't happen. Wentworth tripped on a wet patch on the floor and bruised his face. Understood?"

Everyone nods, including a reluctant O'Sullivan and a fuming Wentworth. We do too. Like our nemesis, we don't mean a word of it.

Gathering our shit, we hightail it out of the locker room.

We say nothing, both of us quietly steaming, until we reach the parking lot. "You get the intel, and I'll grab some equipment," Chad says, unlocking his truck with the key fob. This isn't our first rodeo, and we both know the drill. "It'll have to be late. I need to make a few drop-offs."

It hasn't taken Chad long to pick up a bunch of regular clients. He sells the rest of the drugs at frat and sorority parties. I hate he's selling that shit, but there's no talking him out of it.

Besides, it won't be for long.

The Sainthood is unsanctioned, and Knight Carter has already been tasked with handling the situation. I spoke to the Greed & Gluttony heir last week. He's a freshman too, and we have a couple classes together. Knight is only a few months younger than me, and we spent a good bit of time together growing up. His old man is a misogynistic asshole, but he seems to have evaded that gene. Bree might have some success converting Knight to a more modern, humanity-focused society, but I think he's the only one.

Anyway, I asked him to keep Chad out of whatever his father has planned, and he promised he would. He also swore to keep me updated, and I trust he will.

I wish I could tell my best friend, but I can't. This is far from the first time I have kept shit from him. I have wanted to confide in Chad so badly, at certain times, but it would be more than selfish to burden him.

Plebeians aren't allowed to know about our world. Those that find out—by accident or through selfishness on someone's part—are either killed or their lives are permanently ruined. A favorite punishment is to kill someone they love and then threaten other loved ones to force their eternal silence.

I can't do that to my friend. I won't. All I can do is protect him from any fallout when Rhett Carter decides to intervene.

I should let Ash go, for the same reasons, but I guess my selfishness knows no bounds when it comes to her.

"Will you be able to sneak out unnoticed?" I ask, opening the door to my Range Rover.

"I'll figure out a way," Chad replies. "Will you?"

I let a grin loose on my lips. "I have the perfect distraction. The perfect weapon."

He arches a brow.

"Bree is moving in with me. I'm going over to my parents' place now to grab some of her stuff."

Chad chuckles. "Does your *fiancée* know?"

"Not my fiancée yet, and no. I'm planning to surprise her." I can't contain my grin. Julia is going to lose her shit, but she can't do anything about it. My father has already approved the move, and his word is law.

Bree and Julia are well-acquainted thanks to Luminary social events and the quarterly meetings at HQ. They loathe one another, and I can't wait to see the sparks flying. It took next to nothing to convince my sister. She wanted out of our parents' house, and she has an added incentive to hate Julia now—Ash.

"Maybe you should answer that," Bree says when my cell buzzes again with another call from our big bad brother.

"Nah. He'll only put me in a bad mood, and I want nothing to take away from this moment." I am pretty sure I know why Baz is calling, and I'm determined to avoid him for as long as I can. Steering my Range Rover into the parking space beside Julia's pink Porsche 911, I notice my sister staring at it and shaking her head.

"Will you smuggle me out of the country and help to hide

my ass if I accidentally-on-purpose murder her in her sleep?" Bree smirks as she climbs out of the passenger seat, glancing up at the row of townhomes.

This entire gated community belongs to The Luminaries. The sole purpose in building these townhomes was to house students from the Luminary and master families and occasionally—as in Ash's case—children of respected experts. I suspect luck was on Pamela and Doug's side when they requested one of the properties for their only daughter. If it was any other year, the place would be full, and there would've been no room for her.

This year, my brother and some other luminaries who are seniors chose to live in a new apartment development right beside campus. It was built by Carter Construction, the multi-billion-dollar business owned by the Greed & Gluttony Luminary.

Knight Carter and Toby Salinger live in the other two houses on this side of the street with various friends and family members. Across the way, only two of the four houses are occupied by extended family members attached to the Salinger and Manford lines.

I roar laughing as I get out. It's going to be fun having Bree around. As kids, we were thick as thieves and always getting up to mischief together. Rounding the car, I open the trunk to retrieve her bags. "I solemnly swear to protect your murderous ass, but you should probably refrain from taking it that far. If murder was an option, I'd have slit her throat while she slept the first night we moved in."

"Is it bad my fingers already itch with a craving to key her car?" Bree scowls at the sports car like it has personally affronted her. "Who the fuck orders an iconic car in pink? And it's such a nauseating shade too. It offends me to no end."

I chuckle again. "No wonder Ash likes you. You're like peas in a pod."

"I already liked her before I knew who she was to you. Now, I fucking love her." Bree bands her arm around mine as I set the last of her bags on the ground. "I'm going to help you get your girl back. We're going to find a way to permanently get rid of Julia, even if I have to resort to murdering her in her sleep. I'd make the ultimate sacrifice for you, little brother."

"Your violent offer is tempting, but I'm not sacrificing my sister for that whiny bitch. We'll find another way."

"Come on." Bree snatches up the two smaller bags. "Let's get this show on the road."

"Honey, I'm home," I call out, chuckling to myself as I usher Bree into the house I share with Julia. I'm salivating at the impending fireworks as we deposit my sister's bags on the porcelain floor in the hallway.

"I'm up here, darling," Julia screams from upstairs.

"*Darling*? Really?" Bree scrunches her nose in disgust.

"She's a crazy bitch." I gesture at my sister to follow me up the stairs. "Almost as crazy as that fucker Ares Haynes. He's Ash's stepbrother, and he lives next door," I add in case she isn't aware.

"Oh, I know all about him and his aversion to clothes."

I can't help chuckling. I hate the prick, but it's funny as fuck. Chad is about to lose it big-time. Tonight's nocturnal activities will be good for him. He needs to let off some steam.

We reach the top of the stairs, and Julia shouts, "In here!" from the direction of my master suite, and I'm instantly on high alert.

That bitch has no right to go anywhere near my room. I stomp along the corridor, preparing to rip her a new one as Bree follows a few steps behind me

The instant I enter my bedroom, I slam to a screeching halt.

Julia is lying naked on my bed, propped up on several cushions, save for a pair of high heels on her feet. Brash red lipstick coats her lips as she smiles at me with a come-hither look in her eye. Parting her legs wider, to give me a proper view, she purrs, "We need a do-over, darling. This morning was a complete misunderstanding. Let's bury the hatchet and start things as we mean to go on. I'm adventurous in bed, and I know how to please my man. You can fuck me anyway you want, stud. I'm down with most kinks. Trust me," she adds, licking her lips. "You won't be disappointed."

"Did everything I said earlier go in one ear and out the other?" I ask, purposely shielding Bree.

I know my sister.

She'll want to time her entrance for the perfect moment.

"You couldn't pay me to fuck you." I visibly shudder on purpose. "I feel ill at the thought of my cock anywhere near your vile cunt."

"Ouch." Bree steps around me, grinning as she spots her archnemesis spreadeagled on my bed. "Talk about lamb to the slaughter."

Julia shrieks, clutching the comforter and quickly dragging it up to cover her naked body. "What the hell is she doing here?" she yells, glaring daggers at me. "Make her leave. We need privacy."

"Still so fucking delusional." Bree fixes me with an evil grin. "I definitely think it's time to start things as we mean to go on. What do you say, little brother?"

"I love the way your mind works, PC 1, and I'm game."

Before Julia can make a move, Bree jumps on top of her and pins her to the bed with her much taller frame. Opening the drawer of my bedside table, I snatch a set of handcuffs and ankle cuffs from my stash of goodies. Julia screams and thrashes as Bree holds her down while I grab her arms, one at a time, and cuff them to the bed posts. Then I yank the cover off the bed and toss it aside, exposing her naked body while she curses at me and makes all kinds of threats. Removing her heels, because those things are weapons, I secure her ankles together with the restraints before we both climb off the bed to enjoy our handiwork.

"Untie me now, Jason, or you'll be sorry!" Julia screams.

Bree looks sideways at me. "I think this pathetic bitch needs to be taught a lesson. I say we offer her for sale on Samite. Let some sick fuck buy her and problem solved. No more fiancée."

If that was an option, I'd have made it happen already. But the Greed & Gluttony Luminary controls the underworld and Samite—the dark net. The team assigned to this mammoth task contains masters, experts, and grunts from all four families. Mostly we let it operate without interference, but it takes a lot of manpower to watch over everything and gather intel.

"You can't sell me!" Julia roars. "You'll sign your own death sentence, you dumb bitch."

"It would almost be worth it to see you fucked over like that."

"I think all the drugs you did in South America have rotted your brain," Julia hisses. "It wouldn't get that far, but be my guest. Go for it. See what happens."

Walking over to a chair where Julia placed her clothes, I grab her lace panties and stuff them in her mouth, sick of listening to her whiny self-righteous voice. "That's better," I say, enjoying her muffled protests.

"What will we do with her?" Bree waggles her brows and her eyes light up with all manner of dark and devilish delights.

"Let her stew for a few hours to contemplate her poor life choices," I say before entering my closet and returning a minute later with a video camera mounted on a tripod.

Bree snorts out a laugh. "Do I want to know how you just happen to have one of those lying around?"

"It belongs to Chad." I don't elaborate on why I have it in my bedroom or what we do with it. Bree has an active imagination. I'm sure she can figure it out. Placing the tripod at the end of my bed, I set up the video camera to record, and then I walk over to the side and unbutton my jeans.

"Eh, dude, not sure I want to see this." Bree semi-grimaces as I lower my zipper, and I can only guess where her mind has gone.

"It's not what you're thinking." I flash her an evil grin. "Trust me, you'll want to see this."

"Now I'm all kinds of curious." Bree laughs as she fixes her gaze on the woman tied to my bed.

I whip out my dick and take a piss.

All over Julia.

Tears stab the corners of her eyes, and I whistle as I complete her humiliation. "Golden showers aren't one of your kinks, huh?" Tucking my dick into my boxers and securing my jeans in place, I lean down, chuckling as she squirms uncomfortably. I stare into her face, enjoying the look of panic, fear, and disgust I see in her eyes. "Be grateful I didn't shit on you." Her eyes widen in alarm, and Bree almost chokes on a laugh.

"You are twisted, little brother, but I approve."

I tower over Julia, gaining sick satisfaction as tears stream from her eyes. "Consider this a warning, fiancée. This is a taste of things to come, and I'm capable of much, much worse. I'll leave you here to reflect on your own stupidity. If I ever find you in my room or in my bed again, I won't hesitate to release this video."

It doesn't matter it would be removed. Everyone knows when a tape is out there, it's out there forever. Especially if I share it by text first. She would eternally be a laughingstock, and she knows it. I want to warn her not to make a move against Ash, but that would be counterproductive when I need to convince her I no longer care about our neighbor.

Leaving my bedroom door open, I exit the room with my sister, and we make our way downstairs to grab her bags. "I'll arrange for a new bed to be delivered," she says, already tapping away on her cell.

"Thanks. I have a guy collecting your Ducati in the morning," I confirm. "You can ride with me to school, and it should be here when you get home." Father will throw a hissy fit when he discovers I hid Bree's motorcycle from him after she left for South America. He hates how uncouth it makes her look to ride it. It's the same for Luminary males, so it's not exactly sexist. More like hypocritical bullshit because appearances matter so much in our world.

"Oh, for the love of god." Bree glares at her cell before glancing up at me. "It's Baz. Now he's blowing up *my* phone." She swipes her finger across the screen as I vigorously shake my head.

"You're dealing with it," she demands, answering his call and slapping the cell in my hand.

"What?" I bark into the phone.

"Watch your fucking tone," my brother snaps. "The next time you ignore me I'll haul your ass in and beat the ever-loving crap out of you."

"What do you want, Baz? I'm busy."

"I need you on a job. Don't make plans for Sunday."

Oh, hell to the no. "No. I already told Dad I—"

"Dad's got nothing to do with this. I'm the heir, and I'm telling you it's time you stepped up. I'll even sweeten the deal. Come with me on Sunday, and I'll tell you what I've discovered about Ashley Shaw."

Chapter Sixteen

Chad

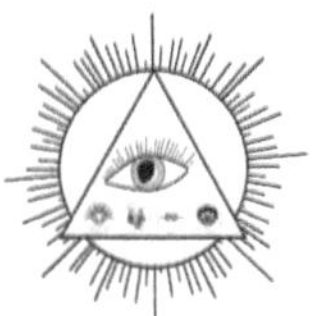

"He's an even bigger asshole than Haynes, and you know how much I hate that guy," I say, running my fingers over the brass knuckles on my other hand as we wait outside a large family home a few miles from campus.

"Truth." Jase agrees, drumming his fingers on the steering wheel of his Range Rover. "O'Sullivan is a fucking idiot too."

"Coach would be so pissed if he knew he was fucking his estranged wife."

"I wonder if that's the reason why they separated," Jase ponders, staring straight ahead through the windshield at the eerily quiet street.

It's almost two a.m. on a Wednesday night, and most folks are safely tucked up in bed. I got delayed doing my rounds thanks to a dickhead who thought he could start a line of credit with me. Luckily, I had stored the equipment for tonight's stakeout in my truck before leaving the house earlier, so I was able to teach the fool a valuable lesson. It didn't even slice the edge off the ever-present rage simmering in my veins.

I'm itching to go nuclear on O'Sullivan's ass.

He won't know what hit him.

My tardiness ended up being advantageous as we trailed our teammate to this house, watching him enter just after midnight, and realized we'd hit the jackpot. "It very well could be," I say. "I wouldn't put it past that sleazy fuck to have had an affair with Coach's wife while they were still together. He's just that arrogant. There's no way Coach knows it's O'Sullivan who is sticking it to his wife."

Jase and I share a conspiratorial grin. "Lucky we got that footage of him entering the marital home," he says.

Coach's wife was more than pleased to see O'Sullivan, flinging her arms around his neck while wrapping her legs around his waist and kissing the shit out of him. There is no denying the evidence. Coach will boot him straight off the team when he sees it.

Not that O'Sullivan will be in any shape to ever play for the Lowell Lions again when we are done with him.

"Prick should've kept his big mouth shut." Jase says it so calmly, but the underlying darkness that always lingers in the shadows surrounding my best friend is obvious in his tone.

"Will this be enough to silence Wentworth?" I ask as light floods one of the upstairs bedrooms.

"We'll make sure it is." Jase runs a hand back and forth across the bat resting on his lap. The look of lethal anticipation on his face matches the way I feel inside.

Thankfully, we don't have to wait much longer.

Jase's blacked-out windows conceal us as the front door of the house opens and O'Sullivan steps out. We put our gloves on and share a fist bump. Exhilaration races through my veins. I'm ready to teach this jerk a lesson.

I film their mushy goodbye, zooming in on O'Sullivan's freshly fucked hair and the woman's skimpy nightdress. Should

Coach have any doubts about what went down, O'Sullivan's hand up the front of her nightgown will seal the deal.

Prick looks smug as fuck as he sets out on foot, walking right by us. He thinks he's so clever, parking his truck a couple of blocks away. Yet he never spotted us trailing him all the way from the frat house.

The dickhead deserves everything coming his way.

In another piece of luck, O'Sullivan parked at the edge of a small park. I hop out when Jase pulls the car up beside his truck, thrusting my fist in the douche's face before he has realized what's happening.

Blood spurts from his nose where the brass knuckles shredded his skin, and he flails against the side of his truck. I land a succession of savage punches to his torso and kick his legs out from under him while Jase parks the car in front. O'Sullivan goes down like a sack of potatoes, and I jump on him, quickly cuffing his hands so he can't retaliate. Stuffing a smelly rag in his mouth, I meet his enraged eyes just as Jase looms over us. "Yes, asshole," I hiss. "Bet you regret spouting that shit about our girl now."

Together we drag the asshole deep into the park, tossing him down on the ground just inside a small, forested area. We don't give him the opportunity to defend himself. We go at him immediately, channeling all our pent-up rage as we kick, punch, and beat him with bats.

He doesn't get to spew that poison about Ash without consequences. How dare he threaten to put his hands anywhere near her. That will be the last time he insinuates Jase and I can't keep our woman satisfied.

We hold nothing back, beating him to a pulp, showing no remorse, only stopping when we reach the point of no return.

As much as I hate this prick, I'm not doing jail time for him.

The smell of urine filters in the air as he pisses himself.

Sweat plasters my shirt to my back, and I wipe my arm across my clammy brow. Both of us are covered in blood, panting and sweating as adrenaline continues to course through our veins.

"Hold his leg up at the knee," I instruct Jase as I kneel on the ground beside the slimy motherfucker. He's moaning behind the rag in his mouth, but it's not enough. I want him to really suffer. I want to hear his piercing cries ring out in the desolate still night air. We're far enough away from the nearest house not to worry about drawing attention.

Removing the saliva-coated rag from his mouth, I use it to rub some of the blood from his eyes. I want to see the look on his face when I shatter his dreams. "If you ever talk shit about our girl again, I will kill you."

"Ashley is a fucking queen," Jase adds, "and you won't ever disrespect her again."

Climbing to my feet, I watch as O'Sullivan struggles to form words through his busted lips, blood-soaked mouth, and cracked teeth. "You really should've minded your own business," I say before slamming my foot repeatedly down on his leg. Jase joins me when O'Sullivan's leg crumples, flopping to the muddy ground. O'Sullivan's strangled wails echo in the silent night air, and it's music to my ears. We slam our feet down on his leg until it's well and truly shattered. Never mind about playing ball. He'll be lucky if he ever walks on two legs again.

Jase rips his shirt over his head, using it to mop up the blood and sweat on his face. "In case it's not clear, we're not to be messed with." His sharp lethal tone conveys considerable warning. Jase crouches down, rifling through O'Sullivan's pockets. Keeping his wallet and his keys, he tosses receipts, coins, and condom packets on the ground around him, making it look like a mugging gone wrong.

When I remove O'Sullivan's cell from the front pocket of

his jeans, it's already destroyed. The screen is completely shattered from our bats. The device isn't even powering on. Still, you can never be too sure. Throwing it to the ground, I stomp on it with my foot, ensuring it's well and truly fucked.

"You tell the cops—and anyone who asks—that you don't know who attacked you," Jase says, kicking him in the ribs for good measure. I'm pretty sure at least a few of them are broken. "If you breathe our names to anyone, ever, at any time for the rest of your life, I will hunt down every person you love and kill them. Slowly and painfully. Starting with that pretty blonde fiancée carrying your baby."

I shield my surprise better than O'Sullivan. Even all bloodied and beaten, shock and fear are evident on his swollen face.

"Then I'll move on to your beaten-down mother," Jase continues. "How many affairs has your father had by now? Does your mom know about the son he has with the neighbor at the end of the block? Do your parents know your sweet sixteen-year-old sister gave her virginity to the local priest? Or how about that time you drove drunk and high and you knocked a middle-aged man down with your car?" Jase kicks him in the balls, and an inhuman sound trickles from O'Sullivan's lips. "Do your parents know what a shitty human you are and how you drove away from the scene of the crime?"

Jase glares at the asshole on the ground as he hovers over him, revealing all the secrets in his family closet. "That's still an open case, you know. All it would take is a call to the cops to give them your name, and they'd turn their attention to you. Plenty of witnesses saw you leave that party drunk and get behind the wheel of your truck. Your parents only live three blocks from the scene of the accident. And CSI discovered shards from your truck at the scene, enough to connect it to the burned-out remains you left at the bottom of Lowell Lake."

O'Sullivan spits out words as he writhes in agony on the ground, but his speech is muffled, slurred, and indecipherable. We don't need to hear it to know he's promising us a vow of silence.

Jase is a scary motherfucker at the best of times. I know he's well-connected, but when he comes out with this stuff, I'm reminded of just how powerful his family is. I have no idea how he gets this intel, but it's an effective incentive. O'Sullivan won't say a word to anyone because he values breathing.

Jase drills the point home when he says, "After I have finished killing your loved ones, I'll hand you on a silver platter to the police, and you'll spend the rest of your miserable life behind bars." He bends down over our ex-teammate. "Have I made myself clear?"

This time, a nod accompanies the litany of slurred words leaking from O' Sullivan's mouth.

Jase pats him on the head. "Good dog."

"The vow of silence extends to Wentworth too," I add. We know Wentworth will point the finger of blame at us first, which is why we are sending him an anonymous copy of the video we took tonight to purposely lead him off our track. The tape plus the location of O'Sullivan's attack should convince him Coach is behind this. He won't say anything because he won't want to risk his place on the team.

I would have loved to teach that asshole a lesson too, but both of them being beaten up so soon after our altercation in the locker room would be too suspicious. Jase managed to talk me down from that ledge. Besides, I got a nice right hook in. The dick will be sporting a nasty bruise for days.

Without his partner in crime, we expect him to keep his head down and not start any shit. If he does, all bets are off, and we'll handle him in a similar manner.

"Especially him," Jase adds, spearing O'Sullivan with a pointed look.

The defeated man on the ground simply nods, all the fight permanently gone from his body.

We leave him there, sauntering back to the SUV with matching grins.

We slash O'Sullivan's tires and beat up his truck, careful not to smash the windows fully and risk someone hearing. Satisfied we have done enough to make it look like a robbery gone wrong, we strip out of our bloody clothes and boots, shoving them in a plastic bag in the trunk. Jase will dispose of them later.

My buddy insists we sit in our boxers on towels so we don't leave any evidence on his leather seats, and then we hightail it out of there.

I make an anonymous call to the cops when we are far enough away, giving them O'Sullivan's location, and then our work here is done.

Chapter Seventeen

Ashley

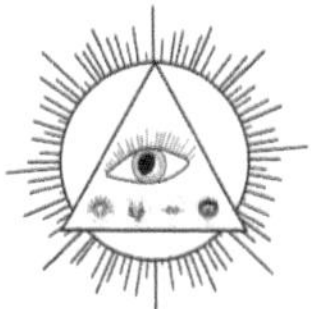

I moan in my sleep, wriggling on the mattress of my king-sized bed as a flurry of tingles emanates from my core, sending tremors cascading all over my body.

If I'm dreaming, I never want to wake up.

Intense pleasure zips through my pussy, gliding up my body and rippling through my thighs. My back bows as an earth-shattering orgasm seizes hold of me, and I cry out as I soar like a bird. Waves of blissful euphoria rock my body, tossing me from side to side as I writhe on my bed.

A satisfied chuckle drags me slowly from slumber as Chad thrusts inside me in one fast, powerful drive.

My back arches off the bed again as a sultry moan filters from my lips. Blinking my eyes open, I watch through blurry vision as my boyfriend hoists my legs over his shoulders and starts pounding inside me. Glancing at the clock by my bed, I'm surprised to see it's three forty a.m. It's been a while since my boyfriend fucked me in my sleep, and it's usually always first thing in the morning.

I don't care if anyone thinks it's wrong. Waking to my

boyfriend with his mouth between my thighs or his cock pushing inside me is one of my favorite ways to start the day.

"Babe," I murmur, lifting my hips as Chad ruts into me while his hands move all over my body, touching and squeezing, kneading and tweaking.

"You're so dirty, sweetheart. You love me eating you out while you sleep."

"I do," I rasp, crying out when he tugs at my nipples in a way that hurts.

"My sexy siren," he whispers, leaning down and smashing his lips against mine. My legs are elevated at an awkward angle, but his cock drives deeper in this position, and I whimper into his mouth.

He ravishes my lips, plundering my mouth, his tongue greedily devouring me as he fucks me into the bed with borderline aggression. Chad roars as I scrape my nails up and down his back and bite his tongue.

"Fuck, Siren. I needed this tonight." Sitting back on his knees, he keeps my legs hooked over his shoulders while he grabs my ass and rams into my cunt with renewed ferver.

A flashing red light behind him draws my eye to the elevated camera in the dark bedroom. "You're filming." I state the obvious because Chad hasn't taken his tripod out once since we moved in.

"Is that okay?" His hands crawl up my body as he asks for permission he already knows he has.

"Sure. As long as you only keep it in the cloud."

When Chad first started filming us—when we were horny sixteen-year-olds fucking any chance we got—he used to keep the videos on his cell. After Jase joined our relationship, he freaked out at that discovery. It doesn't matter that we are the only ones who watch the replays. Jase said it was far too risky to keep on a cell phone, even with a password and encrypted files.

So, we let him set up a secure cloud file, and Chad purchased a couple of specialist cameras and tripods. Now, when he's finished filming, he presses a button, and the file is automatically sent to the cloud and permanently deleted from the camera so it doesn't fall into the wrong hands.

After what happened to Harlow the summer before senior year, I am super grateful for Jase's forward thinking.

"Of course. You know I'd never want anyone to see them but us," he confirms before flipping me around on all fours. "What I meant was are you okay to film without Jase?"

Mention of his name would most likely send me spiraling into a dark hole if it wasn't for Chad's throbbing cock plunging in and out of me, working as an effective distraction. "We filmed before he was involved, and he wasn't always around to watch or participate after we became a threesome. I have no issue with this, Chad. It's a major turn-on knowing you jerk off to videos of us together."

"You're so goddamned perfect, Ash." Gripping my hips hard, he digs his hands into my flesh as he bends over me, planting a line of kisses down my back.

"I aim to please," I tease, whimpering when his fingers find their way to my pussy.

"Prove it, Siren. Come on my dick," he says, smashing my head down into the pillow and thrusting into me in brutal, punishing strokes. My clit throbs as he rubs me vigorously, and I cry out as he brings his hand down on my butt cheek in a harsh, stinging slap, one I know will leave a temporary handprint on my ass.

It works though, and I fall apart on his dick, screaming, crying, and littering the air with a string of dirty words and expletives as I come explosively. I barely have time to enjoy it before Chad pulls out and yanks me upright. He turns me around and shoves me up against the headrest in a seated position. Tangling one hand in my hair, he fists it hard, and I bite the inside of my cheek. My neck stretches at an awkward angle as he positions himself in front of me. "Mouth open, tongue out, sexy. I want to come all over your face."

I do as I'm told because I love when Chad turns all bad. The only place I let him boss me around is the bedroom. Outside of it, I give as good as I get. But I trust my pleasure to my man, and he's never let me down. A hiss slithers from my lips when he tugs hard on my hair, stretching my neck painfully as I stick my tongue out.

"Yes, my little dirty siren. Just like that." The bed rocks as Chad jerks himself hard in one hand while tightening his grip on my hair in his other. He roars out his release a few seconds later, and I close my eyes as ropes of hot cum spurt from his dick, landing on my tongue, my cheeks, my face, my brow, and my eyelids.

Chad sweeps his cum from my eyelids, smearing my lips with his sticky fingers. "Open your eyes," he instructs, and I do, staring at him with complete trust. "Swallow every drop," he commands in a gruff voice, letting go of my hair.

Maintaining eye contact with him, I make a big production out of licking my lips, swiping my fingers through his cum on other parts of my face and shoving it into my mouth as I swallow.

"Fuck." His lips collide with mine as he falls back on the bed, pulling me down on top of him. His tongue dances with mine and the thought of him tasting himself turns me on so much. Grinding on top of him, I moan when I feel him harden underneath me. Chad has unbelievable stamina, and he can go all night. We often do.

Pressing him down into the bed, I sit up and straddle his hips, rubbing my pussy and my ass back and forth along his hard dick. "You make me so fucking horny, babe."

"I am nowhere near finished with you," he grunts, grabbing my hips and pulling me forward as he sits up. Burying his face in my chest, he sucks my nipples as we rock against one another. My hands roam over his cropped velvety-soft hair as I lift my body up, and he positions himself at my entrance. I scream when Chad impales me with his monster dick, and I hope I have woken my asshole stepbrother.

That stunt he pulled with my car yesterday morning deserves payback. I have the ultimate retribution in mind. As soon as we're done with this round, I'm suggesting we put it in motion.

All thoughts of Ares flee my mind when Chad drops down to his back, handing the reins to me. Pressing firmly on his rock-hard chest, I pivot my hips, lifting up and slamming back down, clenching my thighs at the side of his body as I ride him with gusto. Chad gropes my tits, pinches my nipples, and toys with my clit as we fuck, and I'm lost to everything but his touch, the feel of him moving in sync with me from below, and the out-of-this-world sensations he coaxes from my body.

I pick up my pace, my tits jiggling as I bounce up and down on his dick, grinding and moaning as I fuck him. Chad can tell when I need him deeper, and he lifts me up, bending me over the side of the bed as he slides back inside me. Raising my hips and pushing my head down into the bed, he rocks into me savagely, thrusting hard and fast as he drives his cock into my pussy, and I'm clenching around him as I feel another orgasm building. I detonate like a bomb when he pushes his thumb into my ass, screaming so loud I'm sure I've done temporary damage to my vocal cords.

"Take my cum," he rasps, winding his hand around my throat from behind and applying pressure. "Take all of it. Everything I have is yours," he says before he climaxes, depositing his seed deep inside me.

I offer up thanks to whoever invented the IUD because I love he can come inside me without knocking me up.

We collapse on the bed in a sweaty heap, and the only sounds in the room are our mutual deep breathing and heavy pants as we attempt to slow our racing heartbeats down.

"Love you." Chad sweeps my hair aside, kissing the back of my neck.

I angle my head back for a kiss, and he presses his mouth to mine. We kiss slowly and passionately as his arms hold me to him with my back to his chest. "We're going to be like zombies at school tomorrow," I murmur against his lips.

"Worth it." He nips at my ear.

We smile at one another as we remain locked in our intimate embrace, and I'm more content than I have been in weeks. "By the way, we're holding our first party on Saturday. Spread the word."

Chad's first game is this Saturday, at home, so partying Friday night is a no-go. We have decided, while at college, Saturday nights will be party nights except when Chad has an away game. I'm too busy to plan and host weekly parties anyway, so twice a month works perfectly.

"Sounds like a plan." His lips kick up at the corners. "Let's not tell the degenerate. It can be a special surprise."

I snort out a laugh. "I doubt he'll be overly surprised. Parties and me are kind of synonymous, babe."

"True." He hugs me tight before releasing me. "I need to shower."

"I'll join you," I suggest as he climbs off the bed. "Then I think we should put our revenge plan in motion. I got the glue. It's dark out. And by the time we are showered and dressed, Ares should have fallen back asleep." I smirk because there's no way we didn't wake Ares with all the noise we made. "This is the perfect time to do it."

"For sure," he agrees, switching on the bedside lamp.

My mouth drops open in horror as I look at him. "Oh my God." I scramble off the bed. "You're covered in dried blood. Are you hurt?"

He curses as he looks down at the blood stuck to parts of his face, neck, upper chest, and lower arms. "Not mine, don't worry."

I smack his chest and glare at him.

"Ow. What's that for?" he asks, walking toward the camera.

"For not showering before you came to bed. Ugh." A shiver tiptoes over me as I turn on the full light, surveying the mess that was my pristine white bed. He's lucky he gave me multiple orgasms, or I might not be so forgiving. "Do I want to know whose blood has stained our sheets?"

He smirks as he presses a button on the camera to send the latest file to the cloud. "The less you know, the better."

"Did you do this alone or..." I purposely let my question die out.

"Jase was with me."

I'm relieved to hear it. Not that Chad can't handle himself, but there is safety in numbers. Those two have gotten into plenty of fights and scrapes over the years, and they've always had each other's backs. I don't want that to change just because my relationship with Jase has ended.

"Did this have anything to do with the drugs?" I ask, bracing myself for an argument.

A muscle clenches in his jaw. "If you must know, it had to do with you. A couple of guys said some shit we didn't appreciate, and we decided to teach one of them a lesson."

"Aw, you're my hero." I deliberately leave Jase out of my statement, padding naked to where Chad is standing. I stretch up and kiss him. When I pull back, he's looking at me with a funny smile. "What?" I inquire.

"Most girls would freak if their man came home all bloody and sweaty, but you kiss me and tell me I'm your hero."

"I'm not most girls, and I like that you defend my honor. Maybe that makes me twisted." I shrug, not really caring. "Or maybe it's 'cause I'm friends with Harlow and I know a little of the stuff she endured with the guys." I slap his ass before I start stripping the bed. "Perhaps I'm just weird. Blood and violence has always kind of turned me on."

Chad chuckles. "Told you you're perfect." He pinches my ass and I screech, jumping a couple inches in the air.

I roll my eyes as I finish removing the soiled bed linen while Chad returns the tripod and camera to the closet. Then he helps me to change the bed, running downstairs to dump the dirty sheets in the washing machine while I turn the shower on.

Chad fucks me again in the shower, and then we get dressed and head outside to deliver a serving of vengeance to our roomie.

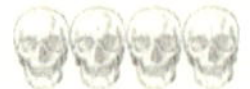

"I can't believe the motherfucker had a late shift today," I grumble, climbing into the passenger seat of my SUV. Chad is driving my car this morning as his truck needs gas and we didn't get up early enough to go to the gas station. "I really wanted to see his face when he tries to start his bike and realizes we glued the lock."

"I know. That's half the fun. Though it's probably best we're not anywhere in the vicinity when that goes down. He's going to lose his shit." Chad barks out a laugh as he reverses out of the parking space.

I smother a yawn as we drive toward campus.

"Tired, sweetheart?" He pins me with a smug look, and I thump him in the arm.

"Some sex-crazed maniac with a giant dick kept me up most of the night." I'm not exaggerating when I say I've had three hours sleep max. And two of those were before Chad got home.

"Giant dick, huh?" He puffs out his chest, and I giggle.

"Don't get all humble on me now, Chad. You know what you're packing in your boxers." I lean over and squeeze his junk.

"Don't start something you don't intend to pursue, Siren," he teases.

"Who said I wouldn't follow through?" I ask, moving in my seat to reach over for him. I wince as my poor overworked vagina reminds me I'm sore.

"That's why." He sweeps his fingers down my cheek as he pulls into a parking space on campus. "As much as I'd love to defile you in the back seat, your pounded pussy needs a break."

"So chivalrous!" I crack up laughing. "You're something else, Chad Lucas Baldwin." Leaning over the console, I kiss him. "Love you. Have a great day!"

I don't see Chad again the rest of the day. Although I'm like the walking dead, I have an assignment due on Friday, so I head to the library after my last class, determined to finish it. I want to hand it in tomorrow and then have an early night with Chad before his first game on Saturday. Hopefully, he might get to play, and we'll celebrate on Saturday night at our first college party. Bree is helping me with the party planning, and we have it all worked out. I'm excited. It'll be fun.

"Ready, babe?" Chad says just as I'm putting the last word down on the page.

"Are you finished already?" I glance at my watch, shocked to see the time. I didn't realize it was so late.

"Yep. I thought we could grab some pizzas on the way home, watch a movie, and have an early night?"

The telltale gleam in his eye gives the game away. "Uh-huh," I say, packing up my shit. "Sure you don't have an ulterior motive?"

He reels me into his arms. "I might have plans to worship my brilliant girlfriend. Sue me if that's a crime."

"Brilliant, huh?"

Chad grabs my bag in one hand and slings his arm around my shoulders with the other as he steers me out of the library. There aren't many students left, but we still get a few shushes as we continue talking while we walk.

"Jase forgot his iPad and went back to the house midmorning to get it. He happened to be there when Ares discovered we glued the lock on his motorcycle. Jase recorded him losing his mind. It's a fucking classic. I thought we could play it on the TV on a loop while eating our pizza and really piss the asshole off."

I burst out laughing, and Chad has to slap his hand over my mouth to stifle the noise.

We're still laughing as we exit the library and head toward my SUV. It's dark out, and there is only a smattering of vehicles in the student parking lot. "He's going to retaliate," I say as Chad unlocks the car and opens the passenger side door.

"He shouldn't. He's the asshole who started this by messing with your car."

I climb up, waiting until Chad is behind the wheel before replying. "We'll need to up the stakes next time."

"We will. That's a promise." He moves to start the car when a noise from the back seat startles both of us. Butterflies swoop into my chest as adrenaline instantly courses through my body. Chad and I share a look as I slowly move my hand toward the glove box, where I stow my gun.

"Don't do that," a man with a gruff voice commands in a sharp tone from behind. "And don't turn around."

My heart slams against my rib cage as fear surges through my veins.

"Start the car and drive as you normally would." His voice is vaguely familiar, but I can't place him over the blood rushing to my head and the panic sounding like alarm bells in my ears. "We need to talk."

Chapter Eighteen

Ashley

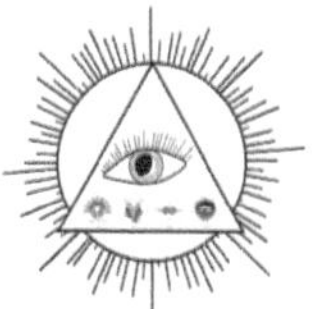

"You don't need your gun, Ashley," the man says as I inch closer to the glove compartment. "I'm not going to hurt either of you. I'm the guy who trained you over at the facility in Grenlow. I'm Harlow's friend. I promise you can trust me."

Chad and I share another look. I don't trust any man who sneaks into the back seat of my car and scares the living daylights out of me. But I trust my friend. Lo said this guy was one of the good guys, so I'm going to give him the benefit of the doubt. Retracting my hand, I sit back in my seat, willing my heart rate to slow down before I give myself a coronary.

"Drive, Chad," he says. "Take the longer route home."

"Why should we do anything you say?" Chad replies, not moving a muscle to start the engine. "This is some legit crazy shit. Give me one reason I shouldn't call the cops."

"Call them if you like, but I won't be arrested. It'll be a waste of all our time. I'm sorry for creeping up on you like this, but it's necessary. I need to speak with Ashley, but no one can know I'm here."

I nod at my boyfriend because I want to find out what's so important this dude needed to resort to such measures. Chad starts the engine and reverses the car. "Why me?" I ask as Chad navigates his way out of the parking lot.

"You're in danger," he somberly replies.

All the fine hairs lift on the back of my neck, and acid churns in my gut. "From who?" I ask, working hard to keep calm as I instinctively turn around.

"Face forward," he commands. "Make it look like you're talking to Chad."

This is weird as fuck, but whatever. I face the front and stare straight ahead.

"Answer the question," Chad barks. "How is Ash in danger and why?"

"I can't get into specifics."

Chad curses. "Why the fuck not?"

"I don't have all the details, and even if I did, I couldn't divulge them. The people who own the organization I work for are some of the most powerful people in the world. There are several anonymous investors and vested partners who sit on the board that I'm not privy to, and I run the organization. Imagine godlike authority. Power and control beyond anything you have ever seen. Way beyond governments and governmental bodies. After I ran your details through our system the other night, I had an unwelcome late-night visit. I was told, in no uncertain terms, to cut you two loose. To forget I'd ever met you. I could be killed for even telling you this."

"Then why are you?" I ask, wondering if he's being a tad overdramatic even though he really doesn't seem the type.

"Because you're Lo's friend and you deserve to know something is going down. I couldn't risk doing any snooping, but I have a hacker friend on the outside who did me a favor. His digging didn't yield much because we couldn't risk delving too deep. But we did discover something suspicious connected to your parents' business. They are involved in this, Ashley. You need to talk to them."

"Involved in what?" He's talking in riddles, and this is starting to stink.

"I have already said too much."

"Really?" Chad says, glaring out the windshield. "It sounds to me like you've told us a whole lot of nothing. Did someone put you up to this?" Chad grinds his teeth, and a muscle pops in his jaw. "Because this sounds like some next-level bullshit."

"I assure you it's the truth, but I'm aware of how it sounds. I didn't have to tell you anything, but it was the right thing to do. Whether you heed my warning is on you now." A shuffling sound emits from the back. "Pull over to the sidewalk behind that black van," he instructs.

"Gladly," Chad snaps, rapidly losing his patience with the dude.

"One more thing," the man says as Chad pulls up alongside the curb and kills the engine. "It's even more important you know how to fully defend yourself. I can't train you, but I know a guy who can. He'll reach out to you in the next few days. Name's Sebastien. I strongly advise you to work with him. He'll equip you with the skills you need. Take care of yourself, Ashley," he adds just before the door opens and closes in quick succession.

"What the actual fuck is going on?" Chad asks as we watch a black-covered figure slip quickly around the hood of my SUV and jump into the back of the van. It takes off instantly, speeding up the road and taking the corner at a sharp angle.

"Drive." I glance left and right, creeped out by the dark, isolated road and thoroughly fucking spooked after that exchange.

"You don't believe that nonsense, do you?" Chad asks as he puts the pedal to the metal and hightails it out of there.

"It sounds preposterous, but why would he lie? What would he gain in doing so?"

Chad shrugs. "I don't know, but it sounds like a crock of shit. Your parents run your dad's family logistics business, and they're as straitlaced and honorable as they come. What kind of suspicious shit could they possibly be involved in?"

"I'm not buying it either, but what if he's right? What if they are involved in something and it's put me at risk? It would explain why Dad felt the need to buy me an armored car."

"Or he's just an overprotective father worried because his only daughter has left home," Chad says, clicking the key fob which opens the security gate at our complex.

"He wasn't overly concerned when he left me alone for weeks at a time while him and Mom traveled overseas for business." I remind my boyfriend. "No, something is definitely not right. My gut tells me not to ignore what that guy just said."

"Maybe your dad feels guilty about that. Realizes he was lucky nothing happened to you while they were gone. Perhaps this is his way of making it up to you."

"I don't know. The car felt like overkill when he gave it to me," I say, turning in my seat to stare at my boyfriend as he slowly maneuvers my SUV through the gates. "But it makes more sense if he believes I'm in danger."

"Sweetheart." Chad swings the car into my parking space and cuts the engine. Moving his seat back, he lifts me into his lap and circles his arms around me. "Your dad loves you. Do you really think he'd say nothing if he believed you were in danger?"

"He might if he didn't want to worry me." I bite down on my lip as another thought lands in my mind. "Maybe that's why he didn't object to Ares moving in. He figured it's extra protection for me."

"What the fuck am I?" Chad raises his brows, looking highly offended.

"Extra protection too." I brush my lips gently across his. "My parents didn't raise any objection when I told them I was moving in with you, and when they gave me the keys to the townhome, they made it clear you were included. I didn't even have to negotiate your moving in."

"Well, I know one way to put this to bed," he says, unlocking the door and placing my feet on the ground outside.

"I need to ask my parents."

"Yep, you do." Chad climbs out and locks the car before slinging his arm over my shoulder. We walk toward the house together.

"It's a conversation best had face to face, which rules Mom out. I'm going home for dinner on Sunday, so I'll talk to Dad then."

"Is the degenerate going too?" he inquires as we walk up the steps.

"Unfortunately, yes. I don't suppose you want to come?"

"Even if I could stomach eating dinner with them, I can't. I told Mom I'd join her and Tessa for dinner. She wants to hear all about the game."

We are stuffing our faces with pizza when the sound of the front door slamming shut reaches our ears. "Quick," Chad mumbles, talking with a mouth full of food. "Switch the channel." We watched the footage Jase recorded of Ares losing his shit over his bike when we first came home, uploading a copy to the TV for this very moment. It's just what I needed to cheer me up after Lo's trainer friend freaked me the fuck out. I was laughing so hard I almost peed my pants as Ares went ballistic on screen.

Chad flicks the channel, and we settle back to watch just as Ares enters the room. Keeping our eyes glued to the screen, we wait to see what he does. No one says anything for a couple minutes until my stepbrother breaks the silence. Tossing a folded piece of paper at me from behind the couch, he says, "You owe me four hundred and thirty bucks."

I open the page as he stomps across the room and turns off the TV. It's an invoice for a tow truck and a new lock for his Triumph. I rise to my feet and thrust the invoice at him, doing my best to ignore the motor oil and grease streaked on his cheeks and smeared across his sleeveless T-shirt. He's wearing dark work pants and scuffed, unlaced boots, and he's the quintessential bad boy biker. Biceps flex and roll as he folds his inked arms across his impressive chest and glares at me. He's not wearing his faux hawk today, favoring a messy flat look that should be banned because ho-lee-fuck.

I hate to admit it—even to myself—but Ares is sinfully hot, and my lady parts are going crazy with a craving to climb his muscular frame like a spider monkey.

"I'm not paying for that," I retort, regaining my composure.

So what if he's hot?

He's still my stepbrother.

Still a jerk.

Still the biggest pain in my ass.

"You had it coming after you let the air out of my tire."

"That wasn't me," he replies, narrowing his eyes as he stands his ground. "As if I'd resort to anything so juvenile." He lowers his arms to his sides and clenches his fists. It's clear he's restraining himself, but why? We expected him to

totally lose his mind, and I'm disappointed he's proving us wrong.

"You're full of shit," Chad says, standing beside me. "We know it was you. You're pathetic, and you need to grow up."

"I'm not the pathetic one." His lips kick up as he tilts his head to the side. "Though I think *desperate* is more the word I'd use to describe Jase."

I snort out a laugh. "Jase didn't mess with my tire."

"Come on, dollface. You're not that dumb. Of course, he did. You won't speak to him. How else can he get some one-on-one time with you?" Ares steps right up to me, rolling the invoice between his large palms. "I bet he was hoping you'd ride his dick in the back seat while parked on campus. He likes fucking you in public, doesn't he? Gets off on the thrill of almost getting caught."

I'm so stunned he has this knowledge I don't see him tugging the front of my shirt down and stuffing the rolled-up invoice in between my bra-clad breasts until after he's done it.

Chad growls as he grabs Ares's shirt, ready to get into it with him. But he can't show up to training tomorrow with visible injuries. Not the day before his first college game.

"No." Clutching Chad's arm, I shake my head as I remove the invoice from my chest. "He's not worth it." I pull my boyfriend away from my loathsome stepbrother, linking my fingers in his and squeezing hard in warning.

"Oh, but I am." Ares grins, winking at me as he whips his stained shirt up over his head. He drops it to the floor as he kicks off his boots and pops the button on his pants.

"You are getting on my very last nerve," Chad says through gritted teeth as Ares slides his pants down his legs revealing he went commando today.

Does the guy ever wear underwear?

"What the hell are you doing?" I subtly press my thighs

together and work on my poker face as I avoid the temptation to stare at his magnificent pierced dick. It's not as if it doesn't already have a starring role in my dreams. It's difficult not to think about his cock when he's constantly shoving it in my face. Not literally, but the way my body responds—involuntarily—he may as well be.

"Putting my dirty clothes in the laundry," he coolly replies, bending down to scoop up his soiled garments.

Releasing Chad's hand, I reach into his bag and retrieve his lighter. When Ares stands, holding his clothes high up his body in one arm—God forbid he not show off his semi-erect dick—I hold the rolled-up invoice over the empty bowl that held nacho chips and set it alight. "I'm not paying for shit," I confirm over a grin.

Ares purses his lips, looking like he swallowed something sour. "That's the last time I do anything nice for you."

I crank out a laugh, dropping the invoice remnants into the bowl. Placing my hands on my hips, I level him with an incredulous look. "Since when have you ever done anything nice for me?" It's like he was put on Earth to piss me the hell off.

"I was late for work the other morning because I came back to the house to pump your tire up."

My eyes pop wide in shock. That's got to be a lie. "I don't believe you."

"Or someone had a guilty conscience," Chad suggests.

"I don't suffer from that infliction," Ares replies, closing the gap between us. "Guilt is for the weak-minded." He puts his face all up in mine. "I own my shit, and I never regret my actions. I didn't mess with your tire, but believe what you want."

He moves dangerously close and there's literally an inch between us. Heat rolls off his body in waves, and I feel his dick pressing against my jean-clad leg. Instinctively, I reach an arm out, holding Chad back. Without looking at him, I know he's seconds from launching himself at my stepbrother.

Ares flicks my nose. "Guess I'll exact payback some other way." Pinning me with an extremely suggestive look, he saunters out of the room, completely naked, whistling as Chad's threats and curses follow him out of the room.

Chapter Nineteen

Ares

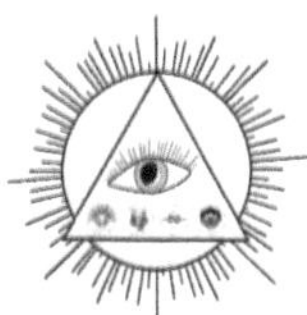

It took colossal willpower not to deck that fucking prick last night when I came home after a shitty fucking day. I wanted nothing more than to take it out on that piece of shit, but the best form of retaliation is to take it out on his girlfriend. Chad turns into a raving lunatic when I go anywhere near Ashley. Stripping naked any chance I get is the gift that keeps on giving. Chad is close to losing it with me, and I fucking love it. Pushing that asshole's buttons is my new favorite pastime, and Ashley makes it so easy.

Dollface can't resist staring at my dick. I'm instantly hard every time she ogles my cock like she wants me to stuff it down her throat and fill her with my seed. If I wasn't still steaming over my motorcycle, I might actually admire the balls on my slutty little sister. There's no doubt it was her idea to glue the ignition switch, and I applaud her ingenuity. She knew exactly how to hit back in a way that would seriously piss me off. Kudos for that. But she won't be laughing when she finds out what I have in store for her now.

I remove a screwdriver and a hammer from the toolbox

before making my way upstairs. My grin expands with every step, and I'm rock-hard behind my jeans, salivating at what's about to go down.

I know she's in the shower, and my man Shoulders has eyes on the jock. Chad is tucked away on campus watching game tapes with his team and the coaching staff. He's unlikely to surface for a couple of hours. Which gives me enough time to reassert my control and have some fun.

Kneeling on the floor in front of the door to the master bedroom, I position the screwdriver underneath the first hinge. I use the hammer to drill the screwdriver upward until the bolt pops up, and I pull it free. I follow the process for the second and third hinges, chuckling at how easy it is to break in. They were idiots to think a little padlock would keep the big bad wolf out.

My stepsister has music on in the en suite bathroom, and she hasn't a clue I'm coming for her. I set my tools down on the ground before adjusting my dick behind my jeans. I'm throbbing with the need to fuck and destroy, but that'll have to wait. My plan to ruin my stepsister only works if she wants me as much as I want her. There is no fun in pushing my agenda before she's ready.

I want her to resist.

To fight me.

To pretend like I'm forcing her.

When we'll both know it's nothing of the sort.

It will really fuck with her mind and her sanity.

She'll hate herself even more than she hates me.

All the touches, stripping, and eye fucking have been on purpose. To plant little seeds in her mind. To watch how her body responds and take note of her tells.

Now it's time to take it to the next level.

And I cannot fucking wait. My cock leaks precum behind

my jeans as I wet my lips and grip the open side of the door. It won't fully open because of the padlock on the other side, but I'm able to stretch it enough to squeeze into the bedroom.

Ash is singing in the shower as I pad across her bedroom in my bare feet. I'm wearing only jeans on purpose. I need to crank her arousal to the max so she's putty in my hands. I've seen the way she drools over my abs and my arms, and it won't take long to bend her to my will.

I couldn't risk being naked because it'd be too tempting to fuck her, and I'm not sure I'm strong enough to resist.

Slowly and quietly, I ease the bathroom door open and slip inside. Ash is singing along to Olivia Rodrigo's latest bestseller, and she's actually got a decent voice. Steam swirls around her inside the shower stall, but I can see enough to know she has her back to me. I hold my breath and focus on not making a sound as I open the shower door and quickly step in before a breeze can alert her to my presence.

I start a slow perusal of her naked body, lingering on her toned back and the delicate curve of her spine. To most men, backs aren't sexy. Hell, I'm not sure I've ever considered any woman's back sexy until now. Ash's back begs to be licked and bitten and sucked until she's stamped all over with my mark. I'm painfully hard and straining against the zipper of my jeans at the thought of bruising and marking all that soft unblemished skin.

Diverting my gaze lower, I drink in the shapely dip of her waist, curve of her hips, and rounded globes of her exquisite ass. I lick my lips as I imagine parting her cheeks and burying my tongue in her puckered hole. My cock is leaking precum like I'm a horny teenager, and my fingers twitch with a craving to explore her naked body.

Grabbing body wash, she begins soaping up her body, and

my gaze is drawn to her long slim legs, visualizing them wrapped around my head as I eat her out.

Fucking hell. This is a hellish form of self-inflicted torture.

A breathy gasp escapes my lips the same time my bare feet squelch on the slate floor. Her spine stiffens as she realizes she's not alone. Before she can react, I dart forward, circling my arm around her waist and slapping my hand over her mouth to stifle her scream. Water streams down on us from the rainforest shower, plastering my hair to my brow.

I press my mouth to her ear. "Time for payback, dollface."

In an unexpected move, she bites down hard on my hand, and I yank it back, chuckling and more turned on than ever.

"Get the hell out!" she yells, wriggling against my hold, and it only makes me more determined.

"No." Pushing her forward, I flatten her against the glass, caging her in with my arm around her waist and my body flush against her back. Her tits are smushed against the glass, and I wish I had thought to put a camera on that side of the bathroom so I could watch the frontal view later. Ash continues to squirm, trying her best to break free, but it's futile. I am way heavier, taller, and stronger, and I've got her trapped.

She's not getting out of this stronghold, and she knows it.

Stretching my fingers up her body, I brush the tips against the underside of her heavy tit and groan at the back of my throat. My slutty little sis has an awesome rack, and I dream of squeezing her tits together and fucking them raw until she bleeds.

Shaking those thoughts from my sex-obsessed, Ash-obsessed mind, I concentrate on what I am here to do. If I don't remain focused and hold our position steady, we'll both go down, and it'll hurt. That's not my goal tonight. Tonight is about inflicting emotional pain as I seriously start toying with her feelings.

"Get your hands off me!" she demands.

I chuckle against her ear, enjoying when I feel her shiver against me. "No."

"How'd you even get in here? My door was locked and bolted."

I tut-tut in her ear. "Did you honestly think that would keep me out? Please." Deliberately gliding my lips against the side of her jaw, I blow warm air into her ear, fanning it across her smooth skin. She visibly shudders, and I give myself a proverbial pat on the back. It really is too easy.

I am thankful she's such a slut and so predictable.

She's gagging for my cock, and I'm going to enjoy giving it to her—when the time is right.

"Chad will be home soon, and he's going to kill you."

"Nice try, but I know exactly where Chad is and how long he'll be occupied." I drag the tips of my fingers back and forth across the underside of her tits. "We have plenty of time to play."

"I'll go to the cops," she threatens. "I'll tell them you raped me. I'll get you put away."

My chilling laughter rings out over the music still playing in the background. "Who said anything about rape?" I thrust my jean-covered dick against her. "When I bury my dick balls deep inside you, it'll be consensual. You'll be greedy for my cock. Begging me to fuck you."

"Hell will freeze over before that ever happens," she hisses.

"Cute how you lie to yourself." I move my arm higher up her body while slightly easing back from the glass so I can cup her tit. My fingers roam over the hardened tip of her nipple, and I chuckle. "You're so turned on right now, but you can't even admit it to yourself."

"Fuck you," she hisses, attempting to get an arm free.

I tighten my hold on her as I squeeze her nipple and knead

her full tit. "Not in the cards tonight, dollface." Dragging my teeth gently across her upper back, I inhale the scent from her bodywash and the smell that is uniquely Ashley.

Focus, dickhead. You have a job to do.

"You had a choice, little sis," I continue, softly biting on her earlobe. As much as I'd love to stamp my brand all over her sexy body, I don't want Chad to know about this. Yet. "Pay with cash or in kind. You chose the latter."

"I chose no such thing." Her voice hitches in a way that lets me know she's now fully aware of how I'm pressed up against her.

"Hmm." Brushing her hair to one side with my free hand, I suck gently on her neck, just under her ear where I know she's sensitive. Her breath oozes out in exaggerated spurts as I glide my lips up and down her neck while thrusting my hard-on against her lower back. "I've seen the way you look at me. The way you drool all over my dick," I say, fondling her tit. "But you don't deserve it."

Cracking my hand across her ass, I slap her hard. "You knew there'd be consequences when you fucked with my motorcycle," I add, landing my hand on her butt in another firm slap. Water cascades down my back as I nudge her legs apart with my thigh, using her body as leverage so I don't lose my balance. "You knew what you were setting in motion when you burned that invoice."

I adjust our position enough to let me move my arm lower on her body. My fingers dip down over her smooth bare pussy, and I bite the inside of my cheek hard as I almost come on the spot. With my other hand, I hold on to her hip, keeping her in place as I run a finger up and down her slit. "What will I find if I slide this finger inside you, hmm?" I lightly graze my teeth along the curve between her neck and her shoulder, and a strangled sound rips from her lips. It's a mix of pleasure and pain, and I know I have her where I want her.

"How often have you fingered your tight cunt imagining my pierced dick sliding inside you? How many times have you ogled my dick and wished you could drop to your knees and take me into your mouth?" I push two digits into her warm pussy and almost die when her tight walls squeeze around my fingers.

My dick throbs with the need to fuck and conquer, and I'm seconds away from saying to hell with it.

Stick with the program, dickhead. It will be all the sweeter when I finally claim her pussy.

"Have you thought about how my dick will feel when I take your ass? How all those piercings will rub against every nerve ending and you'll come so hard you'll black out?"

"I don't think about you," she lies in a raspy tone as her hips buck to meet the thrust of my fingers. She doesn't even realize she's doing it. "I finger myself remembering the dicking my boyfriend just gave me."

Mention of that asshole irritates me to no end. I add a third finger in her pussy and start pumping them roughly. My other hand digs into her hip as I finger fuck her cunt while I rock my dick against her from behind. "Next time, remember how you came all over my fingers while I had you shoved up against the glass in your shower. Remember how fucking soaked you were as you rode my fingers while pretending it was my dick."

I bury my mouth in her shoulder, licking a path along the elegant column of her neck as I aggressively fuck into her with my fingers, feeling her pussy walls clench around me. Her breath is coming out in hostile pants as she grinds down on my hand while fighting an inner battle.

"I hate you," she whispers.

"You hate yourself more."

She doesn't affirm that truth. She says nothing, whimpering when my thumb circles her clit as my fingers continue to plunder her pussy. If we had time, I'd edge her, repeatedly bringing her to the brink and stopping, because I know how much it'd frustrate her. I'd have her begging me to make her come. It's so fucking tempting because I want her desperate and greedy for my touch, my fingers, my mouth, and my cock. But I can't risk that dick returning home before I've completed this stage of my plan.

So, I'll let her come this time.

"That's it, dollface," I say when I feel her tightening around my fingers and I know she's super close. "Come all over my fingers. Fall apart for your stepbrother, slutty little sis." I pinch her clit, and she screams as her orgasm hits. I hold her up as her thighs convulse and her lower body jerks, continuing to stroke my fingers in and out of her while she milks every last drop of her climax.

Her cries and moans hit me on a primal level, and I bite down on my lip to stifle my reaction when I explode behind my jeans, soaking the denim with my cum as I orgasm harder than I have in years. What the actual fuck? I haven't ejaculated without dick contact since I was a horny teen. What the hell is this woman doing to me? Pinning her to the glass screen with my body, I ride my high, holding her there when we're both sated, letting the reality of what just happened seep in.

It's fair to say I'm royally fucked when it comes to Ashley Shaw, and I need to be really careful I don't cross the line I've set for myself.

"Get the fuck away from me," she says in a dead tone, and I know I've accomplished what I came here to do.

I step back and let her go, waiting until she turns around to suck her juices off my fingers, one at a time. "Yummy," I purr, licking my fingers dry while my gaze drops down to her gorgeous rack. It's the first time I've seen her bare tits up close and personal, and they are magnificent. Her creamy skin is flawless, and her tits are perfectly proportioned and a decent handful. There's plenty to grab ahold of. Her rose-colored areolas are small and round with pert nipples currently saluting me in hard peaks.

Fucking hell.

She's perfect. My dream woman, born straight from my fantasies.

I'm instantly hard again, and this is becoming problematic. If I don't fuck her soon, I may die of blue balls.

And that's my cue to leave. Before I say fuck it and throw all caution to the wind.

Time to manipulate her a little further before I go. "Let me know when you plan to tell your boyfriend you let me finger fuck you in the shower. Don't forget to mention how you gushed all over my fingers. I love a good fireworks display."

Rage sparks in her eyes as she shoves my chest, and I almost lose my balance. My arm flies out, and I grab the tile wall on the right before I land flat on my ass. I straighten up and reach over, turning off the shower to be on the safe side.

"You won't breathe a word to Chad." Pain is etched all over her face.

"What's in it for me?"

"You already got a reward," she spits out, purposely eyeballing my crotch.

Guess I wasn't so circumspect after all. "That doesn't count. If you want my silence, you need to pay for it."

"Fine." She glares at me. "I'll pay your invoice."

I shake my head, smirking. "That deal was a one-time thing. It's no longer on the table."

Her nostrils flare, and her hands ball up at her sides. I like that she doesn't attempt to cover herself in front of me. I like that Ashley owns who she is. "What do you want?"

"I'll think about it and get back to you." I have a few ideas, but I want to carefully consider which one will have the most impact. Which one will bring me closer to my end goal.

A muscle clenches in her jaw, but she jerks her head in agreement—it's not like she has any choice.

I grab two towels from the heated towel rack when I get out, passing one to her. She snatches it from me with a glower, and I chuckle. "Hate me all you want, dollface." Wrapping my towel around my body, I peer deep into her angry, fearful brown eyes. "But you didn't hate my fingers inside you." I smack a quick kiss against her lips before she can preempt the movement. "Think about that next time you're masturbating on your bed."

Chapter Twenty

Ares

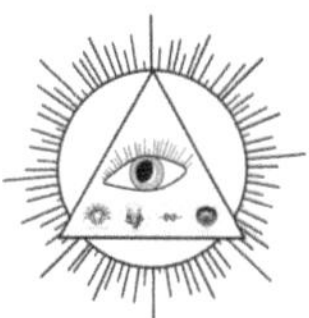

I'm in a super good mood as I head out Saturday morning to meet Shoulders and Rocky. Watching Ash fuss over Chad before he left for the stadium was priceless. She glared at me behind his back any chance she got, but she couldn't disguise the sheer terror lingering behind her bloodshot eyes.

I am going to enjoy dragging this out and tormenting her.

I know she won't tell him. She can't risk it. She's already lost Jase and she knows if she fesses up, she'll lose Chad too. It's why she fixed her bedroom door before he returned home and realized I'd broken into their little sex sanctuary.

I've got her by the balls, so to speak, and we both know it.

Fun times are ahead.

My friends are waiting for me at our usual table in the dingy diner in Fenton when I arrive.

"We ordered already," Shoulders says as I slide into the booth across from him.

His nickname wasn't plucked out of thin air. Dude might only be eighteen, but he's built like a tank. His massive shoulders take up most of the space on his side of the booth. Ewan—Shoulders's real name—got a lot of shit senior year at Fenton High because his shoulders are disproportionate to the rest of his body. The guy works out religiously, and he's seriously ripped, but his shoulders are just so wide compared to the rest of his body it's comical.

The three of us spent most of our senior year flattening assholes for insulting him.

At least it helped to break up the monotony. Pretending to be eighteen and attending high school when you're twenty-one was no picnic, so I took the highs where I could find them.

"Ordered your regular," Rocky confirms from beside me. My other high school buddy is shorter and stockier than Shoulders but no less muscular. With his cropped black hair, face tattoo, full-body ink, and various piercings, my nineteen-year-old fellow Bull is a scary motherfucker.

I picked both of them for a reason, and it's a friendship that continues to pay dividends.

"What do you have for me today?" I ask, removing two envelopes from the inside pocket of my jacket and handing one to each guy.

Spying on the two pussies is bleeding me dry. Most all my wages go toward paying my buddies to keep an eye on them. Thank fuck, Doug is paying for rent, utilities, and groceries at the townhome as part of our deal, or I'd be royally screwed. Mom has tried to offer me money on several occasions, but I'm not taking any more of my stepfather's money. If things go my way later this evening with Marwan at the club, I'll be scoring that meeting I've been wanting for fifteen months and securing a means to earn extra cash I sorely need.

"The boyfriend is a boring, predictable fucker," Shoulders says, holding his mug up for a refill when the waitress appears with the coffee pot.

No one speaks while she pours coffee for the three of us, waiting until she's gone to resume the convo.

"Tell me something I don't know." I glare at him. I'm not spending my hard-earned cash to learn old news.

"Fuck you, Psycho." Shoulders returns my glare and some. "We're doing you a favor."

"A favor you're being paid for," I remind him with a deepening glare.

"You know we have to fit it in around official club business," Rocky says, instantly on the defense. "Marwan kept us busy this week, so we didn't have as much time for surveillance as we usually do."

I hold my palm up. "In that case, give me back half that money." My gaze bounces between them, daring them to challenge me.

Reluctantly, they hand over the cash, grumbling under their breath. I happily stuff the bills into my wallet, ignoring their bitching and moaning. "Tell me what you did see of Chad this week," I ask, eyeballing Shoulders as I settle back against the seat.

"His days are filled with classes and practice, and on nights when he's not pounding the princess's tight ass, he's selling shit around campus for The Sainthood. There was one interesting thing though."

I sit up straighter as I sip from my coffee, waiting for him to elaborate. Shoulders cracks his meaty knuckles. "Followed him and the princess to Grenlow one night. They waited outside a toy warehouse for a while until some dude who looked like he had a stick up his ass came and got them." He leans his elbows on the scuffed Formica tabletop, his eyes lighting up. "I was going to break in and scope the place out until I noticed the biometric scanning system and the heavy-duty cameras all over the exterior."

"What toy shop would need such sophisticated security?" I ponder out loud, drumming my fingers on the table.

We pause when the waitress appears with our food, waiting until she's gone before resuming the conversation.

"That's what I'm wondering. My spidey senses were going crazy, so I didn't get out to investigate. Had a feeling I might disappear permanently if I was caught snooping around that place." He places a large brown envelope on the seat beside me. "Took a bunch of pictures. That has printed copies and a thumb drive if you want to send them to your tech guy."

"Thanks." Removing my jacket, I tuck the envelope inside before placing it on the seat in between Rocky and me. "I'll send the file to Xavier and see what he uncovers." Tearing a piece of crispy bacon off with my teeth, I wonder what Ash and Chad were doing there. "Please tell me you stuck around long enough to see them come out?" I ask my buddy.

Shoulders rolls his eyes. "I'm no fucking amateur."

Debatable. But I say nothing. It's not like either guy is a trained PI. I'm lucky they work full-time for The Bulls since graduating, and they can get away with tailing the two stooges in between official duties. I have a plan to make that easier too.

"They were in there for almost two hours. When they came out, they were all sweaty and messy looking. Like they'd either had a marathon fucking session or gone ten rounds in the ring with McGregor."

Very intriguing. What the hell were they up to? "Let me know if they go back. Call me when it's going down, and I'll come meet you. I want to see for myself."

"Sure thing."

"What about Stewart?" I turn to Rocky. "What's he been up to this week?"

His puffy cheeks are loaded with pancakes and bacon, and he chews noisily as he works to swallow the massive amount of food in his mouth. I eat my eggs, bacon, and toast as I wait for him to finish.

"He's been back and forth to his family home a couple of times," he says when he finally stops chowing down. "I snapped him coming out of a sports bar downtown yesterday. He met with his brother and a couple of other dudes."

My cell pings as he sends me some pics. Opening the message, I examine the photos as I finish eating.

"You know any of them?" Rocky asks before shoving another forkful of pancakes into his mouth.

"That's his older brother, Balthazar," I say, pointing my finger at the dark-haired guy on Jase's right. They look to be arguing. "I don't know who those two are," I add, enlarging the pic to get a good look at the other guys. "Except they're my new neighbors." I didn't pay much attention to them the couple of times I have seen them outside, which was clearly a mistake. This smacks of shady shit, and my curiosity is definitely piqued. I'll get Xavier to take a look at them too.

The taller of the two looks like the youngest. He's got that preppy, pretty, rich boy look down pat with his slicked-back blond hair, big blue eyes, and expensive designer T-shirt and jeans. The other guy is slightly shorter, but he's broader in the shoulders and arms. A silver and navy Tag Heuer adorns his wrist, and he's wearing black pants and a blue dress shirt. His suspicious green eyes are narrowed as he stares straight at the camera.

I cuff Rocky on the back of his head, and he almost chokes on his pancakes. "He made you, you fucking idiot."

"It doesn't matter," he blurts when he's finished swallowing. "I sped away before he got near me."

"That's not the point. Surveillance needs to be discreet, or we'll get played. Be more careful."

He glares at me. "If I'm not good enough, go hire yourself a PI."

"Maybe I will. Then you can kiss future payouts goodbye." His answering scowl is as dark as a thundercloud. "If you're finished pouting, I'd like to propose a change."

"What change?" Shoulders asks, dragging his fingers across his trimmed reddish-brown beard.

"I want you tailing Stewart from now on. Try not to get caught," I tack on the end.

Rocky mumbles something under his breath as he flips me the bird.

I smirk. "I want you tailing the princess," I say, the thought just occurring to me. I can sell this to Doug and get him to pay for Rocky's surveillance. I have a feeling after today I'll be needing to shadow Chad Baldwin myself. Like Shoulders said, he's tied up with college and football during the day, so I can cover his surveillance after I clock out for the night. I suspect he's not going to be a problem for much longer.

"Now you're talking." Rocky waggles his brows and rubs his hands in glee.

I cuff him on the back of the head again. "Don't go getting ideas. It's strictly watching from a distance. She knows you, so you can't let her see you."

"She won't spot me."

"Okay. Good." I toss a twenty down to cover my share of the check before standing. "I'll see you at the club at six, and we'll head back to my place for the party then."

"Who else is going?" Shoulders asks, leaning his arm across the back of the booth.

"A couple of guys from the garage and us three. I have some plans for Stewart's fiancée, which should make for an interesting night." I chuckle as I visualize Ash's face when I make my move. She's going to be spitting blood after last night.

"She's a fine piece of ass too," Rocky adds. "Don't know why Stewart is fighting with her all the time. I wouldn't care if she's a whiny bitch. I'd just stuff her mouth with my cock and shut her up."

"It's like you ripped the idea straight out of my head," I quip, grabbing my jacket from the seat. "See you at six." I turn around to leave but stop. "Don't take a change of clothes," I say over my shoulder. "I want you to show up wearing your leather cuts. It'll seriously piss Baldwin off now he's working with The Sainthood."

The guys grin. "You'll get no complaints from us."

"Good." I salute them before walking away.

I head to the gym for a couple of hours before swinging by Mom's house to get showered and changed for my meeting with Marwan. Luck is on my side as Doug is home. He corners me the instant I step foot in the house, hustling me toward his office.

"Any updates?" he asks the second I enter his study. He looks rough with shadows under his eyes and a thick layer of stubble on his face.

"Nothing to report." It's not like I can tell him I finger fucked his precious princess in the shower and she came all over my hand like a horny cheating slut.

He paces the hardwood floor, scrubbing a hand back and forth across his prickly jawline. "The house is secure and she's driving herself every day, yeah?" he asks.

I nod. "I thought you had access to the camera feeds?" I reply, wondering why he's so highly strung. I installed them in the locations he requested—all the main rooms and hallways. The only place I didn't put them was the bedrooms and bathrooms, like he told me.

"I do, but I'm not actively watching them." A grimace spreads over his face, and I'm guessing he has seen Chad railing his daughter over the kitchen counter or his not so innocent princess blowing the jock off in the living room.

"Should I invite Chad to dinner tomorrow?" I ask with a cheeky grin.

A dark look washes over Doug's features. "Ares," he grinds out. "I told you to respect my daughter's privacy."

"Like you are?" Disbelief radiates from my tone.

"I do a quick check every day to ensure the house hasn't been compromised. I don't linger on anything private I come across." He rubs a spot between his eyebrows. "I expect you to do the same."

"Of course, I do," I lie. I am gathering quite the personal collection of stepsister porn. Ash is insatiable, and they screw at least once a day. I jack off regularly watching it, just like Chad enjoys doing when Ashley isn't around.

I asked Xavier if it was possible to hack into the cloud where Chad has been uploading their sex videos for years, but he told me to go fuck myself. Guess there are limits to what my hacker friend is prepared to do for me, and some lines he refuses to cross.

"You're setting the security system at night and when everyone is out?" he asks, sounding paranoid as fuck.

I push off the wall and walk toward him. "What's going on, Doug? Why am I sensing this is more than you being overprotective?"

"I'm being protective for a reason, Ares."

"And you're not going to share those reasons with me," I surmise.

"I would if I could," he cryptically replies. "Just look out for her, please." The strain is evident in his tone, and I'm starting to get a little uneasy. I have my own agenda and a ticking clock. I can't get dragged into any other shit that might distract me from my goal.

"I'm taking care of her." Why else would I risk getting fired by returning to the house to pump up the tire on her SUV? "I have another idea I think you'll like." I tell him my plan to have Rocky tail Ashley, and he readily agrees.

"Make sure he keeps his distance. I don't want to freak my daughter out. She can't know someone is following her."

"He knows how to be discreet." I hope he doesn't hear the doubt behind my words.

"Pay him double," he adds, swiping his fingers across the screen.

"If that's what you want," I say, planning to use the additional money to cover Shoulders's cost. That way, my wages are my own again. Happy days. My phone pings as he lifts his head.

"I just deposited the first month's payment in your bank account, and I'll set up a regular monthly transfer on the first of every month."

"Okay, cool. I'd better go say hi to Mom." I back away, and my fingers are curled around the door handle when he stops me.

"Oh, and Ares."

I turn around and quirk a brow.

"Quit with all the naked shit. I'm not impressed."

Grinning, I exit his office without saying a word. I'm not promising him jack shit when it comes to that.

Chapter Twenty-One

Ashley

"You can't tell a soul what I just told you," I rasp, panting heavily as I slow my pace when we arrive at a bench. LU is built around a massive park that is strictly for students use only. It's got walking, jogging, and biking trails as well as athletic fields and a full outdoor running track. Today, we took one of the more strenuous walking trails that cuts across the forest on the far side of the park. While I wait to hear from the mysterious Sebastien, I am determined to increase my fitness and stamina, and I've decided on daily walks and runs. Bree wants to work on her fitness too, so we're going to do this as a team.

We had already planned to spend our Saturday together. We're both going to watch the game in a bit, and then we'll be prepping for the party tonight, so she was okay to add a morning walk to our existing agenda. "Let's stop for a minute," I suggest, heading toward the wooden seat.

"You can trust me to keep it a secret. This head is full of them." Bree's wry laugh rings out, bouncing off the trees in this wooded part of the park. We crossed paths with a few other students, but it's not busy. I guess most are probably still nursing hangovers after last night's frat parties.

"What secrets are you keeping?" I ask, uncapping the top on my bottle of water.

"Nothing worth mentioning," she says before slurping from her own bottle. "Besides, I'm here to help with your dilemma. We don't need to get sidetracked with my shit. Trust me, we'd be here all day if we started dissecting my problems."

"You know I'm here for you. If you ever want to talk about anything, I can keep a secret too."

She gives me a quick hug. "I know."

"Is it weird how easily we've bonded?" I take another sip of my water.

"Weird, no. Unusual, yes. At least for me." She brushes stray pieces of blue hair away from her face, attempting to tuck them back into her ponytail. "I have struggled with girl friendships my entire life. I always related better with boys."

"Same here," I admit. "Maybe that's why we get on so well."

"We're kindred spirts." Bree taps her bottle against mine. "Sometimes you just meet people you click with."

"I agree. It was like that with Harlow too though she was gone from my school before we got the chance to properly connect. Now, she's married and attending school in Rhode Island."

"I know who she is."

I grin. "Hard not to. She was all over the news after everything went down last year with The Sainthood."

"She seems cool."

"She is." I finish my water and toss the empty bottle into my bag to dispose of at home. "You'll get to meet her. She's coming back for a short visit in a couple of weeks, and she's promised to drop by the house. I can introduce you."

"Sounds good, but getting back to Ares. What are you going to do?"

I slouch against the bench and sigh. "I can't believe I fucked up."

She snorts. "I can. I've seen the motherfucker, and he's one smoking hot asshole. If he was parading around my house naked making lewd comments and he appeared in my shower, shoving his magical fingers inside me, I'd have done the exact same thing." She throws her arm around my shoulders. "You're only human, babe, and that man is sex on a stick."

"He's the fucking devil," I say over a groan.

"Do you want my opinion?" she asks, and I nod.

"Always."

"Stall Ares until we find leverage to use against him to force him into permanent silence. Then you chalk it up to experience, forgive yourself, and move on with your man."

"I wish it were that easy." It's good advice. I know there's a strong possibility Ares is messing with me, and he could be ready to spill the news of my infidelity any moment, but I am beginning to fully understand how my stepbrother operates. He will use the knowledge to hold me at ransom for as long as possible. Then he'll either tell Chad or find some way to force me into humiliating myself further as punishment.

Either way, this won't end well for me. All I can do is try to protect Chad while I work to find something I can hold over my asshole stepbrother.

"I can help you. I have some resources we can tap to do some digging on Ares."

My eyes pop wide. "You do?" I was planning on asking Lo when I see her if Theo has any time to help, but this works better.

She nods. "Consider it done. I'll set it in motion. That motherfucker must have something he's hiding."

"I appreciate the help. Thanks."

She flashes me a blinding smile. "That's what friends are for."

I rest my elbows on my knees and put my head in my hands. "I'm drowning in guilt, and I don't know if I can keep it a secret. I want to confess, even if I know Chad would break up with me as I rightly deserve. I hate I was so weak and that I have ruined everything." Tears prick my eyes as I think of losing him. "I love him so much, but it won't matter if he finds out what I've done. If Chad cheated and he came to me with it, there would be no going back. I would probably be able to forgive him, given the circumstances, but trust would be a big issue, no matter how remorseful he was. How could any relationship survive when the trust is gone?"

She takes my hand and squeezes it. I look her straight in the eye. "It doesn't sit right with me concealing it. Especially when the three of us live together and I know this is all part of whatever game Ares is playing. I'm not selfish enough that I would hide it so I could hold on to him."

"I don't think it's selfish at all. You love him and plan to be with him forever. Ares doesn't matter in the overall scheme of things. The way I see it, it would be selfish to unburden yourself to ease your guilt. Admitting the truth would only hurt both of you and no one gains."

"I deserve to lose him for cheating. It's unforgivable." It's the truth. I did a bad thing, and I need to own my mistake, but I'm fearful of how it would derail my boyfriend.

"That's not up to you or me to decide. Only Chad could make that call, and I really don't think you should say anything. At least not yet. If we can't find something to hold over Ares, you'll have to tell Chad before he does."

"I know. There's no way I can let him find out from Ares." I heave out a frustrated sigh. "God, it's such a mess."

Bree leans into my side, hugging me. "I would be so hurt if the roles were reversed." I rub at the tight pain spreading across my chest. "It would kill me if Chad did something like that." I gulp over the messy ball of emotion clogging my throat.

"You don't know how you'd feel or how Chad would react. He was okay to share you with my brother. Perhaps he'd be willing to share you with Ares? It could end up being a good thing." She waggles her brows, and her lips twitch.

I think she's joking, but I can't be sure. I stare at her in horror before I erupt in convulsions of hysterical laughter. When I have composed myself enough to speak, I turn to my new friend, wiping tears from my eyes. "Bree, they fucking hate one another. Like it's legit all-consuming loathing. It's why Ares is doing this to me."

Bree rolls her eyes. "It's not the only reason, babe, and you know it. You're gorgeous, and he's a virile male with sex constantly on the brain."

"I know there is simmering attraction between us. I'm not going to deny it or the fact it's been building for months. But that's not his main motivation. Ares has an agenda, and I'm beginning to think it's all connected to Chad. Chad hates him and his mom for destroying his family, and I think Ares is blaming Chad for something his dad did." It's only a hunch. Even I don't think Ares is that big of a dickbag to blame Chad for his father's cheating, so there must be something else going on.

"Like what?" She recaps her bottle and stows it in her bag.

In an unspoken agreement, we stand and resume walking, heading toward the entrance and the parking lot where Bree's Ducati is waiting for us.

I have never thought about buying a motorcycle, but I'm considering it after enjoying rides on Ares's and Bree's bikes.

No doubt my father would have something to say about it, so I might just buy one on the down-low and not mention it.

"I don't know, but I'm going to find out."

"I'll get my guy to start looking there first," she says, and I nod.

If Bree's contact hasn't discovered anything by the time I meet up with Lo, I'll mention it and see if Theo could also take a look. I can't let Ares win this round, and I need all the help I can get. Lo's mystery friend—the one who freaked me out and has me on edge—is the other hot topic of planned conversation.

"So, are you going to hold tight until we dig up some shit on your stepbrother?"

"Yeah. It seems like the best plan. I'll just have to deal with my guilt. Chad is in a bad place right now. He has family problems and money issues, and I'm worried if I tell him what happened he'll seriously go after Ares, and that wouldn't end well. Chad is more than capable of delivering a beatdown, but Ares is a crazy, reckless motherfucker. I doubt there is any limit he won't cross. He already hates my boyfriend, and I'm afraid of what he would do. My betrayal would throw Chad off his game, and he'd risk his scholarship and his football career. I can't let that happen."

I don't mention the drugs or elaborate on his family and financial issues because they aren't my secrets to share, no matter how much I already love and trust Breanna Stewart. Maybe it's because she's Jase's sister, or it's just this incredible connection we have, but I know I could tell her everything and she wouldn't judge or breathe a word to anyone.

If they were my secrets to tell, I would share them with her.

But they're not.

So, I don't divulge how I'm worried his access to a variety of drugs would be too tempting to ignore in the face of his devastation. How I'm terrified he would fall down a black hole there is no returning from.

I can't do that to him.

Chad can never know.

"So here I am," I say as we reach the entrance to the park. "Rock meet hard place."

"We'll figure it out." She loops her arm through mine. "For now, try to put it out of your mind. We have a game and party to get ready for."

Chapter Twenty-Two

Ares

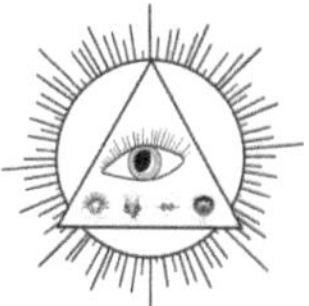

The guys at the door tip their heads up as they step aside to let me into the large industrial warehouse down by the docks in Fenton. Respect shines in their eyes as I enter the building that doubles as a club on weekend nights and The Bulls HQ the rest of the time. I don't know either of them. Marwan—the guy who succeeded Ruben as The Bulls president—has been heavily recruiting, and there are a ton of new members. I guess my rep precedes me.

It's largely open plan on this level except for the enclosed closet and bathrooms, which are situated at the top righthand side of the space. I walk past booths and freestanding tall tables and stools, glancing up at the circular balcony overhead where the man I'm here to meet is hopefully waiting for me.

A couple of members are seated at the bar, nursing beers, as I stride across the empty dance floor, heading for the elevator at the back. Their eyes follow my movements, but they don't acknowledge me, and I don't acknowledge them either. While some of The Bulls are impressed with my actions the night of my initiation, others are more wary. It's probably wise. I wasn't named Psycho for any run-of-the-mill initiation.

I'm not here to make friends even if friendships are what I have gained with Rocky and Shoulders.

I ride the elevator and get out on the top level, heading toward the VIP bar where The Bulls leadership currently conducts all official business. I know they are building a new meeting room and private bar in the extension they had built on to the side of the warehouse, but it's not ready yet.

Members of The Sainthood destroyed the old HQ last year, and they almost succeeded in completely taking The Bulls down. But Ruben and a couple of others took the fall, and Marwan is rebuilding the gang under Ruben's stewardship and with his approval. It's well-known Marwan is only caretaking the role until Ruben gets out of prison. But that's a long time in the future.

The animosity between The Bulls and their previous allies is strong and not dissipating any time soon. Lucky for me because I can use it to fuel my own agenda. The only good thing Jasper Baldwin did was lead us to The Bulls.

"Psycho." Marwan lifts his head in a greeting as I approach, pointing at the seat across the booth from him. "Have a seat."

His VP and sergeant at arms nod as I slide onto the comfortable leather across from the leader. One of the gang sluts brings me a beer, flirting and smiling as she hands it to me. Before she can leave, Marwan tugs her down to plant a hard kiss on her young lips. He kneads her tits through her skimpy dress, and I puke a little in my mouth. He's old enough to be her grandpa, and it sickens me. This is the hardest part of being in this world—seeing how they treat women and young girls and forcing myself to zip my lips instead of interfering to stop it.

I'm not sure why Marwan feels the need to mark his territory. I have zero interest in the girl. Unfortunately, I only have eyes right now for a silver-purple-haired minx with a killer rack and a feisty mouth.

Marwan gropes the poor girl for a few minutes while I quietly sip my beer with a neutral expression on my face. When he's done, he slaps her on the ass before dismissing her. I swallow the bile in my mouth and force a twisted smile on my lips, letting him see my approval. Pandering to his ego should help my cause.

"I've got a proposal for you," Marwan says when he's finished gloating. "One I think you'll be happy with."

"I'm listening."

"I'll set up a meet for you at the prison with Ruben. In exchange, you'll work with a select team to drive The Sainthood from Lowell U. We want full control of the campus, and then you'll manage the operation on our behalf. You'll be well rewarded for your efforts," he tacks on the end.

This is exactly what I hoped to hear today. I bob my head, not giving too much away even though I'm excited. "I want Rocky and Shoulders with me. I need guys I can trust to have my back if I'm to do this."

He trades a look with his number two before refocusing on me. "I'll assign them full-time plus two of the rookies."

Perfect. They can work surveillance for me easily while around campus all the time. "I need time too. Security is tight on campus. I'll need to forge some connections and grease a few palms to ensure the transition goes smoothly."

Tipping his bottle into his mouth, Marwan knocks back his beer as he eyeballs me. "Do what you need to do, but don't take too long. I'm a patient man, but even I have my limits."

"I will update you weekly and work to deliver the campus in the quickest possible timeframe."

"I have no doubt you'll deliver, Psycho." He drills me with

a look, leaving the "or else" part out of his sentence. "Stop by the supply storehouse next week and load up on weapons and artillery."

"Will do." I intend to get rid of the competition without resorting to murder because the last thing I need is to draw attention to myself as I'm getting closer to finding out what happened. But Marwan doesn't need to know that. He won't care as long as I claim the turf for them.

"I'll line up the meet with Ruben, and someone will call you with the details."

"I appreciate it." I drain the rest of my beer in one go before rising.

"See you next week," Marwan says, snapping his fingers at the girl behind the bar.

I tilt my head in respect to the three thugs before making a swift exit.

My guys are downstairs at the bar when I arrive. They quickly finish their beers and hurry out after me.

As soon as I'm outside, I let a huge grin loose on my face.

It finally feels like my goals are aligning. With this deal, Rocky and Shoulders can keep an even closer eye on Jase and Ash, I will get a face-to-face with the man who holds some of the answers I need, and I can implement the next phase of my plan to annihilate Chad Baldwin.

All in all, it's been a good day's work.

And now it's time to celebrate while driving the knife in deeper. I slap my two friends on the back. "It's time to party."

Chapter Twenty-Three

Ashley

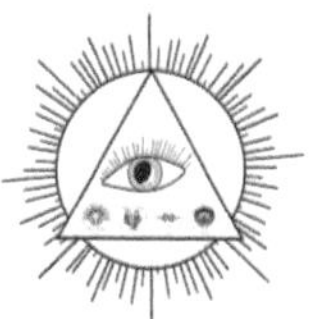

"Looking hot as fuck, princess," Ares's asshole friend says while leering at me. Somehow, my stepbrother found out about the party and showed up with a bunch of friends. Three of the guys are older, and I hadn't met them before. They are some of his new work colleagues, and they seem like okay guys. Why the fuck they're hanging around with Ares is beyond me.

The other two dickheads I unfortunately know. I swear they only wore their club patches to piss Chad off. Unless they actually think wearing gang cuts to a college party will score them pussy. I wouldn't put it past the idiots to believe that. They went to Fenton High with Ares when Ares was pretending to be eighteen and a senior. I wonder if Bree's contact can get to the bottom of that riddle? I add it to my mental checklist to ask my friend later. She's currently in the living room fending off the advances of some prick wearing slacks and a dress shirt to a college party. Obnoxious jerk.

"Whenever you're ready to ditch the jock, give me a call.

I'd happily let you bounce all over my dick," Rocky replies, reaching into the refrigerator to grab some beers.

A few people are congregated in the kitchen, talking where it's a little less loud. Most everyone else is in the living room where one of the guys from the football team is playing DJ with our state-of-the-art sound system.

Chad, Creed, Nix, and a few others went downstairs a few minutes ago to play video games.

Some things never change.

The rest of the team is regaling the crowd with tales of their massive win against one of their rivals today. Chad got to play for a while, and my man did good. Jase was sidelined, but he doesn't seem upset about it.

I flip Ares's annoying friend the bird. "Dream on, Rocky Road." His brows scrunch up at my familiar insult. That dude is too easy to wind up. His full name is Rocky Rose, but I have called him Rocky Road for months, and he's not amused. "I don't fuck meathead gangsters with small dicks and even smaller brains. You couldn't pay me to bounce on that thing." Narrowing my eyes, I pretend to squint as I stare at his crotch.

Predictably, he storms off, and I bark out a laugh. But my good humor doesn't last long. I thought the party would be the best distraction, but I'm struggling to get out of my head. All night, any time I glance in Chad's direction, I'm besieged with guilt. It doesn't help that Ares keeps eye fucking me and making rude gestures with his fingers and his tongue. So, yeah, I'm kinda hiding out in the kitchen right now.

Grabbing a fresh beer from the fridge, I lean back against it as I slowly swallow the cold liquid.

"Temptress."

I close my eyes and silently curse as Jase enters the kitchen. He's here with Julia. She must have forgiven him for tying her to his bed and pissing all over her.

Have to admit, I got an enormous kick out of that when Bree told me. I didn't stop laughing for at least ten minutes. It's good to know he's still putting her in her place, but I wonder how long it will last. Clearly, he's getting over our breakup quicker than me. He hasn't even looked in my direction all night, preferring to drink and joke around with his football buddies.

"Go away," I say without opening my eyes. I can't deal with Jase tonight. I'm already in too much pain, and he'll only add to it.

"Not until you tell me what's wrong," he says as his fingers thread through mine.

Blinking my eyes open, I yank my hand from his and step back. I glance at the now empty kitchen and the closed door, narrowing my eyes in suspicion. This feels like an ambush. "Why do you care? You all but ignore me now."

What the fuck, Ash? I'm blaming the alcohol sloshing in my veins for that stupid outburst.

"I have to," he says, reclaiming the distance between us. His hands land on my waist, and he hauls me up against his rock-hard body. "I'm playing an angle, hoping it will get me out of this mess."

"I can't deal with this shit tonight, Jase." I attempt to wriggle out of his arms, but he only tightens his hold on me.

"Please don't. Just let me hold you, Ash."

I guess there is no limit to my weakness because I stop protesting and sink into his arms. Resting my head on his warm chest, I close my eyes and pretend like it's months ago when everything was perfect.

"I miss you so much," he whispers, running his fingers softly through my hair. "Pretending you don't exist is one of the hardest things I've ever done."

"I know," I whisper, being lulled by the steady, strong beating of his heart under my ear.

He rests his chin on top of my hair. "Talk to me. What's going on? What has put that sadness behind your eyes?"

"I'd have thought it was obvious."

"I know this is more than just me." He tilts my face up with one finger, and we stare at one another for a couple of intense minutes. I wonder if the longing I see in his eyes is reflected in my own gaze.

His gaze sweeps over me from head to toe. Admiration is etched upon his face as he takes his time examining my tight, short, strapless black dress with the cutout panels at the sides. I paired it with sneakers to dress it down a little. Piercing green eyes pin me in place. "You're so fucking beautiful, Ash." His gaze conveys nothing but sincerity, and that's probably the hardest thing of all to handle.

If he no longer cared, if he truly was into Julia, it would make things much simpler. It would be easy to hate him in that scenario.

Knowing he wants me, like I want him, crucifies me.

I still can't make any sense of the situation, and he refuses to give me more than vague answers.

"It hurts so much to see you and not be with you." His slim fingers sweep across my cheeks, and I lean into his touch, wishing things were different.

I long to sink into his arms and lose myself in his body. Jase would be the perfect distraction—if he still belonged to me.

But he doesn't.

My heart throbs with the reminder, and a fresh wave of sorrow crashes over me. "How did all my plans turn to shit so fast?" I ask, lowering my guard further thanks to the three beers I've consumed. "How is everything falling apart?"

"I wish I had the answers," he replies in that deeply sensual voice that speaks to my inner soul. "Is Ares a problem because I can take care of that for you?"

I stiffen in his arms, concerned at his words and the underlying sentiment behind it. It's enough to snap me out of this temporary insanity. "Let me go, Jase." I push at his chest.

"Never." Leaning down, he rubs his prickly jawline against my face as he inhales deeply. "I'm never letting you go, Ash. This isn't the end. I won't let it be."

"Someone could come in, and I've got enough troubles without renewing all that shit with your *fiancée*." I spit the word out, and it does the trick.

Reluctantly, Jase lets me go. "You saw the announcement in the paper."

"It was front page of the *New York Times* today. I doubt there's a single person on campus who hasn't seen it." I only saw it when we returned from the game and Bree showed me. Crossing my arms around my waist, I wish I could snap my fingers and be upstairs alone in my bed.

Why did I think it was a good idea to have a party tonight?

Between Jase's engagement, my guilt over the cheating, concern over this supposed danger I'm in, and Ares's not so subtle eye fucking, I am ready to be done with this day.

"I didn't know our fathers had done that, or I would have warned you." His eyes plead for understanding I don't possess. "It wasn't supposed to be announced yet."

"You have never struck me as the type to let anyone control you, so why are you now?" I hold up a hand before he can give me his well-used reply. "Forget I asked it. I—"

"Well, well," someone with a familiar, most unwelcome voice says. "What do we have here?"

"Who the fuck let you in?" I snap, glaring at Anita Hoare.

Thrusting out her surgically enhanced chest, she pins me

with a superior expression, her collagen-filled lips puckering into a ridiculous pout. "I came as Julia's guest."

I bark out a laugh. "Bitch, she's about as welcome as you are." I only tolerate Julia because she'll whine to her daddy if I kick her out, and then I'll have Mom on the phone berating me for treating her so poorly. The last thing I need to add to my shitty day is Pamela Stewart ripping me a new one from Switzerland.

Stepping around Jase, I head toward the door where that pathetic little narcissist lingers. Her smug grin fades a little as I approach, and I derive enormous satisfaction seeing the glimmer of fear in her eyes. I'm guessing she's remembering how I punched her lights out when she tried to make moves on *my men*.

Smiling sweetly, I grab her arm, digging my nails into her bare flesh as I say, "Get the fuck out of my house, whore. In case it's not clear, you're not welcome tonight or any other night. You're banned."

She screeches as I start dragging her out into the hallway toward the door, screaming for Julia when she fails to halt my forward trajectory. Jase is chuckling as he trails us along the hallway, and it isn't long before we gather a crowd.

Nothing like the sniff of a girl fight to bring all the alpha males running.

"What the hell do you think you're doing?" Julia pushes her way through the guys blocking the entrance from the living room.

"Throwing the thrash out," I coolly reply.

Julia shoves up in front of me, thrusting her barely concealed cleavage in my face.

I'm partial to dressing sexy, and half my wardrobe consists of skimpy dresses, but that scrap she's wearing scarcely covers her boobs or her butt. I wonder who she's trying to snare tonight. It can't be Jase because he's ignoring her like he always does.

"She came with me. She's my friend. She stays." She jabs her bony finger in my collarbone, and I'm less than impressed.

Thrusting her finger away, I let go of the whore and put my face all up in Julia's. "You don't get a say in who comes and goes in *my house*."

"The hell I—" She halts mid-sentence, glancing over my shoulder.

I turn and look, spying Jase leaning against the wall watching the proceedings, looking cool as a cucumber and purposely avoiding my stare.

So, it's back to that.

"What's going on?" Bree materializes at my side, and I have never been more grateful to see a friendly face.

"Sweetheart." Chad approaches from behind, coming over to my side. Creed, Nix, and a couple of others stand behind us. Chad's arm winds around my waist, and his eyes narrow as he glares at Anita. She's standing beside Julia, attempting to look unconcerned but failing to pull it off. The thing about women like Anita is they are all talk and bravado until confronted, and then they turn into scared little mice.

"What's that slut doing here?" Chad asks, peering at me.

"Julia invited her and both of them seem to think Julia has authority over who gets to come into our home."

Out of the corner of my eye, I spot Ares slinking into the hallway with a sly grin on his face.

"Get the fuck out. We told you last year. We're not interested." Chad scoffs, fixing Anita with a derisory look.

"Wait. What?" Julia's brow puckers as she looks at her friend before swinging her gaze to Chad.

"Your new friend didn't tell you how she hit on me and Chad at a party at Ash's house?" Jase says, stepping up on the other side of me. "After she'd slipped a sleeping pill into our girl's drink to eliminate her competition?"

Chad growls. "We still owe you payback for that." He slants murderous eyes at Anita, and she visibly gulps. My boyfriend tightens his hold on me, pressing his lips to my temple before he stabs her with a sneer. "As if any guy would ever pick a pug over a princess."

A chorus of masculine chuckles, catcalls, and lewd comments rings out from the salivating audience.

Anita's face inflames while Julia quietly seethes.

"In case it's not clear," Jase says, drilling a look at Julia. "I was your boyfriend at the time your so-called friend shoved her hand down the front of my jeans."

"I can explain," Anita says in a meek tone, clutching on to Julia's arm. "It was a setup to gather evidence to show you how that bitch was stabbing you in the back and your boyfriend was disloyal."

I clap loudly in a deliberately slow fashion. "I'll give it to you. That's a good comeback, but we all know it's a crock of shit." I cock my head to the side. "Besides, Julia already knew. Isn't that right, *neighbor?*"

Julia looks over at the crowd before lifting her shoulders and tilting her head up high. "I think you should leave," she says, and hurt splays across Anita's face for a split second. "We'll discuss this tomorrow. Come on, I'll walk you to your car." Julia escorts her out the door, and the crowd disperses now the entertainment is over.

Chapter Twenty-Four

Ashley

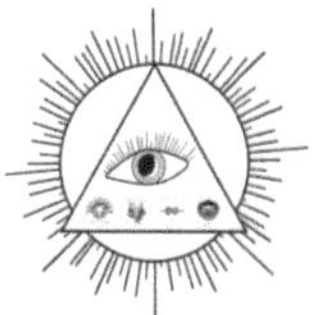

"Nerve of that bitch," Chad says, pulling me around to his front. "Just say the word, Siren, and we'll ensure she never shows her face here again."

I wrap my arms around Chad's waist, peering up at him. "I can handle her, but thanks."

He leans down and kisses me before moving his lips to my ear. "I've hardly seen you all night. Come sit on my lap. I want to celebrate with you."

An additional layer of guilt settles on my shoulders. Avoiding Chad isn't the solution. I'm only compounding the situation. "Of course, babe." I tuck myself into his side. "Lead the way."

I feel Ares's heated eyes glued to my body as Chad guides me back into the living room. Jase quietly follows, claiming a seat as far away as possible, pretending like I don't exist again.

I snuggle into Chad while slowly sipping a beer, listening to the banter, and watching the crowd dancing to the tunes bouncing off the walls. Bree is arguing over in the corner with the guy wearing the inappropriate pants and shirt combo, and I wonder who he is to her and why they are exchanging such heated words. "Babe." I shout into Chad's ear. "Do you know who that guy is talking to Bree?"

Chad looks in the direction I'm pointing while he swigs from his beer. "Jase introduced me to him tonight. He's the son of a family friend. Toby something. He's a sophomore. Lives in the end house."

I thought I'd seen him parking his car one time, but it was dark out, and I wasn't sure. He doesn't remotely resemble a student, and I'm wondering what the story is. Feeling eyes on me, I turn around, my gaze locking with another somewhat familiar guy. I am pretty sure this guy lives in the other house on this side of the road, but we haven't formally met.

He's model handsome with blond hair and striking blue eyes. I watch Jase approach him, whispering something in his ear.

"Who's that guy?" I ask my boyfriend. "I think he lives here too."

Chad turns to look, nodding. "Yeah, he's Knight Carter. Another guy Jase grew up with. He's a freshman like us. Seems cool."

I watch Jase and Knight disappear into the hallway, pondering why all of these so-called family friends seem to be crawling out of the woodwork. Is it just me, or is something off about the whole scene?

I last another hour before calling it quits. It's clear the jock crowd is determined to party all night, but I'm pooped because I had fuck-all sleep last night after the shower incident with Ares. Wolf whistles ring out as I kiss Chad goodnight before making my way upstairs.

I'm yawning as I climb the stairs, so I almost miss the moaning, groaning sounds as I approach the top level. Shaking my head, I wonder what idiots decided to ignore the rules and come upstairs.

There are designated areas downstairs to fuck around, and we left the two guest bedrooms on the second level unlocked. Is it too much to expect them to obey and give us our privacy? I locked our room from the outside anyway, so I don't really care. All I want right now is to crawl into bed and forget the last few days ever happened.

Until I step around the corner and see Julia on her knees in the hallway with Ares's dick in her mouth. His jeans are pooled at his ankles, and he's not wearing a shirt.

Of course, he isn't.

Julia hasn't noticed me yet, but my loathsome stepbrother has. He fixes me with an arrogant grin as he grabs the back of her head, pivots his hips, and drives his pierced cock deeper in her mouth. She almost chokes on that thing, digging her nails into his naked thighs in clear warning. Not that the asshole pays any attention, roughly shoving his dick in and out as he grins at me.

Acid crawls up my throat as heated emotion races through my veins. For a nanosecond, it almost feels like jealousy.

But come on.

This is Ares.

I don't give a fuck about that manipulative douchebag.

So what if he's letting her blow him the day after he finger fucked me in the shower and we both came?

I'm not envious.

Ares means nothing to me.

He clearly thinks this will piss me off.

Well fuck that. I'll show him.

Returning his arrogant grin and some, I video the Manford heir on her knees blowing the devil. I snap a few pics too, using my flash to ensure I get some nice clear shots. Who knows when this might come in handy.

The flash claims Julia's attention, and Ares relaxes his hold on her head enough so she can look up at me. The smug gleam in her eyes is misguided. If she thinks fucking around with my stepbrother will irritate me, I'll go out of my way to prove I'm not bothered.

I saunter up to them, smirking as I repocket my cell. "Glad to see you found your true calling in life, Jules," I tease, knowing she hates when I call her that. "Daddy would be so proud." I pat her head in a condescending fashion. She almost chokes on Ares's dick as she attempts to speak, but he refuses to release his cock from her mouth to let her have her say.

I smile sweetly at my stepbrother. "I couldn't think of two people more suited for a relationship. I hope everything works out for you," I coo, wiggling my fingers as I walk off.

"Oh, and Jules," I say, spinning around and walking backward toward my room. "Your technique looks like it could use a little work. Hit me up if you'd like a few lessons. I've been sucking dick like a pro for years. You could benefit from my considerable experience. Just ask your fiancé if you need a personal recommendation. Jase never had any complaints."

Ares's amused chuckles follow me into my room, and it takes colossal effort not to slam the door shut behind me.

I'm still awake when Chad stumbles into the bedroom a few hours later, seething over Ares and my inability to block the vision of Julia blowing him from my mind.

I know he did that on purpose.

It's all part of his plan to drive me insane.

I hate that it's working.

I should have said nothing, acted disinterested, and came straight to my room. It amused Ares, and that only adds to my frustration.

I pounce on my boyfriend the second he lands on the bed. Pushing Chad flat on his back, I strip him naked and ride him mercilessly until we both collapse in a sweaty heap, overtired, and thoroughly fucked.

I wake the next morning, wrapped up in my boyfriend's arms where I belong. Snuggling into his side, I press my lips over the tattoo with my name on his chest, praying I don't lose him.

"Morning, Siren." Chad yawns as his arm tightens on my waist, and he dusts kisses into my hair.

"Morning, babe."

In a swift move, he slides me under him and nudges my thighs apart with his leg. "Are you sore?" He plants a slew of drugging kisses along my neck.

"Nope," I lie. I will never turn sex down over something as mundane as a little pain.

"Liar." He chuckles against my ear, sending delicious tremors zipping all over my body.

"Fuck me." Reaching up, I clasp his gorgeous face in my hands. "Fuck me until I'm raw. Until I'm aching so much I feel you with every step I take all day."

His eyes flare with primal possession. I knew he'd like that. He hates the thought of me spending the day with the degenerate. This is the perfect way to remind both of us who I belong to. Who I'll always belong to.

Guiding his dick to my entrance, he slams into me in one fast thrust, and I scream. "Yes, babe. Nothing would make me happier." I grab handfuls of his ass as I wrap my legs around his waist and tilt my hips to meet his thrusts.

Chad bites and sucks on my breasts as he pummels my

pussy, and I feel each stroke deep, basking in the pain and urging him to drive harder and deeper.

It helps to assuage the guilt.

I want to feel it.

To throb and bleed for him.

To drown in pleasure-pain as he fucks life back into me.

"Take my ass," I demand after my first orgasm, still not sated. "Fuck it hard and fast, Chad. I want to feel you every time I sit down today."

"Jesus, Siren." He claims my lips in a crushing kiss. "Keep talking like this, and I'll be marching you up that aisle before long."

My cheating heart stutters at his words, and I feel so unworthy.

Shoving him off, I get on all fours while he lubes his dick and his fingers. A guttural groan slips from my lips when he pushes two slick fingers into my ass, working the puckered hole until I'm ready for him. Parting my cheeks, he presses the tip of his dick into me, and I shudder in anticipation. Then he grabs my hips and slams his dick home.

I scream at the top of my lungs, hoping Ares heard me. I have no idea if Julia stayed the night or if she's still here. If she is, I hope she is listening to every moan and scream and cry escaping my lips as Chad ruts into my ass, fucking me like his life depends on it.

He covers my back as he pumps his dick in and out of me, his hand reaching around to squeeze my boob. I push back against him, working in tandem with his thrusts as he grunts and groans and litters the air with a ton of dirty shit. "You complete me," he moans as I slam back against him. "In every fucking way." His fingers find my pussy, and he thrusts two inside me as his cock drives in and out of my ass. When he pinches my clit, I almost rocket off the bed as the most intense body-owning climax rips through me.

I'm writhing on the mattress, whimpering and giggling, as he continues fucking me, and I wish I didn't have to get up soon. I don't want to ever leave the cocoon of this room. "Don't come in my ass," I rasp, brushing knotty strands of hair out of my face. "Come in my mouth."

He pulls out slowly, heading to the bathroom to freshen up while I attempt to wrangle my hair into a messy bun. When Chad returns, wet all over from a lightning-quick shower, he's stroking his hard cock and looking at me like he wants to devour me. An excited shiver ghosts over my skin as I scramble off the bed and kneel at the side. I pat the space in front of me, and he sits on the edge of the bed, eagerly getting into position. Leaning down, he kisses me deep. "I love you."

"I love you." I cup his face, gliding my lips gently across his mouth, hoping he feels the truth of those words. "Fuck my mouth, babe. Don't go easy. Fill my mouth full of your cock, and spill your seed down my throat. I want your cum in my belly when I'm sitting down to eat dinner."

"Fucking hell, Siren. You're totally cock-obsessed today."

"I'm cock-obsessed every day that you're mine."

His pupils dilate, and I squeeze my thighs together when he licks his lips and pumps his dick in his hand. "Open wide, sweetheart, and prepare to choke on my dick."

Pushing his powerful thighs apart, I keep my eyes locked on his as I take his leaking cock into my mouth. Chad roughly grabs my hair, pushing me forward onto his erection as he immediately takes control and fucks my mouth with zero hesitation. Tears seep from my eyes, and drool fills my mouth, trailing from my lips as he rams his dick in and out, stuffing me full of his cock. I widen my mouth and swallow over my natural gag reflex, maintaining eye contact as I swipe my tongue up and down his shaft while he drives into me.

"I'm gonna come," he warns, seconds before he yanks hard on my hair, tilting my head back, and roars out his release into my mouth.

After, he carries me into the bathroom, and we shower together, taking our time washing one another in between hot kisses.

Tears spring to my eyes when he kneels in front of me, gently washing between my legs, before he places a featherlight kiss against my pussy.

Standing, he hugs me against him, with my back to his chest, as he turns off the water and wraps us in a large fluffy towel. "Best way to wake up," he murmurs, kissing that sensitive spot beneath my ear. "And the best fucking hangover cure ever."

Chapter Twenty-Five

Ashley

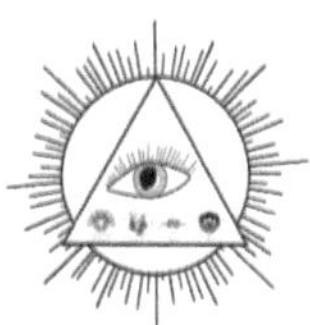

"This smells delicious, Hera," I say, trying not to squirm on the chair as my pussy and ass protest the hard surface.

Ares smirks as if he can tell I've been thoroughly fucked and everything south of my navel aches.

I kick him under the table. 'Cause I'm petty like that.

The asshole tried to cajole me into riding here on his motorcycle. As if I'd go anywhere near him while he reeks of that slut. A part of me regrets showering the smell of Chad and sex from my skin. It would've been nice to taunt him with the evidence of our late-night and early-morning activities. However, I doubt Hera and my dad would've appreciated me showing up looking thoroughly fucked.

"How is school?" Hera asks as we all tuck into our roast lamb dinner.

"Good. I'm enjoying my classes, and I've met some nice people. My new best friend has a bunch of the same classes with me, so that's cool. We've been studying together."

"Who's your friend?" Dad asks, smiling, but it looks brittle.

I take a proper look at him, frowning when I see the bruising shadows under his red-rimmed eyes and the thick growth on his chin and cheeks. His hair is messy, sticking up all over the place, like he's been running his fingers through it continuously. His gray shirt is crumpled and sporting a large coffee stain on the front pocket. He looks like shit, and I'm instantly worried. Dad is always well put together.

Prickles of anxiety sweep over me as Lo's trainer friend's words come back to haunt me. The sooner this dinner is over, the sooner I can quiz my father over what the hell is going on.

"Ashley."

Dad narrows his gaze in concern as he stares at me, and I realize he asked me a question.

"Sorry, I just zoned out for a minute." I set my cutlery down and reach for my glass of water as I try to recall the question. Dad shovels a forkful of lamb and potatoes into his mouth as he watches me. "Um, Bree Stewart. She's Jase's sister, and she's moved in next door."

Dad almost chokes on his food. Hera slaps him on the back before refilling his water glass and handing it to him with concern written all over her face.

"Are you okay, Dad?" I ask, already knowing he isn't.

"Yes, sure. Why wouldn't I be?" He fixes me with another frail smile I'm not buying.

"Do you know Bree or something?"

"I know the Stewart family. I know who Breanna is."

I quirk a brow in silent question.

"Are you aware Richard is related to Breanna and Jason?"

I frown again. "I know Mom's new husband is part of the extended family, but it's large and I thought he was only distantly related. Are you saying that isn't the case?"

Stewart is a popular name around these parts, so I didn't think anything of them having the same name. Mom and

Richard got married at a registry office in Switzerland and they didn't have a wedding, so it's not like I have had the opportunity to meet any of my stepfather's family.

I'm not even sure how it's relevant. So what if Richard is related to Bree and Jase?

"Richard is Eric's—Bree and Jason's dad—youngest brother. There were seven sons, and they've all had big families so it's a lot to keep track of."

"It's great you're making new friends," Hera says, urging everyone to continue eating. "What about you, Ares? How are you getting on with your new workmates?"

Is it just me or did my stepmom purposely redirect the conversation?

"Fine. A few of them came to the party last night."

Out of the corner of my eye, I spot my dad giving Ares the stink eye. What's that all about?

"Oh, while I think of it," Hera says, cutting up her vegetables into small pieces. "Your mom sent me some cute photos of you with Emilie. I printed a couple of them out. I thought you might like to frame them."

"That was thoughtful, thanks. I bet she's getting really big already." I love my adorable little baby sister but hate that we live on different continents.

When I was younger, I used to pray to God to give me a sister or brother, but he never made that dream come true. Of course, now I know my parents weren't ever in love and their marriage was some sort of arrangement, it makes sense. While they have both denied it, I'm guessing I was an accident and they felt obligated to marry and raise me.

Now I have a sibling, but I'll never get to see her. Not unless Mom and Richard return to California. It doesn't seem like it's in the cards, but I can hope.

"I love the baby stage, but they grow so fast," Hera says

before the most heartbreaking expression crests over her face. It's gone so fast I almost wonder if I imagined it.

Not one to look a gift horse in the mouth, I clear my throat and ask my question. "How come you never had other kids?"

"Ashley." Dad's fork clatters to the table as his eyes warn me to drop it.

"What? Am I not allowed to ask that?"

"Most would say it's an extremely rude and invasive question," Ares snaps, glowering at me.

"It's a natural question to ask, and Hera knows I meant no malice."

"It's fine, Ares." Hera knots her hands on top of the table, and tension bleeds into the air. "Ashley is my daughter, and it's not an unusual question." She smiles softly at me as Dad places his hand on her thigh under the table.

Ares growls at me, and I hold his gaze with a challenge, wondering what I'm not privy to.

Because it's clear all three of them know something they're not telling me.

Which really fucking hurts.

"I had a daughter," Hera says, speaking so quietly I barely hear her. "She died," she adds as tears well in her eyes.

I force words out over the painful lump in my throat. "Oh my god, Hera. I'm so sorry."

Ares's chair scrapes across the wooden floor as he stands, the movement so abrupt his chair tips over. He stares down at his mother with a strange look as his hands clench and unclench at his side. His lips curve into a snarl as he whips his head around to me. "Happy now, dollface?"

"I didn't know. I didn't..."

"Mean to be a fucking bitch sticking her nose in things that don't concern you?" he hisses, cutting across me.

"Ares!" Hera clamps a hand over her chest. "It's not Ashley's fault."

"Whatever." He throws his napkin on the table. "I'm out."

Hera gets up, racing after her son as he stomps out of the room.

Dad rubs between his brows as he pushes his half-eaten plate away. "I wish you had come to me with that question."

"I wish you had volunteered that information so I would never have asked it in the first place!" I snap.

"It's not something Hera likes to talk about."

"What happened to her daughter? How did she die?"

"It was a car accident," Dad says. "Her friend's mom was driving when a semitruck smashed into them. Both little girls were killed immediately."

I clamp a hand over my mouth because there aren't adequate words to describe how I'm feeling. Silence trickles into the air for a few beats.

"I'd appreciate it if you didn't ask Hera about it again. It was only two and half years ago. The wound is still fresh."

"Of course. I wouldn't want to upset her." It's no wonder Ares reacted as he did. It's clearly upsetting for him too. I hate the jerk, but I would never be deliberately cruel and mention it to purposely hurt him. "While we're on the subject of keeping things hidden, what the hell is going on with you?"

His spine stiffens. "What do you mean?"

"You look like shit, Dad, and you're jumpy as fuck. What is going on? Does this have anything to do with you giving me that car?"

"Why would you even ask me that?" His brows knit together.

"Am I in some kind of danger, Dad?"

He leans across the table, his eyes widening a fraction. "Has someone said something to you?"

I don't owe Lo's trainer anything, but I believe he spoke the truth when he said he went out on a limb to warn me. Mentioning him would be a shitty way to reward him. Besides, we were told to never mention him or the warehouse. How would I explain it when I don't even know his name or who he works for? Dad will just think I'm cracked, so I play dumb instead.

"Who would say something to me?" I crease my brow and tilt my head to one side. "What's going on, Dad? What aren't you saying?"

He blows air out of his mouth as he drags his hand back and forth across his disheveled hair. "Your mother and I need to talk to you about something."

"What about?"

"I promised your mother I'd wait until she got here. She wants us to talk to you together, in person."

Goose bumps sprout on my arms as an ominous sense of dread washes over me. "Mom's coming here? She only visited a few weeks ago. Why didn't you tell me then?"

He buries his head in his hands, and I'm starting to seriously freak out. "The situation was different then," he admits, lifting his head and stabbing me with troubled eyes.

"What's changed in a few weeks? You're starting to scare me, Dad."

He gets up and moves over beside me. Taking my hands in his, he brings them to his mouth and kisses the backs of my fingers. "I'm not going to let anything happen to you." Releasing my hand, he brings one large palm up to my face and cups my cheek. "You're my daughter."

A fluttery feeling skates across my chest as tears pool in his eyes, and it's an effort to hold my shit together.

Something is very wrong.

I feel it in my bones.

"I love you." He presses a fierce kiss to my brow. "I would kill for you. Die for you." He clasps my face in a firm grip that is borderline painful. "I know I'm not making much sense, but when your mother gets here, we'll do our best to explain it. Until then, I don't want you to worry. But I do want you to be aware of your surroundings, and I want you to carry your gun with you at all times."

"Dad, Jesus," I whisper, more scared than I've ever been in my life. "Just tell me what's going on."

"I will, sweetheart. I promise. All in good time." He bundles me into a huge hug, and I sink into his embrace, hating how badly I'm shivering when I know nothing except Lo's trainer was right.

It's clear now I *am* in danger.

Only the threat is as unknown as the severity.

Chapter Twenty-Six

Chad

I have a couple of hours to kill before I need to leave to visit my mom and my sister, so I decide to go for a run. Sex with my girl cleared most of the cobwebs from my head, but I've still got a throbbing pain in my skull, and I figure some fresh air will chase the last of my hangover away. I don't usually drink so much, but we were celebrating our win, and I was on a high after getting game time.

I grin to myself as I pull on my training shorts and a sleeveless lightweight running top, reliving the highlights of the game in my head. Coach was amped up, and his energy fueled the team, helping us to deliver a stellar performance.

Sending Coach that video delivered the results we'd hoped for. I heard him in the hallway before the game, talking to his lawyer, instructing him to file divorce proceedings against his two-faced, cheating wife. I think we did a good thing. I sure as shit won't lose any sleep over shattering that douchebag's dreams. The conceited asshole deserved it.

I'm lacing up my sneakers when the doorbell chimes. Quickly finishing, I bound down the stairs, checking the peephole before I open the door. This is a gated community and as secure as they come, but I still don't take any chances. Hanging around with The Sainthood has opened my eyes a lot. A place like this would be an obvious target for deviants and criminals, and I don't ever want to let my guard down.

My eyes widen in surprise when I see Pamela standing outside our door. What is Ash's mom doing here, and does she even know her mother is back in the country?

The bell chimes again as Pamela's impatience gets the best of her. I let her stew for another minute or two—I'm not her greatest fan—before I plant a fake smile on my face and open the door. "Pamela. We weren't expecting you, and Ashley isn't here. She's having dinner at Doug and Hera's."

"I know where my daughter is," she says, not waiting for an invitation as she brushes past me into the house.

Make yourself at home, why don'tcha?

"It's you I came to speak with."

Okay, I'm intrigued. I close and lock the door before following her into the kitchen.

Reaching into the refrigerator, she pulls out an unopened bottle of wine and sets it down on the counter. "It smells like a brewery in here," she adds, scrunching her nose in disgust.

I grab a wineglass from the overhead cupboard and hand it to her. "We had people over last night."

We cleared up all the mess this morning after we finally got out of bed, but the place needs a good cleaning and airing out. Not that I'm explaining it to the woman who doesn't seem to give a shit about her daughter. Pamela doesn't get to show up and cast aspersions over how we're living. If she wanted a say in her daughter's life, she should have stuck around for her instead of fucking off to Switzerland with her new family.

Selfish bitch.

"What's this about?" I ask, seriously pissed off now. "I was about to go for a run."

"I'll cut to the chase," she says while pouring a large glass of wine. "Do you love my daughter, Chad?"

"With my whole heart." I don't hesitate to reply. I have nothing to hide, and I'm not ashamed to let her know. Ash is aware of how I feel about her.

"Enough to marry her?" she asks before taking a large mouthful of wine.

Her question takes me by surprise. It's none of her business, but I want to get rid of her, and I'm curious where she's going with this, so I play along. "Yes. I already know Ash is the one."

"Great." She grins at me, and I frown in confusion.

What the hell is she getting at? "Is there a point to this?" I drill her with an impatient look.

"I can pull a few strings and have the paperwork lined up in a couple of days. How does Thursday sound?"

"For what?" I narrow my eyes. She can't be saying what I think she's saying.

"Your wedding." She gulps back more wine while eyeballing me.

I fold my arms and glare at her. "Let me get this straight. You want me to marry Ash this Thursday?"

She bobs her head. "I'll organize it all. You'll just need to show up. How does that sound?" She beams at me, and I examine her eyes, convinced she must be high, but they are clear and hopeful as they peer back at me.

"Like you're swinging from the cray-cray tree."

She scowls, opening her mouth to say something, but I cut across her. "I'm not marrying Ash on Thursday, and I sure as shit am not being rushed into it by you. What the hell is wrong with you?"

"There's no need to be rude, Chad. If you love Ashley, why does it matter when you marry her?"

"Because I haven't even proposed for one!" I throw my hands in the air. "We're not even nineteen, and we're still in college."

"None of those things matter."

"Well, how about you don't get to dictate when we get engaged or married!? It's our business, and it's got nothing to do with you," I snap, seriously riled up now.

"I know it probably seems sudden—"

"Ya think?" I eyeball her like the crazy woman she is.

"I wouldn't ask if it wasn't important."

That captures my attention. "Why is it important?"

"I can't elaborate but it is important. It's about keeping Ashley safe."

All my ire evaporates in a puff of smoke as that weirdo trainer's words replay in my mind. "Is Ash in some kind of danger?" I round the island unit and square right up to her. "If she is, you need to tell me right fucking now what's going on."

"I can't explain until you're married."

"You're legit insane," I say, taking a few steps back. "Unless you explain, you can go fuck yourself."

"Chad, please. If you love her and you want to keep her safe, just do this one thing for me. Please." She drops her guard as she pleads with me. Fear is etched all over her face, and bile travels up my throat.

"Of course, I love Ash, and I always want to keep her safe. If you tell me what's wrong, I promise I'll protect her. But marriage isn't the answer, and I can't do it now. When I propose to Ash, it'll be when I have something concrete to offer her. When I can properly provide for her as a husband should."

"If this is about money, that's easily solved." Opening her

purse, she rifles through it. She pulls out a checkbook and pen a few seconds later. "Name your price, and it's yours."

"What?" My jaw sags in shock.

"Five million? Ten? Twenty? What is it?"

I have never been more offended in my entire life. On my behalf and Ash's. "Get out," I yell. "Get the fuck out and stay out." I'm literally trembling with rage. "I cannot believe you're trying to sell your daughter. You sicken me. I don't know what kind of twisted game you're playing, Pamela, but I'm not buying the bullshit you're peddling. Get the fuck out of our house, and stay the hell away from your daughter with this nonsense."

"Chad, please." She reaches for me, but I move back around the island unit. "It's not what you think. I'm begging you. Just do this one thing, and I'll forever be in your gratitude."

"I won't repeat myself again. Get out, Pamela, or I'll call the cops and have you physically removed from the premises." I point in the direction of the hallway.

"I'm sorry," she says, shoving her things back in her purse. "I'm panicking, and this isn't coming out right. If you'll just let me—"

"Get out," I roar, grabbing her arm and pulling her toward the hallway.

"Okay, okay." She wrestles out of my grip, narrowing her eyes at me. "I clearly made a mistake coming here."

"Damn fucking straight you did."

She hurries to the door, and I trail behind her, wanting to ensure she goes. I can't have her spouting this shit at Ashley when she returns. It'll only freak her out even more. I know my girl is worried. She's been acting strange the past couple of days, and I won't have her psycho mother making it worse. The woman is clearly unhinged. It's no wonder Doug divorced her ass.

"Please don't tell Ashley I was here," she says as she opens the door.

"On that, we agree."

I stand in the doorway as she smooths a hand down over the cream pencil skirt she's wearing. "Please take care of her, and be vigilant at all times." With those parting words, she turns and leaves. I watch as she descends the stairs, gets into her BMW, and drives off before I slam the door shut.

"Damn crazy bitch," I mutter to myself as I walk toward the door leading to the basement. I need to punch something to vent this new frustration.

But beating the bag in our basement gym does nothing to take the edge off my anxiety. The woman is clearly crazy, but she has me spooked. What if she's telling the truth? Not about that bullshit wedding shit but about Ash being in danger? What if her parents are involved in something and they've put her at risk? I will murder them with my bare hands if their actions have endangered her life.

What was with all that wedding stuff? How does me becoming Ash's husband protect her any differently than how I can protect her now? It makes no sense, and I'm seriously questioning Pamela's sanity.

Deciding to head out for a run after all, I call Ash, needing to hear her voice and know that she's safe. It goes straight to voice mail, and that does nothing to quell the fear rising to the surface. I jog past the security gate, heading out on the open road as I try her number again. Same result. "Fuck, fuck, fuck," I mutter as I pick up my pace, pounding my feet on the asphalt as I reason with myself.

Pamela freaked me out, and now she has me worrying over nothing.

Ash's cell is probably out of charge. My girlfriend is notorious for it. Or she's eating dinner and she purposely powered her cell off at Hera's request. Her stepmom is anti phones at the table, so it's not inconceivable. I am probably overreacting because Pamela has rattled me.

I'm sure she's fine.

Except, as I round the bend and spot Ash's SUV in the distance, I immediately know something is wrong. I push my limbs to the limits, speed jogging toward my girlfriend's car, silently praying she's just got another flat and she's in a cell black spot.

I'm panting and breathless when I finally reach her car, and the discovery does nothing to calm my racing pulse. The SUV is empty, and I spin around, looking in all directions, wondering if the car broke down and Ash went looking for help. But there is no sign of her anywhere.

I open the door, cursing when I find it unlocked with the keys in the ignition. Terror sweeps over me like a violent wave, and I'm shaking as I examine the car fully for clues. The only out of place thing I find is an envelope with a bunch of photos of Ash and her baby sister.

All the blood drains from my face when I find her phone, just under the rear wheel, shattered to smithereens. But it's the droplets of blood leading from the back of the vehicle that send me into a tailspin.

Dropping to my knees, I bury my head in my hands, emitting a strangled shout as I realize she's been taken—and she is hurt.

Someone has kidnapped Ash, and when I find them—because I will—they'll wish they'd never been born.

Chapter Twenty-Seven

Ashley

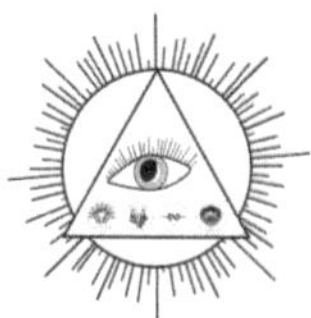

My body jolts, and I wake with a start as something warm presses against my right thigh. My head is fuzzy and sore. Bile collects at the back of my throat, and my tongue is practically glued to the roof of my mouth as I open my eyes. Adrenaline races through my veins when I'm met with pitch-black darkness. I blink repeatedly, wondering if I'm still asleep, but nope, it's dark as shit, and I cannot see a thing. It's as if someone has poked my eyes out, shoving me into a world with no light. Attempting to move my hand, to remove whatever the hell is obviously covering my head, I discover both hands are bound behind my back the same second my shoulders throb with a dull ache.

"She's awake," a man with an unfamiliar voice says, and I jump at his nearness.

A hand clamps down on my thigh. "Stop fidgeting. Stay still and quiet, and this will go much easier for you."

Yeah, not likely.

It comes back to me now. Being ambushed on the road, only a couple of miles from home. I was upset, distracted by the things my father had said—and the things he hadn't—and I stupidly wasn't paying attention. Until I was hemmed in on all sides and figures dressed head to toe in long, black cloaks surrounded my SUV, pointing guns and ordering me out of the vehicle. When I reached for the glove compartment to get my gun, an arm extended from the back seat, and I felt a sharp jab in my neck before it was lights out.

The thought of someone hiding in the back of my car the entire time I was driving creeps me the hell out, but I have more pressing problems now. "What do you want with me? Who are you?" I add, wishing I didn't sound so hoarse and my body wasn't shivering and trembling.

"Stop speaking!" a different man says as a second hand clamps down on my other thigh.

A fluttery feeling skates around my chest as blood rushes to my head. Alarm bells ring in my ears, and this is so not good. I focus on my breathing, quietly inhaling and exhaling in an attempt to calm my racing heart. What the hell is going on, and what do these creeps intend to do with me? The heat emanating from the two men sitting on either side of me makes me uncomfortable and far too warm. Little beads of sweat form on my brow, and my T-shirt sticks to my back.

The hand on my left thigh inches higher, and my breath stutters in my chest. Thank fuck, I wore jeans today. Though it won't stop them if they plan to assault me. Fingers brush against the seam of my jeans, moving upward to the button, and I thrash around as much as I can with bound wrists and within the confines of whatever vehicle I'm in. "Get your fucking hands off me," I hiss, attempting to wriggle out from under both men's firm grip.

"Do you have a death wish?" the first man replies, and initially I think he's talking to me.

"She won't be wearing these for long when we get to our destination. Might as well give us something pretty to look at."

I can almost visualize his pervy smile. A retort lies on the tip of my tongue, but antagonizing these men wouldn't be smart, so I say nothing, waiting to see how it plays out.

"That doesn't matter. If you value breathing, you don't touch Luminary property."

Luminary property? What the what?

The hand at my crotch disappears, and I'm momentarily relieved.

I want to point out *he's* touching me too, but I don't think I'll get any brownie points for it. "I'm not Luminary property," I say, wondering what the hell that even means. "I think you're mistaking me for someone else. You should let me go. I promise I won't tell anyone anything. Just stop the car, and let me out." I doubt it will work, but it's worth saying anyway.

"There is no mistaken identity. Now keep quiet. Unless you'd prefer me to drug you again."

A dull pain rattles around my skull, reminding me of that fact. I grind my teeth to the molars, wanting to retaliate, but I say nothing. Purely for self-preservation. My pulse throbs in my neck as the vehicle moves quickly on whatever road we are on.

Trying to control my errant breathing and keep my rising panic at bay, I focus on my other senses and attempt to get a reading of my surroundings. I listen carefully to the breaths puffing into the air and the slight motion of bodies near me, and I can tell I'm in a vehicle with more than just the driver and the two guys on either side of me. No one speaks, so it's hard to tell how many of those black-cloaked figures are keeping me imprisoned.

I'm jolted forward a few minutes later when the vehicle goes over a bumpy patch of road. A hand grips my upper arm, hauling me back into the seat. I don't know how long I was out for or how far we have traveled, but the road is getting progressively less smooth as we head toward our destination. The vehicle maneuvers over rough terrain, and the grip on my arm tightens.

It's creepy how none of them are talking. I don't hear the telltale swiping of fingers on cellphones either.

It's just weird.

My mind races with possible scenarios. Lo's trainer friend was right about the danger, and my parents knew someone was coming for me. Why else would Dad make such cryptic comments? I am super pissed at them for keeping me in the dark. It's clear I've been in danger for weeks, and they said nothing to me.

If I die today, my blood will be on their hands.

I don't understand any of this. Do they owe money to someone? Or they made a bad business deal? Got into bed with the wrong people and I'm leverage? My brain churns with possibilities while I work hard to keep a lid on my fear and the simmering panic in my veins. I can't help myself unless I can think clearly. So, for now, I'm going to try to stay calm and keep my wits about me.

If my parents know I'm in trouble, they'll realize I've been taken, and I trust them to come for me. I cling to that assertion even if there's a part of me that doesn't fully believe it.

Eventually, the vehicle slows down, and I sit up straighter, remaining alert and ignoring the blood pounding in my skull.

Someone clears their throat, and there's a collective shuffling of feet as we take a sharp right.

"Take the next road on the left," the main man instructs the driver. He is the first one who spoke to me, and he's the chief communicator, so I'm assuming he is the one in charge. "Follow it until you come to a dead end in front of the crypt."

Crypt? WTF? Acid crawls up my throat, and sweat coats the palms of my cuffed hands. My face is hot under the covering, pieces of my long hair sticking to my clammy brow. My shoulders and arms ache, and I'm acutely aware of the need to relieve my bladder. Quietly inhaling and exhaling, I concentrate on my breathing in an attempt to keep my cool. It's challenging, but I'm determined not to fall apart.

The vehicle slows to a complete stop, and I hear the sliding motion as the side door is opened. The sounds of people getting out seem loud to my sensitive ears. "Don't do anything stupid," the main man says. "We are at a private facility in the middle of a forest in a remote location. There is no one around for fifty miles. Run and all you'll receive for your trouble is punishment. I don't advise it." Gripping me by the hips, he helps me out of the vehicle, handing me off to another pair of waiting hands.

"You, you, and you. You're coming with me," the man says, gesturing at some of his colleagues I assume. "The rest of you, stay with the van and await further instructions."

"I want inside." It sounds like the second guy who spoke to me in the van. The asshole who wanted me naked.

"No."

"Why not?"

"Because I don't trust you to keep your hands to yourself. Stay here unless you want to be unalived."

Thank fuck for small mercies.

I'm roughly handed off between the men and then frogmarched forward. "What's going on?" I ask the question even knowing they'll most likely ignore me.

Which they do.

A creaking, clanging sound up ahead raises goose bumps on my arms as I stumble on the bumpy ground, almost losing my footing. I still can't see a damn thing through this head cover, and I'm sweating profusely now.

"Watch your head." He pushes my head down, holding on to my elbow as I'm steered forward. A cool breeze sweeps across my bare lower arms and around my head when the covering is finally removed.

Strands of knotty hair blanket my eyes, restricting my vision, until calloused fingers sweep them aside. My vision adjusts quickly to the dim light of my surroundings. An involuntary shudder rips through me, and I gulp as I stare at the four men, cloaked head to toe in black, standing around me. Voluminous hoods mask half their faces, concealing their identity. All I can see is their chins, mouths, and lower portion of their noses.

"Be careful on the steps. They're old," the man in charge says, gripping my elbow again.

Shivering in the chilly room, I stare at the crypt with my mouth slightly open. It's a massive, tall and wide space with vaulted ceilings composed of stone and marble. A steep set of stone steps lies in front of us, leading down to a lower level. Sturdy pillars, adorned with marble etchings on one side, prop the structure up. The walls are composed of the same beige stone as the steps and the ceiling as is the succession of arches flowing throughout the space.

My heart is in my mouth as I descend the steps, advancing farther into the spooky chamber. Two cloaked figures walk in front of us and one behind. My escort keeps a steady hold of my elbow the entire time. The only lighting is from candles mounted to the walls, casting creepy shadows across the space, adding to the overall sense of dread I'm feeling. Although it is clean, with no visible cobwebs or dirt, and it seems well maintained, I have no doubt this crypt is old as dirt. Smells like it too. My nostrils twitch with the damp, musty scent in the air.

We stride through the vast space until we come to the end of the room with arched doorways on either side, leading to lower levels. I am guided through the right-hand doorway. The staircase is steep, narrow, and winding as we make our way downstairs in single file. Cold air whistles up the steps, and a shiver tiptoes up my spine. All the fine hairs on my arms are standing at attention, and I'm doing my best not to hyperventilate because this is some weird as fuck shit, and I have no idea what is going on or what they have in store for me.

I'm thankful I didn't eat much of my dinner. I have a feeling I'd be revisiting it soon if I had. Panic is an ever-present pressure sitting on my chest as I stumble my way down the stairs. It's not easy to navigate with my hands tied behind my back, and I'm grateful when we reach the lower level without tripping.

A number of narrow hallways branch off in different directions, and we take the one on the far right, passing by several rooms with heavy brass doors. I stumble over a rock on the floor, almost face-planting the ground. My kidnapper straightens me up before that happens, his lips tipping downward in displeasure. "Watch where you're going!" he snaps, his impatience clear.

"Fuck you," I retort, done playing the suppliant mute.

Tightening his grip on my arm to the point of pain, he practically drags me down the hallway until we come to a wide brass door at the very end.

One of the goons up front removes an ancient-looking, skeleton key and turns it in the lock. An ear-piercing creaking sound assaults my eardrums as the door opens. The man shoves it with his shoulder to fully push the door inward, revealing an empty room made entirely of stone with no windows, only two wall-mounted lit candles offering minimal light, and shackles hanging from the ceiling and one wall. Bloodstains decorate the barren well-swept floor and spatter the beige stone walls. The smell of urine is strong, even from out here, and my stomach rebels, retching and twisting with the natural urge to hurl.

Slamming to a stop, I automatically step back, my body refusing to enter the room.

"There is no place to run," my captor reminds me, yanking me forward as I continue to resist, pushing back with my body when he tries to drag me into the room.

A stinging pain whips across my face as he slaps me. "It is futile to resist. This is happening whether you like it or not."

Launching my head back and then forward, I slam it into his skull. His hold on me loosens with the unexpected maneuver, but the dick behind me grabs hold of my bound arms, and he lifts me up, tossing me over his shoulders like I weigh nothing.

I kick and scream as he carries me into the room, pummeling my legs into his body, wishing I'd worn heels instead of sneakers. I land a savage kick near his groin, and he growls, grabbing my hips and preparing to throw me.

"Don't drop her!" the man I headbutted says, coming into the room with one hand under his hood, rubbing his brow. "She can't be marked. You know the rules."

What rules? What the hell is going on? And he's such a hypocrite spouting that crap after he just slapped me.

The jerk places me down on my feet, and I can tell it kills him to be gentle. "Hold her against the wall," the main man instructs, and I gulp over the surge of panic swimming up my throat.

"Gladly." The man shoves me to the wall, pinning my chest with a meaty arm and gripping my face with his free hand.

I bite his hand, digging my teeth in as I lift my leg and knee him in the balls. He lets go of me with a roar, hunching over as he cradles his crotch. "Fucking entitled bitch."

"Enough." The main asshole steps forward, flicking a long

scary-looking needle as he approaches me. "I told you there's no point fighting. You'll only make it worse for yourself if you do." He gestures at my body. "Take your clothes off, or we'll do it for you."

"Eat shit and die." Swallowing the lump in my throat, I level him with a defiant look. I'm not going to help them to defile me.

He sighs. "This is what happens when they're not trained young."

Darting forward, he presses the needle against my neck as his fingers pop the button on my jeans. "I don't want to inject you so soon after the last shot. Don't make me. I promise nothing will happen to you if you just obey."

I crank out a laugh. "Nothing will happen to me? Are you for real?" I glare at him, wishing I could see his eyes. "News flash, asshole. Something already did, or have you convinced yourself you didn't kidnap me?"

"This bitch is giving me a headache," the douche says, snatching the needle from the other man. He presses the full weight of his body up against me as he pricks the surface of my skin with the needle. "Cooperate or we'll put you to sleep and strip you while you're unconscious." His lips pull into an ugly sneer. "There are no cameras in here. No one will know what we do to you, not even you."

The other man grabs hold of my shirt, while his dickhead pal keeps the needle at my neck, ripping it up the front with his bare hands, exposing my bra-covered breasts and my stomach to the other men in the room.

Knots twist in my gut, and I briefly contemplate fighting so they'll stick me and I'll black out. But that'd be the coward's way out. I would rather be fully present for what's about to happen, so I grit my teeth and stare straight ahead, pretending I don't feel ravenous eyes latched on to my chest.

He pulls the shredded shirt away, ripping it at the back to remove it from my constrained arms. A blast of icy air washes over me, hardening my nipples.

A dark chuckle rings out from the dickhead holding the needle to my neck. "She's getting off on this."

"It's fucking freezing, you moron. It's a natural physical reaction to the cold and nothing more. You all repulse me."

I scream when he grabs my breast through my bra and tweaks my nipple hard.

"What the fuck, man?!" the main guy shouts, yanking the dick away from me.

I duck down, ready to nut the guy coming at me when the sound of approaching footfalls claims everyone's attention.

Two figures wearing luxurious full-length gold cloaks appear in the doorway. "Step away from the woman," a man with a familiar voice says, and my brow puckers in confusion.

"We have our orders," my kidnapper says, folding his arms and lifting his head up slightly.

"Now you have new ones," Bree calmly replies, and I almost collapse against the wall in relief.

Chapter Twenty-Eight

Ashley

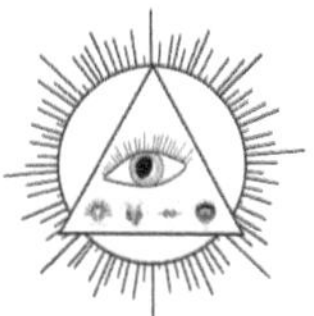

A strangled sound rips from my throat when I hear her voice. I have no idea how they are here or why, but that doesn't matter right now. Bree glances in my direction, shaking her head in silent warning. I can only see the lower halves of their faces, but I know it's them. I would know Jase's profile in my sleep and his voice is hardwired to my brain.

"The Greed & Gluttony Luminary personally assigned us to retrieve the woman. Our instructions were to prepare her for stage one of initiation and leave her in solitary confinement, and that's what we're doing."

"Listen here, grunt." Bree steps up to the guy, uncaring he's towering over her and at least twice her width. "Our authority outranks yours. You know you can't deny us, so move along now."

"We will handle this," Jase confirms.

"Carter said this could happen," one of the other men says, speaking up for the first time as he whips his head to his leader. "This is shady as fuck."

"Agreed." Their leader keeps his focus on the Stewart

siblings. "Unless Rhett Carter instructs us otherwise, we are completing the mission." He shrugs through his cloak. "No skin off my back if you want to watch, but we're going nowhere." He turns around and reaches for me.

Reacting on instinct, I dart sideways, evading his capture.

A clipped noise rings out, and I scream as the guy's legs go out from under him. I take a few more steps back as he falls forward, his face whacking the stone floor with a loud thud. Shock splays across my face as I watch Jase gun down the other three goons, with sharp precision and lightning-fast speed, before any of them can retaliate.

"Fucking hell," I whisper, staring at him like he's a stranger. From the way he handled that and his current cool demeanor, I can tell this isn't the first time Jase has killed someone.

Did I ever truly know the guy I was fucking?

"Did you have to do that?" Bree sounds irritated as she yanks her hood down and glares at her brother.

Jase removes his hood, drilling me with a look as his gaze rakes over me from head to foot. "We don't have time to waste. They weren't going to cooperate, no matter what we said." He kicks the guy slumped at his feet, ensuring he's dead.

"The plan was to drug them," Bree reminds him, bending down to pick up the bullet casings scattered across the floor.

My heart is jackhammering against my rib cage, and my ears are pounding as adrenaline shoots through my veins.

"It's better not to leave witnesses." Jase steps over the blood pooling on the ground to reach me.

I open my mouth, but no words come out.

"It's okay, Ash," he says in that deep seductive tone of his. "I know you have a million questions. I promise we'll answer them, but we need to get you out of here first." His eyes close momentarily before he presses a kiss to the top of my head. "I'm not letting them do this to you," he whispers.

"Do what?" I'm still completely in the dark.

"Catch," Bree hollers, and Jase's eyes snap open. Lifting his hand, he deftly snags the pliers his sister throws at him.

With gentle fingers, he turns me around and makes quick work of breaking the metal cuffs. They clang to the ground with a screeching sound as Jase tenderly massages my sore wrists.

I rotate my shoulders, trying to loosen the knots as I watch Bree remove a cloak from one of the guys. "Here, put this on." She thrusts it at me. "It doesn't have any blood spatter. It'll keep you warm and disguise you until we get off the compound."

"Where are we?" I ask, finally finding my voice. "And how did you know where to find me?" I add as I place the cloak around my shoulders with trembling hands.

Jase takes over, buttoning it under my chin before tucking my hair behind my ears. He pulls the cloak up over my head before kissing me quickly. "We're at Luminary HQ. It's in a valley deep in the forest in a remote part of California. It's spread over hundreds of acres. It's all private land and heavily guarded with maximum security systems."

Bree pockets the shells before gesturing at the four dead men littering the floor. "We can't leave them here."

"We have no choice." Jase drills her with a look, and she curses under her breath.

"We should have brought Baz."

"No fucking way. He's not on our side, Bree. The sooner you realize that, the better."

"I wouldn't be too sure about that, little brother."

"How did you get in?" I ask, remembering the guys outside.

"We entered via a secret tunnel," Jase supplies. "Not many know about it."

"There's a bunch of other guys outside the main entrance.

My kidnapper told them to wait for his instruction." I point at the man in question.

"Did they hurt you?" Jase asks in a clipped tone as Bree hunches over the dead leader.

"Not really. They drugged me when they took me, and my head's a little groggy, but I'm okay."

Jase snarls, glaring at the dead men like he wishes he could resurrect them and kill them all over again. "I should have tortured the fuckers."

"They're not the ones who requested this," Bree says, shoving the dead guy's cloak up to his waist. She digs through his pockets and retrieves his cell. Lifting his finger, Bree swipes it across the screen, activating it. Her fingers fly across the keypad as she taps out a message. "The other grunts are dealt with."

"What's a grunt?" I ask before remembering how badly I need to pee. "And please tell me there's a bathroom. My bladder might explode if I don't go soon."

Flashing me a grin, she walks to the corner of the room, returning with a bucket I hadn't noticed. "Knock yourself out, babe."

I stare at it for a few seconds before realization dawns. Jase chuckles at whatever expression is on my face. Fuck it. Beggars can't be choosers, I think as I set it on the ground, away from the dead guys, and unbuckle my jeans. I'm so desperate to go I don't honestly care. Jase has seen everything anyway and the cloak acts as an effective shield. A blissful sigh slips from my lips as I relieve myself and the pressure in my bladder slowly dissipates.

"A grunt is a low-ranking worker in our society. They follow instructions and are tasked with duties as part of missions and assignments," Jase explains though I'm not any clearer.

"Your society? You mean the...luminaries? Who are they?" I ask, wanting to know and needing to disguise the sound of my peeing.

Jase turns his back to me, granting an illusion of privacy.

"A secret society of powerful families that has existed for generations and thousands of years," Bree explains, tossing the dead dude's cell away.

I finish my business and secure my jeans, leaving the piss bucket where it is.

"We'll explain more when we're free of this place. We can't linger. Nothing gets past The Luminaries, and it won't take them long to figure out what's happened here." She narrows her eyes at her brother as he ushers me forward.

"Don't look at me like that!" he snaps. "Whether they were found drugged or dead doesn't matter. They're only grunts. The board won't care."

"They were just doing their job, Jase, and they were innocent! They didn't deserve to die."

Jase tugs me out of the room behind his sister, and we take off running after Bree. "I don't give a fuck about some dead grunts, so quit busting my balls. Saving Ash is my sole priority. I don't care how many assholes I have to kill to protect her."

That declaration shouldn't turn me on, but it does. I have an irrational urge to slam him against the wall and kiss the shit out of him, but it'll have to wait.

I squeeze his hand. "Thank you for coming for me."

"I'm not letting anything happen to you."

"Don't make promises you can't keep," Bree calls out over her shoulder. Her expression is solemn. "We didn't have any time to put thought into this," she explains, dropping back beside me. "We just knew we had to get you out of here before the ceremonial process began."

I open my mouth to ask what a ceremonial process is, but

this isn't the time or place. Instead, I add that question to the mental checklist I'm writing in my head.

"Will you get in trouble for this?"

The siblings trade a wary look, and I guess I have my answer. "Don't worry about that now," Jase says.

"Are *you* luminaries?" I inquire as we pass the stairwell I came down earlier, taking a narrow hallway to the left instead of going up the stairs.

"Our father is the Lust & Envy Luminary," Jase says, and my mouth trails the ground.

"What does that even mean, and what's with the seven deadly sins?" There was talk of Rhett Carter being the Greed & Gluttony Luminary back there. I shiver under my cloak, and it has nothing to do with the cold.

"Eight if the separatists had their way," Bree cryptically replies, taking a sharp left.

I add that question to my list.

"Keep your head down," she instructs as we follow hot on her heels. "The tunnel is just up ahead, and the ceiling is much lower."

"The foundation of our society is built upon the seven deadly sins. There are four Luminary families—Stewart, Salinger, Carter, and Manford—and each family is responsible for controlling different sins," Jase explains.

"They're obviously doing a piss-poor job of it," I deadpan, thinking of the state of the world and how often people *sin*. "Unless that's the goal—in which case, they are excelling."

"You'd be surprised how much they actually do control," he replies, squeezing my hand.

"Your marriage to Julia is part of this," I say. The Manford name jumped out at me when he mentioned the Luminary families. It's probably the last thing I should be focusing on when I'm escaping my kidnappers and whatever kind of fate these luminaries have lined up for me, but I need to know.

"It is," he confirms. "It's the way of our society."

"And you're not allowed to talk about it," I surmise, guessing this is the secret part Bree referred to.

"We swear an oath of silence and loyalty at an early age. Everyone involved in our world is sworn to secrecy in some guise, even if they aren't privy to all the truths." Bree comes to a halt in front of a raised section of the wall.

Curiosity ensnares me as I watch her press a hand to the edge of it and push in. There's a subtle click, and then the wall pops out.

"I feel like I've stumbled onto the set of *Tomb Raider*," I mumble.

Bree spots my slack jaw and wide eyes, grinning as she pulls the door back, revealing the hidden passageway behind it. She wasn't kidding. The space is low and narrow, and Jase will have to basically crawl to navigate his way through.

"Stop!"

The command comes from behind us, and all the blood drains from my face. Jase reacts superfast, whipping us around and shielding me with his body as he points his gun out in front of him.

I peek around him, tears automatically welling in my eyes as my parents run toward us. Mom is wearing a gold cloak, like the one Bree and Jase are wearing, while Dad is wearing jeans and a sweater.

What's with the different cloaks? Honestly, I'll have to start an actual written list if this continues 'cause there's no way I'll be able to keep track of everything I need to ask.

"What the hell do you think you two are doing?" Mom glares at Bree and Jase.

"What you failed to do!" Jase's snippy tone is laced with unspoken aggression.

"This is insanity! You're going to get us all killed." Mom scrubs her hands down her cheeks as her eyes rake me from head to toe.

"Are you okay?" Dad asks and his brow furrows in concern.

"Why do you even care?" I retort, moving to Jase's side.

His arm winds around me as he tucks me protectively into his body. Bree comes up behind me, offering silent support.

"Of course, we care, princess. You're our daughter. We love you."

"I didn't want this for you," Mom says. Strain is etched upon her face, and her eyes are bloodshot and troubled as she silently pleads with me for understanding that's in limited supply.

Jase harrumphs. "Maybe you should've thought about that before you married Richard. You were out from under their clutches, for fuck's sake!"

Mom scoffs. "Don't be ridiculous. No one gets out from under their clutches unless they end up in a body bag. We were still under Luminary control and always will be."

My eyes pop wide in shocked surprise.

"Ashley was free, and now she's fucked," Jase yells.

Yep. I'm beginning to see that.

"This wasn't the way it was meant to go down!" Mom shouts back.

"What did you think would happen, Pamela?"

"Not this!" Her tone is borderline hysterical. It's so rare to see her rattled I believe she's genuine. "She turned eighteen. The danger had passed."

"How could you be so goddamned naïve." Jase bundles me in his arms, holding me tight to his chest. His heart is beating crazy fast under my cheek. "If I'd known, I would've—"

"You would've what, Jason?" Mom snaps, moving closer as I eye her from the safety of Jase's protective arms. "Done something less foolish than going against a direct Luminary order, breaking into the crypt, killing a bunch of grunts, and trying to steal my daughter away from her fate?"

"We didn't have time to plan anything because we didn't know," Bree says in a clipped tone. She's been quiet up to this point.

"I literally only discovered the truth a few days ago," Jase says. "We were told special dispensation was given to my uncle to marry you because of the circumstances under which he lost his first wife. I had no idea you were a Luminary or that Ash was. I was trying to find an angle when I got the call she had been taken." Jase lifts his gun and points it at my parents, waving it from side to side between them. "Give me one good reason I shouldn't put a bullet in both your skulls."

"You're holding it in your arms," Dad quietly replies.

"You know who I am and what it'd mean for you if you kill me." Mom bores a hole in his skull while I try to figure out what she's inferring.

As much as I'm confused, scared, hurt, and angry, they are my parents, and I don't want them dead. Straightening up, I lock eyes with Jase. "Please don't."

A heavy sigh leaves his lush lips as he lowers his gun and puts it back in the holster on his hip.

"I need answers," I say as tension bleeds into the air.

"You will get them," Mom replies in a calmer tone. She whips her head to Dad, and he nods. "But first we need to fix this mess before anyone finds out."

"No." Jase holds me tighter. "I'm not letting them take her."

"Jason, be reasonable." Mom steps forward, briefly touching his arm. "We don't want this either, but there is no choice. You know there is nowhere you could run they wouldn't find you."

"We won't know until we try," Bree says. "We know how to cover our tracks, and we'll move around so it's harder to find us."

"I remember wanting to rebel at your age too." Immense sadness ghosts over her eyes, and I don't think I've ever seen such strong emotion on my mother's face before. She's an ice queen. Devoid of showing emotion.

Now, I'm beginning to realize that may not be the truth.

Mom has been hiding secrets, and I realize I don't know her at all.

"From what I've heard, you did, and you're still standing," Bree says.

"Only because I had a powerful ally."

"Your brother helped you," Jase says.

I frown as I stare at my mother. "You don't have any siblings."

Her tongue darts out, wetting her lips. "That's not exactly true."

My features harden, and my eyes blaze. "Has anything been true?" Right now, thinking my parents had gotten into bed with the wrong business partner would be preferable than the truth. I know, whatever this Luminary society is, my parents are all mixed up in it, and they have been for some time. "You have both lied to me my entire life."

"Not about everything," Dad says.

"And it was done out of love." Mom reaches for me, but I push her hand away. "Everything we have done was done to protect you. To keep you out of this lifestyle. To give you the freedom and choices I never had."

My spine stiffens as I slip out of Jase's embrace. I square off with my mom. "I want the truth. Who are you? And who is your brother?"

She casts a glance over her shoulder at my father, and he nods.

When she turns back around, there are tears in her eyes. "My maiden name is Pamela Manford, and James is my brother."

Chapter Twenty-Nine

Ashley

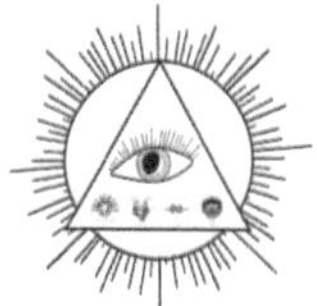

I blink profusely, unsure if I heard her correctly. Jase slides his arm around my waist from behind, holding me tight. Briefly, it registers that neither of my parents are in any way surprised by the PDAs between Jase and me. I thought I had been clever to hide my forbidden relationship from them, but it's obvious they have known all this time. Is there anything they don't know? My brain is close to shutting down. This is all so overwhelming, and I have barely scratched the surface of the things I need to know.

Clearing my throat, I try to focus on the horrifying new reality. "Do you mean that James Manford is my uncle?" Mom nods as I start fitting the puzzle pieces into place. "Is he a Luminary?"

"Your uncle is the Sloth Luminary, and Julia is his heir."

"Oh my god," I splutter as it dawns on me. "She's my cousin."

Her head bobs.

Oh fuck. This is...I have no words to describe this fucked-up situation. I've been screwing my cousin's fiancé this whole time, and I never knew it.

I'm in love with the man she will soon call her husband.

I hate Julia Manford with the intensity of a thousand suns, and now I will forever be tied to her through blood and this Luminary shit.

All the times she has spouted "I'm the Manford heir" at me, I have scoffed at her super-inflated sense of self-importance. I thought she was referring to inheriting her father's media business, but there is clearly a lot more to it than that.

I start laughing because it's either that or shoot my parents myself. Once I start laughing, I can't stop. It feels like I'm unraveling from the inside out.

Mom and Dad exchange a worried look.

I'm wiping tears from my eyes a minute later. "No wonder you were forcing me to be friends with her. Now I get why you stepped up when her mom died."

"Julia is my niece, and I owe James my life."

"Why?"

"It's a long story." She holds up a hand when my face pulls into a grimace. "Which I will tell you after you come back to the cell. We need to clean the scene and get Bree and Jase out of here before someone finds and reports them."

"Will you be killed?" I look up at Jase as the horrifying thought lands in my brain. Judging by the way he just killed a bunch of people in cold blood without breaking a sweat, I am guessing that is the usual way things get resolved within the Luminary world. Fear for him and Bree surges through my veins.

"It's against the law to kill a Luminary or a member of a Luminary family," my dad explains. "Breanna and Jason are the children of the current Lust & Envy Luminary. No one can kill them without signing their own death warrant and that of their loved ones."

I blow air out of my mouth as relief sweeps through me. But it's only short-lived. "What form of justice would be handed down?" I ask no one in particular.

"There are various punishments," Mom says. "It would be up to the Board of Luminaries to decide on the appropriate sanction, but we can stop it if we act now."

"We're wasting precious time," Dad says, looking over my shoulder at the Stewart siblings. "Go back through the tunnel, get into your car, and leave. I have called in a favor. A couple of guys will meet you on the road, and you can switch vehicles with them. They'll plant the car on a couple of known carjackers. I'll backdate a police report of the robbery and manipulate the camera feeds, wiping all trace of this."

"They won't know you've ever been here," Mom supplies, tugging me out of Jase's arms.

"What about the dead grunts?" Bree inquires.

"There are no cameras inside or outside the crypt, so we'll put them in our trunk and dispose of them later."

I stare at my dad like he has three heads.

"I'll create a false digital trail," he adds. "Make it look like they have absconded overseas, and then I'll kill them in a car accident, and problem solved."

My jaw slackens at how flippant he appears. So much for him being an accountant.

All of them make this sound so normal. I am beginning to realize it is for them.

Shock renders me mute as Mom wraps her arm around my shoulders and hugs me. I stare at Jase through dazed eyes, wondering how much of our relationship was real. I had already suspected it wasn't true recently but for vastly different reasons.

"I love you," Jase blurts, stepping forward and softly pulling me back into his arms. "I didn't tell you before because I couldn't offer you a future. I still can't, but I'm done hiding the truth." He cups my face and tilts my chin up. "It was real, baby. All of it." He crashes his lips to mine, and my dad makes a strangled sound from behind.

"Jase, sweet and all as this is, we need to go," Mom says. "This isn't safe for any of us."

Her words reel me back to reality. I break our kiss, placing my hand on his chest. I don't know much of anything. Jase is still engaged to Julia, and there seems no solution is in sight. But I know his words are sincere. And I know now he was telling the truth when he said he was being forced into the relationship. That's what counts. I don't know where we go from here, or if there is any future path for us, but I'm done fighting him. "I love you too."

"You don't have to do this. We can still escape and take our chances," he offers.

Mom mutters under her breath.

"It doesn't sound like that's any way to live our lives, and I don't shy away from challenges." I fling my arms around him and kiss him passionately. "We'll find another way."

"The other car is in position," Dad confirms, lifting his head from his cell. "Go now before it's too late."

Jase looks over my head at Mom with the most tortured expression. "I don't want her to initiate. I can't..." His voice cracks, and I squeeze him tight before releasing him. They need to leave before someone finds them here.

I move back beside Mom. Sympathy splays across her face while Dad looks like he wants to murder someone with his bare hands.

This time, Bree steps in. "Ash is strong. She'll get through it. At least this way, it buys us time to figure out a permanent solution that doesn't involve hiding and running forever. C'mon, PC2. Time to hit the road." Bree slants me a pointed look.

"Go. I'll be fine. I need both of you safe."

"You're my world, Temptress," Jase says, before slamming his lips down on mine again for one final kiss. Then Bree drags him away, and they both slip into the tunnel. Dad shuts it behind them, and I pray they get to safety. I don't want to see them suffer for trying to rescue me.

"Come on." Mom pulls me forward. "We have lots to do and little time to do it."

Mom sends a message to The Luminaries confirming she is with me and helping me to prepare. It will buy us time, apparently. The three of us work together in silence, carrying the dead men from the cell up the stairs and out to my dad's armored SUV. Everything is surreal, and I'm still in shock. I have so many questions, yet at the same time, I can't form a single one.

We stuff the guys in the trunk and set about cleaning up all the blood inside and outside the crypt. By the time we are done, we're all sweating and red-faced and in desperate need of water.

Dad returns to the car, coming back a few minutes later with three bottles of water and a variety of protein bars. We eat and drink in silence.

I'm trying to grasp everything that has happened today, but my mind is blown.

"I want to show you something," Mom says when we are finished. Standing, she offers me her hand and hauls me to my feet.

"I'll go now," Dad says, glancing at Mom. "I want to get rid of the bodies, and I shouldn't be here when they arrive."

"Who's coming?" My gaze skates between my parents.

"I will explain everything in due course." Mom pats my hand. "The Luminaries won't be here for a few hours."

"Why can't you be here?" I ask Dad.

He reels me into his arms. "Fathers aren't involved in this part of the process. Plus, I'm only an expert. It's a pay grade up from the grunts," he adds before I can pose the question. "Ordinarily, I wouldn't be involved at all."

I open my mouth to ask why, but he responds again before I have asked the question.

"You'll learn more about the structure in the coming days, weeks, and months ahead, and we'll tell you whatever you need to know." He kisses the top of my head. "I hate it has come to this, but at least we don't have to keep any more secrets from you."

My parents share another one of their looks.

"Go, Douglas," Mom says. "I've got it from here."

"Be brave, my princess." His words send ripples of fear crashing over my skin. "I love you. You're the very best thing to happen to me, and I'll do everything in my power to protect you." He hugs me tight before releasing me with tears shining in his eyes.

"Daddy," I croak, reeling him back for another hug. I cling to him, fighting tears as emotions try to smother me. "I love you too."

He smooths a hand down the back of my hair. "It will be okay. Stay strong." With a kiss to my cheek and a quick nod to Mom, he turns around and leaves.

Chapter Thirty

Ashley

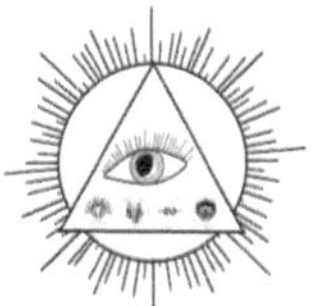

"Come on. I have much to show you and explain." Mom takes my hand, leading me down to the end of the room, and we take the left-hand door down to the basement level. "Even if your father was a Luminary, he wouldn't be permitted to stay with you tonight. Only mothers are permitted to prepare their initiates for the ceremonial process."

"What does that mean, and what's involved?" I hold on to the wall as we descend the narrow winding stairway.

"Our society has existed in secret for thousands of years and many, many generations," she explains as she walks in front of me. "It is steeped in traditions and rules and laws that date back to the fourth century."

I gasp when we reach the end of the stairs and enter a large, cavernous space. This level is wide-open with the exception of a couple of doors at the rear indicating enclosed rooms. A myriad of candles is burning. Some are mounted to walls, like the other parts of the crypt, and many more are freestanding, forming a perimeter around the space and resting on ledges and shelfs.

An earthy, woody fragrance tickles my nostrils as we slowly make our way into the center of the room. My nose twitches as other scents reach me—sweet citrus notes balancing out the heavier aroma. "What is that smell?" I ask, clutching Mom's hand as she leads me into the room. There's an air of reverence about the space as I glance up at the rudimentary etchings on the ceilings and the plain tapestries lining the walls.

"It's frankincense." Mom steers me past the altar and long table in the center of the room toward four stone coffins. "Grunts were here earlier to start the preparations for the ceremony. Usually, initiations take place twice a year in January and June. While every initiation is an individual one, they are usually successive, so anyone who has come of age is initiated on the same day."

Releasing my hand, she places hers on one of the stone coffins. "These guys are to blame." Her mournful expression is tinged with a hint of reverence. "These coffins house the original luminaries. The ones who started our society. This crypt is considered the holy grail within our world. Our most sacred place."

I know which place I'll target first should I want to burn their world down around them.

I have a feeling I'll be consumed with murderous thoughts and ideas after I'm forced into whatever this induction is. "Where did they come from because it can't be the US if the society has been around since the fourth century," I inquire.

"Ancient Rome."

"Wow." I don't want to be impressed, but that period of history has always fascinated me.

"The original luminaries were obsessed with the seven deadly sins. They were consumed with fear for the future, if humans couldn't control their unhealthy desires and behaviors, so they made it their mission to save humanity. The structure for our society was born from that goal."

"Is it religious then?" I place my hand on the top of the coffin next to the one Mom has her hand on. They are very basic in design with the same five carved drawings on the top of each one.

"It started out like that," Mom confirms as I bring my face closer to examine the marks. "But as our society has evolved, it has become less religious though our rules and laws are still heavily imbued with the traditions of Christianity."

"It sounds like something someone dreamed up while high on psychedelics," I muse, running my fingers back and forth across the etching of the sun. In the center of the wide sun is a big eye and underneath it are four small circular symbols. "What do these drawings mean?"

"Those four smaller insignia represent each Luminary family." She points them out one at a time. "Two intertwined snakes symbolizing lust and envy. The lion and the peacock for pride and wrath. A sloth for sloth." Her lips kick up briefly. "And the wolf and the eagle representing greed and gluttony." She places a hand on her chest, just over her heart. "I have the sloth emblem branded here."

I can't say I have ever noticed, which is weird.

"That main one is the Luminary symbol," Mom continues explaining, tapping her finger on the larger drawing of a sun. "Every member of a Luminary family and a masters family has that mark branded on their upper arm."

"What is a master?"

"They are the next level down from a Luminary family. These are very important people in our world. They operate at the grass-roots level, implementing The Luminaries' plans on their behalf. They are the lynchpin linking the four levels of our world."

"I want to ensure I'm grasping this correctly. So, The Luminaries are on the top, then the masters, then experts and grunts?"

A proud smile coasts over her mouth. "Yes." She squeezes my hand. "Think of it like a business. The Luminaries are the business owners with the money and the ones who dictate the strategy and direction of the business. The masters are the management team who execute the strategy. They oversee the entire operation, and the employees—in our case, experts and grunts—report to them."

"How many employees are we talking about?"

"Millions and millions the world over."

This is so much to grasp. My eyes drift to the symbols again. "Does everyone have to wear this brand?"

She shakes her head. "Grunts and experts don't know The Luminaries exist. They think they work for a secret division of the government. Your father is the exception to the rule because he was married to me. Masters have their own form of initiation, but it's not the same as our ceremonial process. They must swear an oath of loyalty and silence and bear the Luminary symbol on their arm. All members of a Luminary family bear their own insignia over their heart and the main symbol on their arm."

My brow puckers in confusion. "If the grunts and experts don't know about The Luminaries, how come grunts kidnapped me and you mentioned some were here earlier preparing for the ceremony?"

"We have some special task forces made up of grunts and experts who are assigned to classified work. They still think it's for the government. They may be suspicious, but they don't question it. Anyone who has is never seen from again."

"Well, shit."

"Yeah. Think of it like the military special task forces. They receive their orders, and they obey without question."

I nod, my attention returning to the symbols on the coffins. "Why have I never noticed your brandings?"

"I wear a skin-colored patch over them in public, so as not to draw attention. Secrecy is pivotal within the Luminary world. Only those in the inner circle are aware we exist. You need to understand the significance of this world, Ashley, and how much power The Luminaries wield. It is like nothing you have ever conceived before."

Her expression is somber as she continues explaining, and my chills are multiplying.

"These four luminaries are at the helm of the world, pulling strings and making things happen from the shadows." Her eyes bore into mine. "These men, these families, *our* family, have unrivaled power. Forget what you think you know about governments and royalty and the people you presume are in charge of our modern world. It's not true. They are mere puppets. The Luminaries are all knowing, all acting, all-seeing." She runs her finger back and forth across the eye. "Hence this emblem."

"That's why we couldn't run." I wrap my arms around myself as a deathly chill wafts over my body.

"There is no place you can go to outrun them. It warms my heart to know Jason and Breanna were willing to risk everything for you." She cups my face. "To know you are loved like that brings me comfort. But it was foolish and ill planned, and they would not have succeeded." She runs a hand along the back of her neck. "I am proof that you cannot rebel and get away with it."

"In what way? What did you do?"

"I let a man who wasn't my fiancé knock me up."

I let that shock settle for a few seconds before I clear my throat. "You're talking about Dad," I surmise, and she nods. She pulls herself up to sit on the top of the coffin.

"Should you be doing that?"

She shoots me a mischievous grin. "Fuck them! There are no cameras here, so they won't know."

"I hope I'm not damning myself for eternity by being so sacrilegious," I joke, hauling myself up to sit on the coffin beside her.

"Nothing has happened to me yet. Trust me when I say if anyone was to be struck down with divine retribution it would be me. You're good."

Perhaps I should be mad my mother has hidden her true persona from me my entire life—and maybe I will be at some point in the future—but right now, I am loving this different side to her.

Today, despite the clear danger I'm in, I don't feel afraid because she is here. I have never felt closer to her, and I don't want that to change. If anything good is to come out of this shit show my life has just turned into, maybe it's this. Maybe now Mom and I can forge a new relationship.

"Who knew my mother was such a rebel." I can't contain my grin.

Her smile fades a little. "God knows they tried hard to stamp it out of me."

"What happened? And why was it so bad you got pregnant with Dad's baby?"

"There is a system of checks and balances in our world. Luminary blood must be kept pure, and to do that, we have to marry from within our own circle."

"That sounds...incestuous."

"It must have been, back in the day, but now the Luminary families are extensive, and the structure is designed in such a way that it is morally acceptable in the modern world without risking tainting the bloodlines."

My brows knit together as I think it through.

"You look confused."

"I am. This is why Jase is supposed to marry Julia, right?"

She nods. "The Stewarts are the Lust & Envy Luminary and the Manfords are Sloth. It is forbidden to marry within your own Luminary family, so matches are made with other eligible Luminary offspring."

I chew on my lip as a thought occurs to me. "All of this," I say, waving my hands around the room. "This is because I'm a Manford now, yes?"

"That is correct."

"So why can't I marry Jase?" It's not like I want to get married before I've even turned nineteen, but if it saves him from that witch and it's a way for us to be together, I'll do it. It's only a fucking piece of paper anyway. The commitment is one I'm prepared to make with or without a marriage certificate because I love him. Chad too.

They are both as vital to me as breathing.

Sympathy splays across her beautiful face. "I wish it were that simple, but it's not. Matches are not chosen on a whim. There is a lot of thought put into them. I told you it's about checks and balances, and it's important to ensure no single Luminary family grows too powerful. Otherwise, the whole system would collapse. It works because power is shared equally among the four families. Matches are carefully planned to ensure this balance isn't upset. Julia is an heir, which means she can't marry another heir. Ideally, her match must be a second son, which Jason is."

"Because his older brother Baz is the heir."

"Correct." Her proud smile is firmly back in place.

"You said *ideally*." A kernel of hope flares in my chest. "So, can someone else marry her instead? Because I got to say, Mom, family dinners are going to be hell on earth if Julia marries the man I love."

"It's a foregone conclusion, honey. I'm sorry, but I really don't see how Jason can avoid his fate. Their match was decided when they were kids. When both of them graduate LU, they will be married."

A familiar pain spears me through the heart. "But Dad isn't a Luminary, and you got to marry him. I don't understand."

"I rebelled, and it's not something I'd recommend." She wets her lips and looks down at her lap. "I got pregnant on purpose to avoid marrying the man I was supposed to marry. I was desperate for a way out." Her lower lip trembles as she lifts her head, and I'm trying not to take this personally, but it's hard. "Honey." She clasps my hands in hers. "You were wanted and adored. Don't ever doubt that."

"But I do," I truthfully reply. "I always seemed like an inconvenience."

Tears pool in her eyes. "I am so sorry, Ashley. I truly, truly am. I was so busy trying to protect you from this world, doing what I needed to do to pay the price for my rebellion, that I didn't leave enough time to parent you. I cut myself off from emotion, and in doing so, I didn't show you affection. It's unacceptable. I know I have failed you. I wasn't there for you when you needed me." Her chest heaves as she pauses to draw a breath.

She squeezes my hands, and her eyes glimmer with sincerity. "I can't turn back the clock, but I am hoping we can start over. You're going to need me in the months ahead, and I am here for you. Richard is packing up our house in Switzerland as we speak. We're moving back to Lowell permanently so I can help you to adjust."

"I would like a do-over," I admit, staring deep into her eyes.

"But there can be no more lies, Mom. I'm an adult now and you can't shield anything from me anymore."

"Agreed." She hugs me.

"So back to you and Dad," I say when we break our embrace. "Tell me the rest."

"Your dad was best friends with your uncle James. They met when they both attended Lowell U." She avoids eye contact as she meanders through her past, staring off into space. "My brother didn't want me to marry my intended either, so we concocted a plan. I would get knocked up by another man, and James would negotiate for a lenient sentence."

"What should've happened in that scenario?"

"Children are a gift from God. Our society still believes that, so no harm would have ever come to you if that's what you are asking."

I run my fingers back and forth along the curved top of the coffin, hoping the crusty dude underneath is cursing us from above for our disrespect. The more I hear about this society, the less I like it. "I wasn't, but good to know I can cross baby-killing off the list of things I might have to do."

"Ordinarily, I would be banished to a remote part of Europe and forced to live out a frugal, solitary life with my child, and the father would be killed."

"Jesus." I rub my hands down my face. What kind of a warped world is this?

"But James was the newly appointed Sloth Luminary, and he was already doing things differently, building alliances and developing his influence beyond anything known at that time. It was clear he was a force to be reckoned with. The other luminaries were much older and keen to hand the reins to their heirs, so they didn't want to ruffle any feathers. James proposed Doug and I work as experts for the society as penance while being allowed to remain in Lowell as members of the lower echelons of our world."

"So, you were demoted in a sense?"

"I was stripped of my Luminary identity and told my baby would be considered filius nullius unless I married Doug and you became a plebeian. A normal lay person," she explains.

I arch a brow. "So, I was either to be a bastard or a pleb."

She smiles softly. "You are grasping this a lot quicker than most would."

"I'm not sure about that. My head is mush right now." I rub a tense spot between my brows. "If you and Dad weren't in love, like you told me, why did you marry him? You could've co-parented."

"Yes, but then you would've been expected to work as a grunt when you came of age. It's kind of like a punishment on the child for being a bastard. Because I married Doug, you were considered more respected, I suppose." She purses her lips and grimaces. "It's such bullshit, but I did what I could to protect you from this life. As a plebeian, you had no inherited rights, and there was no expectation."

"You sacrificed your happiness to free me from obligation."

Her hazel eyes pin me in place. "It wasn't a chore, Ashley. Yes, I was forced to work for The Luminaries, and they still controlled many aspects of my life, but at least I was freed from a life of hell with that prick." Her eyes harden.

"Who was he? The man you were supposed to marry?"

She brushes hair back off her face. "It doesn't matter now."

Anger rushes to the surface. "Why won't you tell me? We agreed no more secrets."

"He isn't a secret. He's a monster I try to forget," she whispers.

I drop it, for now, but only because of the look of sheer

torment on her face. I am sensing there is a lot more she hasn't said.

She stands. "I want you to know I don't regret what I did. My only regret is that I wasn't there for you in the way I should have been. I wasn't unhappy, Ashley. Doug is a wonderful man, and he's my best friend. I couldn't have picked anyone better to be your father. He readily agreed after I gave him a basic explanation, knowing what he was giving up."

I push air out of my mouth as I climb to my feet. "This is a lot to take in. I'm feeling overwhelmed."

"I know." She glances at her watch. "Time is ticking. We need to hurry. I have to prepare you before they arrive."

An icy chill creeps up my spine. "The Luminaries are coming here tonight?"

She nods, linking her fingers in mine. "It's all part of the ritual. I must formally present you to them."

"And then what?"

"Then you'll spend the night in the ancestors' room cleansing your soul before the ceremony tomorrow."

LUMINARY

LUMINARY FAMILY

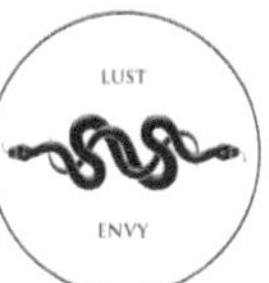

The Luminaries

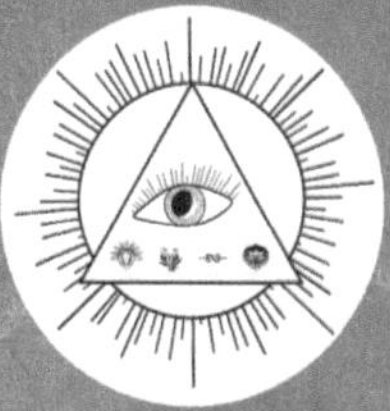

CARTER	MANFORD	SALINGER	STEWART

RHETT CARTER LUMINARY	JAMES MANFORD LUMINARY	WALTER SALINGER LUMINARY	ERIC STEWART LUMINARY
KNIGHT CARTER HEIR	JULIA MANFORD HEIR	TOBIAS SALINGER HEIR	BALTHAZAR STEWART HEIR

Family Tree

DOUGLAS SHAW
Now Divorced
PAMELA MANFORD
HERA HAYNES SHAW
WIFE
ASHLEY SHAW
DAUGHTER
JAMES MANFORD
BROTHER
Stepsiblings
Cousins
ARES HAYNES
SON
JULIA MANFORD
NIECE
Engaged
CHAD BALDWIN
BOYFRIEND
Best Friends
JASE STEWART
LOVER
Enemies/Rivals
BREE STEWART
SISTER
BAZ STEWART
BROTHER

Chapter Thirty-One

Ashley

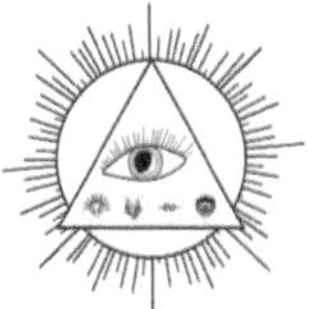

I still have a ton of questions, but I don't have the brain capacity to handle any more tonight, so I'm quiet as Mom helps me to prepare, listening to what she tells me about the process without interrupting her.

We're in one of the rooms at the back of the ceremonial hall that has been transformed into a bathroom-slash-beauty room. Although it has the stone walls and ceiling like the rest of the place, everything else is modernized. A bright light hangs overhead, and there is an abundance of electrical sockets and equipment. Propped against the wall is a spa bed, and on the other side is a hairdresser station with a round mirror, comfy adjustable chair, and a sink. The other side of the room hosts a toilet, shower, and a massive tub Mom had me soaking in at first.

Every hair on my body has been waxed, my nail polish removed, and my nails cut shorter. I only protest when she applies a color remover to my hair. "Silver-purple hair will not be acceptable. You need to be in the most natural raw state for initiation when you offer yourself in obedience and loyalty."

A scowl automatically appears on my face.

Ignoring my obvious distaste, she continues, "Appearances matter to The Luminaries. You are one of us now, and you need to present yourself accordingly. Both in how you look and how you conduct yourself."

I'm thinking Julia must not have gotten that memo. For sure, she *looks* the part. She's always groomed to within an inch of her life. I have seen her parading all over campus in the most ridiculous outfits. But she doesn't *act* the part. She's an idiot. People only tolerate her because of who her father is.

The Luminaries are insane if they think I'm going to change who I am just to appease them. I don't care what Mom says. I already know they can't kill me. My Luminary blood and status protect me now, so they can go fuck themselves if they think I'm going to dress like Campus Barbie.

"Bree dyed her hair blue," I say, stating the obvious. "If she's able to do it and she's more important than me, why can't I keep my hair like this?"

"Bree's mother didn't christen her a 'problem child' for no reason. Dying her hair blue is the least of her parents' worries," she says, applying the treatment to my hair whether I like it or not.

"I'm dying it back after the ceremony. I like not being a blonde."

Mom sighs, looking down at my face as she rubs the treatment into my hair. "I know you like being independent, and I hate asking you to conform, but you must, Ashley. There will be a spotlight on your head in the coming months. Pick your battles wisely." She pauses to let that sink in before continuing. "Your case is pretty unique. Most all your peers have been groomed for this life since they were young. They went through initiation at ten. The board will be watching you closely, and you can't step out of line."

"I thought they couldn't kill me."

"There are other things worse than death." Her cryptic words and clear warning filter into the silence between us.

"Why now, Mom? Why have they decided this?" I close my eyes as she massages my hair.

"It's my fault," she whispers, and I blink my eyes open. Tears coat her lashes. "I waited until you were eighteen to marry Richard and have his child because I thought you were safe. Everyone is initiated young and fully trained by the time they graduate high school. There is no precedence for what they are doing with you. At least not in recent times."

"Then why are they?"

She leans back, squirting more liquid into her hands. "I presume it's because of your Manford blood and the fact I have just been approved to return to the fold. We had to seek permission to marry because Richard is of the Stewart line and I'm of the Manford line. They agreed and told me I was pardoned for good behavior and I would be warmly welcomed back into the circle. It hadn't been made official yet, but an announcement was forthcoming. They told me my unborn child would be born into the society, but they mentioned nothing about you. A friend suggested they were looking at you a few weeks ago, but we received no official news, and James had heard nothing, so we were hoping he was mistaken. Until I received a call yesterday." Her features darken, and her fingers tighten on my scalp. "They told me your initiation was next week. I don't understand why they lied or why they felt the need to kidnap you in the manner they did. I will be having stern words with my brother."

She wraps a plastic covering over my hair before urging me to sit up. "Thank god, I hopped on a plane the second I hung up after the call." Her jaw looks tense as she rinses her hands. "It's happening so fast they haven't even given us adequate time to properly prepare you. I asked for time, but it was immediately denied. The board has said you must be initiated and trained immediately. I'm sorry, honey. I wish I could have stopped it, but there is nothing anyone can do."

Silence descends again while I mull over all of it. It's such a crock of shit, but I have seen how Jase has been controlled despite his protests. I'm not going to get away with denying them.

"This has all been sprung on you, Ashley. I remember how much I struggled to accept everything expected of me, and I was brought up in this world, so I fully understand how challenging this will be for you, but I'm begging you." She looks straight in my eyes. "Please go along with it. Don't fight back or challenge them, especially on something as trivial as your hair color."

"It's not trivial. It's about freedom of choice!"

She puts her hand on my shoulder. "I know, honey. Believe me, I do. For now, just promise me you'll obey, and we'll work something out."

I don't dignify that with a reply. I'm in no position to make promises to anyone, not even myself.

After the beautification is finished and my blonde hair is styled and dried, Mom hands me a gold cloak. "What's with the different colored cloaks?" I ask, reaching for my bra and panties.

"Gold is for luminaries, silver is for masters, and black for those grunts who make up the special task force teams."

"Degrading but functional," I admit, moving to put my bra on.

"You can't wear anything underneath," Mom says, interrupting me.

I stab her with a pointed look as acid churns in my gut.

"Why?" I'm pleased my voice sounds calm even if I'm anything but on the inside.

"Part of preparing for the ceremony is to be at one with nature. To exist in our raw state as we were first born in this world."

"And?" I want her to just spit it out.

She wraps the cloak around my body. "You will be naked for your inspection."

Bile floods my mouth. "Inspection?" I say it low, almost under my breath.

"Come." She walks to the door, not looking at me or answering.

"Mom." My sharp tone warns her not to bullshit me.

She exhales heavily as she casts a glance over her shoulder. "I'll explain when we get to the ancestors' room. Follow me."

With little choice, I trail her back out into the main room and over to the other door. It makes a creepy, eerie sound as she pushes the door open. I stop in the doorway, staring inside in initial horror, my fear over this so-called inspection instantly forgotten. "What the hell is this place?"

"This is the ancestors' room." Slowly, she spins around in the circular space, encouraging me with her eyes. I take a cautious step inside the room, trying to take it all in. In the middle of the space is an ornate rustic wooden table resting on top of a stone podium. Around the edges is a row of lit candles. But it's the walls of this room that equally fascinate me and creep me out.

"Are those real skulls?" I ask, tipping my head back and staring skyward. The room extends upward like a tower, far beyond the line of my vision. Everywhere I look, wrapped around the entirety of the walls, stretching as far as I can see, are shelves packed full of old skulls. Lights are dotted among shelves and behind some of the skulls where the eyes used to be. It's super creepy, and a chill dances down my spine.

"Those are the skulls of every Luminary leader from each of the four families dating back for centuries."

Although I'm a bit freaked out, I am also intrigued. "It's like the catacombs in Paris and Rome." I remember seeing a program on the History Channel, and I definitely have those on my bucket list.

"Yes, it's exactly like that." She rubs a hand over her chest and looks at her watch. "It's almost midnight. They will be here any moment, and we need to get you into position."

"I don't want to do this."

"I know, honey, but you must." Mom grips my arms. "Count yourself lucky you didn't have to do this at age ten like I did. Like all the Luminary children did. You can't show any weakness, honey. They will crucify you if they think you aren't strong."

"This is lunacy. It can't be real. Please tell me some wacky TV presenter is going to pop out of the shadows and tell me I've been punked."

"Unfortunately, this *is* your new reality. You don't have the luxury of falling apart. I know I raised a strong, independent daughter. I know you can do this. The next twelve hours will be hard, but you will get through it."

Get a grip, Ashley, and just get the bullshit over and done with.

"If you need extra motivation, think of Jase. You saw his face earlier. This is devastating for him. If he sees you struggling, it will kill him, and I fear what he'll do."

"Jase will be here?"

"Not tonight. But tomorrow at the ceremony. The four luminaries, their heirs, and their immediate families always attend the initiations. Your dad and I will be here too. We're permitted as we're your parents and we have to hand you over to the sanctity of The Luminaries."

Super. That means Julia and my uncle will bear witness to it as well.

"What happens at the ceremony?" I ask, letting her steer me toward the table.

"You have to swear the oath, drink some blood, and you'll be branded." She curses under her breath when her cell pings. "Shit, they're outside." Dragging me over to the stone podium, she quickly unties the cloak from under my chin. "You need to get up there." Jerking her head at the table, she fully removes my cloak, folding it up and placing it on the stone floor.

"I really have to be naked?" I mean, I guessed that's what she meant by inspection, but this is still scary and creepy.

"Yes. Quick, climb up and be careful."

I grind my teeth to the molars, wondering how I might get away with killing these fucking Luminary bastards because this is some crazy weird shit.

"Think of Jase," she blurts, looking panicked when I haven't moved a muscle.

"Emotional blackmail at its finest," I hiss, stepping up and hauling ass onto the hard table.

"It doesn't make it untrue."

No, I guess it doesn't. I won't let any harm come to Jase or Bree. If this is what I need to do to play my part, I'll do it, no matter how disgusting and distasteful I find it.

"Lie down with your legs and arms stretched," she commands, coming up beside me.

I say nothing as she cuffs my wrists and ankles to the circular chains on each corner of the table, waiting until she is done to ask, "Are they going to touch me? Rape me?"

She vigorously shakes her head. "They will just look and

ask questions. The purpose of the inspection ritual is to ensure you are pure of spirit and soul to undergo initiation."

"What if I'm found lacking?" I ask, purposely not looking at all the creepy skulls surrounding me. It feels like thousands of ghostly eyeballs are watching me as I wait for the four pervs to arrive to inspect my naked body and deem me worthy of this bullshit.

"You won't be, as long as you cooperate. You don't speak unless spoken to, and you don't look at them unless they make direct eye contact with you."

"This is some next-level bullshit."

"For the love of God, do not curse." Mom is rattled, sounding more stressed than I can ever recall.

"How long will this take?"

"Not long."

"And what then?"

She jerks her head up at the sound of approaching footsteps. Mom pulls the hood of her gold cloak over her head and steps down. "Then you will have to spend the night in this room to bond with the spirits of ancestors past and prepare your soul to make your vows tomorrow."

Chapter Thirty-Two

Ashley

The air distorts, and candles flicker as the men enter the ancestors' room. Mom told me not to look at them, so I stare straight ahead, my gaze tunneling up the towered view overhead as I will my naked body not to tremble.

Won't lie. Being laid out in a demeaning pose, like the proverbial sacrifice, as creepy old dudes inspect every inch of me, wasn't in my plans for tonight. I thought I'd come back from dinner, mess around with my new camera until Chad returned from visiting his mom and sister, and then we could pick up where we left off this morning and fuck like demented bunnies.

Remembering how I caught Jules blowing Ares and how pissed off it made me, seems like a distant memory now. How was that only last night?

I'm doing a good job of distracting myself while the men move around the table. The soft thud of their shoes and gentle swish of fabric is the only sound as they examine me. Out of the corners of my eyes, I catch glimpses of heads covered with gold cloaks, and bile swims up my throat.

This is so wrong.

Every single part of what I have learned today.

I'm trying not to think about the fact my uncle and Jase's dad are two of the men currently circling my body 'cause that's all kinds of wrong.

And now I can't stop visualizing their faces, and I'm creeped out on a whole new level.

I concentrate on my breathing, feeling my chest inflate and deflate and reminding myself I am alive.

This doesn't matter. It's only naked flesh. As long as they don't touch me, I can get through this.

I bite on the inside of my cheek and let my thoughts turn to Jase when they start chanting low under their breaths. Someone moves behind my head, and I almost choke as that spicy, earthy, citrusy smell assaults my nostrils. The frankincense wafts over my head and down my body like a barely discernible fog.

"Who presents this girl for inspection?" an unfamiliar man asks. His deep commanding tone rings out around the eerie room, and I flinch.

"I do and her father," my mother says, her voice unruffled and emotionless. That's more like the Pamela I know.

A hand lands on my thigh, and I barely manage to trap my scream in time. "Don't move," a different unfamiliar man says.

I'm afraid to even breathe until he removes his hand.

A face looms over me, half-hidden by the cloak and I'm actually glad for it. It's somehow not quite as bad when I can't see their eyes. Even if it is still creepy as fuck. He doesn't say anything, just stares at me, as I wonder if I should avert my gaze sideways or keep looking up.

"She's not pure," another man says.

"She is eighteen, not ten. Of course, she isn't pure," the man staring at me says.

"Don't act surprised," someone else says. "It's your son she's fucking after all."

"It's our most sacred initiation rule. I think this is wrong," the man I have identified as Eric Stewart says.

"As do I." My uncle finally speaks. "She's too old and too far behind to be of any real use."

"This has been discussed and agreed. There is no going back now."

"She's a prime breeding specimen, and the stats don't lie. The Manford line needs more females, and we need to ensure the checks and balances are righted."

Anger swims in my veins at their words. Prime breeding specimen? What the actual fuck? Mom said nothing about this. Is that all women are to this society? Baby-making machines to continue their fucked-up bloodline and sentence more innocent children to a world where they have minimal control?

No thank you.

I do not volunteer.

Still, I say nothing. Playing my part. For now.

"This should not be discussed here."

"There is no further discussion needed. It's agreed, and she is worthy."

The man hovering over me withdraws, and my body screams silently in relief. It's only temporary though as another figure approaches. I can't see his full face, but I see enough to know it's my uncle this time. "How many men, besides Stewart and Baldwin, have been inside your body?" he asks.

I want to tell him to go to hell. That it's none of his business, but I know I can't. So, I adopt my mother's bland emotionless look as I reply. "None."

"How many other men have you had intimate sexual contact with short of penetration?" someone else asks.

"Why does that even matter?" I blurt before I can stop myself.

Tension bleeds into the air, and I can almost hear my mother berating me.

A meaty hand wraps around my throat, squeezing tight. "Answer the question. The next time you are disobedient, we will be forced to punish you. We would rather not do that before your ceremonial initiation."

The hand leaves my throat, and I suck in a big lungful of air. "Only one," I reluctantly reply.

"Name."

I close my eyes before quickly blinking them open. I don't want to admit this and have my mother know, but it doesn't seem like lying would be in my best interests. Not if these men truly are all-seeing and all knowing. "Ares Haynes," I quietly admit, hating my stepbrother with every facet of my being.

Complete silence greets my response. I wonder what this means for Ares and Chad. If they are in danger because of their involvement with me. I tuck that question away to ask Mom later.

"Hold still," my uncle instructs. "No flinching. No nothing."

I don't know if he expects me to respond, but I don't say anything, gulping nervously as they start chanting again. A soft rattling sound echoes in the eerie chamber as thick incense creeps over my body. Although it's warm in this room, a sudden chill washes over me, hardening the tips of my nipples and adding to my humiliation.

Hands touch me all at once, and I bite down so hard on my lip I taste blood. Their fingers sweep over me as their chanting becomes louder. The words are in a language I don't understand. Given their religious backstory, I wonder if it's Latin. I can't help flinching when hands land on my breasts and my pussy. I expect a reprimand, but their chanting increases in velocity. The hands don't grope, they merely remain still on my most intimate parts, but it's disgusting.

One of these men is my uncle, and one is my lover's father.

I hold my breath, more scared than I want to admit even to myself.

I am going to kill Mom. She said they wouldn't touch me.

To distract myself, I zone out, thinking about Jase and what today's revelations mean for our future. I want him back now I know he was telling the truth and why. I love him, and he loves me. I'm going to fight now. To find a way to replace Julia as his intended because I won't lose him to her.

I almost cry out in relief when the chanting stops and the hands disappear.

"This completes the first part of the process," James says.

"Your body is ready. Now it is time to cleanse your mind," Eric says.

"You will remain in this room overnight to bond with the spirits of our ancestors," another man says.

"Open your mind and clear it of all preconceived notions," the fourth man says.

"Let go of your past life, forgive yourself your sins and indiscretions, and emerge born anew, ready to begin this new life, to enter into the protection of The Luminaries," James adds.

That is the biggest load of bull I have ever heard, and it's quite possible these luminaries are insane.

Tender fingers release my wrists and ankles from the chains. "I will be back in the morning to prepare you for the ceremony," my mother softly says, peering into my eyes and silently telling me to trust her.

She helps me off the table and guides me over to where the four men are lined in a row, fully cloaked, their heads slightly bent. Mom pushes me down onto my knees. "Bow before each Luminary, and thank him for his belief and support. Confirm you are ready to give them your loyalty and silence."

You have got to be kidding me! Mom's eyes bore into me, instructing me to do what I'm told.

It goes against my every instinct to obey, but I do it, bending my head and spouting the words before each Luminary. A hand on my head and acceptance guides me on to the next man until the charade is done.

"You will remain naked on the table for the duration of the night," Eric says as Mom helps me to stand.

"There is a bucket for your needs."

"Use this time wisely to make peace with the passing of your old life and embrace new possibilities," my uncle says. "You will represent our family, and it is a responsibility you will undertake with the greatest reverence and severity."

Like your precious daughter? I snarl it in my head while keeping a neutral expression on my face.

Mom helps me back up on the table, discreetly squeezing my side before she takes my cloak and exits the room with the four luminaries. The turning of the key in the lock is loud as they secure me inside. I wait until the footsteps have fully receded and I can hear nothing outside before I slide off the table.

There are no cameras in here, so fuck them. I'm not sleeping on that hard thing. I'd rather take my chances with the floor.

Grabbing the large bottle of water on the ground beside the table, I move over to the corner of the room. I sit down with my back against the wall and my knees pulled up to my chest, trying not to freak out as thousands of skulls surround me in the dim light.

It's going to be a long night.

The candles die out after a few hours, plunging the room into pitch darkness. The light would have faded earlier if I hadn't had the foresight to blow out all but a couple of candles. When they got close to burning out, I relit another two, and in that way, I staggered them so they lasted longer. Now, there is no light, and I feel the eyeballs of ancestors past watching me as I lie on the cold dusty floor, in the fetal position, desperately trying to sleep. But it's useless. The air has turned progressively colder, and I'm shivering and shaking as I huddle in a ball, willing my heavy eyes to shut.

Eventually, after what feels like hours, I slip into a restless sleep.

My shoulders shake as I slowly come to. "Ashley," Mom hisses, and I blink my eyes open.

I'm disorientated for a moment until I take in my surroundings, and it comes back to me. I'm expecting her to rip me a new one for disobeying the rules, but she surprises me.

"Get up. It's time to get ready." She helps me to stand without mentioning my transgression.

I stretch my arms up over my head and rotate my neck to loosen the tightness in my muscles. "I ache everywhere," I grumble, "and I badly need to pee." I refused to piss in a bucket again, so I held it. Mainly because I wanted to do the opposite of what those assholes told me. Now it feels like my bladder is ready to explode, and I'm questioning the intelligence of my small rebellion.

"Come on. Let's get you to the bathroom." She drapes a

gold cloak around me before escorting me from the room. Outside in the main space, a number of cloaked figures are lighting candles and dressing the altar.

Mom closes the door behind us when we enter the bathroom, and I sigh in relief as I attend to business. Then I shower the dust and grime off my body and wash my hair. Mom blow-dries it again until it's hanging in straight lines down my back. It's so weird looking at my reflection and seeing myself with blonde hair again.

"You told me they wouldn't touch me." I pierce her with a lethal look as she begins applying some gold-tinted oil to my skin.

"If I had mentioned that, you would have been freaking out the entire time."

"So, you thought it was better I was unprepared?" My tone conveys my disbelief. "It's a miracle I didn't scream when they all put their hands on me." A shudder skates over me. "It was disgusting and pervy."

"In our society, the body is just a vessel," she says, lathering my body with the oil. "It's the soul that is most important. It's why The Luminaries go to such lengths to eradicate sin and keep the soul pure."

"Please tell me you don't really believe that."

"I believe what is in my best interests to believe." She stops massaging oil into my skin and stares at me. "There is a lot I don't agree with but a lot I do."

I arch a brow, and she continues. "The basic beliefs and the original mission were altruistic. Before the corruption and before it became so political, there was truth in the goal. I know how this all looks to you now, but I suggest you keep an open mind when learning about our origins. A lot of it is fascinating and believable."

She stares off into space. "Things could be so different," she muses before snapping out of it. She begins rubbing oil into my skin again. "They still could be with the right Luminary leadership." Her eyes stab mine. "The things you and your peers do can influence change. The next generation of heirs could choose to do things differently."

"Now you just sound naïve."

"Probably." She sighs before dipping down to work on my legs and my feet.

"Tell me again what will happen today."

"You will repeat the oath in front of all the witnesses, committing yourself to The Luminaries. Then you will be branded with the Luminary symbol and the sloth symbol before there is an exchange of blood."

"Please tell me I get to wear the cloak."

She stands, wiping her hands on a towel as she pins me with a sympathetic look.

"Wow, that's just fucking great." I throw my hands in the air. "I get to be naked in front of a bunch of people including my dad, my best friend, my cousin, my lover who is already on edge over this, and his entire family. Awesome, just awesome."

"Like I said, the body is a vessel. It is to be celebrated as it gives new life, and it hosts the soul, but it doesn't matter in the grand scheme of things. Nudity is commonplace in our world and not something to be ashamed of."

"Right. Got it." Sarcasm drips through my tone.

"You have always seemed comfortable and body confident. I didn't think this part would be an issue for you."

"I'm not ashamed of my body, Mom, but I'd challenge anyone to parade around naked in front of their parents and a bunch of strangers and not find it uncomfortable." But by God, will they not know it. I will *own* my body in front of them, especially Julia. She will *never* know I'm uncomfortable.

"It will all be over in a couple of hours."

"What's with the oil?" I ask as she leads me to the sink. She works some cream into my face and dabs something under my shadowed eyes before handing me a toothbrush and toothpaste.

"It's just part of the ritual," she says, watching as I clean my teeth. When I'm done, she applies a sweet-smelling salve to my lips. Then she rubs her finger against my skin, testing whether the oil has seeped in.

I cast a glance at my reflection in the mirror. My skin has a slight golden hue, and it shimmers when I move my body. It compliments my lustrous blonde locks. My face is glowing, all trace of my sleep-deprived state eradicated. I've got to admit I look pretty spectacular. Like a goddess the ancestors would have worshipped, no doubt, but it doesn't disguise the fact I'll be completely naked. I can already see Julia's sneering expression in my mind's eye.

I make a vow to purposely ignore her. That will infuriate her. I'll focus my attention on Jase and Bree. Their silent support will help to get me through this ordeal.

I notice a circle of clean non-oiled skin just over my heart and at the top of my upper arm, which is obviously for the brandings.

Since Ares came into my life, and more recently when Chad got inked, I have considered getting a tattoo. I hate that the first markings on my skin will be these. That this choice has been denied me too.

Mom sprays a light body mist over my skin before helping me into my cloak. At least I don't have to enter naked. I'm grateful for small mercies.

A knock on the door startles me. "It's just me, Pamela," my dad says. Air whooshes out of my mouth in relief.

She opens the door quickly, pulling him in.

"Princess." Dad stalks toward me, wearing a black cloak,

immediately pulling me into his arms. "How are you holding up?"

"I'm okay," I lie.

He tilts my face up to his. "I hate this. I hate this so fucking much. I want to kill every motherfucker out there, but this is about survival now. Get through the ceremony and this week, and then we'll figure it out." He presses a kiss to the top of my cloaked head. "Keeping you safe and protected is our main goal."

"What's happening this week?" I ask, eyeballing my mother.

"After the ceremony, you'll be taken up to the main compound for training. It will mostly consist of attending lectures and a few meetings with The Luminaries."

"What?" I screech. "Why am I only hearing about this now?"

"Honey." She clasps my face over my hood, careful not to mess up her work. "I'm telling you what you need to know to get through this." She levels a soft glare at my father. "If I told you everything in advance, you would only worry, so I'm relaying information in a piecemeal fashion. I was just about to tell you this."

"What else haven't you told me about?"

My parents share a look, and an involuntary shiver fingers up my spine.

"What is it?" I ask in a low voice, my nerves jangling on all sides.

"The last part of the ceremony involves—"

Chapter Thirty-Three

Ashley

The door swings open, cutting Mom off mid-sentence.

A tall man wearing a gold cloak says, "It is time."

"I just need five more minutes," Mom calmly replies.

Grabbing my arm, he shakes his head. "It is time," he repeats in a robotic tone.

Mom's dispassionate mask drops, showcasing her fear and her pain. "Just do as they say, Ashley. Don't resist."

"No more talking!" the man snaps.

Dad glares at Mom as they come to stand on either side of me. They clasp my hands and walk me out of the bathroom and into the main room.

About twenty people fill the space, most standing in a loose circle around the altar and the table. Four figures—The Luminaries I'm guessing—stand behind the altar. Behind them are five large tapestries hanging from the ceiling. Each one depicts a symbol from the coffins—the Luminary eye symbol and the four family symbols with various animals.

A plain cream and gold tablecloth covers the altar, and

three stone tabernacles rest upon it. Two tall freestanding candles are perched at either end. In front of the altar is a wide rectangular table. A similar cloth covers this table. Little bunches of daisies, tied with string, line the perimeter of the table. Beside it, flames jumping brightly, is a small fire pit. On a table alongside it are some tools and equipment, which do nothing to calm my ever-racing mind.

Several candles are dotted around the room, casting flickers of subtle light off the stone walls. As there are no windows down here, I have no idea what time it is or if it's even daytime or nighttime.

Everyone is wearing gold cloaks with their hands joined and raised in front of them and their heads bowed. I can't tell who anyone is, and I silently panic.

I need to look into Jase's eyes to remind me why I'm going through with this bullshit. His attention will help to steady me as I subject myself to shit that feels like it's come straight out of a horror movie.

The circle parts to let us step inside. Tension comingles with excitement and anticipation in the air. I clutch my parents' hands harder as I try to ignore the pounding of my heart and the screaming bouncing off the walls of my skull. I feel eyeballs glued to my back as we walk, and I wonder where Jase and Bree are. Remembering Mom's words and the tormented expression on Jase's face yesterday, I lift my head more confidently and promise I will be strong, so as not to make this more difficult for either of us.

I'm a fucking queen, and nothing these assholes will do to me can change that.

That resolve helps to slice the edge off my nerves.

Mom and Dad guide me around the table and up to the front of the altar where we come to a stop.

"Who presents this initiate today?" the four luminaries ask in tandem as they step closer to the altar.

"We do," my parents say in unison.

"Bring the initiate forward."

Adrenaline shoots through my veins, and I can scarcely hear over the thrumming of blood rushing to my head and in my ears. I focus on my breathing to keep myself calm, reminding myself I can do this.

"Remove your cloak and kneel."

With trembling fingers, I take the cloak off. Mom gathers it up before stepping back. I kneel, barely feeling the cold ground underneath my exposed knees.

"Bow before your luminaries, and prepare to swear your oath of silence and loyalty," my uncle says.

I gladly bow my head. This charade will be easier to survive if I don't have to see them.

Eric Stewart reads out the oath in English. It's a load of crap about respecting the traditions and laws and offering my lifelong servitude and loyalty. The second part focuses on the vow of silence and my commitment to maintain the utmost secrecy in relation to Luminary business, to not speak a word of our society or responsibility outside the inner circle and official assignments.

"Do you understand and agree?" James asks.

"I do," I lie.

"Have you purged your sins and cleansed your soul?" Either Carter or Salinger poses the question.

"I have." I lie again, hoping I won't be struck down.

"Very well. Repeat this vow after us."

They start spouting the oath, in that foreign language, and I'm grateful they go slow and do it one line at a time. I repeat it after them, sure I'm mispronouncing some words, but what do they expect when I don't speak Luminary?

After what feels like an eternity, they stop. "We accept your oath and welcome you into the Luminary family. You may kiss us."

What the what? My head automatically turns to Mom as firm fingers grip my chin, forcing my face back around. The man shoves his hand in front of my face, and a shuddering breath leaves my lips when I realize they mean kiss their hands.

Oh, thank fuck.

I never want to know what old man tongue feels like in my mouth.

One by one, I kiss their hands, working hard to contain my shiver of disgust.

"You may stand," the last man says, and I rise awkwardly and inelegantly to my feet, my knees half numb from kneeling for so long.

"Come with us." My uncle takes my left hand as a different man takes my right.

I keep my head up, my shoulders back, and my gaze straight as we walk toward the table. Nerves are firing at me from all angles as I feel copious eyeballs locked on my naked body.

"I am the Greed & Gluttony Luminary," Rhett Carter says, lifting me up onto the edge of the table. He lowers his hood, letting me see his face. He's handsome for an older guy with dirty-blond hair and brown eyes. He's around my dad's age, if I had to guess, so early forties. He stares at my face with a neutral expression, but his eyes drill into mine as if he's trying to burrow his way into my skull and hear what I'm thinking.

Behind him, my uncle moves in the direction of the fire pit.

"Knight." Rhett Carter's voice elevates as he calls his son forward.

My neighbor, a guy I was only introduced to on Saturday at the party, steps up beside his father. He lowers his hood and looks at my face. I appreciate that both men don't gawk at my body.

"This is my heir, Knight Carter. I believe you have already met." I nod, and Knight gives me a little jerk of his head before returning to his position in line.

Another man steps up beside Rhett. He too lowers his hood, fixing me with a ravenous smile as his gaze roams my body from head to toe.

Perverted prick.

I channel my inner Pamela and stare straight ahead while he drinks his fill.

"I am Walter Salinger, the Pride & Wrath Luminary," he says, puffing out his chest. "And this is my son and heir, Tobias," he adds as another guy I just met comes up alongside him.

Toby leers at me, licking his lips as he feasts on my breasts and my pussy. He makes no attempt to disguise his interest. He's a good-looking guy, but his inner ugliness shines through, negating any attractiveness. He makes my skin crawl, and it's hard not to cover myself or punch him in the nuts.

Angry whispering tickles my eardrums as vile Toby continues ogling me like I'm his next meal.

"Quiet." Eric Stewart's command rings out around the room, and the whispering stops. He comes up in front of me as Toby reluctantly walks away. "I am the Lust & Envy Luminary." A gorgeous guy with dark hair and Jase's green eyes approaches, and Eric introduces him. "This is Balthazar Stewart, my eldest son and heir."

More heated murmurs are exchanged in the background, and I'm guessing it's Jase and Bree.

Eric Stewart's expression doesn't alter as he turns around, leveling his gaze to the left, and the murmurs stop again.

Walter Salinger smirks. Rhett Carter looks like he's two

seconds from murdering someone, and Eric Stewart looks unconcerned and disinterested. My uncle is still doing *whatever* over at the fire pit, so I can't see his reaction.

Unlike the Salingers, Jase's father and brother don't ogle me, keeping their attention focused above my neck. I appreciate it until I realize what I'm thinking and dismiss it. They may not be outwardly ogling me, but they are still facilitating this humiliation.

Baz walks away a few seconds later, and then it's my uncle and cousin's turn.

"I am the Sloth Luminary," James says, peering deep into my eyes. His expression conveys no familiarity. The cold dead look in his eyes mirrors my mother's when she's wearing her mask, and I don't know how I didn't spot the family resemblance before. "And this is my heir, Julia."

I stare straight through her as she fixes me with a smug grin, her eyes sweeping over my body in a derisory fashion. I hold my breath for a few seconds until she walks away and Uncle James returns to the fire pit. Then it's only me and The Luminaries around the table. My uncle comes forward, wearing heavy gloves and carrying a black cast-iron stick with a raised circular piece at the end.

All the blood drains from my face. Maybe I should be grateful it'll be far quicker than a needle, but it's going to hurt like a bitch.

Chapter Thirty-Four

Ashley

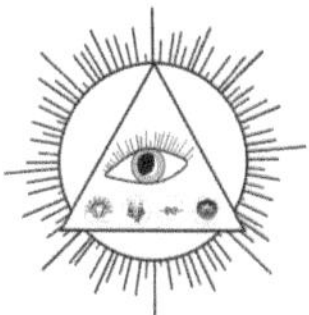

"Hoods down." My uncle's voice projects around the vast space as collective hoods are lowered.

Rhett Carter gloves up as Salinger and Stewart push me down on my back on the hard table. My legs are dangling over the edge, and if the men weren't standing in front of me, the people at the end would have a nice view of my bare pussy.

Salinger and Stewart hold me down firmly, the former with a heavy arm draped across my collarbone, tight up against my neck, and the latter with an arm across my thighs.

My uncle swipes a damp cloth over the clean circular shape on my upper arm. His eyes lose their coldness for a brief second when our gazes lock together, silently cautioning me to be brave. With the iron stick in his hand, Rhett Carter wastes no more time, leaning over me and firmly pressing the hot iron on my skin.

An anguished scream escapes my throat as my skin burns with the brand. Carter's eyes probe my face as he keeps the brand pressed to my arm, and I continue screaming. Sweat beads instantly dot my brow, and I'm struggling to breathe as tears cling to my lashes. The pain is intense and all-consuming, and I only vaguely hear sounds of commotion on my left.

I almost pass out when Carter removes the branding stick and air washes over the raised burned skin. My uncle is wearing plastic gloves now, and he dabs some salve over the wound. I can't help whimpering as it stings and burns like a motherfucker. James's gaze latches on mine, and he subtly nods. I would glare at him if I had the strength, but I'm in too much pain, and I know there is more to come.

Salinger moves his arm, pressing his hand down firmly on my shoulder while Stewart restrains my other one. Carter holds my thighs down until I'm firmly pinned on the table. Tears leak involuntarily down my face as my arm throbs and burns. Salinger's leery grin is firmly in place as he stares at my bare breasts. My nipples are hard, not from arousal but from the shock skittering over my body. Stewart looks to the left, his eyes carrying a warning, and I know he's staring at his son and daughter, cautioning them to settle down.

I cannot see my love or my friend, so I visualize their faces in my head and try to remember happy times with Jase to distract me from the pain.

Howls rip from my throat as searing-hot pain presses down on my chest, just over my heart. My body bucks and writhes of its own accord as the four luminaries hold me down. My uncle stares into my eyes as he keeps the iron pressed on my chest, but I can't see his expression through the tears blurring my vision to know if he feels any remorse for inflicting such pain on his niece. Nausea swims up my throat, and briefly I wonder if they didn't feed me so I wouldn't puke all over them.

Out of the corner of my eye, I see my parents. Uncaring if I'm punished, I twist my head a little so I can see them better. Mom is in Luminary mode, hiding her emotions behind a wall.

Dad has tears streaming down his face and murder in his eyes. I try to reassure him with a slight smile, but it's hard when it feels like I'm on fire.

The brand is removed, and like the last time, the pain intensifies, and my eyes roll back in my head as my screams bounce off the walls. Tears leak from my eyes, and I'm moaning as nausea swirls in my gut and black spots dance behind my retinas.

Hearing Jase's voice, I force my eyes to focus, roaming my gaze over to the left until I find him. His tortured eyes lock on mine as he pushes against the bodies restraining him.

Bree, Baz, and another girl—his younger sister, Jocelyn, I'm guessing—are holding him back as he strains toward me, shouting and screaming. Bree looks from me to him as she whispers frantically in Jase's ear. An older woman standing beside them looks on with fear tripping across her face. Apart from the eyes, Jase looks so much like her, and I instantly know it's his mother.

I stare at Jase, willing him to back down. This is torturous enough without the thought of him being punished. I won't lie and try to pretend I'm not in immense pain, but I hope he can see all I'm trying to convey with my eyes.

Julia steps in front of him, blocking my view. Hate fills her eyes before a familiar sneer ghosts over her face. He is humiliating her in front of their elders and peers, and she won't take that lying down. For now, she'll put on a front and enjoy seeing me compliant. She's a cruel, coldhearted bitch lacking in empathy.

Imagining her enduring this at ten, I don't feel a smidgeon of sympathy. What kind of a monster knows what it's like to undergo this ordeal and gloats watching it happen to another? She is a twisted, sick bitch, devoid of humanity.

I don't feel sorry for her, because a lot of it she has brought on herself, but I do pity her. She will never know what it's like to love and be loved or what it feels like to be genuinely happy because nothing will ever be good enough. Her desire to control and hurt others will always take precedence and always ensure I'm the winner in life.

I snap my gaze back to the four luminaries as I am straightened up, sitting on the edge of the table. My limbs feel heavy, and pain radiates throughout my body, and mixed with the lack of food, it's making me feel weak.

James places a salve on the brand on my chest before helping me to drink from a bottle of water. My dry lips and aching throat welcome the cold liquid. In the background, there is movement and activity, but I'm too exhausted to worry about it. Whatever is coming next cannot be as bad as what I have just been subjected to.

Salinger and Carter return carrying two big gold chalices. Carter hands one to my uncle along with a slim dagger. The Luminary symbols are etched into the silver handle of the dagger, and it's a replica of the dagger Salinger drags across his palm. My eyes pop wide as I watch him hold his hand over one of the chalices to capture the blood droplets. After a few seconds, he passes it to Carter. He does the same, adding his blood to the mix, while Salinger presses a large clear Band-Aid over his sliced palm.

James reclaims my attention when he hands the dagger to me. "You know what to do."

Mom mentioned a blood exchange, but it would've been nice if she had elaborated. Without thinking about it, I drag the dagger across my palm, opening my skin. The sharp sting barely registers against the throbbing pain in my arm and my chest. My uncle places my hand over the second chalice, keeping his palm on top of mine.

Around the room, every member of the Luminary's close family is doing the same, sharing the dagger and chalice from person to person. My eyes find Jase again, and we stare at one another as the blood drips from my cut into the chalice. My heart pounds as I stare into his gorgeous emerald-green eyes. My fingers twitch with a craving to touch him, and I long to feel his strong arms around me. Everything around me disappears as we stare at one another, and his gaze helps to comfort me. Concern lingers in his eyes, and I try to reassure him I'm okay.

"That will have to end," my uncle murmurs under his breath, so low only I can hear him.

It drags me out of my bubble, breaking the spell Jase and I are under. I turn my head to look at James.

"He isn't destined for you." He removes my hand from the chalice before setting the goblet down on the table behind him, the one beside the fire pit. "We will talk about this again," he adds as Salinger retrieves the second chalice and walks toward us.

"Stand," Carter commands, taking the elbow of my unbranded arm and helping me to my feet.

I glare at him as I stand on wobbly limbs, almost at my breaking point. His eyes bore into mine, warning me to keep challenging him. A throat clearing grabs my attention, and I look over at Mom. She subtly shakes her head, nodding subtly in Jase's direction, reminding me why I must obey.

Air expels from my mouth as I stand straighter, reminding myself this is almost over.

"We share blood to reinforce our vows and strengthen our bonds," Stewart says, raising the chalice with my blood to his lips.

My face twists in horror as I watch Stewart, Carter, and Salinger drink my blood before passing it to my uncle. Their lips are coated with little droplets of blood before the chalice is passed over to the rest of the crowd.

My uncle hands me the other goblet—the one that was sent around the room and now contains blood from every person present. "Drink."

My nose scrunches up as I peer into the chalice. There is a decent amount of blood in here. Surely, I'm not expected to drink all of it?

Raising it to my lips, I swallow my fears and tip it back. The metallic coppery taste hits my tongue as the thick liquid drips down my throat. I zone out, thinking of sexy times with Jase and Chad as I drink because it's the only way I can do it without gagging or puking.

James removes the cup from my lips unexpectedly, and blood spills from my mouth, dripping over my lips and down past my chin. The chalice with my blood is returned with only a small amount of liquid remaining. I watch in horrified fascination as Rhett Carter dumps the remaining blood into one chalice and swirls his finger around to mix it.

My uncle pushes me back down on top of the table. "Hold still," he warns, dipping his fingers in the blood and swirling it across my stomach.

What fresh hell is this?

I look up at the ceiling as all four luminaries touch me, painting my body in bloody brushstrokes, covering my breasts, my stomach, legs, arms, and face, careful not to touch my brandings.

I look over at Mom, and her eyes plead with me for understanding. Chills creep over my body as I realize there is something else to this ritual. Something she waited until the last second to tell me because she was afraid of how I would react. Something she never got to tell me because she left it too late.

My eyes harden as I glare at her. No matter how horrifying

this is, I would rather have known and had the time to psych myself up for it.

"No!" Jase's panicked shout claims my focus. I turn my head as Salinger and Carter tie my wrists to chains at the side of the table so I can't get free. I watch Jase shouting and fighting as his mom, sisters, and the Carter and Salinger heirs restrain him.

In front of me, Eric Stewart, removes his cloak and begins undressing. Jase roars, screaming obscenities at his father.

A cold sweat coats my skin as realization dawns. This cannot be happening. I'm shaking all over as he sheds his shirt and his fingers move to the button on his pants.

"No, Dad!" Jase roars. "Touch her, and I'll kill you!"

Chapter Thirty-Five

Ashley

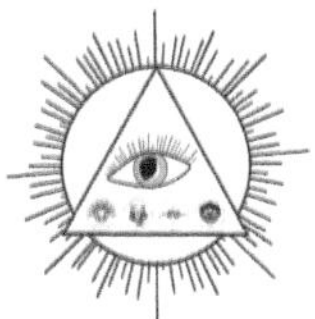

"Cuff him," Walter Salinger commands, eyeballing Toby.

"No!" I plead as all the men in the circle around us advance on Jase. "Leave him alone!"

"He needs to be taught a lesson," Rhett Carter adds. "This insubordination is the utmost disrespect during a ceremonial initiation. Tie him to a chair, and bring him forward."

Julia grins as she watches Jase being restrained to a chair. He's bucking and thrashing, but six men have him pinned and he has no fighting chance. In record time, they have his arms, legs, and waist bound to the chair. Lifting him up, they carry him over, depositing him at the side of the table.

"This is what I was trying to avoid. I wanted to protect you. We should have ran away," he says. Pain radiates from his body in waves, and it's etched upon every line on his face.

He is dangerously close to undoing all the work my parents did last night to protect him and Bree. I can't let him do this, no matter how badly I'm shaking at the thought of Jase's father forcing his way inside me with an audience. "Shut your mouth,

Jason," I snap, glaring at him. "I made an oath, and this needs to happen. Deal with it."

The barest hint of respect curves the corner of Carter's mouth though it's gone so fast I may have imagined it.

Walter Salinger steps forward. "This is why I suggested I be the one to fuck her." He licks his lips as his eyes fixate on my pussy.

I squeeze my legs together and narrow my eyes at him, uncaring if he sees exactly what I think about him.

"Stewart is the next on the list," my uncle says. "There can be no deviation from the plan."

"I invoke the heir's right," Balthazar Stewart says, stepping forward.

A hushed silence descends, broken a couple of seconds later by Jase. "The same applies to you, brother," he hisses, angling his head back to look at Baz as he walks toward us. "Touch my girl, and you die." He pins pleading eyes on the four luminaries. "If a Stewart has to do it, let it be me. Please, I will do anything you ask. I'll marry Julia without protest, just let me be the one to do this."

"It can't be you, son." Eric Stewart has that same impassionate expression on his face as he eyeballs his son, his fingers temporarily stalled on the waistband of his pants. "You are not a Luminary or an heir."

"Heirs don't fuck the initiates," Salinger pipes up.

"They do if the initiate is over eighteen and the heir has claimed the heir's right," my uncle says.

"We are wasting time," Carter interjects. "Balthazar has claimed the right to fuck the girl as the Stewart heir, and tradition demands we accept. Let him through."

"Fuck you, Baz!" Jase shouts. "You're dead. I will kill you if you lay one finger on Ash."

"Shut that disrespectful asshole up," Carter demands,

pointing his finger at Eric Stewart. "Or I'll gladly take him off your hands and teach him what it means to be a second son of a Luminary!" His anger is rising, and I'm terrified of what he might do to him.

I look over at Jase, softening my tone and my expression. "You need to let this go. It has to happen, and I'm okay with it." That isn't even remotely true. Letting Jase's brother fuck me without protest is not something I would ever be okay with. But this is life and death, and at least it's not his father.

"Don't lie, Ash! I know you."

"Then know this. If you let anything happen to yourself, I will never speak to you again. Do you understand? Stand down, Jase. This isn't a fight you need to fight."

My father comes up behind Jase, clamping a hand down on his shoulder in solidarity. His eyes are red-rimmed and angry, his expression forlorn, but he knows better than to argue. He's not a Luminary. He's not protected if he tries to stop this. He knew coming here today he had no way of preventing it. Still, his eyes convey his pain, and I know he's beating himself up for not protecting me.

"I love you both," I say, my gaze jumping between my dad and my lover. "This is not on you. It's the way it has to be, and I have made my peace with it." It takes a lot out of me to say those words, but I do it for them. Mom stands in the background, quietly nodding at me. I am so pissed at her, and we will be having words when this is over and done with.

"Enough of this!" Salinger snaps. "Get on with it, young man."

"You're dead to me," Jase says as Baz begins undressing. "I will never forgive you for this."

Oh my god, does he have a death wish?

"I'll remove him from the room," Eric says, moving toward his son.

"No." My uncle's voice projects around the room. "He needs to see this. He is far too attached to my niece. She is not meant for him. Maybe this will help him to come to terms with it." James steps forward with a folded-up handkerchief, stuffing it into Jase's mouth. He wraps a bandage over his mouth and behind his head, securing it in place and effectively silencing his protests.

My heart aches for Jase. If the roles were reversed and I had to watch my cousin fuck him, I would be destroyed. I don't think the images would ever leave my brain. My uncle knows what he's doing insisting Jase watches this, and I hate him for it. I have always liked James Manford. He was always kind, generous, and welcoming, taking interest in my hobbies and my schoolwork, and he seemed like a good guy.

I take it all back. He's a prick. I don't care if he helped my mom in the past.

Surely, he could have stopped all of this, and he did nothing.

As of now, he's as dead to me as Baz is to Jase.

Baz strips down fast, stroking his dick as he approaches me on the table. Jase's muffled cries behind his gag aren't helping. I glance over at him, begging him with my eyes. I can't do this if I am constantly aware of how much this is hurting Jase. I can only do this if I lie back and focus on my pain and distract my mind with happy images while his brother takes from my body.

Jase nods, his eyes filling with unshed tears as he understands my silent communication. He won't make this harder for me. We will both suffer in silence.

Rhett Carter plants a hand on Baz's shoulder as he brushes up against my legs. I turn to face him. "This is the last part of the ceremony," Carter explains, staring at me. "Where you pledge your body to The Luminaries. It is ours to command as we please."

Suck a dick, asshole.

"After this, we own you. Body, mind, heart, and soul. You exist only to obey the Luminary calling," Salinger adds.

I don't know if that means it's a free-for-all when I am fully initiated because Mom hasn't explained anything about what happens after, other than I need to obey and present myself accordingly. If it's as lewd as it sounds, I would rather kill myself than let that creepy old perv or his vile son anywhere near me.

Horror engulfs me as I consider the other initiates went through this at age ten. My god, this is how they lost their virginity! When they were fucking ten years old?! And what about the boys? Were they fucked by men, or were female Luminary members chosen to take their virginity? I am more than grossed out. I can't even count myself lucky I got to choose who to lose my virginity to. Or that I wasn't scarred for life being forced into sex before my body was ready because Jase's brother is getting ready to fuck me against my will, and I'm not okay with it.

But I must pretend. For Jase and my dad's sake.

I avoid looking at Baz as he pumps his dick and parts my legs, stepping in between my thighs.

My eyes close when his fingers part my folds, and he rubs them up and down my slit. His fingers are slick, and I guess he must have lubed them up when I wasn't watching.

"Eyes open," Salinger instructs, coming up beside Jase. I force my eyes open, willing my mind to go numb. The four luminaries remain right beside the table. Got to make sure they have a bird's-eye view. My dad is back in the circle beside my mom, and they have their arms wrapped around one another.

I focus on the throbbing pain radiating from my arm and my chest as Baz slides two fingers inside me, warming me up. My heart feels like a block of wood in my chest, and I can scarcely swallow over the messy ball of emotion in my throat. Lying here mute and still goes against my every instinct as Baz leans over me, pressing his body down on mine as his fingers work to loosen me up. His mouth grazes my ear. "I'll be gentle, and I'll be quick," he whispers.

Does he want a medal or something?

I give him nothing when he peers into my eyes, hating how much he looks like his younger brother.

He straightens up, running his hands all over my body, massaging the blood into my oil-slickened skin as he rubs his cock against my entrance. His fingers tug at my nipples, his large hands kneading my flesh, and I want to die. I zone out, trying to think of happier times, but it's challenging when he lifts my legs, pressing them back against my stomach, and I feel heated eyes watching my exposed pussy.

I stifle my cry of surprise when he slams his cock into me in one fast move. The urge to close my eyes is hitting me hard, but I resist. I focus on the pain, both physical and emotional, as Baz fucks me fast. I wouldn't call it gentle, but he's not overly rough. My tits jiggle as he thrusts in and out of me, jolting my body. I don't dare look at Jase. His pain will unlock my own, and I can't fall apart. Julia appears in my line of vision, a cheery grin spread across her face as she watches me.

In this moment, I vow I'm going to kill her. I don't know how, but that bitch is going to die.

Baz leans down over me again, kissing my lips before moving to my jaw and slowly working his way up to my ear. He dots kisses all over my face, disguising his intention. "You've got to come," he whispers. "They will make me keep going until you do."

A fresh wave of horror crests over me.

"Imagine I'm Jase," he adds. "Remember a time you were together, and replay it in your mind." He kisses my neck and my collarbone, lifting his head before his lips touch my tits, and I realize he did this for Jase and maybe a little bit for me. So neither of us would have to suffer the alternative.

A shared understanding passes between us when we next lock eyes, and I discreetly nod, doing as he says when his fingers move to my clit and he starts toying with it as he picks up his pace and ruts into me harder.

I let my mind wander to the first time Jase fucked me in public. It was at the library of our high school. We had only been together a couple of months, but I was head over heels in love with him. Our time together was always limited because of school, football, family, and his Julia commitments, so we had to be creative.

This day, he hunted me down in the library, dragged me between the shelves, and fingered me under my uniform skirt until I came all over his hand. Then he pushed me up against the books and fucked me from behind. The thrill of being discovered heightened our arousal, and we'd both come in record time.

It was only when we were done we realized we weren't alone. Chad had been watching, cock in hand and eyes darkened with lust. I noticed him just as he spurted all over his fingers and the library floor. I knew Chad liked to watch, but it was the first time I realized his voyeuristic tendencies were more than a passing whim.

Chad likes to tease Jase over his exhibitionist kink, but the truth is, we all get a kick out of it.

Those thoughts are floating through my mind as I come all over Baz's cock while he climaxes inside me, and the ordeal is finally over.

Chapter Thirty-Six

Jase

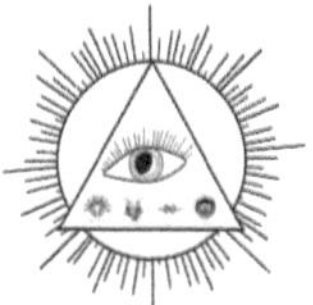

I have lost track of time down here in the basement of Luminary HQ, trapped in physical pain and my own torturous mind as I replay Ash's initiation on a continuous loop. I'm sick to my stomach every time I think about it. Every man's eyes on her gorgeous body. Her pain-filled screams as those bastards branded her. The disgust on her face as she was forced to drink blood. Her strength and bravery as she succumbed to their final demand, accepting it calmly for me.

All of it hurts, but it's the image of my brother thrusting inside her, taking something that wasn't his to take, that elevates my rage into murderous territory.

A snarl rips from my lips in the confines of my small cell, and my fists clench into balls. I meant what I said. My brother is dead to me, and he'll be sorry when I get my hands on him.

Lying on my back on the single cot, I stare at the plain white ceiling of the windowless room, wondering when they will deem my punishment served so I can return to my life.

I am well acquainted with the lower levels of the compound, having spent plenty of time down here for various rebellions and misdemeanors while growing up. Bree spent a good bit of time here too. They don't discriminate against females when it comes to beatings. Which is really fucking hypocritical because in every other aspect of our society women have less rights.

They have a ton of single cells down here. All small rooms with narrow cots and en suite bathrooms. The small desk and stool are nailed to the floor, like my bed, so there is nothing I can use to hurt myself or them. The only time I've been removed from this room is to be punished.

They have a large hall with all manner of torture equipment and tools and various sadistic bastards more than happy to teach me a lesson.

I'm sure Dad has smoothed things over with Coach and LU. The Luminaries do own it after all. I know Ash is here, being subjected to a crash course in all things Luminary, and I'm desperate to see her. I need to kiss every part of her to check she's okay and to remind her she belongs to me.

They can beat me and starve me and threaten me, and it won't make any difference.

Ashley is my girl, my future, my life.

I don't know how I'm going to swing it, but she *will* be mine.

Turning on my side on the bed, I ignore the pain lancing across my stomach with the motion. Dried blood has crusted on my lips and my nose, and one eye is half shut from the beating I took this morning. They worked me over good but made sure nothing was broken, which must mean they plan to return me to LU sooner than later. I couldn't be bothered cleaning up when they dragged me back here and tossed me on my bed. I like the pain. It feels like penance for failing to protect the love of my life.

I don't lift my head when the door opens and a couple of people enter my room.

"Sit up, son. We need to talk," my father says.

"I have nothing to say to you."

"Well, we have plenty to say to you," James Manford replies.

Reluctantly, I turn over and sit up, placing my bare feet on the ground.

"You look like hell," my father says.

I just glare at him as he walks across the room and enters the bathroom.

"This kind of conduct is beneath you, Jason." James leans against the wall beside the desk and folds his arms. "You are smarter than this. You are destined to be the future Sloth heir, and quite frankly, this latest behavior concerns me."

"If you're that worried, cut me loose. Find someone more worthy."

"Don't be facetious, Jason," he replies. "You know that's not how these things work. Julia and you were matched for a reason, and those reasons haven't changed." James purses his lips. "If this juvenile behavior is a deliberate attempt to thwart your marriage to my daughter, think again. This marriage is happening. The only thing your behavior will achieve is a delaying of the transfer of power from me to you until I have groomed you to be the perfect replacement. You will just prolong the situation."

"You are a second son," Dad says, returning to the room and handing me a wet facecloth. He was clearly listening to our conversation from the bathroom. "And I won't tolerate this rebelliousness any longer. Your blatant disrespect of me and James on Monday was completely unacceptable." He looms over me, pinning me with a lethal look. "You will do as you are told or face the consequences."

"Which are?" I quirk a brow as I press the wet cloth against my dry lips.

"You're close with your friends on the team. Chad, Nix, Creed, right?" James says.

I don't bother replying to his rhetorical question.

"Step out of line, and your friends will pay the price," Dad confirms.

It's classic Luminary behavior—threaten the innocents who can't defend themselves. It's an effective strategy though. It's why most luminaries don't mix with outsiders. They can't use innocents to hurt you if you haven't befriended or fallen in love with any.

My father doesn't need to elaborate for me to understand. I toe the line, or they will kill my friends.

All rebelliousness flees my veins, and I nod.

It's one thing to place myself in danger.

I won't do that to my unsuspecting friends.

I need to formulate a more sophisticated plan. One which will legitimately extract me from the marriage to Julia and let me marry Ashley instead.

For now, I need to stop outwardly rebelling and play the game. "I understand."

"I hope you do." James flicks a piece of fluff from the arm of his navy suit jacket. "You are engaged to my daughter now, and I expect you to conduct yourself accordingly. You have your Luminary commitments, of course, and those are sanctioned, but for now I expect you to demonstrate loyalty and faithfulness to my daughter as your future wife. Your engagement is public and official, and I won't have her disrespected."

Of course, he won't. These assholes bend the rules to suit themselves. As long as I'm discreet, I am allowed to fuck whomever I want while engaged. He is only doing this to enforce his power over me, and to appease his whiny daughter.

"I have tolerated your indiscretion with my niece for years." He stabs me with a look. "It ends now."

"A marriage contract is being worked out for Ashley," my dad says, and I work hard to hide my reaction. It's not like I haven't considered this already, but I thought I had more time. Ash isn't familiar with our ways, and she won't be fully up to speed for some time. I didn't think they would rush to find her a match this soon. It complicates things.

"You will not interfere," James cautions one final time.

"Understood."

"Ashley is new to our world, and she has a lot to learn. She doesn't need this complication either. If you love her like you profess to do, you will walk away and let her deal with her fate," my father says.

"You need to make the point very clear to her," James warns. "Ensure she hates you so there is no doubt you and her will never be."

I'm in a shitty mood the rest of the day after that little visit, and my mood doesn't improve when my brother shows up later that night.

Despite my earlier promises, I lunge at him the instant he steps foot in my room, throwing a punch at his face. His head whips back, blood spraying from his mouth as my fist connects. My bruised body screams at me in pain, but I ignore it, thrusting my fist at his solar plexus.

My brother blocks the punch, fisting my hand and holding it against his stomach. "I let you have one, but that's it." His cool demeanor pisses me off, and I growl. "Don't make me hurt you, little brother."

I bark out a harsh laugh as I glare at him. "Too fucking late."

I detect motion at his wrist, spying him clicking something

tucked underneath his shirt sleeve. "Quick," Baz says, his entire expression changing. "We don't have much time."

"What did you do?" I yank my arm back.

"Scrambled the connection so the camera feed goes down. It won't take them long to fix it." He grips my shoulders. "I know you hate me, but I was only trying to help. As was Dad."

"Yeah, it sure looked like that."

He taps my temple. "Use your fucking brain, Jase, and stop thinking with your dick. Dad promised you we would protect the girl, and he meant it. Walter Salinger was next in line. He's who should have fucked your girl. Dad went out on a limb to hack into the system and mess with the intel. It could still come back to bite him. Salinger is suspicious and salty as fuck he didn't get to screw her."

"Oh, and I suppose you offered yourself out of the goodness of your heart."

He shakes his head, stepping back from me. "You are an idiot. Love truly has blinded you." He pauses for a couple of beats. "I found that old heir's right rule so it would be me. Or would you rather it had been Dad? Ashley understood I was trying to help."

"You fucked my girl in front of everyone! You made her come, and you came inside her. Do you have any idea how much that hurt both of us?"

His features harden with anger. "I'm not going to apologize. I was helping you, and it's not like I had any choice. You've been attending initiations since you were ten. You know how these things go. Get over yourself, and start worrying about the important stuff."

"Like?" I rub a hand across the back of my neck.

My brother and I have never gotten along. He thrives on this shit while I have spent my life rebelling against it. It's not like he has ever done anything for me or tried to understand my perspective, so sue me if I have a hard time believing he did this to help me or Ash.

"Like finding a way to be with your girl, and I think I have the answer."

Shock splays across my face. He glances at his watch and curses. Grabbing my head, he whispers in my ear. "The cameras will be back online any second. Knock her up, brother. It worked for her mother. It got her out of marrying that piece of shit. They'll be mad, but how bad can the punishment be? You're both luminaries, the child will be pure-blooded, and they can't kick you out. Not with the precedent they set with her mother." He waggles his brows as he takes a step back. "You can thank me later."

Chapter Thirty-Seven

Ashley

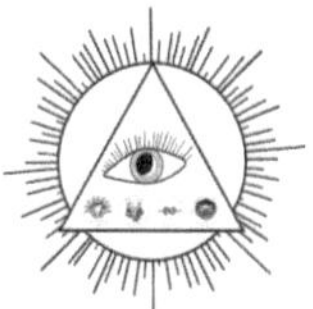

Standing outside the Luminary HQ entrance, waiting for my ride, I have never been more grateful to see the back of a place. Although, it's only the first of many such visits I've been told. My head is about to explode with all this new knowledge. I got a rundown of the history-slash-origins of The Luminaries, a crash course in Latin, and a high-level breakdown of the Luminary structure, each family, and their businesses.

I've also been sick with worry over Jase. When Rhett took me into the observation room and I saw what they were doing to him, I threw up everywhere. No one will tell me anything about him. I couldn't get past security at the lower level to visit him, so I've been going out of my mind.

I hardly slept a wink all week, concerned about what they were doing to punish Jase, troubled over all these new expectations of me, and worried about Chad. I have no cell, and they wouldn't give me access to a phone. The Wi-Fi only works for approved websites so I could complete my assignments. It wouldn't connect to social media or any communication sites, so I had no way of contacting my boyfriend. I assume my parents spoke to him, but I have no idea how they explained my absence or what they told the school. I'm less worried about the latter now I know The Luminaries actually own the entire campus. It's not like I'm going to get kicked out.

"Temptress."

I spin around so fast I almost trip over my feet. Jase stands behind me, looking much better than the last time I saw him. He still has the remnants of a black eye and some bruising around his nose, but boy is he a sight for sore eyes. "Jase," I rasp, stepping toward him and wrapping my arms around his waist. "I have been so worried."

"Me too." He presses a lingering kiss into my hair before removing my arms and putting distance between us.

Pain spears me through the chest at his rejection. "Do you hate me now?"

"Never, baby," he says and then mouths "I love you" before subtly jerking his head at the camera tucked into the corner of the entrance.

We're being watched. I hope that's all it is. Part of the reason I haven't been sleeping is worry over what went down with me and Baz and whether Jase and I will ever be able to get past it.

"Here comes our ride," he says, and I turn around in time to see my SUV pull up in front of us.

My eyes startle in happy surprise when Bree hops out of the driver's side and races toward me. She envelops me in a gentle hug, careful of my brandings. She knows from personal experience they take weeks to heal. Mine have only just started scabbing over, and they are still sore. I hug her back, grateful to see a friend after a week spent with strangers and scary men with crazy expectations.

"Missed you," she says, squeezing me one last time before letting me go so she can hug her brother. "Missed you too, little brother. Still living up to your PC2 moniker, I see." She gives him a thumbs-up.

"What's that mean?" I ask, recalling Jase referring to her as PC1 on another occasion.

"I'm problem child two," Jase explains, bending down to swipe my bag. "And Bree is problem child one."

"It's our mom's attempt at humor." Bree rolls her eyes as she pops the trunk.

Snagging my hand, Jase pulls me with him as he shoves our bags into the very back of the trunk. "Let Bree drive. We need to talk," he whispers.

I don't question him, climbing in the back seat as Bree gets behind the wheel and Jase takes shotgun. "Wait until we are through the gates." Bree glances at her brother as she turns on the radio.

"Can they see us through tinted windows or hear us somehow?" I ask, wondering if there are bugs inside my new car.

"No. Your dad checked before I left." Bree eyeballs me through the mirror as she drives down a long straight road bordered by tall trees on both sides. All I can see for miles is dense woodland and wide fields with the odd building dotted into the landscape. The main compound is behind us, and if I never see that creepy crypt again, I'll die happy.

"It's just better to be safe than sorry." Jase throws a quick look at me over his shoulder. "Big brother has nothing on The Luminaries."

"So I'm learning."

"You look beautiful, baby," he says, looking straight ahead as he reaches back for my hand.

I sit up straighter, threading my fingers in his as I connect with him through the mirror. "You look a lot better than the last time I saw you." He frowns, and I worry my lower lip between my teeth, wondering if I should have said anything. But I don't want there to be secrets between us any longer. It's going to be hard enough having to lie to Chad. I don't want to lie about anything to Jase. "Rhett Carter took me to the observation room when you were being beaten." Tears stab my eyes as I remember the things they were doing to him.

"That fucking prick." Jase's eyes narrow.

"If it helps you to feel better, I puked all over his dress pants and his shoes."

Bree howls with laughter, and a glorious smile spreads across Jase's gorgeous mouth. "That's my girl."

"Am I?" I ask as Bree takes a sharp turn up ahead.

"Yes." Confidence rings out in his tone.

"I thought after what happened with Baz..."

"You can't let that come between you." Bree eyeballs me through the mirror again. "Otherwise, those bastards have won."

"It's easier said than done," I quietly admit. No matter that we were forced into it, I still fucked Jase's brother. I don't know if he can ever get over it. Maintaining eye contact with him, I squeeze his hand. "Thank you for trying to stop it. You knew they would punish you, and you still tried."

"I didn't care about the punishment. I knew it was a long shot, but I had to try. I didn't want any of that for you."

"I know, but it could've been worse." Jase opens his mouth to argue, but I place a finger on his lips stalling him. "Baz was trying to help, and he talked me through it. He told me to imagine it was you touching me, fucking me, and to think about one of our sexy times. That's the only way I could do it." Tears well in my eyes. "I know that must have been awful for you, Jase, but you were all I was thinking about."

"Fuck this." Jase yanks his hand from mine, unbuckles his belt, and climbs into the back seat. "Put the pedal to the metal, PC1. Get us the fuck off this compound."

"Yes, sir." Bree mock salutes him, and he flips her the bird as he lands on the seat beside me, instantly circling his arm around my shoulders.

"Temptress." Jase cups my face in his hands. "I don't hold any of that against you. Not a single thing." He tilts my face up. "You hear me? None of it was your fault." He dots kisses all over my face. "You were so strong. So brave."

"You carried yourself with grace," Bree offers. "Julia was spitting fire."

I don't want to think about that bitch now. Not when Jase is staring at me like I hung the moon in the sky. "I love you." I loop my hands around his neck. "I love you so much, Jase. I was so terrified I had lost you."

"Never." He rests his forehead against mine. "They want me to break up with you and commit to Julia. I agreed purely to get them off my back, but I'm not giving up, Ash. I won't stop fighting for you."

"I won't either," I say before brushing my lips against his.

"Breanna," Jase says in a clipped tone. "I need away from here now."

"I'm almost at the gates. Chill."

Jase winds his fingers through my hair, and my core pulses with need when he fixes me with a lustful look. His green eyes are so dark they are almost black. "I've been on a countdown until you were back in my arms." His eyes are greedy as he drinks me in. "I wanted to kill every one of those motherfuckers for looking at you. I still might," he adds, nipping at my earlobe.

Jase holds me against his chest as Bree slows down when we approach the gate. A couple of armed guards stand outside a large gatehouse, watching as a scanner scans the plate on my car. The gates open automatically, and one of the guards waves us through.

Bree floors it, the tires squealing as she peels out of there. The second we are away from the compound, Jase slams his lips down on mine and hauls me into his lap. We devour one another like it's the first time we kissed. Angling my head, I grant him better access, and he pushes his tongue inside my mouth, exploring as we get reacquainted.

It's been weeks since we were intimate, and I'm aching for him all over. Our tongues tangle together, and he moans into my mouth when I straddle him, pushing my crotch against the bulge in his jeans.

"Shit, guys, you're making me all horny," Bree protests from the front seat.

"You're about to get hornier," Jase jokes, breaking our kiss and reaching for the bottom of my shirt. His eyes beg the question, and I nod.

"Eww. Seriously?"

"I am starved for my woman," Jase admits, lifting my shirt up and tossing it on the ground. "And I refuse to wait another minute."

"If you don't want to know, keep your eyes on the road and turn the music up to drown out the noise," I suggest, waggling my brows at Jase as I unclip my bra.

His fingers trace gently over the plastic wrapping covering the brandings on my chest and my arm. "How sore are you?"

"I can manage." Grabbing fistfuls of his hair, I pin him with a warning look. "Don't you dare hold back. Fuck me hard and fast, baby, and talk dirty to me. Just how I like it."

The music blares, and Jase and I laugh until our eyes meet in a marriage of lust and need, and all bets are off. His hands move to my breasts, and he plucks my nipples before taking them in his mouth. "I've missed my girls," he says, lavishing attention on my chest. "I want to fuck you here after I've fucked your cunt, your mouth, and your ass. My cock is starved for you, baby, and I want to fill you with my cum until your body remembers who you belong to."

Bree raises the volume on the radio again.

Oops.

"Yes to all of that," I pant, grinding against his lap while I hold his face to my tits. "Though it might push your sister to the limits if we try that marathon in here." He chuckles before his tongue darts out, licking a circular path around my breasts before he grazes my nipples with his teeth. He works me into a frenzy in no time, and I'm all out of patience. "I need you inside me now." I yell into his ear, so he hears me over the music, while grabbing his shirt and pulling it up his body.

He flings it aside, and I ask a silent question as my fingers brush over the discolored skin painting his arms, his chest, and his stomach. "I'm fine, Ash." He kisses my lips. "I would do it all over again if it meant protecting you."

"You made it all bearable, Jase," I say, tracing the tip of my finger around the intertwined snake design on his chest. "Did you wear skin patches to hide these from me before?" I run my fingers over the design on his arm. The same one I now have.

He nods. "I had no choice. It would have invited too many questions."

"I'm not criticizing. I understand." My hands gently trail the dips and curves of his abs. "They didn't tell me what responsibilities each family has yet. My uncle said he'd talk to me about our family duties when I got home." It could be my imagination, but it feels like he tenses underneath my hands. I peer deep into his eyes. "What do you have to do?"

His Adam's apple bobs in his throat as he tilts his head to one side and pierces me with a dazzling smile that instantly nukes all brainpower. "Is this really what you want to talk about now?" His sultry voice sends shivers cascading along my skin as his expert fingers pluck my nipples.

"No," I admit in a breathless voice, not even remembering what I asked him now. "I need you, dirty boy."

Jase pushes me back flat on the seat behind Bree's chair. His fingers reach for the button on my jeans, and I lift my hips, helping him to peel them off me. Hooking his fingers in my panties, he tugs them down my legs and tosses them aside. Then he parts my thighs and buries his face in my pussy.

I cry out as he licks my slit and drives his tongue deep inside me. Yanking fistfuls of his hair, I arch my hips and buck against him, riding his face as my orgasm quickly builds. Jase laps at my clit the same time he pushes three fingers inside me, and I explode, coming with a loud scream as I soak his gorgeous face.

As if it's a race, he tugs his jeans and boxers off and slams inside me in one powerful thrust. I scream again, forgetting all about our audience in the driver's seat. Jase ravishes my mouth as he fucks me into the seat with my legs wrapped around his hips. We're a bit cramped for space, especially with his strong body and long legs, but we make it work.

It's not like it's the first time we have fucked in a car. Though this is the first time anyone other than Chad has witnessed it.

Jase pulls up into a seated position, bringing me with him. My back is to the door as he ruts into me, holding the back of my head so it doesn't slam against the window. Pivoting my hips, I rotate them to match his thrusts, but it's not deep enough. I need to feel him nudging my womb. I crave him as deep as he can go. I want his seed deposited inside me when he comes. "From behind," I pant, nipping at his lower lip. "I want you to fuck me really hard, Jase, and you can't do it like this."

He buries his face in my breasts, biting and sucking on them, before getting us into a new position. I'm on all fours with him behind me when he grabs my hips and drives inside me in one hard thrust. I scream, and Bree yells something at us, her words lost in the music. We are both too lost to lust to care anyway. Jase maintains a firm grip on my hips as he pounds into me. "Yes, baby," I hiss, seeing stars when he shoves his dick real deep. "Fuck me harder, Jase. I want to feel you for days."

He obliges without question, rutting into me like a wild beast. One hand goes under my body to grope my breast while he rocks into me. I push back, in sync with his movements, whimpering and moaning as I feel another orgasm cresting. The second Jase pinches my clit, I erupt into a frenzy of fireworks, my body arching and writhing as waves of heavenly bliss rip through my body, sending me into outer space.

Jase roars as his release hits, pressing his lips to the back of my neck as he spills inside me. He keeps fucking me as we come down from our high, only stopping when we collapse on the seat in a sticky, sweaty mass of limbs. Our joint ragged breathing trickles in the air as Bree lowers the music.

"Well, that was just awesome, assholes."

My lips kick up at the obvious amusement in her tone.

"Now I know what my brother's O-face looks like, that my bestie is a screamer during sex, and exactly how she sounds when she comes."

Jase grins, and I giggle. Nuzzling his head in my neck from behind, he moves his mouth to my ear. "I have a solution to our problems," he whispers, and his warm breath sends a new wave of delicious tremors coasting over my body.

My pussy throbs with fresh need as desire pools in my belly. Reaching around, I grab hold of his hardening dick and begin stroking it. "Please tell me it involves more sex," I half joke.

He holds me tighter against his hot body, pressing a soft kiss to my neck, making me shiver, before he says, "Let's make a baby."

Chapter Thirty-Eight

Ashley

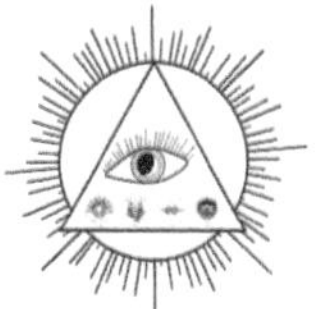

"What are you doing here?" I ask Mom when I step into my kitchen and find her seated at the island unit drinking a coffee.

"Waiting for you," she coolly replies, sliding off her stool when Bree and Jase appear in the room. "We need to talk."

Jase drops my bag on the floor and leans against the doorway as Bree comes up alongside me.

"Don't be shy, Jase. Come in." Mom smiles as she reaches for three mugs. "I'm pretty sure I know you've been warned to stay away from my daughter in the same way I know neither of you will heed that warning."

She has ditched her long wavy hair and the more casual attire she was favoring in recent months for a stern look I'm familiar with—the chignon, pearls, silk blouse, pencil skirt, and heels are her staple wardrobe as a Luminary. Guess she is fully back in the fold now and there's no need to pretend otherwise.

All it does is irritate me more. "Would you have?" I imbue sass with my tone and my petulant stance.

She looks over her shoulder at me as she pours coffee into

the three cups. "Definitely not." She grins as she distributes the coffee. "Who do you think you inherited your rebellious streak from?"

Ugh. It's just like her to try to claim credit for that. "I'm pissed at you," I admit, narrowing my eyes at her over the rim of my mug as I blow on the steam.

She nods. "That's understandable."

"But I don't have the time or the energy to get into it now. I need to find Chad. Is he here, and where does he think we were this past week?" We discussed this in the car on the ride here. Chad must have assumed Jase and I were somewhere together. Bree says she hasn't seen him, and all my mom told her was that it was handled.

"That's what I wanted to talk to you about." Mom gestures for us to follow her to the dining table.

When we are all seated with our drinks, she begins explaining. "The first thing you should know is I came here on Sunday when you were at Doug and Hera's. I asked Chad to marry you."

I spit coffee all over the table. "What the hell, Mom?"

"I thought if you did what I did, married a plebeian and got pregnant, they would leave you alone."

Jase and I share a knowing look. It's a version of what we have planned.

"Chad wouldn't agree," she adds.

Her words slice a line through my heart, which is ridiculous because, of course, he wouldn't agree to marry me. It's not the normal thing when you're still young and a freshman in college.

Jase grabs my hand under the table, giving it a comforting squeeze. "Chad would marry Ash in a heartbeat if he had money. I'm guessing he declined because he isn't in a position to take care of her the way a husband should."

"You know your friend well." Mom traces her finger around

the rim of her mug. "Yes, money was the issue. I offered to pay him, but I'm afraid that only made things worse." She shrugs, like it's no biggie.

I jump up, gripping the table as I glare at her. "You did what?" I yell, ready to tear her limb from limb. Chad is very proud, and he won't accept a penny from me or Jase, so Mom offering this would have seriously insulted him.

"You're as dramatic as he is. Relax, Ashley, and sit back down."

Did I really feel like I bonded with this woman in the crypt? How on earth did I believe this experience would draw us closer together? It's clear to me Pamela's Luminary indoctrination is embedded far deeper than she realizes. "How dare you offer to sell me to him! It's as demeaning as what happened to me in that crypt."

"Sit down, Ashley." Her sharp tone matches the sour look on her face. "I was trying to protect you the only way I knew how. It's only money. How was I to know he has a major chip on his shoulder?"

Jase pulls me down on his lap and wraps his arms around me. "I know your actions came from a place of love, Pamela, but the fact is, you insulted Chad in a big way coming here and asking him that."

She throws her hands in the air. "I was desperate! And it doesn't matter now anyway. It's too late."

I work hard to keep my tone civil. "Where does Chad think I was?"

She clasps her hands on top of the table, composing her face into a serene look, and I instantly know I'm not going to like what she says. "I had to get creative because he saw your SUV. He knows someone kidnapped you." She flips her head in Jase's direction. "He tried calling you, but when you didn't answer, he called the cops."

"I only saw his missed calls on the way back from the crypt Sunday night. I tried calling him back, but he didn't answer, and he wasn't at home when we arrived or the following morning. I have been gone since then with no way of contacting him," Jase responds.

"What did you do, Mom?" I chew on the inside of my cheek. "If you have hurt him, I will kill you with my bare hands."

"Give me some credit," she snaps. "I know you love him. I would never hurt him."

"So, where is he?" I am beginning to feel like a broken record. Evasiveness is obviously a skill The Luminaries excel at.

"Upstairs sick in bed," Julia says, appearing like a nasty apparition in the doorway.

I slide off Jase's lap, inwardly cursing whoever left the front door open. Our plan hinges on The Luminaries believing we are staying away from each other. Julia cannot know we are back together.

"How did you get in?" Bree narrows her eyes in suspicion. "I know I locked the door when we came in."

Julia preens as she walks toward us, her heels clacking off the tile floor. "Ares gave me a key."

"He did what?" I ball my hands into fists under the table.

"We're fucking," she adds. "And it's getting serious." She dangles a key from her finger. "Hence why we exchanged keys."

"Puh-lease." I toss out a laugh. "He is playing you, and you're too dumb to see it." You only have to take one look at Ares Haynes to know he doesn't do relationships. He also doesn't tolerate fools. If he is fucking my cousin, and he may well be, he's doing it for a reason.

News flash—it's not 'cause he likes her.

"Whether he gave me a key or not doesn't matter," she hisses. "My father owns this house as well as next door. I can come and go as I please."

I whip my head to my mother, and she nods.

I was told my parents bought this place for me. But it's just more lies.

Great, this is just great.

"You've outstayed your welcome." I waggle my fingers in her face in a condescending manner. "Bye, cuz."

Bree and Jase stand.

"This wasn't a social visit." Julia rolls her eyes in a derogatory fashion. "Not that I expect you to understand Luminary business. You're barely a step up from a pleb."

"Julia, that is quite enough. Ashley is your cousin and a Luminary. You will not disrespect her, or I'll be having words with your father," Mom says, standing and coming around the table.

Julia snorts out a derisory laugh. "That's rich. That slut has been sneaking around with my fiancé behind my back, yet somehow that's not disrespectful?"

"Wasn't your fiancé." I correct her.

"Semantics, bitch."

"Julia, enough!" Mom's exasperated tone conveys her rapidly growing impatience.

I am glad she is getting to see who her niece truly is behind the fake civility and all the ass-licking.

"Knock yourself out, Auntie Pam. See if I care." Stalking to the island, Julia slams a small medical kit on top of the counter. "I brought the antidote you requested."

"What the fuck is going on?" Jase folds his arms, leveling a glare at my mom and Julia. "What have you done to Chad?"

"My brother handled the situation with the cops, but Chad was still mouthing off and causing trouble," Mom explains. "I was worried the order would be given to kill him, so we found a way to silence him."

"So you what? Made him sick?" I ask because this is what they seem to be implying.

"We have had teams working on creating a virus for years. Weeding out the ineffective, weak, and lazy elements within the modern world is a tedious task growing more insurmountable by the day," Julia says, extracting a couple of vials and a long needle from the medical bag. "So, Daddy's plan has been to create a virus we can use to wipe those people out in one fell swoop. Of course, we can't make it obvious." She giggles. "So our scientists also created an antidote, and they are working on a vaccine. That way we can pick those elements we want to save and those we want to die."

My mouth slackens as she explains, and bile swims up my throat. I don't even have words to describe how ethically reprehensible that is.

"It will be some time before we're ready to roll it out, but it's just entered the testing phase." She attaches one vial to the needle before handing it to Mom. "Your mom and I decided Chad would make an excellent guinea pig."

The smug grin is wiped off her face when my punch lands squarely in her mouth. "You could have killed him!"

She teeters on her high heels, falling to the ground on her ass. Her dress rides up, exposing her bare pussy because she isn't wearing underwear.

So classy.

"You will pay for that," she yells, mopping up blood from her lip.

"Ashley." Mom grabs my elbow and pulls me back. "You cannot go around punching other luminaries. Especially not an heir."

"Fuck you, Mom." I wrangle out of her embrace. "I would

highly recommend you leave before my fist finds your face next."

"You are overreacting again."

Jase wraps his arms around me, lifting me away before I can swing at my mother. "We need to pick our battles, remember?" he whispers in my ear. "As much as this disgusts me, we need your mother on our side."

Those are the only words he could say to get me to back down. I nod, signaling he can let me down, as Mom helps Julia to her feet.

"I think it's best you leave, Julia. I can administer the antidote," Mom says.

"Fine," she clips out, smoothing a hand down her dress. "It's no skin off my back if the jock dies." She jabs her finger in the air at me. "You're going to get what's coming to you."

"I said that's enough, Julia!" Mom shouts, shoving her up against the wall in an unexpected move. "I might have helped to raise you, but you're still only my niece. Ashley is my daughter. Threaten her again, and you won't like what I do next."

Julia thrusts Mom away. "Watch who you push around, Auntie Pam. My father won't always be in charge." She smooths a hand over her hair. "You'd all do well to remember who will."

"It sure as fuck won't be you, you delusional bitch," Bree says. "You couldn't organize an orgy in a brothel without someone holding your hand."

Julia flips us the bird, in what I assume is very unLuminary-like behavior, before flouncing out of the house.

"I'm going to see Chad," I announce, striding toward the door.

"Wait!" Mom races after me. "You can't tell him where you've been."

"I am not an imbecile, Mother!" I hiss over my shoulder as I take the stairs with Jase and Bree hot on Mom's heels. "I know he can't know anything. Jase and I will tell him we were together this past week repairing our relationship. Jase arranged to kidnap me as he was desperate."

"I can send some backdated messages to his cell," Jase adds. "He won't dispute it. He'll be too happy to see us back together."

"That aligns with what we have told him the few times he's been lucid."

I spin around on the top step with my fist raised, ready to level my mom, but Jase shakes his head, reminding me of our convo in the kitchen. "You will give him the antidote and then get the fuck out of our house."

"I'm on your side, Ash," she pleads, trailing behind me as I stomp up the next set of stairs.

"Try telling that to my sick boyfriend!" I whirl around again. "You are fucking with his health and his life, and that's not okay! What about football and his family?"

"I visited his mother and sister and ensured they were looked after."

I know what that means. She gave them money. Probably paid their rent in advance and stocked up on groceries. The motives weren't entirely pure, but I like she thought to look after them. Still, it will cause issues between me and Chad when he realizes. But that's not my mother's fault. The chip is on my boyfriend's shoulder. I force myself to calm down. "Thank you for that. What about Coach?"

"As far as Coach is concerned, both Jase and Chad came down with a fever. There will be no issues on campus, for any of you. It's all been taken care of."

"It's the least you could do." I glare at her again. "I can't believe you injected him with something that could have killed him!"

"It would not have killed him. I have been here every day taking care of him, monitoring his vitals, and ensuring he wasn't in any danger. I'll give him this, and then you can sneak him a couple of doses of the vaccine along with some supplements, and he'll be totally fine." Mom pushes past me, looking aggrieved. "A little thanks would be nice," she murmurs, walking down the hallway toward the master suite.

"Hell will freeze over before that happens," I spit out.

Jase hauls me back against his chest as we reach the door to my bedroom. "I know you're mad. I am too, but you need to calm down before we go in there, or you're going to tip him off there is more to this."

Air whooshes out of my mouth as he spins me around and envelops me in his arms. "You're right, but it's not easy. She told me no more secrets or lies, but she still hasn't been truthful. You can't tell me she couldn't have asked her brother to speak to me about this at HQ when he escorted me to the compound after the ceremony. She never gave either of us the opportunity to have a say."

"I know, baby." He pecks my lips softly. "What's important is Chad is okay, and look at it like this. You have an excuse now to avoid sex with him for a while. We'll get your mom to tell him it's infectious for at least four weeks and he needs to take precautions and avoid intimate contact with others."

We hadn't come up with a workable solution yet to that part of our plan. I can't use the skin patches to cover my brandings for another few weeks, so I can't get naked with my boyfriend. And after I get my IUD removed, I can't have unprotected sex with Chad either. Not until I'm pregnant with Jase's baby.

It sucks because I love Chad and we are very sexually active. I hate adding more lies on the pile, but we have to protect him. He can't know about us or The Luminaries. To do so would be signing his death warrant. Ergo, we have no choice. I hate it, and it will be hell on earth resisting temptation. I'll just have to remind myself this is a life-or-death situation, and that should be all it takes to stick to my resolve.

"What about Ares?" I ask Mom as she curls her fingers around the door handle to our room. "What did you tell him?"

"He believes you were staying at my new house, helping to unpack and take care of Emilie, while I took care of Chad. I told him I had a nursing degree, and he seemed to buy it."

"I wouldn't be so sure." Ares is no dumbass, and he's sneaky.

Mom turns, planting her hands on her hips. "While we're on the subject of Ares Haynes, do you want to explain what you said to The Luminaries Sunday night?"

Oh, hell to the no. She did not just go there in front of Jase.

"Nope." I flash her a "butt out" look as I push her out of the way and open the bedroom door, rushing inside to see my boyfriend.

Chapter Thirty-Nine

Ashley

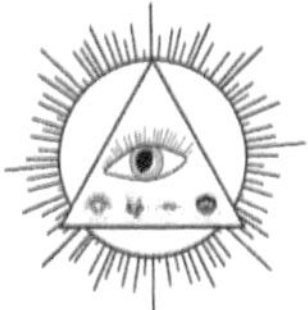

"That went better than expected," Jase says, bundling me into his arms the second I enter his bedroom.

"He looks terrible though." I link my arms around his neck. "And he's clearly exhausted." Chad was only awake for about twenty minutes after Mom administered the shot. She insisted on staying to monitor him. Hence why we came next door. Julia's car is gone, and Bree has gone to the library, so we have the house to ourselves.

Poor Chad. I am sickened at what's been done to him, and Mom and Julia better pray he makes a full recovery, or I'll be out for their blood even more than I already am.

"Chad will recover. He'll be fine." He kisses the top of my head. "At least he was thrilled we have resolved our differences and the three of us are back together."

"He won't be so pleased when he realizes what being contagious means for his sex life."

Jase grimaces as he pulls his shirt off over his head, revealing that sexy-as-sin body I'm eager to climb all over. "I know what it's like not to have you in my life or my bed. It won't be easy, but it's only temporary." He devours me with his eyes as he grips the hem of my shirt. "At least you have me to take care of your needs." He waggles his brows suggestively as he rips my shirt off. "And Chad likes watching. We can include him so he doesn't feel left out."

"Good thinking, Batman." I press a firm kiss on his lips. "I won't enjoy sneaking around again," I admit, helping him out of his sneakers and jeans. "And I hate we have to lie to Chad."

He kicks his jeans away before popping the button on mine. "That seriously sucks. I have been so close to telling him, telling both of you, over the years, but ultimately that would be the most selfish thing I could have done."

I lean my hand on his chest as I remove my sneakers and shimmy my jeans down my legs. "I know we can't tell him to keep him safe, but it still sucks." Pushing my jeans away, I stand in front of him in my bra and panties. I run my hands up his broad tan chest. "I don't want to lose Chad. If we pull this off, how long can we keep him?"

Jase removes his boxers and his impressive cock springs free, already hard and raring to go. He pulls me up against his naked body. "Like I said, when you get pregnant, they'll have to let us marry. Then, when the dust has settled, and we've paid whatever punishment they deem necessary, we can fuck whomever we want within the privacy of our marriage. The rest is up to Chad."

"What do you think he'll say?"

"He'll say yes, Temptress." Jase unclips my bra and carefully drags the straps down over my still-healing brandings. "He loves you too fucking much to ever let you go."

Jase pulls my hand to his lips, pressing a soft kiss against the small scar on my palm. We have matching scars now too, but Jase's line is much deeper than mine from participating in countless initiations. He had told me he got the injury from repairing fences on his grandpa's estate in France during successive summers as a kid, but that was only a cover story.

"Don't stress about it. Chad isn't going to let you go."

I hope he's right, but there's no point worrying now. Why borrow tomorrow's troubles when I've got enough to be concerned with today? One day at a time, one problem at a time, is my new motto.

He swats me on the ass before lifting me over his shoulder and sauntering toward his bed. "I haven't had the chance to show you this yet," he says, tossing me down on the bed on my back.

My breasts jiggle as I land on the giant four-poster bed. A dazzling shine glints off my face, and my eyes startle as I look up. "Oh my god." I stand on the mattress, examining it more closely. "You had mirrors installed."

"Told you I was going to do it." Hooking his thumbs in my panties, he slides them down my legs as I stare at the mirrored panels built into the top of the bed. "And before you ask, this is a brand-new bed. Bree tossed the old one."

I laugh as I remember Bree telling me how Julia tried to seduce Jase, and he humiliated her by tying her up and pissing on her. She even showed us a short video, and it was priceless.

I hold on to him as I step out of my panties, watching as he brings them to his nose, inhaling deeply before stuffing them in the drawer of his bedside table. I grin. "Such a pervert."

He pulls me down on top of him, and I squeal. "*Your* pervert." He nips at my bottom lip, and I sigh into his mouth.

He cracks his hand over my ass in a few firm slaps, sending tingles shooting all over my cheeks, while he kisses me. Nuzzling his nose against mine, he threads his hands in my hair and clasps my head in his large hands. "I missed kissing you, fucking you, holding you." Dropping soft kisses all over my face, he adds, "Missed talking and laughing with you." He sweeps his fingers across my face. "I just missed you, period."

"I missed you too." I wince a little when my branding touches his warm chest as I lie down fully on top of him.

"I've got an idea," he says, carefully lifting me to the side. His eyes twinkle with wicked intent. "I want to eat your ass and then fuck it while you watch." Reaching out, he fondles my boobs before turning me over and propping me up on all fours. "This position will make it easier not to put pressure on your wounds." Sliding a pillow under my head, he urges me to lie my face sideways on it so I can look up at the mirror and see everything. I lean down on my right side, so I'm not putting pressure on my sore chest or arm.

I watch him open the second drawer in his bedside table, rooting through the multitude of sex toys and aids before finding wipes and lube. He flings them on the bed near my legs and settles behind me. "I have been fantasizing about this for weeks," he says, parting my cheeks and cleaning me up. "Your tight hot ass is the stuff of dreams, Temptress." He rubs the head of his cock up and down my ass crack, and my body quivers in anticipation.

A whimper flies from my mouth when his hot tongue lands on my puckered hole, and he proceeds to eat me out. "I'm addicted to your ass, baby," he murmurs in between licks. "I jerk off remembering how tight it feels when I shove my cock inside it while fingering your pussy and thumbing your clit. Those sounds you make are like manna from heaven."

He tongues my ass in a slew of successive, lingering strokes like I'm his favorite ice-cream cone. My pussy is already drenched and pulsing with the need to be filled. "Watch me," he commands, looking up at himself with his face buried between my ass cheeks.

Through the mirror, I watch as he ravishes me with his

mouth and his tongue, and I buck my hips while kneading my tits as desire washes over me. After lubing his fingers, he pushes them inside slowly, one at a time, until he has three fingers inserted. Curling them with skill, he massages my tight hole in precise slow strokes, igniting all my nerve endings, and I almost come already.

"Holy fuck, Jase," I pant, moving my fingers down my body to rub my clit. "You are so fucking good at that."

"You're good at taking it up the ass, Ash, and I can't get enough." He pulls his fingers out and wipes them before slathering lube on his cock. "I need inside, baby. I'm going to drive my dick all the way in, hitting your G-spot, as I finger your cunt and play with your clit." He dusts a line of kisses up my spine. "But you won't come until I tell you."

I moan when I feel his dick nudge my hole, relaxing my inner walls and watching as he slowly pushes his big cock inside. The only sounds are our excited breaths as he carefully inches inside, pushing all the way in. He holds himself still for a couple beats, grinning at me through the mirror, before he begins to move.

I'm so close already it's hard to hold my orgasm. But I do because Jase stops when he feels me getting close, letting me settle before moving again. Jase slowly thrusts his cock in and out of my ass, and I feel the intense drag of his erection with every stroke. The moans leaving my lips are animalistic, and I push back against him, needing more friction. Two fingers plunge into my pussy, and he pumps them in and out fast.

"Fuck, baby. Please. I need to come," I say after a few rounds of edging, so turned on I'm ready to explode.

"Hold tight, Temptress. I'm going to blow my load all over your hot ass."

Jase grips my hips, urging me with his eyes to keep watching, and I hold on to the pillow as he fucks me hard and fast. I shatter into a thousand pieces a few minutes later as he fucks my ass, fingers my cunt, and rubs my clit.

I scream at the top of my lungs as the most incredible orgasm rips through me. Jase roars his release seconds later, pulling out and jerking his dick over my ass. Cum sprays across my lower back, my cheeks, and my legs, and I watch it all through the mirrors, which only heightens the experience.

After, Jase carries me to the shower and washes me while I struggle to keep my eyes open. The lack of sleep this past week is catching up with me. I should go home, in case Julia returns and to check on Chad, but when Jase lays me down on his bed and pulls me under his arm, I am asleep in two seconds flat.

"Shit!" I hiss before clamping a hand over my mouth so I don't wake my lover. I'm standing at Jase's window, staring out into the dark nighttime sky, cursing the glaring pink Porsche parked outside.

"What's wrong?" Jase mumbles, sitting up and rubbing the sleep from his eyes.

I pad back to the bed as naked as the day I was born. "I'm sorry. I didn't mean to wake you. It's three a.m., and I need to go home, but Julia is here." Falling asleep in Jase's arms while Chad is so ill was a total bitch move. I know Mom was with him until midnight, but I should have been there to relieve her. I need to get home ASAP.

"I wasn't expecting her. She is gone more nights than she is here."

"Really?" I ask, pulling on my bra. "Where does she sleep?"

"Don't know and don't care." He pulls my face down to his, kissing me deeply. "I don't want you to go."

"I know, but we agreed to be careful. And I need to check on Chad."

"Of course." He presses a kiss between my breasts. "I'm just being greedy."

He watches me shimmy into my jeans, sans panties, and grab my shirt off the floor. He trails a finger up my uninjured arm. "What did your mom mean about Ares?"

I stall with my shirt halfway over my head. Fuck. I knew he wouldn't let that go. I might as well come clean. He's going to be my husband, my baby daddy, and I can't keep secrets from him. Letting my shirt fall down over my body, I turn to face him. "You can't tell Chad."

He nods, wrapping a finger around my blonde hair. "What did Ares do?"

I tell him everything about that night in the shower, and his features grow angrier with every word out of my mouth. "That fucking manipulative bastard!" he growls when I have explained it all. "Just say the word, and I'll kill him."

I laugh until I see he's serious. "Jase." I cup his gorgeous face. "You can't just offer to kill him like that."

"Why not?"

"Because it's not fucking normal!" I kneel beside him. "I know it's the way you've been brought up, but you can't go around killing people who piss you off."

"It's more than that, Ash, and you know it! He took advantage of you."

"He did, but I didn't fight him. I let it happen."

"Do you think he would have walked away if you said no?"

"I don't know for sure, but yes, I think he would have."

Jase stares at me for so long I wonder if he's turned into a statue. "You're into him," he quietly says.

"What?" I rear back, offended. "No! Of course not."

"It's okay to admit it, baby. I won't be mad."

"You wouldn't?"

"No. You can't help who you're attracted to. Even if the guy is a jerk, I can admit he's a hot jerk."

"Well, I'm not into him." I slide my feet into my sneakers. "So, you don't need to worry. And I can deal with this myself." I pierce him with a pointed look. "Bree is looking for dirt I can use to blackmail him, and I'm confident I can handle him. You are not to do anything, Jase. I won't have you fighting my battles for me."

"Okay." He readily concedes without argument, and I'm grateful. He pulls me in for one final kiss, and I go willingly, sighing into his mouth as I melt against him. Jase is an unbelievable kisser. It's like he is making love to my mouth every time, and he casts a spell on me. "Message me when you get home." His lips tip up when he spots the lovestruck, dazed expression on my face.

Fucker knows he's a freaking god in the bedroom.

I roll my eyes. "Jase, it's only next door."

"I don't care. You know the world we live in now. Always expect the unexpected."

I suppose it's good advice. I just need to wrap my head around all the ways in which my life has changed. It's not something I can get used to overnight. "I'll see you tomorrow." I ruffle his hair and sneak one last kiss before I tiptoe out of the room.

Quietly closing the door, I turn around just as Ares slips out of Julia's room. He notices me instantly, and we stare at one another for a few silent beats. Then he smirks his usual annoying smirk, and that snaps me out of it. I flip him the bird as I walk past, glaring at him over my shoulder when he swats my ass.

We walk in silence back to our house, neither of us saying a word as we make our way upstairs to the bedrooms. Jase's words bounce around my head, and I wonder if that's why I'm irrationally pissed off at the thought Julia was telling the truth earlier. Why does it bother me if they are fucking? What is Ares to me but a nuisance foisted on me by our parents' marriage.

Julia is welcome to the asshole.

Hopefully, she'll annoy him so much he'll slit the bitch's throat and do us all a favor.

I slip inside the guest bedroom where Chad is sleeping and ease myself down into the tub chair pulled up beside the bed. Mom had texted earlier to say she moved him here and changed the sheets on my bed. I can't recall a time when my mother ever changed my bed, so I guess she is trying. Still, it's not enough to instantly forgive her for all the ways in which she has failed me and lied to me.

I stare at my boyfriend sleeping for a couple of minutes with a tight pain in my chest. I haven't forgotten Ares's threat. I know he hasn't said anything to Chad yet because, if he had, my boyfriend would not have welcomed me back so enthusiastically earlier.

No, Ares is planning something humiliating.

He is going to wait until I think the threat has passed and then spring something on me. I just know it.

But like I vowed earlier, I'm not going to borrow tomorrow's troubles.

Whenever Ares strikes back, I'll be ready for him.

Chapter Forty

Ashley

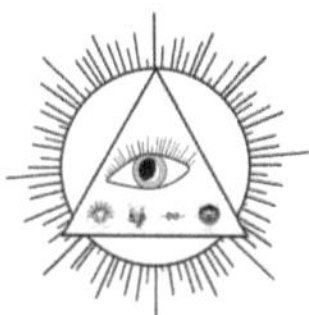

My face breaks into a huge smile the second I open the door. "It's so good to see you!" I exclaim, genuine happiness lighting up my face as I pull Harlow Westbrook into a hug.

"I was thrilled when Chad called and said your birthday party was this weekend. For once, the timing was perfect!" She hugs me back, and I'm glad I popped a couple of pain pills earlier.

I knew everyone would want to hug me tonight. The brandings on my chest and arm are healing well, and I'm disciplined in applying the salve morning and night, so hopefully in a couple of weeks, I won't feel any pain.

"You look amazing, as always," I say when we break our embrace. Lo is drop-dead gorgeous with long, thick, dark hair, the prettiest face, and a body to die for. I know plenty of guys at our old school who were hopelessly in love with her beauty and her feisty personality.

"You went back to blonde."

"It's only temporary. Parental bullshit." I roll my eyes.

"Happy birthday, Ashley," a man with a deep masculine voice says. I stare over Lo's head at the men currently crowding the top step. Harlow's four husbands are the stuff of dreams.

"Thanks, Saint." I step aside to make room for them. "Come in. The party's in full swing, as you can hear." Saint, Caz, and Theo pile in, giving me a quick hug or kiss on the cheek.

I'm not sure if it's my imagination, but those guys seem to get hotter every time I see them. Caz is muscular and seriously ripped with killer biceps and a matching killer smile. Saint is the kind of bad boy who looks like he stepped off the pages of a magazine. His blond hair is longer than he used to wear it, but it suits him all messy and falling into his blue eyes. Theo has a gorgeous face and the kindest eyes. His long blond hair falls to the nape of his neck, but tonight he's wearing it in a man bun, which is seriously freaking hot.

They are all so different in looks and personality but equally as hot as one another. Caz and Theo are holding hands, and my ovaries swoon. According to Lo, it took them forever to admit their feelings, but now they are solid, and the five of them have the kind of relationship I can only aspire to.

For a while, I tried my best to tempt Jase and Chad into fucking one another, even as an experiment, but they are steadfastly into pussy, so I had to let that fantasy go.

"For the birthday girl," Galen adds, coming up at the rear. Lo's other husband thrusts a box at me, and I try not to swoon. Galen has a face and body that belongs on a catwalk. He is insanely stunning with dark hair and smoldering fuck-me eyes. Like his cousin Saint, he is tall and ripped with various tats and piercings.

Lo is a lucky bitch, that's for sure.

My friend is smirking at me with a knowing smile. I return it and some. She knows the kind of reaction the guys invoke in the female, and male, population. When they made up the junior chapter leadership of The Sainthood, they were as lusted after as they were feared. Now, they have all retired from that world, and they live an idyllic polyamorous life in Rhode Island.

"You guys! You didn't need to bring a gift, but thank you so much." I press a kiss to Galen's cheek before looping my arm through Lo's.

"Every girl deserves to get spoiled on her birthday, and we don't see enough of one another," Lo says as we trail behind Caz, Theo, and Saint. Galen closes the door and follows us.

"The guys are in the basement playing pool and video games," I call out, pointing at the door to the right of the stairs. "They have beers and a weed stash down there, so knock yourselves out."

Saint tracks back, grabbing Lo and slamming his lips against hers in a brief hard kiss. "Watch your back, Queenie," he says. "Especially if Ares and other members of The Bulls are here."

Lo flips him the bird before patting her thigh. "Fuck off, Saintly. I know how to protect myself."

Caz chuckles, stepping forward to kiss her. "Behave, babe."

Theo comes up next, hugging her tight before pecking her lips. "Love you. Stay safe."

Galen wraps his arm around her from behind, leaning down to kiss her cheek. "We may be out of the game, but we still have plenty of enemies in Lowell. We know you can take care of yourself, but a warning is not out of order." She yelps as he cracks a loud slap against her ass. "Later, angel." He kisses the corner of her mouth before they all disappear down the stairs to the basement.

"Overprotective assholes," Lo mutters as I steer her into the living room where the party is raging.

Bree outdid herself with the party planning this time. She did most of it while I was incarcerated in Luminary HQ, insisting on keeping it a surprise because it's my nineteenth birthday.

"Would you recommend marriage then?" I ask with a wide grin.

"Actually, I would." A glorious smile spreads over Lo's mouth. "I would highly recommend it. Tell anyone who says you're too young to go fuck themselves." Tilting her head to one side, she studies my face. "Is that something you guys are considering?"

I wish I could tell her, but I can't. "Not right now." I steer her away from the boisterous crowd in the living room toward the kitchen. "But it's definitely in the cards for later."

"So, things are good with you?" She leans against the counter as I open the refrigerator door.

"Yep. Name your poison."

"I'll take a beer," she replies, glancing left and straightening up.

I grab two beers, pop the caps, and hand one to her.

"I know Ares is a giant ass, but holy fuck is he hot." She stares in the corner where Ares is deep in conversation with Rocky Road and Shoulders.

"Says the woman married to four of the hottest guys on the planet." I clink my bottle against hers. "You did good, Lo."

"I did, didn't I?" She flashes me a grin. "But don't change the subject. What's the tea with your stepbrother?"

"Same ole, same ole."

"Has he said anything about payback yet?" she asks, lowering her voice. I've had a couple of calls with Lo since we moved to LU, so she's up to speed on everything but the Luminary bullshit.

"No, but Bree has a guy working on digging up some shit, and we're expecting a report this week."

"I mentioned it to Theo. If you want him to investigate it, you only have to say the word." Theo is an IT genius with some mad hacking skills. I was planning on asking him to help, but I think it's best to keep my friend and her husbands away from my bullshit. They only just extricated themselves from a nightmare with Saint's dad and The Sainthood. They don't deserve to get dragged into anything else.

"Thank you both. I'll let you know if we need assistance."

"There you are." Bree bounces into the kitchen, looking like she's ready to commit murder.

"What's up? Did something happen?" I ask, instantly grabbing another beer from the fridge for her.

"Toby is here, and we got into it again." Bree explained this week how she is promised in marriage to Tobias Salinger. Apparently, he makes Ares look like a puppy dog. The wedding can't take place until she graduates, so we have four years to find a solution to her dilemma.

Fucking luminaries and their arranged marriages and bullshit checks and balances.

"Tell me who I need to gut, and I'm there." Lo lifts the side of her short black dress, revealing the dagger strapped to her thigh. She is legendary in these parts for her blade skills and sharpshooting expertise.

"Girl, don't fucking tempt me." Bree snatches the beer from my hand. "If murder was an option, I'd have gutted that prick the second he came out of the womb."

Lo bursts out laughing as Bree grins, bringing the bottle to her lips. We all knock back a few mouthfuls, and then I introduce the girls to one another. We are chatting and drinking when Baz appears in the doorway. This is the first time I have seen him since my initiation. He jerks his head toward the hallway, and I excuse myself for a few moments.

I hold my head up as I walk out to meet him, projecting confidence even if I'm a teeny bit nervous. It's more than a little weird after what went down, but it was just sex. It's only awkward if I make it so. "Hey, what's up?" I say when I stop in front of him.

His lips fight a twitch. "Not my dick this time, you'll be glad to know."

"Oh my god." A giggle bursts from my mouth. "I can't believe you went there." I'm glad he did though because it breaks any possibility of tension.

"I'm not known for my filter." He waggles his brows and tilts his head to the side in a gesture reminiscent of his brother. "I just wanted to check in and make sure everything is cool."

I know Jase doesn't get along with his brother, but I don't understand why. I actually really like Baz. "I appreciate that, and everything is fine."

"You and my brother worked things out?"

"We did."

"Good. I'm glad. I know he thinks the world of you. Now that I've met you, I can see why."

His grin is flirtatious in the extreme, but I've heard he's a major player and the biggest charmer on campus. "That legendary charm won't work on me, buddy." I playfully thump him in the chest. "Besides, you already got in my panties."

Now it's his turn to burst out laughing. "Not how I wanted our first meeting to go, but I'm not complaining." He winks and dazzles me with a blinding smile. I can see why girls go gaga for him. He's every bit as gorgeous as his younger brother.

Shaking that thought from my mind before it goes someplace it shouldn't, I fasten a solemn look on my face. "Thank you for what you did."

He arches a brow, and his grin expands.

I burst into laughter again, realizing how it sounds. Perhaps I should take it easy on the beers. "Wow, that sounds so wrong even if I mean it."

"I hear ya. It's a fucked-up world we inhabit."

"For sure, and I have only barely scratched the surface of my knowledge."

"Be careful," he says, turning all serious. "I know what you and Jase are planning, and I approve, but they can't find out."

"We know."

He leans in and plants a soft kiss on my cheek. "Watch your back." Pulling back, he salutes me before dazzling me with another megawatt smile, and then he's slipping out the door before anyone even realizes he was here.

Blinking my eyes to clear my head, I return to the kitchen and my two friends.

We shoot the breeze for a while before Bree leaves to deal with some unruly dicks causing a commotion in the living room.

"Could we go somewhere quiet to talk?" Lo asks, and I nod, lifting a shoulder.

"Follow me."

"Hey, beautiful," Ares says, licking his lips as he winks at Lo when we approach. "Didn't know you were back in town."

She coolly flips him off. "None of your business, Haynes."

"You're Harlow Westbrook," Shoulders says, glaring at her with unconcealed hatred.

It's well known around these parts that The Sainthood and The Bulls used to be allies until the former turned on the latter and set them up. It's what led to Ruben's arrest and imprisonment. It almost brought The Bulls to their knees the same way The Arrows, another local gang, were eliminated. Lo and her guys were in the thick of it, but I don't know exactly what went down because I didn't ask, and she didn't volunteer the information.

I have zero interest in gang warfare, especially now I know they mean next to nothing when compared to the power and control The Luminaries exert. I knew there was a chance Ares and some of his Bulls friends would be here, so I warned Lo and the guys in advance. They weren't concerned, and I'm glad it didn't stop them from coming.

Lo pushes all up in Shoulders' face, undeterred he's a couple of inches taller than her. "And you're two seconds away from having your dick separated from your body." He stiffens and panic races across his face. I look down, smothering a laugh when I see Lo has her dagger pressed against his crotch. "We didn't come here to cause trouble. We're out, and we've no beef with you unless you start it."

"He won't." Ares grabs Shoulders by the scruff of the neck and shoves him. "You're an idiot. Apologize or fuck off."

I arch a brow, surprised. Then again, I don't know why I am. I have seen Ares be civil and act almost normal toward other women.

It's just me he seems to have an issue with.

"I'm not apologizing," he says, straightening up. "But I won't cause trouble at the princess's party."

Ares shakes his head before grabbing his friend and hauling his ass toward the front door. Rocky doesn't move. He just drinks his beer as he slowly eyes me up and down.

"You're a disrespectful perv," Lo says, pointing her dagger at his face. "I'll poke your eyes out if you don't stop eye fucking my friend."

"Fuck this shit." Rocky drains his beer, slamming it down on the table behind him. "I'm out too."

Lo and I grin as he storms off, and I loop my arm through

my friend's. "Who needs security when Harlow Westbrook is in the building?!"

We push past couples making out in the hallway as I lead my friend to the study, grateful to leave the noise behind when we step inside. I sit in one of the high-backed navy velvet chairs in front of the open fireplace, and Lo takes the one beside me.

"I have a message for you from D," Lo says after a few seconds. "I didn't want to risk saying anything on the phone."

I frown. "D?"

"My trainer friend."

"Ah, yes, the hot older guy."

An instant grin appears. "He is definitely hot."

I take a swig from my beer. "What's the story with you two anyway?"

"My dad hired him to train me when I was a kid. After the kidnapping. We worked together for years. He taught me everything I know, but I owe him so much more. He's a good friend."

"Is that all he was because the look he had on his face when he talked about you was something else."

Her features soften. "We were a thing for like five seconds the summer before senior year."

"Wow." I tap my bottle against hers. "You already know how much I admire you, but you've just gone even higher in my esteem. Fucking an older man while still in high school is pretty impressive."

"I'm glad we didn't lose our friendship. He means so much to me."

"And the guys are okay with it?"

She cracks up laughing, wiping tears from her eyes. "I'm not sure *okay* is the word I'd use. I mean, Theo and Caz are fine with it, and Galen tolerates him, but Saint." She shakes her head, still grinning. "Let's just say Saint calls D granddad and D calls Saint punk and leave it at that."

Now I'm laughing too. "Man, I would love to be a fly on the wall for that!"

"Fun times for sure." She waggles her brows before her expression turns serious. She sits up straighter. "D said Sebastien was warned off training you. He says he's sorry, but you'll have to find someone yourself." She reaches out, taking my hand. "What is going on, Ashley? Are you in some kind of danger?"

Fucking asshole luminaries know goddamned everything. "I wish I could tell you, but I can't. I'm not in danger, per se, just that certain stuff has come to light recently, and it's changed a lot of things for me."

She nods in understanding. "I get that." She squeezes my hand. "Just know I am here for you. If there is anything we can do, you only have to ask."

"Thanks, Lo. I appreciate it." I reach out and hug her because I truly do appreciate her support.

"Well, isn't this cozy?" Ares says. The door slams against the wall as he bursts into the room. "Though I'm a little disappointed you weren't getting it on," he adds, grabbing his crotch like the Neanderthal he is. "Some live girl-on-girl action would be just what the doc ordered."

"Get out, perv." I jab my finger at the door. "This is a private conversation, and you're not invited."

The asshole holds his hands up as he strolls toward us. His T-shirt lifts with the motion, showcasing a tantalizing strip of toned, tan skin, defined V-indents at his hips, and a trail of dark hair creeping down under the waistband of his low-slung ripped black jeans. Tipping my chin up with one finger, he closes my mouth shut. "You were drooling."

I slap his hand away and growl. "Fuck off."

Leaning down, he puts his face all up in mine. "It's okay, little slutser. I know you can't help it. You're only human."

"Your ego is so big it lives on its own planet." I shove his shoulders. "Get out of my personal space and get lost."

Ignoring me, Ares perches his butt on the arm of my chair and turns to face Lo. "I was hoping you could tell me about The Sainthood."

Lo is cool as a cucumber as she stares at my stepbrother. "Why would I do that?"

"You're out now, but I know you have intel. I'm just looking for a list of names of current members." He shrugs and cocks his head to one side, and I just know he's fixing her with one of his sexy looks. The kind of look that renders most women to mush. But Lo is not most women, and all it's liable to achieve is a punch to the nuts.

"Sorry, can't help you. The last thing I want is to get dragged into more Sainthood shit." Lo levels him with a look, clearly telling him to drop it.

But Ares is like a dog with a bone, and he's a crazy motherfucker who just can't help himself. "Don't be a cunt. I'm only looking for a favor." He puts his face all up in hers, which means his butt is all up in mine. Like, his ass is *literally* in my face, so I'm struggling to pay attention to the conversation with such a tempting distraction right in front of me.

"And like I said. I want nothing to do with whatever you have planned. Now, back off, buddy, or I'll make you."

Of course, Ares still doesn't back down. "I know you can get what I need. If you don't volunteer the information, I will fucking force it from you through any means necessary." He grabs a handful of her dress, yanking her face up to his, and I instantly see red. "You feel me, bitch?"

If I wasn't so mad at how rude he's being, I would actually enjoy seeing Ares make an ass of himself. He must be desperate to threaten the one woman everyone knows you shouldn't threaten. Maybe it's a Bulls trait. Or Ares and Shoulders are both missing an intelligence gene.

No matter what is driving it, he doesn't get to speak to my friend—a guest in my house— like this. Lo and I share a quick look and act simultaneously. I bite down hard on one ass cheek, through the denim of Ares's jeans, as Lo grabs his balls from the front and twists.

Ares yelps in pain.

Am I a sick bitch for deriving pleasure from this?

Lo and I exchange another look, and I dig my teeth in harder as she tightens her grip on his balls.

And that's how Saint, Galen, Theo, Caz, Chad, and Jase find us when they charge into the room. As if they are psychic and knew what was going down.

"What the actual fuck?" Jase asks as Saint storms across the room, grabbing hold of Ares without asking any questions. He yanks him to his feet and headbutts him.

Lo rolls her eyes, muttering stuff under her breath.

"We had it handled," I say as Jase comes up to me.

Ares lets out a roar before lunging at Saint, and they go down, legs and arms flailing.

Idiot boys.

"Do I want to know why you were biting his ass?" Jase sounds mildly amused. His arms wind around me as Chad comes up on the other side of me. He keeps his distance, like he has been doing all week, and my heart aches for him.

"He was rude to Lo, and his ass was right there in my face. I didn't think. I just acted."

"Girl, we make a good team." Lo reaches around Theo and Caz who are holding on to her protectively, and we high-five like we're back in sixth grade.

"I've been spitting in his breakfast all week," Chad says out of the blue. I crack up, and Jase's chest rumbles with laughter behind me. "Hopefully, he'll get whatever bug I had, and when he's lying in bed, barely able to breathe, I'm going to beat the absolute shit out of him for all the crap he's been pulling," he adds, watching Saint, Galen, and Ares throw punches and jabs with a massive smile on his face.

Mom says the virus he was injected with actually *is* infectious, and it's not known how it might spread, so we weren't actually lying when we told Chad that even if we didn't know it at the time. It's quite possible he may have infected Ares. And Ares is screwing Julia, so she may get infected too.

Wouldn't that be karma? I can only hope.

I know it's killing Chad not getting involved, but Monday is his first day back on the team, and he won't risk turning up injured, no matter how much he hates Ares Haynes and would love to join the fight.

"Oh shit," Jase says, holding me closer as a bunch of guys rush through the door, yelling and pumping their fists in the air. I'm guessing someone shouted "fight," and that's like waving a red flag in front of a bull.

"Men are such idiots," Lo says, shaking her head as we watch it become a general melee with about ten guys swinging punches at everyone just for the hell of it.

"There's way too much testosterone in here," I agree.

One thing's for sure. I won't ever forget my nineteenth birthday party.

Chapter Forty-One

Ares

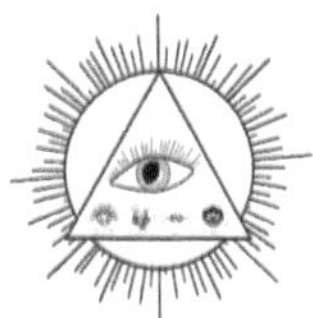

"We had a deal," I say through gritted teeth, itching to knock Marwan's teeth down his throat. If he didn't have a full table of assholes around him, I might be tempted. I am beyond done dealing with gang bullshit. I'm sick of it and beginning to think it's been the biggest waste of my time.

"I haven't reneged on it." Marwan wipes wing sauce off one cheek while licking his fingers. "You'll get your meeting with Ruben when you deliver Lowell U to me."

"That wasn't what we agreed," I argue.

"Plans change." He stands, wiping his grubby fingers on a napkin before tossing it down on the table. He thrusts a greasy finger into my chest. "I'm running out of patience, Haynes. We let you join on a part-time basis due to your work commitments, but I'm failing to see what The Bulls are getting from your membership. You promised you would deliver the campus, and you haven't come through with it yet."

Removing his finger, I glare at him. I'm done being pushed around by this fat fucker. "I told you I needed time."

"You've had almost three weeks!"

"Are you insane?" I snap. "That's not long enough. I am making progress, and in another two or three weeks, I will have the intel we need to take The Sainthood down. We can coordinate a planned attack and take them out in one fell swoop. They won't know what's hit them."

"I'm all out of patience, and we have a new plan."

"What plan?" I rub a tense spot between my brows. I have the motherfucker of all hangovers, bruised ribs, and a beat-up face after the party last night. It became a free-for-all, so I didn't even get to do much damage to those Sainthood assholes, but at least it felt good to beat the shit out of a few frat boys.

"We're setting up an ambush. A decoy deal to bring them to the surface. Then we'll bury them for good." Marwan clamps a firm hand down on my shoulder. "Don't worry. You'll get a chance to redeem yourself. We'll expect you at the fight, and you'll handle the transition on campus. Manage that and you'll get your meeting."

This is such bullshit, but there's no point protesting. "When is it going down?"

"You'll receive a message soon."

I stomp off, infuriated that I'm at a disadvantage. If that Westbrook bitch had just played ball, I could have the upper hand right now. I know she knows everything. She could have gotten me the intel. I considered using Ash to do my dirty work. But writing off her IOU for something so mundane isn't appealing. I felt sure I could charm Harlow fucking Westbrook into giving up the goods, but wouldn't you know she is the one woman on the planet immune to my charms.

Getting on my bike, I drive a few miles down the coast and park at the far side of the docks. I walk along the promenade, sitting on a bench that faces the ocean. My actions last night weren't smart, and I'm losing my cool. The longer this goes on, the more desperate I become. Burying my head in my hands, I will the burning pain in my chest to go away. But I know it won't. Not unless...

My cell pings, dragging me out of my inner depression. It's not my normal cell. It's the burner one my tech friend scored for me. I swipe the screen and answer immediately. "You better have answers for me," I grunt into the phone.

"Well, some asshole got up on the wrong side of bed today," Xavier says. "Let's try this again."

He hangs up, and I briefly consider throwing my phone over the railing into the ocean. Silently counting to ten, I redial his number when I'm a little less manic. "Hey," I say in my least grumpy voice when the line connects.

"Hey?" Xavier scoffs. "That's all you've got for me? A hey? Pathetic, dude."

"Bro, seriously, can we not do this today?" Xavier is a crazy fucker, and normally I buzz off him, but I'm feeling low right now, and I'm not in the mood to fuck around.

He drops it, clearly picking up on my tone. "Talk to me. What's going on?"

"I'm not making any progress, and Mom has been getting on my case. She wants to give up. She thinks it's too late. It's like she's all loved up now, and it doesn't matter anymore."

"I'm sure that's not true, man. It's a stressful situation for both of you, and it's been years."

"I won't give up. I can't."

"I know, and it's why I have been helping you."

"I appreciate it. I know you're some big hotshot now with your own company and a fuck ton of VIP clients who actually pay you, and I'm just the pain in your ass who expects your expertise for free."

"No, that would be Sawyer."

I convulse with laughter, and it's the first time in days my mood has lightened. "How is your new husband?"

"Fine as fuck and horny as fuck. I hope the honeymoon period never ends."

"Good for you, man. I'm glad you're happy."

"What about you? Has your spectacular new stepsister caved to your charms yet?"

"She's halfway there. I'm working on it."

"Put her on a call with me. I'll tell her you're one of the good guys."

I crack up laughing again. "Yeah, she'd never believe that, and I've given her no reason to."

"Boo. I hope you're not being mean to sweet Ashley."

"May I remind you you've never even met her. Sweet is not the word I'd use to describe Ashley Shaw."

"Oh, that reminds me. Did you know Ashley is Sydney's cousin?"

"Sydney? As in Sawyer's ex-wife?"

"Fake wife, and the marriage was annulled, but yes, that's her. Her dad and Douglas Shaw are brothers. They aren't close. Like at all, but they're still blood."

"No, I didn't know that. Wonder if dollface even does?" I muse.

"You have nicknames for one another already. I love it!" I can almost see him doing cartwheels in his living room. "What does she call you?"

"Asshole. Psycho. Crazy motherfucker. Perv. Weirdo. Or any number of similar names. She's got quite a colorful vocab. It's all so romantic," I tag on the end in my best dreamy voice.

"You are an asshole but the lovable kind."

I roll my eyes. "Tell me you have something for me."

"I wish I could, man, but it's not good news."

"Seems to be that kind of weekend. Lay it on me."

"So, you were right. The dudes in the photo from the bar are Tobias Salinger, Balthazar Stewart, Jason Stewart, and Knight Carter. All rich kids, squeaky clean, no records, which makes them suspicious as fuck in my mind. I dug as deep as I could, and nothing, nada. It's like everything that's to be found has been planted there. I stopped looking because I don't want to draw the wrong kind of attention. Which leads me nicely on to that thumb drive." There's a muffled sound in the background.

"Hunt, I'm on a call," Xavier says. "Just give me five minutes."

I lean back and close my eyes as there's more hushed talking down the line.

"Shit, sorry about that. Ares, are you still there?"

"I'm here."

"Sawyer is insatiable. He has sex on the brain nonstop."

"My blue balls don't thank you for that admission."

"I so want to know what that's about on our next call, but I'm under pressure now. I don't like keeping my man waiting."

"I was going to say you're pussy-whipped until I realized the error of my ways. You're dick-obsessed, dude."

"I am, but stop distracting me with cock talk. That thumb drive brought me a whole world of trouble, dude."

I sit up straighter. "In what way?"

"Your guy got a nice clean shot of the man outside the toy warehouse. One minute after I uploaded it to the facial imaging software I use, my whole system got shut down. Like I mean everything. Hunt went ballistic. In a way he rarely does. Had to blow him and let him top to calm him down."

"What does it mean?"

"It means I got a call from a guy I've met a few times telling me in no uncertain terms to drop that line of inquiry."

"What guy?"

"Sorry, man. Can't say." I know Xavier works with a lot of government bodies as well as mercenary groups. "But I can tell you this. It's got nothing to do with Lilianna. And nothing to do with Ashley either. Don't bother wasting your time pursuing that angle."

"And Stewart, Carter, and Salinger?"

"There's something there, man. I feel it in my bones. I'm not sure what, but there's definitely something there."

"That's what my gut is telling me too. The trail didn't lead to Baldwin and Stewart for no reason."

"I'll see what I can find on Samite. Do a little more digging, but I need to be extra covert, and that'll take time."

"I appreciate you, man. Go ride your husband's dick."

"Hang in there, dude."

He hangs up, and I return to my bike and head home.

I'm lying naked on my bed, stroking my ever-hard cock as I scroll through the camera feeds from the past few days. For some reason yet to be explained, Doug shut down the cameras I installed on his behalf, citing guilt over Ash's privacy, but I smell a rat. Thank fuck for my stalker tendencies and the cameras I planted in the master bedroom and bathroom, or I'd go insane.

"What are you up to, Julia?" I mutter to myself a couple of minutes later as I watch her sneak into Ashley's room. I only gave the bitch a house key so she'd give me one to her place. The fact it pissed Ash off was an added bonus. I needed access to the house next door so I could put a camera in Stewart's room and bathroom.

It's already paid dividends.

I came so hard watching him nail Ashley in the ass I almost gave myself a coronary. I'm pissed the audio isn't working, but if it came down to a choice, I'd much rather have the visual. I have already jerked off three times watching it. Imagining it was my cock driving into her puckered hole.

Continuing to stroke my cock, I zoom in on the whiny whore searching Ash's bedroom the day after my stepsister relocated to her mom's new house and the jock mysteriously disappeared. Pamela fed me a pack of lies when I asked where Ashley was, but I pretended to buy it.

I refocus on the screen. It doesn't look like Julia has taken anything or left anything, but it's hard to tell when her back is to the camera so much. I had planned to plant another camera in the bathroom and move the one in the bedroom, but Chad returned before I had the chance, and Pamela was in and out too often playing Florence Nightingale for me to risk it.

Switching out of that file, I open my stepsister-porn folder and pump my cock harder. I'm gathering quite the collection, thanks to my sister's insatiable need to be fucked six ways from Sunday. Chad is in temporary retirement, thanks to his infectious illness, but Jase is taking one for the team. It's interesting how Ashley returned seemingly all loved up with an engaged man when she was apparently unpacking and babysitting.

The whole setup in this gated community is shady as fuck, and I intend to get to the bottom of it.

I pull up the video of Ash riding Chad from a couple of weeks ago. It's my new favorite—because it's reverse cowgirl and I have a full-frontal view of her banging body. Her fuckable tits are bouncing all over the place, and she's moaning and writhing as she slams up and down on his cock while he fingers her clit. I'm close to coming when I hear Ash call up the stairs.

"Chad. Are you home?"

Grinning to myself, I shut down my laptop and climb off my bed, palming my dick slowly to keep my load in reserve. I wait until I hear her pass my room before I come out. The door to Chad's room is open, so I stroll inside, whistling as I pump my erection.

Ashley turns and stares at me. "You really are a crazy bastard." She tries not to look at my dick, but she can't help herself. My slutty little sister is still in denial. But others have seen what she refuses to see. It's the only reason Julia made a play for me. And the only reason I'm entertaining it is because I know it's the fastest way to have Ashley where I want her—begging for my cock and writhing underneath me.

When I finally get her in my bed, I'm chaining her up and fucking her relentlessly for days. Maybe then I will quench this voracious thirst I have for her. Until then, I'll continue to push my agenda. "Get on your knees, and open your mouth."

The slut laughs. "Nice try, but no."

"Fine." I grab her elbow before she can walk past me. "We'll consider our debt paid when you swallow my cock."

She stares at me like I've grown wings or some shit. "Do you seriously think I'm that dumb? I'm not going to blow you so you don't blackmail me over fingering me in the shower. You'll just blackmail me over blowing you then, and the cycle of abuse will never end."

I yank her into my body, grabbing her hand and wrapping it around my straining shaft. "Delude yourself all you want, but we both know you wanted it." Her eyes swirl with heat, and her fingers curl around my dick of their own volition. "Like we both know you want me to push you to the floor, straddle your shoulders, and shove my cock so deep in your mouth you gag on it."

"I think you are clinically insane," she says, removing her fingers from my dick. "Like seriously a bona fide nut job. You think I want you?" She huffs out a laugh. "I loathe you, Ares. I lie in my bed at night dreaming up creative ways to murder you."

"Hate fucking is the best sex ever. When you give in to me, you'll see." I start pumping my cock harder, unable to hold back my release any longer.

"You have the nerve to call me delusional." She shakes her head, attempting to walk past me again, but I'm faster.

Racing ahead, I bolt the door and flatten my back against it, trapping her in here with me.

"Open the door, Ares," she says through gritted teeth.

"I will." I flash her a devilish grin. "After I come."

"Let me out. I don't want to see this."

"Course you do, dollface." I jerk my dick harder, and her eyes gravitate to it like a moth to a flame. "I'm imagining you on your knees," I tell her, working my cock harder. "You're naked, cupping your big tits and tugging on your nipples before you crawl to me, desperate to have my cock in your mouth." My balls tighten, and familiar tingles shoot up my spine. "You take me between your fuckable lips, and your tongue glides between the rungs of my ladder, your pussy leaking the evidence of your arousal as you moan around my dick."

Her pupils are dilated, and she's discreetly clenching her thighs together.

"Say the word, and I'll come all over your face." Pumping my dick faster, I walk right up to her, licking my lips as I wonder what it would be like to taste her mouth. Her cheeks are flushed, her gaze lowered as she watches me jerk myself off. "Your loss, dollface," I say as I fall over the edge. I call out her name as my dick explodes, spraying her shirt and the floor with my cum.

Walking over to the bed, I spurt some semen over the jock's pillow as I stroke my shaft to completion.

Ash stares at me in shock, and I wink, holding my dick at the base and wiggling it at her. "Want to come clean me off?" I waggle my brows and lick my lips, my loud laughter following her out of the room as she yanks the door open and darts out into the hallway.

Chapter Forty-Two

Ashley

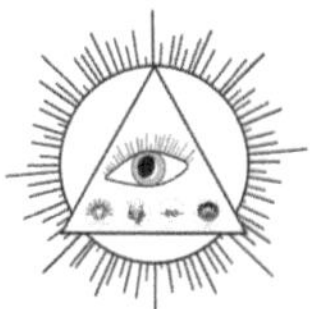

We settle into a new routine in the week ahead. I get up early and go walking or running with Bree before school. Jase and I are sneaking around campus, fucking any chance we get in an attempt to get me pregnant now my IUD is gone. I got that removed the day after I returned from Luminary HQ.

That was a massive covert op.

Jase insisted on coming with me, so we dressed in disguise and changed vehicles three times, ensuring all had dodgy untraceable plates and blacked-out windows, before visiting the guy Bree found in an unregistered office building down by the docks in Grenlow.

Such subterfuge. All to get my IUD taken out!

It was a taste of what my life has become. I swear I feel eyeballs on me all over campus, and I'm super spooked. The Luminaries are watching everything, and our sneaking around has to be even more discreet. Jase has been scouting the campus for camera-free zones and dragging me into storage closets, supply offices, and staff bathrooms to fuck my brains out. At home, Chad is relegated to watching with his cock in hand, from a distance, jerking off as he watches his best friend nail me in all manner of positions.

It's a miracle I can walk straight.

I administered the final vaccine to Chad today, so only one more week before we can resume sexual activities. I know he's dying for it because he's conditioned to daily sex and screaming for my pussy.

So, life is good even if I'm on edge a lot of the time.

Ares still hasn't called in his IOU, and I'm on pins and needles every time he steps into the room when I'm with my boyfriend.

It's Friday evening, and I'm giving my overworked pussy a break while the guys are at practice. They have an away game tomorrow, and I have a reprieve from party planning, so I plan to catch up on schoolwork and get ahead on a few assignments. Halloween is next week, and we're hosting a massive event. We have even rented a function room on campus to hold the party so we can go all out with the decorating. I'm meeting Bree tomorrow to go shopping for costumes, and it's going to be fun.

The doorbell chimes, and I set my pen and notepad down, sliding off the stool and going to the front door. I check the peephole, opening the door when I see my friend. "Hey, is something up?" I ask, stepping aside to let Bree enter.

"I finally got a report on Ares." She holds up a bottle of wine. "Thought we could have a glass and dissect it."

"You're such a bad influence," I say, closing the door behind her. "I was working on an assignment."

"It's the weekend. You deserve a drink after working so hard this week." She pins me with a grin as she plonks the wine down on the counter. "All that fucking must be exhausting." She snickers, and I laugh as I retrieve two wineglasses while she unscrews the cap.

"Jase had better not be sharing specifics, or I'll kick him in the balls." I grab a bag of chips and some salsa from the cupboard as Bree pours the wine.

"Ha!" Bree snorts out a laugh. "You are in no position to judge." She narrows her eyes at me while fighting a grin. "Not after the front-row seat I had driving you guys home from HQ."

"I should probably apologize for that." I dump the chips in a bowl and pop the lid on the salsa.

"But you won't." Bree finishes pouring the wine and puts the bottle in the refrigerator.

"Nope." I pop a chip in my mouth and chew. "Hottest sex of my life and there isn't a damn thing I regret."

"You're a shameless hussy." She grabs the wineglasses while I take the bowl and salsa.

We walk toward the living room side by side.

"Says the woman caught riding a cock and eating a pussy, at the same time, naked on the couch of the house she shares with her brother and my bitch of a cousin." I try to avoid referring to Julia as Jase's fiancée 'cause I see red every time I think about their engagement.

"I owed PC2 payback, and I love grossing Julia out. I got the dude to come all over her favorite pink cushions. Then I rubbed his jizz into the material until you couldn't really see it. She was sitting on them for days before she sniffed one and realized why it smelled funky. She threw an epic hissy fit. Best entertainment I've had since the guy fight at your party."

"Oh my god, I wish I'd been there to see that. She is so anal about stuff." Placing the goodies down on the coffee table, I kick off my sneakers and bounce on the couch.

"Tell me about it. She's definitely borderline OCD."

I settle into one corner, sitting cross-legged while Bree settles into the other corner in a similar position. She hands me my wineglass, and we clink them together. "Cheers, babe." We take a healthy mouthful before getting down to business. "What did your contact find out about Ares? I'm telling you there is definitely something going down with him. He's been in a foul mood all week, though I haven't seen much of him. He disappears after dinner and rarely comes home before midnight. Has he been hanging at your place?"

She shakes her head. "Nope." She sips from her drink, studying me. "You know I won't give a fuck if you like him. He's a dick, but he's sexy as hell. I'd bounce on his cock if I got the chance and you weren't into him."

"I'm not into him."

"Babe, the sexual chemistry between you two is enough to fuel a small planet."

"My life is already complicated enough without adding him to the mix. Jase might be cool with it, but Chad would never go for it. Nothing is worth losing Chad over, and I'm not entertaining notions of adding Ares Haynes to my little harem. In case you've forgotten, he's blackmailing me."

"That's why I'm here." She hands me a thumb drive. "Everything my guy found is on that."

I slip it into the pocket of my hoodie to check it out later. "Give me the CliffsNotes version."

"He's a ghost. Hera too."

I dribble wine down my chin as I almost choke. "What does that mean?" I wipe my chin with the sleeve of my hoodie.

"It means there is no record of Ares Haynes or Hera Haynes beyond the last two and a half years. Hera was in Cali the whole time, but Ares was in Boston for eight months before moving here with his mom."

"So, there is nothing to be found before that?"

"Nope. There is no trace. Like they didn't exist."

"What about birth certs and social security numbers and other official records?"

"All issued two and a half years ago. Births are listed as US, but the parentage is fake."

"That isn't possible."

"Their history has been wiped for sure."

I put my wineglass down on the end table and wrap my arms around my knees. "What are they trying to hide? Are they luminaries?" I ask the obvious question.

She shakes her head. "They can't be, or I'd know about it."

"Ares mentioned living in Europe. Isn't it possible he's part of some European Luminary family?"

"If he was, there would be records." She puts her glass down and scoots up closer. "Babe, the only way this could happen is if someone within Luminary circles wiped the records. It's the only explanation that stacks up. Though it's stupid because it makes it so obvious. It's why we all have fake records so it's not as suspicious if someone comes looking."

"Why would someone within the Luminary world do this then?" I bite down on my lip. "Could this have happened when Hera started dating my dad? Would her background have been checked? If they found something disagreeable or unsavory, would they have done this to cover it up?"

Her nose scrunches up. "That's actually a clever theory."

I swat her with a cushion. "Don't insult me. I did graduate high school with a four point oh GPA. I'm not some bimbo."

"I didn't mean it like that. I know you've got smarts. That theory could totally explain why there is no fake profile. They aren't Luminary, but Hera is married to an expert, so they couldn't have anything shady on her profile, but they don't care enough to create a false history."

I shake my head as another thought occurs to me. "It couldn't be that. Dad didn't even know Hera two-and-a-half-years ago."

"Oh, good point." Bree purses her lips. "There's got to be another reason."

"What did they do that warranted such drastic action?" I ponder out loud, grabbing my wineglass again.

"I don't know, but we'll find out."

"I'm glad I didn't ask Theo to go snooping now," I admit in between sips of wine.

"Definitely don't involve outsiders. I told you our experts are the best, and each family has their own contacts. My guy is a fucking genius, and he's discreet. Whatever you need to know, he'll find it, or it's not there to be found."

"Keep digging. I want to know what they're hiding."

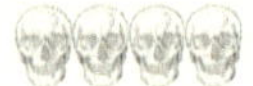

I return to the house Saturday afternoon, after shopping up a storm with Bree, to discover my uncle waiting in the kitchen for me. It's really starting to bug me how he and Julia just let themselves in all the time. He might own the house, but it's my home, and I am entitled to my privacy. God knows I have fuck-all privacy as soon as I step foot outside. I know they have people watching me because I sense eyeballs on me anytime I leave the house. It's really starting to aggravate me.

"Uncle, to what do I owe this pleasure?" I ask, working hard to keep my tone pleasant. Mom's "pick your battles" mantra is one I'm trying to live by.

"We need to talk about your family responsibilities. It's time you started pulling your weight."

I dump my bags by the door and walk to the coffee pot.

"I'll have a refill." He thrusts his mug at me. I'm tempted to crack it over his skull, but I simply smile and do as he asks.

When we are both sitting on stools at the counter with steaming hot mugs of coffee, he begins filling me in. "While at university, siblings and children from Luminary families are expected to excel. You represent our Sloth Luminary on this campus, and your attitude and behavior must reflect the highest levels of respect and responsibility. Maintain high grades, and set the best example for your student peers."

"Understood and agreed." That I can do.

"However, Luminary students are also required to attend to tasks, missions, and projects as assigned, and they hold responsibility centered around the sins under their family's control."

"They mentioned that at HQ, but it wasn't elaborated on," I explain.

"You will learn more in time. For now, you need to understand what that responsibility means in terms of our family and the role you will play."

"So, what is it you are asking of me?" I inquire, clutching both hands around my mug.

"Luminary family members become the sins and vices they control in order to lure others out."

Perhaps that explains why Julia is such a lazy bitch.

"Eradicating the weaker elements in our society, those who cannot resist falling prey to sins and vices, is the core work we do. There are various ways to draw these weaklings to the surface, and it differs from family to family."

"How do Luminary families stop themselves from falling prey to temptation if they are having to succumb to it themselves?"

"That is an intelligent question and one we contemplated for years before reaching a solution which kept us all pure. In order to stop us from becoming corruptible, every two years we undergo a period of virtuosity to curb our baser desires, control our human nature, and ensure we remain Luminary and above reproach."

Sounds like the biggest load of bologna to me, but I don't voice that sentiment.

"You will learn more about this during your classes."

"Okay, so what about now? What do I need to do?"

"We are the only family with one sin under our control because laziness and apathy are the biggest threats to our modern society along with pride, but that is for Salinger to address. Other families have direct vices they control as part of their remit, like drugs, guns, the underworld, sex, and other addictions, but our responsibility speaks to the core of human nature, which is demonstrated in all manner of ways. As the biggest problem to tackle, we focus on characteristic traits and the people themselves."

He pauses to drink his coffee, watching me as his words sink in.

"Lazy, unambitious, unfocused people will not be tolerated as they will drag society down," he continues. "Those who are indifferent to duties and obligations. Those who give in to boredom, inertia, apathy. God gave us talents to be used. Not using gifts bestowed on you by our maker is a heinous sin. Younger generations have an entitled attitude that must be eradicated if we are to maintain control of the world. Though we see it in all walks of life, at all levels, which is why it is such a huge undertaking. Picking off individuals is no longer feasible, so our strategies are becoming more focused on groups of people."

"Like this virus you're creating." It takes colossal willpower not to snap at him or pin him with the full extent of my disgust.

"Exactly. It has been necessary, at certain times in our history, to instigate such situations. Only through mass eradication will we remove this blight from our world."

I am sickened at the casual way he discusses killing innocent people. These luminaries are nothing more than serial killers and psychopaths. The level of control and power they wield is incredibly disturbing because there is literally no one to stop them.

"Your role, like Julia's to a lesser extent, and other Sloth family members is to identify behaviors in others and compile watch lists. Our teams handle the rest."

"So, I'm like a spy?"

He bobs his head. "Of sorts."

This is terrifying. If the unsuspecting public knew this was going on, it would create mass panic and global unrest. These people are playing at being gods and it's so wrong. What gives them the right to stand in moral judgment over other humans? The original luminaries may have had noble motives and naïve goals, but it's abundantly clear this current generation does not. They are high on power and greed and feeding the monster, not curbing its appetite.

My uncle's voice drones on, snapping me out of my head. "In order to do this, you need to immerse yourself in your surroundings. Get involved in everything on campus and socialize. Get to know as many students as possible. It is why the Sloth heir is often referred to as the party heir or the people heir."

I am beginning to understand why Julia is not home that often and why I see her with different groups around campus. She's already gained a reputation for attending sorority and frat parties. But she's not liked. People let her in because of who she is as the only daughter of the owner of the world's largest media corporation.

"Doors are opened for Julia because of her name," James says as if he has a hotline to my thoughts. "We cannot change your name at this juncture without drawing attention. The Shaw name will not open the same doors, but I don't believe you need it. You have a sparkling personality that naturally draws people to you, and you are well-connected. Your boyfriend is a jock, and that will open doors. You're a sociable host, and people already gravitate to your parties, so this shouldn't be too big of a transition for you." He drains his coffee and stands. "You will go out with Julia tonight to a party. She will require you to attend other functions with her. When you aren't working with her, you must attend other events and mingle."

He closes the button on his suit jacket. "Get to know everyone. Ingratiate yourself into their world and profile them. Anyone who is weak must be documented so we can investigate them and their families. You will be expected to submit your first monthly report at the end of November. Talk to your mother if you run into any issues. She is familiar with the process."

There goes all my free time.

This is such bullshit.

I walk him to the door, delighted to see the back of him.

"One final thing," he says, turning around in the doorway. "Quit fucking Jason Stewart. He is engaged, and it's unseemly for one cousin to be screwing another cousin's fiancé. It makes us look weak in front of the other houses. A marriage contract is being sought for you," he adds, and all the blood drains from my face. "We will find someone suitable for you to marry." He eyeballs me with a dark look. "Jason Stewart is not for you. You need to let him go. This is the last time I will warn you."

Chapter Forty-Three

Ashley

I'm pacing the kitchen, panicking over my uncle's words. I have lost control over every aspect of my life. James expects me to devote all my time to my studies and socializing on campus. He wants me to spy on fellow students and submit their names so he can wipe them out in some future mass pandemic. And now he thinks he can force me into marrying some asshole at a time of their choosing, pop out a few kids to continue this disgusting society, and I won't rebel?

The more I mull it over, the more I realize Chad has no place in my future. How could he? They will never permit it. And it's selfish of Jase and I to want to hold onto him.

We should cut him loose before he ends up dead.

Stabbing pains pierce me through the heart, like a thousand tiny daggers puncturing the soft organ, as that thought lands in my mind.

I love Chad, and I want to be with him, but I just don't see how.

Fuck it. I need to get pregnant and fast. It's the only way to possibly hold on to some control.

Even though I took a pregnancy test this morning, I go up to my bathroom and do another one.

A lone tear rolls down my face when the test comes back negative. How ironic I spent years on birth control to prevent pregnancy, experiencing a couple of scares before I got an IUD implanted, and now I *want* to have a baby, and I can't get knocked up. I know it's only been a couple of weeks, but I stupidly Googled it and discovered most young couples don't get pregnant for four to six months after IUD removal.

We don't have that long to wait!

The doorbell chimes again, and I pull myself together and hurry down the stairs.

"What now?" I murmur to myself when I see who is standing on my doorstep. Planting a fake smile on my face, I open the door and greet Jase's dad. "Mr. Stewart. How lovely to see you. Do come in." I go full-blown Stepford wife.

"Would you like a coffee?" I ask when we enter the kitchen.

"This is only a short visit, so no thank you."

"Okay." I spin around, leaning against the sink as I wait for him to speak. Jase and Bree's dad is a very handsome man for his age, and I see definite physical traits in both his sons. But that's where the resemblance ends. Where Jase is expressive and warm, and Baz has shown he is charismatic and capable of compassion, their father is cold and lacking emotion. It's like looking at a robot. Someone who goes through the motions without any empathy or feeling.

"I know you are trying to upskill in combat and self-defense."

Masking my surprise, I nod. I so wasn't expecting that to come out of his mouth. At least now I know it was Eric Stewart who put a kibosh to my original plan.

"I have arranged sessions for you at this gym." He hands me a card that says Fox Fitness on the back. On the front is a contact email and phone number for a Vincent Fox. "It's owned by a master attached to the Pride and Wrath family. He's an old, trusted friend. Vincent is an excellent trainer, and he will look after you."

"Thank you." I pocket the card and fold my arms. "Why are you doing this? Surely, it's my uncle's responsibility to train me?"

"Your uncle doesn't believe women need to train. I don't agree, which is why both my daughters are proficient in combat, weaponry, and self-defense."

"That still doesn't answer my question."

"I know you are friends with my daughter, and I believe you'll be a good influence on her, so I have a vested interest in your future."

Ha! So much for good judgment, and how rude to slight his daughter like that. I school my face into a neutral line, giving nothing away.

"And I made a promise to my son," he adds, straightening up. "Unlike him, I keep mine." He tips his head forward. "Good day to you, Miss Shaw."

I'm still mulling over my uncle's and Eric's words the following night as I wait for Chad to get home. I glance at the clock, frowning when I see it's almost two a.m. I know Chad meets his dealer late on Sundays, but he's usually home by now, and I'm starting to worry. Risking his wrath, I dial his cell, but it automatically goes to voicemail.

Getting out of bed, I wrap my fluffy robe around my body and head downstairs to call Jase. I'm not expecting him to answer as he was already half asleep when I left his bed a few hours ago, so I'm surprised when he picks up after a few rings.

"Baby, I can't really talk right now," he says, and I can hardly hear him over the commotion in the background.

"What's going on? Where are you? Is Chad with you?"

"Nix and Creed were in a car accident," he says in a clipped tone. "I'm at the scene. The firefighters are just cutting them out of the car now."

"Oh my god. Are they okay?"

"I don't know." Strain is clear in his voice. "Creed has regained consciousness, but Nix hasn't woken at all. They are being airlifted to the hospital as soon as the paramedics can get to them."

"Shit, that sounds bad."

"Yeah."

"Have you heard from Chad?" I ask, guessing he didn't hear that part of my question.

"No. Why? Isn't he home?" Fear is palpable behind his words, and it does nothing to reassure me.

"No and he's not answering his cell either. I'm worried."

"Let me make some calls."

"I could drive to South Lowell. We both have each other's devices on that Find my Device app."

"You don't anymore," he says, as shouting and a loud noise echo in the background. "The Lum will have deactivated that. A pleb can't have access to your location, Ash. Anyway, you need to sit tight. Do not go on a wild goose chase. I'll find him and call you back. Gotta go, baby. I'll be in touch."

The line dies. I blow air out of my mouth as I move to the coffee pot to make fresh coffee. I will need it to stay awake as I'm exhausted.

The frat party I attended last night with Julia went on for hours, and she wouldn't let me leave. I don't take orders from that bitch, but I didn't want her ratting me out to her father. Jase and I have enough of a spotlight on us as it is. So, I stayed, stumbling home at five a.m. and collapsing into bed. I got up early to get a head start on schoolwork and to spend some time with Chad before he left to go to his mother's place. He went straight to meet Deke from there, so I haven't seen him since four p.m.

While the coffee is gurgling, I look for the app on my phone. Lo and behold, Jase is right. The app is gone from my cell. I'm tempted to smash it against the wall, but then Jase won't have any way of contacting me.

I am pouring my second cup of coffee when my cell pings with a message. It's from Bree, telling me she's at the front door and to open it.

"Hey." She rubs her hands together as she brushes past me. "I came as soon as Jase called me. Any news?"

"Nothing yet, and still no sign of Chad. I am really worried."

She slings her arm around my shoulders as we enter the kitchen. "Jase will find him. Try not to worry until we know more."

Bree grabs a mug from the cupboard and pours herself a coffee as I hop up on a stool. "Do I want to know why your shirt is buttoned all wrong and your hair looks like it got dragged through a bush?" I ask when she jumps on the stool across from me.

She winks. "I was in the middle of fucking twins when Jase called. I was literally just about to come when my cell buzzed."

"Sorry I ruined your night."

She shrugs. "You didn't. I came all over twin one's cock two minutes after getting off the call."

I laugh. "Girl, your sex life is on fire." Bree is stunning and sassy and into dick and pussy, so I'm not surprised she has no trouble finding willing bed partners. She seems to spend most nights hooking up and never goes back for seconds. I might be slightly envious even if I'm deliriously happy with my two guys.

"It's not all it's cracked up to be," she cryptically says just as there's a loud thud against the door.

We get up at the same time, racing to the front door. Bree gets there first, cursing when she looks through the peephole. She swings the door open, and Ares falls into the hallway, clutching his head and groaning as he lands on the floor.

Bree darts outside at the sound of screeching tires as I drop to my knees beside my stepbrother. His black shirt is torn in several places, his jeans are filthy, all his clothes smell like smoke, and he has several cuts and abrasions all over his face, arms, and chest. "What the hell, Ares?" I lean over him as I check the rest of him for injuries. "What happened?"

"I'll get the first aid kit," Bree says, coming inside and closing the door.

"Who was that speeding off?"

Her expression darkens. "I don't know. It was dark, and I couldn't see."

"Who dropped you off?" I ask my stepbrother, reaching for him as he attempts to sit up. It must be someone sanctioned if they got through security at the gate. He winces, his face contorting in pain. I help to prop him up against the wall in the hallway while Bree goes to get some supplies. "Ares, what's going on?"

"I don't know who dropped me here," he pants, lifting his shirt and prodding his lower abs. Blood pumps from an open wound across his lower belly.

"Were you stabbed?" I ask, horrified at the state of him.

"Slashed, it's not too deep," he rasps, poking at it.

"Stop." I pull his hand away. "It could get infected. Your hands are dirty."

Ripping the remnants of his shirt, I pull it away, leaning down so I can get a good look at the injury.

"If you want to see my dick again, dollface, you only have to ask."

I shoot daggers at him. "Do not fucking joke at a time like this."

"Aw, are you worried about me, little sis?" Grabbing a handful of my hair, he pulls my face to his and kisses me. A smokey, coppery taste lingers on his lips as he devours my mouth, and I momentarily get lost in it before sense returns.

I rip my lips from his and glare at him. "Are you kidding me right now?"

"I've been wanting to do that for months."

He reaches for me again, but I slap his hands away, peering deep into his eyes. "Did you hurt your head too?"

His dark chuckle rings out in the hallway as Bree's racing footsteps get nearer.

"I don't have a concussion. I thought I might die tonight, and one of my biggest regrets was that I never kissed you."

"Did he knock his brain loose?" Bree asks, hearing the tail end of Ares's statement as she drops to her knees beside me.

"Don't ask," I murmur, taking the bowl of water, a cloth, and towel from her. "Why did you think you'd die?" I ask him, dipping the cloth in the water.

"The warehouse blew up," he says, and panic floods my body.

"What warehouse? Was this gang shit? Please tell me Chad wasn't there!"

Bree shares a look with me as I begin washing the blood, dirt, and grime from his chest.

"Chad was there," he says, and a strangled sound rips from my mouth.

Ares grabs my wrist. "He's okay, Ash. Someone pulled him out too."

"Oh god." I slap a hand over my chest, willing my pounding heart to calm down. "Do you swear it? You saw him and he's okay?"

"He's alive. I swear it. I would not lie about something like that. I hate that prick, and I wouldn't be sorry to see him dead, but he made it out." He lowers his hand to his lap, and my shoulders slump with relief.

Bree is already tapping away on her cell as she unpacks the first aid kit. She stands. "I'll be back in a few minutes. Fix him up, and I'll find out what's gone down."

"Why do you hate him? What has he ever done to you?"

"He's not one of the good guys, Ash. He's not who you think he is."

"I know him, Ares. Whatever you think he did, you're wrong."

He grinds his teeth, and his jaw pulls tight. "Whatever." He attempts a shrug, grimacing with the motion, and I push our animosity aside again. He's hurt, and he needs help. I won't withhold that.

"Where did this happen?" I ask as I drag the wet cloth over his stomach and chest. Most all his other wounds are bruises and minor cuts. I carefully clean the knife wound, but he's right. It's not too deep. Still, it will need stitches. I rummage through the first aid kit as he explains.

"There was a big fight between The Bulls and The Sainthood at a warehouse on the outskirts of South Lowell. It was supposed to be a Bulls ambush," he says, hissing as I attempt to dry the skin around the knife wound.

"Sorry. I need to dry it before I can apply the butterfly bandages."

"It's okay. Do what you need to." He pulls a silver flask from his back pocket. "This will help."

"Go on," I encourage as I begin applying the paper stitches.

"I don't know who double-crossed us, but The Sainthood was waiting for us, and it was a bloodbath. We were fighting," he pants, pausing for a second to drink from his flask, "hence how I got the injury and then the whole place exploded. Literally thirty seconds before the bomb went off, a group of guys dressed in black grabbed me and Chad and dragged us out of the building. We weren't fully clear when it detonated, and the blast threw us back. I passed out, coming to as I was being carried into an SUV. I saw Chad; he was crawling away. Then I blacked out again, and the next thing I know, I'm being tossed out on the sidewalk outside."

"Who planted the bomb?" I ask, applying the last butterfly bandage.

"I don't know." He takes another swig from his flask as I wash the cloth in the bowl of warm water and wring it out.

"If The Bulls planned the ambush, it must have been them," I suggest, carefully cleaning his face.

"Not a chance it was them. It wasn't The Sainthood either." He stares off into space. "Both gangs were wiped out tonight, Ash. I doubt anyone but the two of us survived that explosion."

Icy chills sweep over my body as I consider this was a Luminary kill. I know The Sainthood was selling drugs on campus because my boyfriend was one of the dealers. Now that I know LU is owned by The Luminaries it would make sense. I continue cleaning his face. "Were The Bulls planning to take the campus territory for themselves?" I innocently ask as I grab the rubbing alcohol.

"Yes."

That's got to be it. The Luminaries didn't want gang rivalry on campus, and what better way to eliminate a group of sinners than staging an ambush and having them go at one another so they're distracted when the bomb goes off? It's actually genius if I wasn't so sickened by the loss of life. The finger of blame will be pointed at one of the gangs, so they don't need to look for any third party. It will be an open and shut case, and no one will mourn the loss of two local gangs except for their loved ones.

I feel Ares's eyes on my face as I wet some cotton wool with the rubbing alcohol.

"What do you know?"

"Me?" I feign innocence as I dab at the cuts on his face.

He flinches and grabs my hand to stall my movements. "I know you know something. I just saw the look on your face."

"Ash!" Bree dashes back inside with perfect timing. "Jase found Chad."

I stand, walking toward my friend. "Where is he?"

"At the cop shop. He's been arrested."

Chapter Forty-Four
Ashley

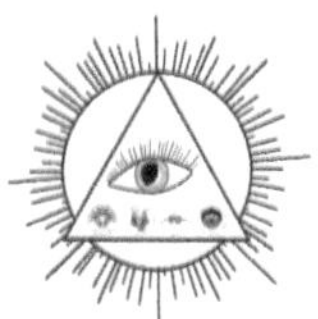

"Chad. It's eleven a.m. Seriously?" I eyeball the beer in his hand wishing I had some magical powers so I could whisk it away.

"Fuck off with the nagging, Ash. I'm not doing this again." He swings his bare feet up on the coffee table and raises the volume on the TV.

Infuriated at his clear dismissal, I stomp around the couch, grab the remote from his lap, and turn the TV off. I stand in front of him, hands on my hips. "You are throwing your life away, Chad, and I'm not going to sit by and watch it happen."

"Go to class, Ash," he barks, bringing the beer to his lips.

"Not without you." I was out late at some bullshit house party Julia dragged me to last night, and I slept through my alarm. I can't afford to miss classes and have the Sloth Luminary getting on my case, but this bullshit with Chad has gone on for two weeks, and I'm done playing nice.

"I'm not going, so you're wasting your time."

"Why the hell not?" Pushing his feet down, I sit on the coffee table in front of him. "I know you're devastated, babe.

I'm devastated for you too. Football was your life, but you knew you were risking everything dealing drugs on campus. I warned you this could happen, and you didn't listen."

He stands, steam practically billowing from his ears. "If this is your 'I told you so' speech, you can save your breath."

His words anger me. I have been tiptoeing around him since he was arrested for drug possession and discharging a weapon in a public area. My parents got the charges dropped, but they couldn't save his football dreams. Coach kicked Chad off the team, and he lost his scholarship. Jase pleaded with Coach to give him another chance, but he was adamant there was no going back. He refuses to give Chad any leeway.

I know The Luminaries could fix this. The fact they have refused to let Mom intervene, and they told Jase there was nothing more to be done, means this is deliberate. They are punishing Chad to send me a warning. I suppose I should be grateful they saved him and Ares the night of the bombing. The fact they were the only two men pulled out alive confirms it was a Luminary kill and that someone connected to me requested they be dragged out in time.

"Man the fuck up, Chad, and stop this bullshit. Drinking yourself into an early grave won't do your mom and sister any favors. You fucked up. Now own it. Jase paid your college fees, so you still have a chance to get a degree and salvage your future. You can go into sports management or open a fitness business or go into coaching. Or you could apply to another school. If you stay clean, you can get on another football team." It would be challenging as his rep will follow him, but I'm sure Jase could make that go away. I don't like the thought of Chad moving to another college, but I would support him if that is what he decided to do. "There are still options, and you're throwing it all away."

"I don't want to be a coach," he roars, getting all up in my face. "I want to play ball for the Lowell Lions and progress to the NFL. And I sure as fuck don't want my so-called best friend's charity."

"Maybe you should have thought about that before you made a deal with the devil. You had choices, and you chose wrong."

"Fuck you, Ash. What the hell would you know? You have had everything handed to you on a silver platter. You don't know what it's like to have everything you had planned ripped out from under you."

"I relate more than you know." I sigh as I stand. "Your pride will be the death of you, Chad." I grab his face. "I love you, and seeing you like this is killing me."

He removes my hands and avoids my gaze. "You've got to give me time, Ash." Defeat is etched all over his face. "My whole world has come crashing down, and this is the only way I know how to deal with it."

"Wow, thanks for nothing." Hurt splays across my face, and I don't disguise it. I have done everything to support him and hearing him say that, like I mean nothing, crushes me.

"Stop being so fucking sensitive. You know I didn't mean it like that."

Do I? We haven't been intimate in weeks. He hasn't even kissed me, and he's been virus free for over a week. All we are doing is arguing, and I hate it. Instead of leaning on me, he's pushing me away and spewing hurtful comments. A future with him is looking less and less likely. It's as if I don't exist except to provide a roof over his head and beer.

Everything has turned to shit. I'm still not pregnant. I'm still on edge knowing they are watching me while I wait for them to decide which Luminary prick I'm to marry. Ares is back to his usual douchey self, but he has been quieter than usual. He's grieving the loss of his best friends, I assume.

Both Rocky and Shoulders died in the warehouse bombing along with fifty-eight other gangsters. The Sainthood and The Bulls are only shells of their former selves, and I doubt they will ever recover from this. At least it means Ares appears to have forgotten about my debt for now. He has been winding Chad up any chance he gets, but my boyfriend doesn't even have the energy to fight back, so Ares is quickly losing interest in both of us, which suits me just fine.

Jase has been avoiding me. He's denying it; claiming work, family, school, and football are keeping him fully occupied. He has been visiting his friends at the hospital too. Thankfully, Nix and Creed survived their horrific car accident, but both suffered serious injuries, and they will be out of action for some time.

I get it to an extent. I am super busy too, but I'm willing to find time for him, and it doesn't seem like he's willing to do the same for me. I wonder if our plan even matters to him anymore. It's not like I can get pregnant when he isn't fucking me.

So, yeah, everything is falling apart in my world too. But you don't see me sitting around in dirty sweats, not bothering to shower or shave, and swallowing beer for breakfast.

"I'm leaving. Are you coming or not?" I ask, already knowing what the answer will be.

"Not." He heads toward the kitchen to grab another beer.

Emitting a frustrated scream, I turn on my heel and stomp out of the house.

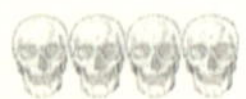

"Don't you get sick of this?" I ask Julia as we enter our third party of the night. My day started off like shit when I slept through my alarm and had another fight with Chad, and it only got progressively worse. I received a B on my cognitive psychology assignment, which almost made me cry, and now I'm subjected to another night being dragged around various frat parties by Julia as we socialize and spy on our fellow students.

"What's to get sick of?" Stopping at a mirror in the hallway, she preens at her reflection before blowing herself a kiss. Vain bitch. "We get to party for a living. There could be worse things." A wicked glint gleams in her eye as she turns around to face me.

"Like what?"

She tweaks my nose, and I swat her hand away.

"You'll see." She waggles her fingers in my face. "Go mingle."

I curse her and her father and The Luminaries under my breath as I make my way into the main room and head to a group in the corner I know from my History of Psychology class. I knock back a few beers, which isn't like me, but I've had a shitty day, and tomorrow is Saturday, so at least I don't have to get up early.

I'm dancing with a few girls when Julia comes up to me. "I need to leave, but you're to stay."

I flip her the bird, fully intending on bouncing as soon as she's gone and the coast is clear.

"You're exasperating," she says, inspecting her nails. "But fine." She drags out the E. "If you need the bathroom, go now while I pull the car around. I haven't been drinking, so I'll drop you off at home on my way."

I narrow my eyes at her. "What are you up to?"

She feigns innocence. "Moi? Nothing." Taking my arm, she pulls me over to the wall. "Look, I know we don't like one another, for obvious reasons, but we have to work together. I'd like to call a truce. I'm tired of all the snarking."

Honestly, I am too, but I don't see how she and I will ever

get along with the Jase-sized elephant in the room. And I don't trust this bitch as far as I'd throw her. She's up to something. I'd bet on it. Still, I'll play this game for now. Make her think I buy her crap while I figure out what she's planning.

"Me too." I sling my arm around her shoulder, giving it a firm squeeze. "We are blood related, and it makes sense we should try to get along."

"I'm glad you think so." She removes my hand from her shoulder. "Hurry, babe." She leans in and kisses me on the cheek. "Bathroom is at the top of the stairs, two doors down on your right. I'll be waiting outside, so don't be long."

I message Jase as I head up the stairs, wondering if he's still up so I can drop by when I get home. Julia has made it clear she's going somewhere else, like she often does after we party. I think I'll start following her to see where she goes. But I'm too beat to play spy tonight. I just need to lose myself in Jase's arms and forget this shitty day ever existed.

I'm too busy tapping on my phone to properly notice where I'm going. Lifting my head from the screen, I spot the bathroom door and open it, pushing inside with my head bowed over my phone as I close the door behind me.

"Oh, fuck, yes, just like that."

My head whips up, and I freeze. My cell slips through my fingers, landing on the carpeted floor. It's not a bathroom. It's a bedroom.

And the man currently under the sheets with a stunning redhead is the man I was just texting.

The woman's hair is spread across the pillow like spilled blood, and Jase's fingers are threaded through some of the strands. His cell vibrates on the bedside table as he thrusts against the woman, leaning down to kiss her neck. She has her eyes closed, moaning and whimpering, as she writhes underneath him, neither of them noticing I'm in the room.

I watch with a pain in my chest and a lump in my throat as Jase checks his cell, glancing briefly at my message, before tossing it on the bouncing bed.

"We have an audience," the woman says, her eyes now open and fixated on me.

I know her. I've seen her around campus. She's one of the professors. As her hand lands on Jase's shoulder, the gold band around her ring finger glistens and shines under the ceiling light. She continues to stare at me, unconcerned about who I am or that she's been caught in bed with a much younger man because, now I can see her more clearly, she is way older than him.

Nausea swims up my throat, and my stomach twists into knots at the sheer horror of what I've stumbled upon.

Jase continues fucking her as he slowly turns to face me. His Adam's apple bobs in his throat, and emotion shimmers in his eyes for a fleeting moment before it's gone.

I want to yell at him, throw things at him, berate him for doing this, but I can't move, and I can't speak. Silent tears roll down my face as I watch him whisper something to the woman before kissing her softly.

A part of me dies inside as he gets off her, swings his legs to the side of the bed, and holds the sheets to his waist. "Wait outside, Ash. I'll be there in a minute."

When I don't move, he fixes me with a hard glare. "Ashley! Go outside. Now."

I obey in a bit of a daze, keeping a hand on my chest as if that will hold my rupturing heart together.

"Oh my god," I pant when I'm outside, slumping against the wall. I hold on to the doorway as I inhale and exhale, struggling to pull myself together in the face of that discovery.

I straighten up when the door opens, and a shirtless Jase emerges. Grabbing my elbow, he pulls me down to the end of the hallway, away from the door. "What the hell are you doing here, Ash?"

Anger spikes in my blood as I wrench my arm from his hold, finally snapping out of my fugue state. "That's what you have to say to me?" I yell, furiously swiping at the hot tears dampening my cheeks.

He looks anxiously around. "Keep your voice down. I don't want Meredith to hear."

"What the actual fuck?" I push him back into the wall, beating my fists into his chest. "You're worried about *her*? Who is she, and how long have you been fucking her?"

"She doesn't matter." He grabs my wrists. "Stop, Ash. Let me explain."

"Your actions did all the talking!" I roar. "You motherfucking cheating bastard!" I hate how my voice cracks as emotion comes crashing down around me.

"You are overreacting, and you need to calm down. You can't act like this in public, Ashley. You have a part to play now, or have you forgotten?"

His words incense me, and I lift my knee, ready to drive it into his balls, but he reacts fast, grabbing me by the throat and spinning us around. He presses me flat against the wall, keeping his hand around my throat as he pins me in place. "This is why I didn't tell you. I knew you wouldn't understand."

"You expect me to *understand*?" I shout. "Fuck you! There is nothing to understand! How long have you been cheating on me?" I wriggle against him, trying to break free, but he is strong, and I am wedged against the wall.

The hand on my throat tightens, and I gasp for air. "This is what I have to do, Ash!" he snaps. "This is my Luminary responsibility! Why the fuck do you think Bree is out there fucking men and women day and night?"

All the blood in my veins turns to ice. "What?" I croak, barely able to force words out through my constricted airway. My head is muddled in confusion as I try to decipher his words because he can't mean what I think he means.

He releases me and steps back, correctly reading my body language. I turn around, rubbing my sore neck. "You do not seriously expect me to believe you are in there fucking *Meredith* because it's your *job*?" I hiss.

"It *is* my job, Ash. You and Julia are the party heirs. Bree, Baz, and I are the player heirs." He shrugs, like it's no big deal. "We prey on the weak too, luring males and females into indulging their lustful and envious desires. We entice married people to cheat, like the older, married professor waiting for me in bed, or the priest Bree is currently blowing in the campus chapel a few blocks away. We coax perverts to act on their fantasies, enable twisted pricks to entrap kids, and exploit others they plan to hurt and degrade so we can stop it and stop them from trying again."

"There are other ways to trap those kinds of people," I say in a low tone.

"That isn't the Luminary way. They like to be hands-on." A hint of a sly smile curves the corners of his lips, and reality dawns.

"You like this."

He closes the distance between us, piercing me with a sultry stare as he twirls a lock of my hair around his finger. "Who wouldn't like fucking for a living?"

I shove him away, appalled at his gloating grin, smug expression, and utter lack of remorse. "Me," I say, "I don't like it." Another horrifying thought lands in my mind. "Is this why you were too busy to see me these past two weeks? Because you were busy fucking other men and women?"

"Just women. I don't fuck men. It's not allowed."

"Of course, it isn't. It's okay for Bree to fuck both sexes but not the men."

"Bree likes pussy," he says, glancing down the hallway. "Are we done here 'cause I've got to get back before Meredith has a crisis of conscience."

Tears prick my eyes. "How many women have you had sex with since we last slept together, Jase?"

He considers it for a few tense beats. "Twelve, thirteen." He shrugs. "I don't exactly keep count."

The glue holding my fragile heart together breaks apart, and I can almost feel the physical cracks as they rip my heart wide-open. "You unimaginable bastard."

"It means nothing, Ash. It's only sex." His eyes plead for understanding I don't have. "None of those women have my heart. You're the only one with a claim to that."

"Did you even use protection?" I ask as fresh horror engulfs me. I've been letting him fuck me bare in an attempt to get pregnant, and all this time he's been fucking other women. I clutch the wall as another layer rips off my heart.

"Of course, I did. I would never risk you like that. I'm clean. We get tested every month."

I guess it's necessary when you fuck so many women.

I think I'm going to be sick.

"I won't share you with others."

He shakes his head, his eyes narrowing. "Of course, you won't. It's okay for me to share you with Chad, and I see how badly you're panting after that prick Ares, but you won't even consider doing the same for me."

"It's not the same, and you know it!" I shove his chest again, irritated when he doesn't even flinch. "Don't you dare try to compare what we have with what you are doing."

"I don't have a choice, Ash!" he yells back before he gets a hold of himself. I watch him shut down before me. "This is my responsibility. This will always be my responsibility. I have no choice."

His words heap more horror on the pile as it sinks in. Even if we were to marry, he would always be fucking other women for his *job*. There is no way I can handle that.

"If you can't deal with my job, then we're done." He stares at me, and I stare back at him, desperately trying to paper over the cracks in my heart. There's a vast ocean between us now. I'm on one side, he's on the other, and there is no way to close the gap because he has the boat and I have the oars, and no matter how we try to resolve our dilemma, it doesn't add up. Because it's unresolvable, and there is no choice to be made.

It's already been made.

I thought I knew who Jase was, but I don't know him at all.

"You call it a job. I call it betrayal," I say. "Fuck you, Jase. You're right about one thing. We *are* done. You just shit all over everything we shared. I hope you're proud of yourself."

I walk off with my head held high, praying I can make it out of this house before I fall to pieces. A whimper escapes my lips when the telltale click of the door shutting confirms he's gone back to that woman—to resume fucking her. My lower lip wobbles as I fight to keep it together. I begin descending the stairs, slamming to a halt when I discover Julia standing on the steps just out of sight but close enough to have heard every word.

It all clicks into place. "You bitch. You did that on purpose."

"You needed to know, and Jase was too much of a pussy to tell you. I did you a favor. You should be thanking me." She smiles sweetly, and I growl.

"Get the hell out of my way, bitch."

"Aw, boohoo. Has Ashley finally realized she can't get everything she wants?" She jabs her finger in my chest. "I told you I would win. Jase is *mine*. I don't care that he fucks other women. I understand, which is why we are so well matched. You're too weak to handle this life. It's what I have been telling him for weeks, and now he sees. With you out of the picture, he and I can finally get our relationship on track. I'll be the one riding his cock tonight. Now run along and cry into your pillow."

Her words are pointed, and they hit home, ramping my anger into murderous intent. I see red and react without thinking it through, pushing her hard and feeling nothing as she teeters on her heels, her eyes widening in shock as she loses her balance. I step to the side when she reaches for me, letting her tumble down the stairs, her loud screams drawing people from the main room.

I calmly walk down the stairs and hover over her as she lies simpering and crying at the bottom of the stairs, clutching her leg and screaming for help. "Enjoy my sloppy seconds. You two deserve one another. I wish you a lifetime of unhappiness chained to a man who will never be faithful and never give you his heart because he already gave it to me." Avoiding eye contact with anyone, I exit the house and head for home.

Chapter Forty-Five

Ashley

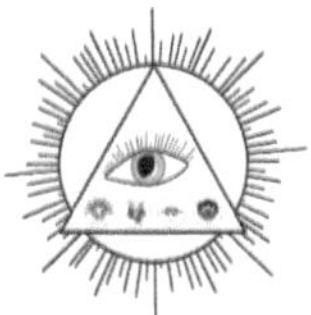

The door slams against the wall as I stumble into my bedroom on shaky legs. Reaching behind me, I shove it closed, instantly muting the sounds of the party raging downstairs in the lower level of the townhome I share with Chad and Ares. The place is packed with coeds, jocks, members of frats and sororities, and our personal friends from Lowell University. Along with the degenerates Ares is hanging out with tonight.

The room spins, and I sway a little as I hold on to the wall while removing my heels and kicking them away. I'm not feeling so hot as I flop down on my king-sized bed, staring up at the stark white ceiling, wondering why I thought it was a good idea to drink so much.

Usually, I am pretty smart when it comes to alcohol. Drinking enough to generate a nice buzz without losing control of myself.

Tonight is different.

Tonight, I am trying to forget my broken heart.

Seeing him walk through the door with *her* draped all over him sent me over the edge. I knew I would never survive the party unless I blotted it all out and numbed myself to the harsh reality of my current existence.

Pain slices across my chest as intense as if someone has plunged a knife into my flesh.

A lone sob travels up my throat, surging for freedom, and it's an anguished, strangled, desolate sound as it rips from my lips.

Fuck, it hurts.

It's not getting any easier.

Turning on my side, I pull my knees up to my chest and wrap my arms around myself as if that will keep me together.

Everything is turning to shit, and I seem powerless to stop it.

The more I learn about the secret world of The Luminaries, the more I lose control of my life. Sometimes, I wish I had a time machine so I could go back to senior year of high school and warn myself of the danger lying in wait for me when I started college.

To think my biggest worry coming here was extracting Chad from the deal he made with The Sainthood.

Gang warfare is a normal way of life in this part of California, but The Luminaries make The Sainthood and The Bulls look like kindergarteners.

What a fucking joke.

It's not true what they say—ignorance *isn't* bliss.

Most everyone in my life was hiding huge secrets from me, and I was walking around, living a lie, like the biggest fool.

I have been ignorant my entire life, largely thanks to my mom and her misguided sense of protection. Blood boils under my skin as Pamela's image surfaces in my mind's eye. I dig my nails into my knees, enraged as I think of all the ways she has fucked up my life. Some mother she turned out to be.

Music blares, hurting my ears, and a burst of light from the hallway has me squinting in the darkened room as the door swings open. I glance over, scrubbing my eyes as a tall, muscular form kicks the door shut with a booted foot before stalking toward me. His familiar hulking frame is a shadowy blur as he strides across the room.

"I want to be alone, Chad," I say, my words slurring slightly. I angle my face away without looking at him. Things have been increasingly strained between me and my boyfriend since arriving at Lowell University a few months ago.

Especially these past few weeks.

I'm not the only one who has lost Jase. I met Jase through Chad, and it was my boyfriend who proposed I take his best friend as my lover too. They have been best friends and teammates on the football team for years. This is the first time they have stopped talking to one another, and I'm not sure if the damage to their relationship can ever be repaired.

The bed dips as Chad climbs up behind me, ignoring my wishes, as per usual. Warmth coats my back as he presses his long, hard, ripped body up against me. Firm fingers land on my hip as he thrusts his hard-on against my ass. Lust stirs low in my belly despite my frustration and melancholy. Pushing my hair aside, he plants a slew of drugging kisses along my neck, and my skin tingles from his addictive touch. I close my eyes, and my drunken brain conjures my dreams to life. I imagine it's Jase touching me, eliciting little moans and whimpers, and dampening my panties as Chad's hands begin to wander.

Shoving those images aside, I am immediately remorseful and shamefaced. Chad doesn't deserve to have me check out on him, no matter how fragile our relationship is right now. We haven't had sex in weeks, and I need to feel closer to my boyfriend.

I can't lose him too.

Notes of citrus, spice, and sandalwood tickle my nostrils as he moves, and the heady scent of his cologne hits me like a direct stab to the heart.

I would know that scent anywhere.

My eyes pop wide in realization, and I attempt to turn around, but firm hands stop me. My heart is thrashing against my rib cage, pounding in excitement as adrenaline charges through my veins and lust elevates my arousal to dizzy heights.

He came looking for me.

Jase is here.

Touching me. Kissing me. Holding me. Comforting me.

Does he miss me as much as I miss him? Does he walk around with a constant pain in his heart and an ache in his soul?

I need to see him. To peer into his gorgeous emerald-green eyes as I reclaim his lips. I attempt to turn around again, but he stops me once more, and my newfound hope stutters to a halt.

He won't face me because nothing has changed.

He can never be mine.

This is as much as he can offer me.

But it's not enough.

It never will be.

That horrific night replays in my mind, like it often has these past couple of weeks, and my heart ruptures again in my chest as the pain of his betrayal slays me anew. His arms tighten around me in the dark, holding me steady as I thrash around, desperate to get away from him before my treacherous body gives me away.

No matter how much I want this, want *him*, I can't give in.

But it's not that simple.

Every nerve ending on my body craves his touch, and I'm like an addict chasing a high I know isn't good for me, but I'm struggling to resist.

I'm waging an inner battle as much as I'm fighting him.

How can I still want him after everything he has done?

My body so needs to get with the program. Determined to be stronger than my base desires, I continue fighting him, trying to escape his embrace, but it's a weak effort, at best. My head is at war with my body and my heart, and my inebriated limbs can't muster the appropriate strength to get away from him because my man is ripped. Tall, strong, muscular, and a force to be reckoned with.

No longer *your* man, my snide inner voice reminds me. *He never truly was*, the voice adds, driving the knife in deeper.

No matter how futile it is, I continue to fight, thrashing around in his solid hold. "Fuck off, Jase," I hiss. "I don't need you. Don't want you," I lie. "Go back to that bitch." I grip his arms, ready to drag my nails through his flesh if it's the only way I can break free, but my fingers meet material. My brows knit together as I look down at the long sleeves of the dress shirt he's wearing. Jase doesn't dress like this. Anger churns in my gut. This is *her* influence. She's already turning him into something he's not.

I hate her.

As much as I hate The Luminaries and their stupid rules and traditions.

And I have a hate-love thing going on with the man currently holding me to him. I hate Jase for what he did to me, yet I can't stop loving him. I wish there was an off switch in my heart and my head so I could bury those feelings and forget I ever loved Jason Stewart.

"Let me go," I snap, digging my nails into his clothed arms and lashing out with my legs.

One beefy leg clamps down on mine, restricting my movement, as I sense, rather than see, him shaking his head. His lips go on the offensive, planting addictive kisses along my neck and my jawline, his teeth tugging on my earlobe before his mouth suctions on that sensitive spot just under my ear.

He isn't playing fair.

Fuck him to the high heavens.

I am losing the battle and I know it.

If he's so determined this is happening, maybe I'll let it. A good hate fuck might be just what I need to sever the lingering ties to my ex. It might be good to remind him of what he has destroyed. And if it gets back to *her*, it'll be the cherry on top.

Let her know she'll never have him the way I did.

The intense chemistry and connection we share will never be broken.

Jase will never love her the way I know he loves me.

He chose me in a way he never chose her.

What good is having a man if he's forced to be with you?

She might think she's won, but she's lost. She will always know he's unfaithful and that he's still in love with me. She will always know he's incapable of loving her.

It doesn't sound like much fun.

He may no longer be mine, but at least I know what we had was real.

So, I stop fighting, going placid in his arms.

If this is the last time I get to be with him like this, I am not going to deny myself what I need right now.

I will fuck him one last time, and then I'm moving on and shutting him out completely.

His fingers trail up my leg, and he moves my thighs apart while keeping me on my side, rocking his erection against my ass through our clothes. Closing my eyes, I succumb to the myriad of sensations rioting in my body. A whimper escapes my lips when his hand continues its upward trajectory. Brushing his fingers against my lace-covered pussy, he rubs me aggressively through the flimsy material for a couple minutes, rocketing my arousal into the stratosphere.

Cool air wafts over the bare cheeks of my ass when he lifts my dress from behind and pulls my panties down. Shoving them to my knees, he leaves them there, like a restraint, as he repositions my legs so he has access to my weeping cunt. The arm around my waist moves lower, joining his other hand as he parts my pussy lips with his thumbs before driving two fingers inside me.

I can't see his wicked smile, but I know it's there as his fingers glide easily through my slick channel. Wrapping my long hair around his fist, he tugs my head back slightly, enough to grant him greater access to my neck. I keep my eyes closed as he peppers kisses along my neck, my collarbone, and the swells of my ample breasts.

If he insists on doing this without looking at me, I'm going to do the same—we can pretend together.

A grunt tumbles free from my lips when he tweaks my nipples through my dress, sending darts of desire shooting to my core. He tugs roughly on the hardened peaks and a pleasurable painful sensation ricochets across my sensitive skin. I'm not even aware I'm rotating my hips and riding his hand until he adds another digit and increases his pace. My climax is already building because Jase is just that good.

Releasing my hair, he continues pumping his fingers in and out of me as his thumb makes circles on my swollen clit, swirling my juices around my tightening bud as I chase a familiar high.

I shriek in surprise when his free hand lands on my bare ass with a sharp slap. My pussy throbs with need, pulsing and gushing as he lands a succession of hard slaps on my ass. I'm not in the least bit surprised when his thumb presses against my puckered hole because Jase is a big fan of anal.

Memories of better times flip through my mind on a loop. Happy times spent with both my guys in bed as we explored and fucked for hours, none of us ever getting enough. Our insatiable fucking never satisfying us for long.

I come apart at the seams, shattering completely the instant he plunges two fingers all the way into my ass. My pussy clenches around his fingers in my cunt while I tighten and pulse around the digits in my ass. I'm a writhing mess of hormones and incoherent mumbles as he works my body like a pro.

I don't even hear his zipper lowering in my blissed-out drunken state. A scream rips from my mouth when he thrusts his cock in me in one claiming stroke, pushing so far inside it feels like he's nudging my womb. He's half draped over my back as he fucks into me, pushing my body farther into the bed with my face mushed against the comforter. The angle is a little awkward, but the constriction of my legs makes him seem fuller and bigger inside me, his thrusting tighter, hotter, and so much more.

"Yes," I hiss, rocking my ass back against him as he drives his big dick into my cunt in a feverish pace, rutting in and out like a wild savage, brutalizing me in a way that speaks volumes.

This is an elevated form of hate fucking. And. I. Am. Here. For. It.

He slams in and out of me over and over, and I'm moaning and whimpering like this is the first time I've had sex. Sex is always phenomenal with my guys, but this is next level.

Why does his dick feel so much bigger at this angle? And is that...?

A primitive groan filters from my mouth as I feel the additional friction sliding against my inner walls, and it clicks into place. "You got your dick pierced," I rasp, reaching back to grab hold of his ass because I need to be touching him. "I never thought you'd do it." I squeeze his ass as I pivot my hips, as best as I can from this angle, working in sync with his rough thrusts. I feel impossibly full, and the sensations his magical cock is evoking in me is out of this world.

In the past, I have suggested the guys get some metal in their cocks, but neither Chad nor Jase seemed interested, so I hadn't pushed my agenda. Now, I wish I had pushed harder, because ho-lee fucking shit, nothing feels better than this. "Oh my god, Jase," I pant when stars burst behind my closed eyes. "That feels incredible."

A dark chuckle ripples through the air, raising goose bumps all over my arms. My pulse picks up, and my heart beats faster against my rib cage as an ominous sense of dread sweeps over me.

I stop moving.

Stop breathing.

His hand wraps firmly around my throat as he presses his mouth to my ear. "Wrong dick. Try again." His warm breath fans across my earlobe while his fingers grip my neck painfully.

This cannot be happening.

"No!" I croak, pushing past my restricted airway as he continues fucking me. "No! Stop!"

This time, his chuckle is downright menacing as he rams his dick inside me like he's trying to stab me with the damn thing. "Don't pretend you don't love my dick inside you, slutty little sis. You're so wet I'm practically drowning. Your hungry cunt is hugging my cock so hard it's almost suffocating it."

"I thought you were Jase!" I scream, clawing at Ares's arm as his fingers squeeze my neck.

"No, you didn't. Deep down, you knew it was me."

I don't dignify that with a response because I'm terrified he speaks the truth. "Get off!" I yell, my voice raspy and strained. "Get the fuck away from me!" I try to pull off his dick, but it's impossible at this angle. His hand locks on to my hip, holding me in place as he continues driving his monster cock into my slick channel. Angry tears prick my eyes, but I refuse to let them fall. I won't give my despicable stepbrother the satisfaction. Not when he's already reveling in my bodily reactions. I hate how I'm still reacting to him, and I bite the inside of my cheek to stop myself from crying out in pleasure.

"Stop lying to yourself. You're fucking loving this, and Jase doesn't want you. He used you up and tossed you aside when you passed your sell-by date," Ares cruelly replies. "I saw him in the hallway on my way to your room. He was balls deep in his fiancée, and she was screaming his name as she exploded all over his dick."

His words dig deep, carving new scars in my heart. "I hate you," I rasp, the words squeezing out of my narrowed airway.

"Now, now, dollface, let's stop with all the lies."

He thrusts deep inside me, and I almost come again. Biting down hard on my lip, I trap my moans because I'd rather choke on my tongue than let him know how much I'm enjoying this.

"You might think you hate me, but your greedy cunt says otherwise," he taunts.

"My body is responding the way it would to any dick inside me," I lie. "But I don't want this. I don't want you. I want you to stop. If you don't, I'll scream."

"Go for it." He bites my ear, and a choked scream tears from my throat. "There's no one up here to rescue you, and no one downstairs will hear over the music."

In a lightning-fast move, I'm flipped onto my back as he straddles my thighs. The instant his hand releases my throat, I suck in greedy lungsful of air, and then I lunge for him, reaching to slap him, but he's quick, restraining my wrists in one of his meaty hands. He tut-tuts. "Always so eager for violence."

"Only when it comes to you," I bark.

It's embarrassing how easily he restrains me with his powerful thighs and one firm hand. His free hand reaches behind him to his jeans, which are pooled halfway down his legs, and he yanks his belt free. I buck and writhe underneath him, but it's pointless because he's got at least eighty pounds on me, and he's fueled by months of pent-up aggression when it comes to me. Hooking his belt around the top of my bedframe, he loops it around my wrists, securing it tightly.

My back arches off the bed as my arms stretch over my head, and I try to buck him off, but it's useless. My legs are still restrained at the knees by my panties, and he's too heavy. He barely even moves as I work up a sweat trying to get him away from me.

"Chad!" I roar, ignoring the soreness in my neck as I scream for my boyfriend, hoping he'll miraculously show up and save me.

Ares chuckles as he slides down my body and climbs off the bed. "Are you sure you want your boyfriend to come up here? I doubt he'll be sympathetic when he hears what we've been up to and how incredible you think my dick is." He puts his smug face all up in mine as I wrestle with the belt securing my wrists to the headboard.

"You're going to pay for this, asshole," I snap before I resume screaming for help.

In an unexpected move, Ares rips my panties from my legs and stuffs them in my mouth, grinning like the maniac he is as my muffled shouts go nowhere. Anger churns in my gut, and I react on instinct. Swinging my leg to the side, I shove my foot into his upper thigh, narrowly missing my intended target. Ares falls back a little, chuckling with amusement as a scowl spreads across my face. A growl forms at the back of my throat as I wriggle on the bed, pleased when my movements cause my dress to lower, hiding my bare pussy. I'm sweating from all the exertion involved in trying to get free, and strands of my hair are plastered to my face.

Adrenaline courses through my veins as I watch Ares kick off his boots, jeans, and boxers before whipping his shirt over his head in a typical one-armed guy move. He is completely naked, standing before me like a resurrected Greek god, teasingly stroking his dick and licking his lips. He hovers over me like a looming dark threat, a salacious smug grin curling the corners of his lush mouth.

Desire coils low in my belly, and my pussy throbs with raw need. Heat flares in my cheeks as my body reacts to the jerk, and I fucking hate it.

I hate I'm so attracted to him.

Why isn't there a pill I can pop to cure this disease?

Purposely, I jerk my head to the side, not wanting him to see me ogling his naked body.

Ares has spent months parading around the house naked and semi-naked, in a deliberate move to piss me and Chad off, and I know what I'll see if I let my eyes linger—a body carved straight from my fantasies. Powerful thighs. Chiseled abs. Broad chest. Rippling biceps. V-shaped indents at his hips. A monster cock with impressive piercings laddering the underside of his shaft.

Ares is not shy about whipping his dick out any chance he gets. It's where my new obsession with metal has come from. He's not shy about any part of his body, and who could blame him? He's all sharp lines, hard edges, and rock-solid muscle—a testament to hours of daily dedication in the gym.

But it doesn't matter how hot his body is. He's a crazy

motherfucker with a giant chip on his shoulder. Chad hates him, for obvious reasons, and the feeling is mutual.

"Fuck the hell off," I shout when he climbs back on the bed, aiming for me. My words are muffled behind my gag, but he doesn't need to hear it to know what I've said.

"Nah," he replies, stroking his monster dick. "I'm just getting started." His grin is downright evil as he pushes my dress up to my waist, parts my thighs, and spreads them wide. I fight him, trying to close my legs, but he tightens his grip on my inner thighs and forces them wider.

Dipping his head, he blows across my exposed pussy, chuckling when my hips buck of their own volition. Angry tears prick my eyes as I resume an internal battle. My entire body jolts when he slides his hot tongue up and down my slit, and I let my tears fall as my body responds positively to his touch. Frustration comingles with anger, fear, and lust as he thrusts his tongue inside me and buries his face in my pussy.

I close my eyes, unable to bear witness to this.

Ares knows what he's doing.

This is his payback. He waited until the most opportune moment to catch me vulnerable and drive the knife in all the way.

He knows this will be my utter ruination.

Like I know nothing short of a miracle can stop this from happening.

"Salty and sweet," he says in a voice that's gruff and deep. "My favorite flavor." Plunging three fingers inside me, he drives them in and out in rough strokes. "I could eat you all night, but you don't deserve it."

Air trickles over my chest when he shoves my dress up higher and removes my bra. My eyes pop open as pain shoots through my body when he bites down on my nipple, tugging on it with his teeth as he continues shoving his fingers inside me. Angry tears leak from my eyes as he plucks my body like a damn guitar. He alternates his attention from one breast to another, sucking, biting, and licking, and I'm so fucked because I like it.

I really like it.

But he will never know that.

Narrowing my eyes, I glare at him because it's the only power I have.

Except my fucked-up stepbrother likes it.

"Keep pretending if you like, but we both know you don't want me to stop."

I glare harder at him, trying to deny the mountain my body is ascending in a rush to reach the peak. Just as I'm there, ready to fall off the cliff, Ares yanks his fingers out of me with a smirk, denying my body its release.

More frustrated tears cling to the corners of my lashes, and I scream behind the panties in my mouth. In my head, I toss obscenities at him and plot creative ways to murder the fucker.

Lifting my legs, he forces them back until my knees are pressed up against my stomach and I'm spread wide before him. "Look at you," he says in a voice thick with need. His eyes are glued to my exposed pussy and ass as he pumps his dick hard in his free hand while licking his lips. "You're dripping," he adds, gathering my pussy juices on his fingers before smearing them around my puckered hole. Panic mixes with molten desire when he pushes his thumb into my ass. "I would fuck you here, but you'd like it too much." His eyes are dark pools of wicked intent when he lifts them to meet mine as he removes his thumb. "This isn't a reward. It's a punishment."

His body covers mine as he presses me down into the mattress. "I meant what I said that first day I was at your house with my mom. I won't stop until I've ruined you, dollface." His fingers sweep over my cheeks as his erection presses against my raised leg. "It's what you all deserve." He grips my chin painfully, tilting my face up. "You should make wiser choices in the future."

Pressing my raised legs back farther against my upper body, he stretches my limbs almost painfully as he brings his thick cock to my entrance. His engorged head is leaking precum as he rubs it against my folds. Fear spikes in my blood as he slams inside me without a condom. This cannot be happening. I'm not on birth control right now, so pregnancy and STDs are a concern. Who knows where his giant dick has been?

I glare at him as he fucks into me, helpless to stop him. His devilish grin expands as he nips at my breasts with his teeth, tugging my sore hard nipples as he pummels my pussy with manic energy. Lifting up on his knees, he keeps one arm across my bent legs to hold me in place while raising my hips and shoving into me deeper.

He fucks me raw, pounding and thrusting into me like a demented man. Sweat glistens on his ink-covered chest as he screws me into the bed and tightens his grip on me in a way I know will leave bruises.

But that's the least of my worries now because he's edging me, and I'm close to the brink of insanity. Every time my orgasm rises and I'm ready to fall apart, he stops, stilling his cock and halting his fingers.

And every time, I cry inside in sheer frustration.

He will pay for this. The gloves are off this time, and it's all-out fucking war now.

Beyond frustrated, I shout against the gag in my mouth and move what parts of my body I can even though I know there is no way I can break free. I refuse to lie here docile and just take it.

His dark chuckle is quickly becoming my least favorite sound as he smirks at me with amusement. "You can try to deny this all you want, but your body gives you away every time. Your cunt can't get enough of my cock," he says, sliding it in and out in a more leisurely fashion. "It doesn't matter what you say; Chad will never believe I forced you into this. Not when he sees the evidence."

Pressure sits on my chest as alarm bells screech in my ears at his words. It's how he's able to untie his belt from my headboard and flip me around until I'm on my stomach. My wrists are still restrained at my back when he lifts me up on my knees and slams back inside me. We are both kneeling on the bed with my back to his sweat-slickened chest and his cock buried deep inside my cunt when he grips my chin and angles my head toward my bedside table. His cell is propped up against my lamp, and I see the flashing red light, confirming he's recording this.

Silent tears spill down my cheeks as he pivots his hips and fucks into me from behind.

His thrusts are rough, aggressive, possessive, celebratory, and all the fight seeps out of me.

One muscular arm traps me across my middle while his free hand covers my gagged mouth as he picks up his pace and screws the shit out of me. "Come, slutty little sis. Come all over my cock like you've been dying to." His fingers creep down my stomach, reaching my clit and rubbing aggressively. The second he pinches my oversensitive bud, I explode, detonating into a thousand tiny pieces, hating how much pleasure he has given me while simultaneously destroying me.

Ares continues fucking me after my climax has abated before pulling out and pushing me flat on my back. Kneeling over me, his winning smirk pins me in place as he fucks his hand in a fast skillful manner. A loud roar bounces off the walls, and his dick jerks as he starts to come. Ropes of hot cum stream over my bare breasts and across my face as he unleashes his release all over me, completing the ruination.

I know what he's done.

I know what happens next.

I just lost Chad too.

Chapter Forty-Six

Ashley

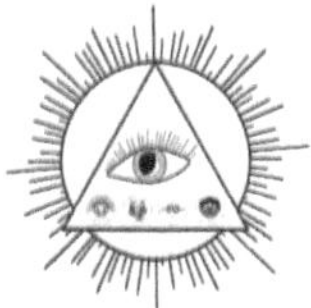

I sit on the bottom step of the stairs, carrying the weight of the world on my shoulders as I watch Chad lift the last of his bags. Pushing up, I stand in front of him, blocking the doorway, before he can walk out of my life forever. "I'm so sorry, Chad. If I could take it all back, I would."

"I might have believed that until the prick sent me the video."

I didn't sleep a wink all night knowing what I needed to do. I knew Ares would send the video to Chad, so I snuck into his room and took Chad's cell, deleting the video, because I wanted to be the one to tell him what I had done.

I fessed up to everything at six a.m. this morning when I woke Chad. I told him about the shower. Ares jerking off in front of me in Chad's bedroom. The kiss in the hallway, and my biggest mistake of all, fucking him last night. I didn't play the manipulation card because it wouldn't have been the truth.

Deep down, I knew it wasn't Chad or Jase in bed with me. All the clues were there. And Ares was right. I told him to stop, but I didn't mean it. I was loving it too much to end it, even knowing how it would ruin things with Chad.

I am glad I told Chad the truth because Ares covered all his bases, sending a copy of the video to Chad's email, which he discovered a couple of hours after he broke up with me for cheating on him with his rival.

I fight tears because I have no right to my hurt feelings. I did this. I'm the one who broke us up. Yes, we were teetering on a cliff, but my actions pushed us over the ledge. "It is the truth. I never wanted any of this to happen."

"I don't believe you." He folds his arms and glares at me. "That prick has been pushing you for weeks, and you didn't say one word. Not a single fucking word. This whole time my world has come crashing down around me, and you've been fooling around with him."

His eyes fill with disgust as he looks me over. "To think I wasted years of my life with you. You're nothing but a cheating whore. You're some bitch for criticizing Jase for cheating when you're no better. To think I broke my friendship with him over that for you. I'm just glad he has forgiven me. At least I know I can always count on Jase to have my back."

"I've had your back too, and I only ever wanted what's best for you."

He grinds his teeth as he puts his face all up in mine. "News flash, whore. It's not you. Now get the fuck out of my face."

I step aside, swallowing painfully over the messy ball of emotion in my throat. "I'll always love you, Chad, and I'll always regret how we ended."

His lips twist into an ugly sneer, and I brace myself for whatever will come out of his mouth. "I'll always hate you and regret we didn't end sooner."

"I deserve that."

"No, you deserve so much more."

With those hate-filled parting words, he leaves. Like a glutton for punishment, I stand in my door, watching Julia and Jase greet their new roomie. Even the sight of my archnemesis on crutches doesn't cheer me up.

"Ouch."

I jump, not even hearing Ares creep up behind me.

"Julia has all your men. That's got to hurt."

"Eat shit and die, asshole," I say, slamming the front door shut and escaping to my room.

Thankfully, his bike is gone when I leave an hour later after finally dragging my heartsick ass in the shower. I need to get the morning-after pill because it would be just my luck to get knocked up by that fucking prick—even though he came on my tits.

When I return from the pharmacy, Bree is waiting outside my door. I appreciate she didn't just let herself in, like everyone else does, but that doesn't mean I want her here. "I don't want to talk to you," I say when I reach the top step.

"I get you're pissed but please let me explain." Bree has been trying to talk to me since my discovery at the frat party.

"I have no interest in whatever you have to say." I open the door and step inside, knowing she will follow me. I figure if we're doing this now, we might as well do it without an audience.

"I'm sorry I didn't tell you," she says, following me into the kitchen.

I whirl around and glare at her. "I thought you were my friend!"

"I am your friend, Ash. It killed me not telling you about our responsibility."

"So, why didn't you?" I fetch a glass from the overhead cupboard.

"Jase asked me not to. He wanted to tell you himself."

"Bullshit." I fill the glass with water and open the package from the pharmacy.

"We argued over it, and I was so close to telling you—"

"But you didn't," I finish for her before popping the pill and swallowing it down with water.

"I'm so incredibly, unbelievably sorry. How can I make it up to you? Just tell me, and I'll do it."

"You can't." I finish the water and put the glass in the sink. "Jase was fucking other women the whole time we were together. Every single part of our history together was a lie. You knew that, and you said nothing. You should have told me the day you came to HQ to pick me up. I reunited with him without knowing the facts. You can't call me your friend and hide something so huge from me."

"He wasn't fucking other women the whole time. Our responsibilities only kick in when we come to college. He was faithful to you, Ashley, and you should know he fought against this for as long as he could."

"Well, it wasn't long enough." I have considered The Luminaries put pressure on him to do this, knowing it would split us up. It's what they wanted after all. But if that was the truth, he should have come and talked to me about it before jumping into bed with other women.

Not that it would have made a difference, so I don't really know why it matters. It's not like I could have given him a stamp of approval. There is no scenario where my heart could tolerate this level of constant pain.

Maybe Julia is right, and I am too weak for this world because I hate it. It sickens me, and I don't know how I am going to do the things expected of me.

"You have had so much dumped on you these past few weeks, it's completely understandable you are angry. We have had our whole lives to wrap our heads around this, and you've been thrown in at the deep end." Tears pool in her eyes as she takes my cold hands in hers. "Please don't shut me out. I want to be here for you. I want to prove I can be worthy of your friendship. I promise I won't ever keep anything from you again, no matter what anyone says."

I snatch my hands back and wrap them around myself. "It's too late. You should have told me. You knew what we had planned. You let him have unprotected sex with me knowing he was screwing other women. How could you do that? How could you both take another choice away from me? And don't spout that responsibility shit at me. He should have told me, and when he didn't, *you* should have. End of."

"You're right. I made a bad judgment call."

"It's more than that. You were fucking different men and women and letting me believe it was sexual freedom, but it's the opposite. You lied to me about that too." I rub at the tight pain spreading across my chest. "Just go, Bree. I need to be alone."

Tears spill from the corners of her eyes. "I've never had a true friend like you before, Ash. I'll give you space because I understand how badly I have let you down." She wipes at her tears. "But I'm going nowhere, and I'll always have your back."

The next few weeks are some of the hardest of my life. My punishment for pushing Julia down the stairs is I have to take over her party heir chores as well as my own. It would've been a lot worse if my uncle had proof I acted deliberately, but I lied through my teeth, insisting I tripped over my heels on the stairs, causing me to lose my balance and knock into Julia. She was spitting blood, stating it was no accident, but without evidence, my uncle had no choice in the matter.

I got off lightly by Luminary standards.

Still, carrying her duties on top of mine is no picnic.

I'm running on fumes, barely getting four hours sleep most nights.

At least I'm too busy to think and too tired every night to lie awake, lamenting my lost loves. The other bonus is I don't have to spend any time with Julia although I know that's only a temporary reprieve.

Chad has returned to campus, and he's attending classes. He's permanently off the team, but at least he seems to have stopped drinking, and he's focusing on his studies.

If our breakup helped with that, then I'm glad.

I miss him.

I miss him so much, and I wish things could be different.

But maybe it happened like this for a reason.

I don't see how there was any future for Chad in my world. Perhaps it's best that he hates me and glowers at me any time we bump into one another on campus. At least I can't put him in harm's way anymore.

Unfortunately, I bump into Jase at parties a lot, and he's usually with different women. He is discreet in fulfilling his responsibility, slipping upstairs when no one is watching so he doesn't tarnish his rep or Julia's now everyone knows they are engaged.

He always pretends like I don't exist, and I ignore him too. I hate how much I miss him and how I'm going to be reminded of it all the time because he'll be my family when he marries Julia, and there is no getting away from it.

Ares and I living together is a constant test of my willpower. He has stopped his daily naked routine and taunts about Chad, Jase, and Julia in favor of a new routine. I'm calling it "killing me with kindness." He's trying to be nice to me while flirting at the same time. He has breakfast ready for me each morning, rushes home from work to cook me dinners, and plies me with hot chocolate at bedtime. Hera obviously taught him how to cook because he knows her full repertoire. But it doesn't matter. I don't have much of an appetite these days, and even though Ares nags me until I've eaten at least a few mouthfuls, my clothes hang off me now.

He even insists on watching movies with me, and he hasn't been going out as much. I have spotted him hanging around some of the parties I attend. On other occasions, he is outside when I'm leaving in the early hours to whisk me home on his bike. It's like every time I turn around he is there, and it's borderline stalking.

I think I preferred it when he was mean to me.

If I didn't know better, I'd say it's remorse and guilt. But Ares's mantra is guilt is for the weak-minded, and he proudly boasted to Chad that he doesn't suffer a guilty conscience, so I'm not sure why he is going overboard. Perhaps Dad and Hera asked him to do it. That's the only explanation that makes sense.

On weekends, when I manage to find some downtime, I train with my new trainer Vincent, or I drive off in my car with my Nikon and take pictures. Sometimes, I head to the lake, or go into the forest, or hike a mountain, snapping pictures of everything I see. Other times I walk around downtown, capturing interesting people, or chalk murals on the sidewalk, or birds converging around the fountain as little kids throw them pieces of bread, or tourists throwing coins into the well along with their unspoken dreams.

I attended the photography expo, but it wasn't as enjoyable going alone.

Sundays are alternated between visits to see Dad and Hera

and Mom and her new family. Relations are still frosty between me and my mother, and I mainly visit to spend time with my cute little sister, Emilie.

I'm still not talking to Bree. I'm so hurt she was keeping secrets from me. I understand, to a point, but she was still deceiving me even if she believed her motives were justified. So, I'm wandering in this weird space, devoid of the people I love and those I came to rely on, living with the person who helped to derail my life, and socializing with a bunch of strangers I am only befriending as part of a job that aims to hurt them and their families.

I handed in my first report recently, and I hated it. I don't want to issue regular lists of so-called weak people to be punished. But if I don't, *I'll* be punished, and I know next time my uncle won't be so lenient.

Chapter Forty-Seven

Ashley

"Are you heading next door?" Ares asks on Saturday night as I slip my feet into my heels in the hallway.

"What's it to you?" I snap, still pissed at my stepbrother and riled up because my uncle personally called to tell me I had to attend the pre-Christmas party Julia is hosting at the townhome she shares with Jase, Chad, and Bree. I would rather yank my eyelashes out with pliers than step foot in that house, but I'm sure the punishment would be worse.

Mom called and warned me to go, spouting appearances and the need to mend bridges, yada, yada. She has truly embraced her inner Luminary, and she's fully back in the fold.

"Woah, no need to bite my head off. I just thought you could use some moral support." Ares holds up his hands, flashing me a flirtatious grin, and I try not to notice how totally hot he looks in a plain white and black tee with ripped jeans and biker boots.

"From you?" I snort out a laugh. "I'm well and truly screwed if relying on *you* is what my life has come to. Or have you forgotten how you destroyed my relationship with my boyfriend and fucked my archnemesis? And that's before I mention all the other shit you've pulled over the past year. Fuck you, Ares. I don't need moral support from the likes of you."

His black hair falls in sexy waves across his brow, and his hazel eyes are smoldering as he drinks me in. It's like he didn't even hear what I just said, or it just rolled off his back. Man, what I wouldn't give to be that indifferent. "Stop eye fucking me!" I snap, clasping the strap at my ankle and standing.

"You are sexy as hell in that dress, and I can't help it." He stalks toward me with dark intent, licking his lips and undressing me with his eyes.

I hold up my palms, screaming at my rapidly pounding heart to calm the fuck down. My body hasn't gotten the memo this asshole is part of the reason my life is one giant shit show. "Step back, dickface. Don't come any closer, or I'll drive my heels into your balls killing any chance you have of ever fathering kids." I lift my leg a little, showcasing the pointed black stilettos with the sharp silver spikes all over them that clasp around my ankle. They cost a small fortune, and I'm not even sure I can walk in them, let alone dance, but I guess we'll soon see.

He chuckles, and I glare at him. "You know your threats turn me on." He shrugs. "Sue me for being obsessively attracted to you if you want, but at least I'm being honest. You're still pretending you don't feel the same."

"Fuck this." I grab my purse and stride to the door. "I'm not doing this bullshit with you again." He is constantly showering me with compliments and making sleazy jokes. It's messing with my head, which I'm sure is the intent.

"I think I love the pink more than the silver-purple," he says, trailing me out of the house.

"Quit touching me," I snap, shoving his hand away as he fingers my newly dyed hair. I got it done this morning purposely for the party. Plus, I know it will piss Mom and James off. I cling to the railing as I inch my way down the steps. Not an easy feat when my short, tight, strapless leather dress barely leaves space to breathe. The skyscraper heels don't help.

"Holy shit." Ares slams to a halt when we reach the bottom of the steps. "Did you buy a Harley?"

"How do you know it's not Bree's?"

"Because it's parked in one of our spaces." He moves over beside my new bike, tracing his fingers reverentially along the bodywork. "You should have told me you were thinking of buying a motorcycle. I would have helped."

"I don't need help. As you can see, I did fine by myself." I did my research and visited a few showrooms.

"Have you taken her out yet?" he asks, and I shake my head. "I'll take you out tomorrow. Give you a few pointers. We should stretch her legs and see what's she got."

It's on the tip of my tongue to tell him to piss off when Julia pulls up in her stupid pink Porsche.

"Ares, darling." She prances toward us wearing a bright red minidress with a giant bow over the lowcut chest. "I haven't seen you in ages." She places her hand on his chest. "I'm crutch free." She glares at me before pressing herself up against Ares and giggling. "You can help me to celebrate."

My blood boils, and I'm seconds from digging my new heels in her crotch, destroying her pussy so she can stop hitting on my men.

Huh? What the fuck, Ash?! Ares is not *your man.*

"No thanks." Ares pries her body away from his. "You couldn't pay me enough to let your skanky ass near me again."

Stepping back, he wraps his arm around my waist in a protective gesture. "Now, fuck off. Ashley and I were having a private conversation about her new bike."

Julia narrows her eyes at my motorcycle before throwing

back her head and laughing. "Oh my, this is priceless. I can't wait until Daddy hears about this."

"Run along and tell him then." I flip her the bird, glaring daggers at her back as she totters off.

"You shouldn't let her get to you. It's obvious, and she gets off on it."

I remove his arm and chew on my lip. "Thanks for those words of advice, oh wise one. Now if you don't mind, go fuck yourself."

I walk up the steps toward the enemy lair, conscious Ares is still behind me and most likely staring up my short dress. "Stop ogling my ass," I toss over my shoulder.

"Can't help it when it's right in my face," he says from way too close. "Maybe I should do like someone else I know and take a big bite."

I yelp when his teeth nip my ass through my dress, almost losing my balance on the top step. But Ares is there to steady me, wrapping his arm around my waist from behind and pushing his warm, hard body up against my back. "Someday soon, this ass will be mine." He squeezes one cheek before nibbling on my ear just as the door opens, revealing Jase and Chad.

Wow. Their timing couldn't be any worse.

I freeze, going numb as they rake their gazes over me, before noticing the jerk at my back.

"Yeah, just what I thought." Chad glowers at Ares before turning that hate-filled lens on me. "You look like a whore." He sways a little on his feet as he swigs from a bottle of beer. "And I can see your panties."

Jase clamps his hand down on Chad's shoulder. "Come on, dude. Don't do this."

"Why the hell not?" Chad turns the daggers on his best friend. "She has the nerve to show up here with *him*, and I'm not allowed to call her on that bullshit? Why the fuck were they even invited?" He storms off without waiting for a reply.

Pain cuts me in two at the reminder he hates me. I'm sorely tempted to turn around and go home. Yet, I came here for a reason, and I am dressed to the nines so I would at least look composed on the outside. I'm not falling apart at the very first hurdle. It's not like I didn't know this was coming

Jase steps out, folding his arms and leveling Ares with a deadly look. "You're not welcome."

"That's not what my invite text from Julia says." Ares waves his cell in front of him.

"She just uninvited you, so bye." Jase grabs my hand, yanks me inside, and slams and locks the door before Ares can retaliate. I stumble on my heels, falling into his chest, inhaling the familiar scent of his cologne, and almost dying. His hand lands on my lower back, and his eyes dip to my mouth.

I straighten up and slide out of his embrace before we both do something we will regret.

His lips pull into a tight line. "Drinks are in the kitchen, and people are split between the basement and the living room. Enjoy your night, Ashley." He walks off, and I try to calm my racing heart. He stops at the door leading to the basement and turns around. "For the record, you don't look like a whore. I love the new hair and you look sexy as hell." He opens the door and disappears down the stairs as a clicking sound reverberates behind me.

"I said it first," Ares says, coming up behind me.

"How did you—"

He waggles a key in my face and grins. "The bitch never took her key back."

I laugh, and it's the first time in weeks I've exercised those muscles.

His features soften as he sweeps his fingers down one cheek. "I have missed that sound."

"Don't go getting all soft on me now, Ares." I gently remove his fingers from my face. "I don't know what your new game is, but I have no desire to play it." Before he can reply, I walk off toward the kitchen to grab a beer.

I move around the living room, chatting to a few people I know while knocking back a few beers and counting down the time until I can leave. Ares is dipping in and out of the room, staying in the shadows, but his eyes rarely stray from mine.

You would have to put a gun up my vajayjay to get me to admit I like his possessive attention. It feels good to have someone in my corner again. Even if that someone has questionable morals and motives.

"Hey." Bree comes up to me the second she sees me in the living room. "How have you been?"

I shrug, knocking back a mouthful of beer as Ares slips back into the room, planting himself in the corner, with a fresh beer in hand and his gaze firmly fixed on me.

"Chad is going crazy you showed up with him," Bree says, sipping a vodka cranberry as she jerks her head in Ares's direction.

"It was a coincidence. Nothing is going on."

"I believe you, but I don't think Chad does."

I turn to face her. "What does it matter? We broke up weeks ago, and he hates my guts. He doesn't get to do this. He knows the kind of person I am. He knows how truly sorry I am for cheating on him. He knows I would not show up with his enemy on my arm even if something was happening between us."

"He's hurting, and he's a man. Emotion and logic don't always cohabit easily in the male mind."

"Isn't that the truth." I spot Toby Salinger watching our interactions like a hawk dissecting his prey.

"How are things with Toby? He's watching us like he has lip-reading ability and he knows everything we are saying."

I haven't forgotten how he leered over me at my initiation.

He's a creep.

Bree turns around and flips him the bird. "He's a prick, and I might have made it worse and slept with him last week." The words rush out like verbal diarrhea.

"Well, that's an unexpected development."

"I was drunk, and in my drunken state, I thought I should sample the goods before I'm forced to purchase them."

"Something tells me that didn't work out quite how you planned."

"It was awful."

I quirk a brow.

"His dick is a beast. Like seriously, it's the biggest cock I have ever seen, and I have seen big cocks. Unfortunately, he also knows what to do with it." She glares at him as she emits these little dreamy sounds, and that is true multitasking talent.

"That sounds positively horrific." I fight a smile.

She looks at me when she has given up giving him the evil eye. "It is. This is a major problem because he has ruined me for all others, and now I can't stop thinking about how hot the sex was, and he fucking knows, and he's all down for a repeat and turning all possessive and shit which is crazy 'cause hello"—she points at herself—" Lust and Envy slut here. It's making my skin crawl, and okay, my lady balls might be salivating at the prospect of round eight, but I refuse to be ruled by my hormones!"

"Breathe, babe. You need to draw air into your lungs." I laugh as she pants while scowling at her fiancé. "Shit, that sounds like a truly terrible problem."

She punches me in the arm. "It is. He's still a giant asshole. His monster cock doesn't magically fix his dysfunctional personality."

"I've missed you," I quietly say.

"Girl, I've missed you too."

We stare at one another.

"I won't ask if I'm forgiven, but could we just hang out?" she asks, hope written all over her pretty face.

I can stay mad at her and cut my nose off to spite my face or find it in my heart to forgive her. She has been a good friend to me, and there were extenuating circumstances. Jase and I are no longer together. The damage is done, and there's no going back. But I can work to repair things with Bree, to rebuild the trust, and I want to. "Yeah, I would really like that."

She squeals, pulling me into a hug before stiffening. "Uh, oh, trouble at nine o'clock."

I whip my head left as Ares approaches like a dark warrior hellbent on whisking me off into the night. "We should go," he gruffly says, shielding me with his large body.

"Why?"

"It's way past your bedtime, and I'm tired." He fakes the worst ever yawn while tucking me under his arm. "Snuggle into my chest, and I'll get us out of here."

"Shit." Bree's expletive confirms Ares strange behavior is an attempt to hide something from me.

"Whatever it is, I'm not hiding from it," I say, shucking out from under his arm.

Chapter Forty-Eight

Ashley

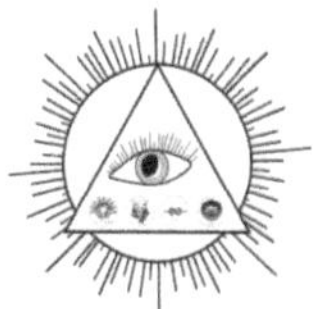

"I can't believe he's gone there," Bree says, staring at the open doorway with her mouth trailing the ground.

"He's an immature punk and predictable as shit." Ares slides his arm protectively around my waist.

I follow their line of sight, already suspecting what I will find. Hot, slicing pain glides through skin and bone, flaying me on the inside as I watch Chad kiss and grope Julia in the hallway.

"I can't say I'm surprised. He watched me fuck his enemy. Now he wants me to see him fuck mine."

"He's an idiot and he was never worthy of you," Ares says. "Say the word, and I'll flatten him. He's been knocking back beers like they're going out of fashion. One punch, and it'll be lights out."

"What is with you?" I yank my hand from his. "Violence is not the answer."

"I'm with Ares on this one." Bree looks over at my step-brother. "How about you throat punch him and I'll kick her in her conniving cunt?"

"Deal."

"No deal," I refute even though it's very tempting. I will adopt the moral high ground and leave with my head held high. I won't let either of them see how much this hurts me. I grab my purse from the end table. "What was it you said to me on the way in?" I ask Ares.

A slow smile spreads over his mouth.

"Chad is a free agent now. He's not doing anything wrong except letting his anger drive poor judgment. I know he can't stand her, and he'll hate himself tomorrow. If he thinks it'll even the score or make him feel better, he'll soon realize it won't."

I turn and kiss Bree on the cheek. "I'll text you tomorrow, and we'll do something."

"I'm proud of you, babe. Maintain your dignity and ignore the bitch."

"That's the plan."

Ares tries to take my hand again, but I shake my head. I'm doing this my way, and I refuse to give Chad any more ammunition. He's making a big mistake. Maybe if he sees I'm not reacting, he might come to his senses and kick her to the curb.

Ares walks by my side as I stride toward the exit. Julia sees me coming and says something to my ex. Chad grabs her boobs, and she giggles while I fight the roll of nausea creeping up my throat. Channeling my inner Harlow Westbrook, I walk confidently to the open doorway as Chad spins Julia around in his arms and throws her over his shoulder. His eyes are rolling back in his head when he turns to look at me. A smirk spreads over his lips as he smacks Julia's ass and moves toward the stairs.

Pain besieges my body, thrashing me from all angles, but I keep a neutral expression on my face as I step into the hallway.

Chad slaps her ass again at the bottom of the stairs, and she squeals and moans, really putting on a show. I don't look at them, walking toward the front door with my game face on and my shoulders back.

"Enjoy my sloppy seconds," Chad shouts as my fingers curl around the door handle. I'm holding my breath and clinging to my sanity by my nails. I need to get out of here before I exhaust the last of my bravery supply.

"Oh, trust me, I plan to," Ares retorts, and I want to smack him in the head.

Of course, he can't follow the advice he dishes out.

"I'd say enjoy mine," he adds, "but you'll find out soon enough she can't suck dick for shit." Ares fondles my ass as I open the door, and I am going to murder him. "Unlike my doll-face who sucks cock like a pro."

I yank him outside before he can do any more damage, slamming the door shut behind us. I glare at him as I rub my throbbing temples.

He arches a brow. "Don't get mad at me for defending your honor."

"You compared me to a prostitute in front of everyone!" I toss back.

"Porn star was more what I had in mind, and I don't see why it's such a big deal." He shrugs.

I cling to the railing and attempt to hurry away from him. It's challenging in these ridiculous heels, so I take them off and rush down the steps in my bare feet.

"Every guy knows that's a compliment."

"How the fuck would you know anyway? I haven't sucked your dick."

A sly smirk washes over his face. "Yet."

"Dream on, asshole."

His eyes fixate on my mouth. "One look at those cock-sucking lips, and a guy can just tell." He adjusts his dick behind his jeans. "I'm already hard just imagining that mouth wrapped around my—"

"Just shut up, Ares." I point my finger in his face. "This all started because of you. If you'd stayed home like I asked, none of this would've happened."

"Bullshit." Scooping me up, he carries me along the sidewalk toward our house.

"Put me down, you ass." I beat on his chest, and I'm sorely tempted to poke his eye out with my spiky shoe.

"You'll cut your feet. For once, let me do something nice for you." He peers into my eyes, and I'm shocked at the sincerity I see radiating back at me. "Please let me take care of you," he adds, lowering his tone.

I'm so shocked at how genuine he is that I stop fighting. I give him a curt nod before wrapping my arms around his neck and burying my face in his chest. He smells nice, but it's not how he smelled the night he pretended to be Jase.

Knowing Ares, he purposely wore Jase's cologne to confuse me. He has a key to their place and could easily have snuck into Jase's bedroom. I can't even find it in me to be mad because I'm so sad. And the dedication he put into the whole ruse is begrudgingly admirable.

A strangled sob slips from my mouth as the weight of everything finally comes crashing down around me. I'm so tired of it all, and I'm so lost and lonely. I'm tired of blocking my feelings and acting strong all the time. Everything in my world has upended, and I'm scared of what my future holds now.

Ares cradles me closer as he wrestles with the key in the lock while silent tears pump out of my eyes.

The alarm pings when we enter, and he punches in the code before setting it on the nighttime setting. There is something so sweet about the way he is looking after me that loosens whatever remaining control I have over my emotions, and the dam breaks. I fall apart in his arms as he carries me up the stairs, sobbing against his chest as weeks of pent-up emotion break free.

I didn't cry after I lost Jase and Chad. I bottled it up inside, knowing it would find an outlet at some point.

I cling to Ares, soaking his shirt as he walks to the top level and heads toward my bedroom. He continues to hold me as he opens my door and steps inside the dark room. With supreme tenderness, he lays me down on the bed. I turn on my side, sobbing into my pillow as I curl into a ball.

My mind loves torturing me, sending visual slideshows of what is most likely happening next door. Every image I have stored in my brain of the guy I gave my virginity and heart to first replays unhelpfully behind my eyes. Yet in this version of my memories, it is Julia Chad is sliding inside. It's her lips he's kissing, her pussy he's devouring, and her ass he's pounding. It's her Jase is joining as he too slips into the bedroom.

My cries grow louder as the bed dips behind me. Ares circles his arms around me, and I lean back into his touch, needing his warmth and the comfort he's offering.

I know I will regret this tomorrow.

That he'll find some way of turning my vulnerability around on me, but tonight I don't care.

I need him because I have never felt more heartbroken or more alone.

"It's okay," he whispers against my neck, his warm breath sending shivers rippling over my skin. "You're going to be okay. He never deserved you, Ashley. Jase didn't either. You were always far too good for them."

I cry harder because it's not true.

We were perfect together.

Until we weren't.

Jase tore apart what we had, and Chad and I took a machete to our relationship together.

Although I was the one who dealt the deathblow—I cheated, and that is unforgivable—Chad is far from innocent of blame. Distance had grown between us from the moment his family's fortunes changed and he made one bad decision after another. His actions derailed his life, yet in those few weeks before we split, he did nothing but turn it around on me. As if it was my fault. He seemed to resent me when all I was trying to do was help. I'm not saying it excuses my cheating. It doesn't. But he gave me no emotional support when Jase and I broke up despite supposedly taking my side.

Tonight confirms it. Chad and I are truly over forever. He won't ever forgive me for sleeping with his enemy, and I will never forgive him for sleeping with mine.

Our joint choices led to this place, and there is no point crying over spilled milk.

It's done, and there is no going back.

That realization lands hard, and my sobs slowly subside as I mourn the ending of my first love. Turning around, I face Ares. Pushing my body up close to his, I gently cup his face. God, he's so gorgeous when he's holding nothing back like now.

I see the full extent of his adoration, and this time I believe it.

Does it excuse his shitty behavior? Nope, but maybe it's time I stopped fighting the feelings I have for him.

"Why did you do it? Just tell me that," I ask.

"It started out as revenge for reasons I will explain if you want to know."

"I do."

He nods. "Okay, I'll tell you. But not now. Now isn't the right time or place, but soon, I promise."

Maybe I'm a gullible fool, but I believe him. "Okay."

"It started as vengeance, but it became so much more." Taking my free hand, he places it over his heart. "You're in here, Ashley." He doesn't often say my full name, but I love hearing it tumble from his lips. "And you were always meant to be mine. *Only* mine." He brushes his lips against my mouth. "Don't ask me how I know, I just do. We were meant to find one another."

"That's some heavy shit for the middle of the night when I'm still nursing a broken heart," I admit, snuggling into his chest.

His chest rumbles with light laughter. "True." He presses a kiss to the top of my head. "Sleep, dollface. I'll be here when you wake."

"Ares." I lift my head and stare at him. "Thank you for being there tonight. Despite what I said, I don't think I would've been brave enough to step up to that door if I'd been alone."

He brushes my pink hair back off my face. "You would have, Ashley, because you are stronger than you know."

My eyes lower to his mouth the same time he leans in, and we move as one, our lips colliding in a slow, sensual, passionate kiss I feel all the way to my toes. His kiss is unhurried and worshipping, and I'm melting against him because it's everything I have been denying myself for months.

I thread my fingers in his silky-soft hair, and he presses his large palm flat against my back, holding me close. He nips at my lips, and his tongue prods at the seam, asking for entry. I don't deny him, readily parting my lips so his tongue can slide inside. I moan into his mouth as every nerve ending in my body sparks to life. He ignites a fire inside me with every expert sweep of his lips and flourish of his tongue, and I have never been kissed like this before.

"That should have been our first kiss," he whispers over my lips when we break apart sometime later.

I nod, fighting a yawn as the emotional trauma of the night finally creeps up on me.

"Sleep, beautiful." He holds me tight, and I rest my face on his chest as I close my eyes. "Tomorrow is a new day."

Chapter Forty-Nine
Ashley

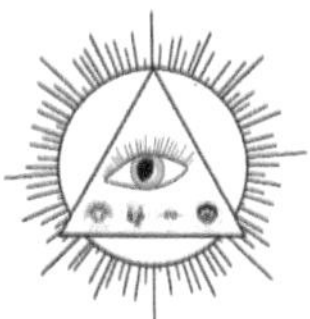

"It's so weird being around the house and not snarking at one another," I tell Bree as we leave the cafeteria on Monday after sharing lunch together. "He keeps grabbing me and kissing me like he's afraid I'm going to disappear on him or something."

"Are you sure you didn't have sex with him again?"

I arch a brow. "I think I'd remember."

"You should just climb back on that horse and fuck him stupid. That's what I'd do."

"Lucky I'm not you then." I sling my bag over my shoulder. "I want to take it slow. I still don't know what this thing is between us, and I'm not ready for a new relationship. I doubt that's even something Ares would want. He doesn't strike me as the relationship kind of guy. Shit is already confusing, and I'm still grieving the guys I lost. I also can't forget the part he played, and there's more I don't know yet. Until then, I don't want to rush into something new and end up making things worse. So, for now I'm happy with the PG kissing."

"Is he a good kisser?" she asks, tossing her empty water bottle in a trash can we pass en route to the library.

I smirk at her. "Do you really need to ask?"

"Damn. You're so screwed."

"Not yet I'm not," I quip.

We separate when we enter the library 'cause we'll get no work done if we are together.

Bree leaves a couple hours later because she has a family dinner to attend, but I stay for another hour before packing up my shit and heading home. I usually stay longer, but tonight I want to get home before Ares and cook him dinner. Not really sure why, but I'm not going to overanalyze it either.

I have only taken three steps away from the entrance when I'm accosted by the next-to-last person I would want to see.

Anita Hoare purposely stands in front of me, blocking my route to the parking lot.

"Move," I demand, planting my disinterested face on.

"It must really kill you to know Julia now has everything that once belonged to you." She grins, like this is the best news ever.

"For starters, I didn't own either guy. That's such a sexist, archaic sentiment, not that I'm surprised it's part of your vocab. Secondly, Julia has shit all. Jase is forced to be with her, and Chad used her to try to make me jealous. She will never have what I had with them because she's an insipid, spineless, selfish, conceited, spoiled bitch, and they could never love someone like her."

I lean down into her face. "Exactly like you. It's why they were so quick to shut you down when you hit on them." Her cheeks turn red. "And finally, it doesn't kill me. I'm getting over them, and I'm moving on." I push her back. "I seriously advise you to do the same because we're not in high school anymore, and the way you lick the ground Julia walks on is pathetic."

"Yeah, we'll see." She waggles her fingers in my face and grins.

I don't know what I said that was so amusing. Weird bitch. Shaking all thoughts of Anita and Julia from my mind, I walk toward the parking lot, eager to get home. Tripping over a loose stone on the sidewalk, I almost face-plant the ground. Glancing down, I see one of my laces is undone. I bend down to tie it when a whistling sound blows over my head, quickly followed by a loud scream.

"Oh my god," a woman shrieks. "She's been shot. Help! My friend has been shot!"

Alarm bells ring in my ears at her words, and I whip my cell out as I crouch down and crawl toward the direction of my car. Panic sluices through my veins as I press Bree's number, willing her to pick up.

A second shot rings out, and I lunge forward on the sidewalk as it whizzes over my head. A car explodes behind me, and I dump my bag and get up, running toward the safety of my car as Bree's line rings out. I am almost to my armored SUV when she picks up, just as pain rips through my skull and I scream, dropping the phone and instantly blacking out.

"We need to move her now," Mom says in a hushed tone as I slowly come to.

"I agree," Jase says, "It's too dangerous in a public hospital. We need to get her to Luminary HQ."

"You heard what the doctor said," Dad says. "He doesn't advise moving her for twenty-four hours. I don't want to risk it."

"Someone just tried to kill our daughter, Douglas." Mom's tone is borderline hysterical as I try to blink my eyes open.

"I am aware, Pamela! But moving her against medical

advice could hurt her. I understand security is a concern, so let's put a guard on the door and one inside the room until we can safely move her."

"That won't stop whoever did this. I'm not sitting around twiddling my thumbs while they try again," Jase snaps, his words laced with concern.

"That's not your decision to make," Dad replies in a snotty tone.

You tell him, Dad.

"You shouldn't be here, Jase," Mom replies. "Nothing has changed in relation to your situation."

I purposely keep my eyes closed now, wanting to listen. They might spill some secrets if they think I'm still sleeping.

"Try keeping me away, Pamela. Go on, I dare you," he sneers. "Someone just took potshots at the woman I love. No one is keeping me away from Ashley right now."

There's a loud noise, and I jolt on the bed as heavy footsteps approach. "Is she okay? What happened?" Ares pants, sounding out of breath. "Jesus, fuck. What happened to her head?"

"You need to leave," Jase says as Mom clasps my hand and says, "Ashley, can you hear me?"

I guess the game is up. I slowly open my eyes, wincing at the stabbing pain in my skull and the harsh bright lights.

"Turn the lights down," Bree says as more footsteps race into the room.

I am pretty sure I must be in the ICU. I'm almost positive they only let two or three visitors in at one time. With the way my head is pounding and my body is aching, I understand why, and I fully support that rule. I'm guessing Luminary influence is at play, and that's why there are no nurses around and my room is crowded with noisy idiots fighting with one another.

"Jase, is she okay?" Chad asks, panic clear in his tone. "The news is all over campus. It said one girl was killed and Ashley was shot. Is that true?"

"What the fuck are you doing here?" Ares says as Mom squeezes my fingers.

"I have more right to be here than you," Chad retorts as I attempt to open my eyes again.

It's less bright this time, but the sharp pain in my head remains.

"I disagree. After the stunt you pulled Saturday night, you have no right being anywhere near Ashley," Ares says.

"Neither of you should be here, and you need to leave now," Jase says.

"I want all of you out because this isn't about you," Dad grits out in a clipped tone.

"Shut the fuck up, all of you," I croak, pushing the words out of my scratchy throat. "You're making my head hurt worse."

The instant silence is golden.

"How do you feel, honey?" Mom asks in a soft voice.

"Like I just got shot." My vision focuses as I look at her. "Is that true? It all happened so fast."

"You were extremely lucky, princess." Dad comes around the other side of my bed. "The shot just grazed your temple."

"You have a bad concussion, and you banged your hip when you fell, but it's just bruised," Mom says. "You'll be sore for a few days, but there is no serious damage."

"Did you see who did this?" Bree asks, coming up alongside me.

I am deliberately not looking at Chad, Jase or Ares.

"No. I had bent down to tie my laces when the first shot was made. That other girl, the one who got hit, that bullet was meant for me."

"We know, princess. The police are canvassing the area, trying to find witnesses who saw where the shots came from,"

Dad adds, throwing a warning look in Chad's and Ares's directions. Meaning The Luminaries are on the case, and they'll have the culprit locked in their basement in no time.

The moments leading up to the shooting come back to me, and I hiss under my breath.

"What?" Jase leans down, putting his obnoxiously gorgeous face in front of mine. "What have you remembered?"

"Anita Hoare," I rasp. "She was there, being annoying on the sidewalk, stopping me from walking to my car."

"She was stalling you," Ares says.

I nod without thinking, almost crying when pain spreads across my skull with the motion. I sink back against my pillow, briefly closing my eyes. "This was Julia," I say after a few beats. "Anita doesn't have the balls to try to take me down or the contacts to make it happen, but Julia does."

Shocked silence rings out for a few seconds.

"This is your fault. Both of you," Ares says, and I don't need to look at him to know he's glaring at Chad and Jase.

"Ashley, you can't accuse your cousin of something like this." Shock splays across Mom's brow. "I know you two have your differences, but she wouldn't do this. She couldn't." The meaning is clear, but Mom can't verbalize it with two plebs in the room.

"Let's go grab some coffees," Dad says to Ares and Chad. "You boys can come with me."

"Fuck no. Take the jock, but I'm staying."

"Ares, please." I plead with my eyes. "Just go with Dad."

Darting forward, he presses a soft kiss to my lips. "I just needed to touch you to know you're okay," he whispers in my ear. "You gave me one hell of a fright, dollface."

"I'm okay. Go sneak me a coffee. You know how I like it."

He places another kiss on my brow before straightening up.

Jase chuckles at the furious expression on Dad's face.

"I warned you she was off limits," Dad hisses as he ushers the two guys out of the room.

"Ashley," Chad calls out, twisting away from Dad and staring at me with the most tormented expression. "I didn't fuck her. I never could. Not when I'm still so in love with you."

If that's true, it means he deliberately set it up to look that way to hurt me. He purposely planned it to inflict the worst pain, and I'm not sure I can ever forgive him. I know I hurt him deeply, but I didn't plan it, and I tried—albeit weakly—to stop it from happening. He can't say the same.

Mom mutters something I can't hear under her breath.

Ares scowls at Chad as Dad yanks them both out of the room.

"When did that happen?" Mom slants me with a knowing look.

"I'm not discussing it now."

"Temptress." Jase occupies the space vacated by my father, threading his fingers through mine.

"You lost the right to call me that," I say, immediately extracting my fingers from his.

Bree slants a sympathetic look in her brother's direction, and if I find out she has been keeping other things from me, our friendship is forever dead.

Mom glares at Jase, furiously shaking her head. "Need I remind you of the danger?"

"What don't I know?" I ask, my blurry gaze bouncing between the three of them. My eyelids are growing heavy, and I'm fighting to stay awake.

"It's nothing for you to worry about now," Jase says, softening his voice and his expression. "I'm glad you're okay." He lifts my hand to his lips, placing a kiss on my knuckles. "I almost crashed my car when Bree called."

For the second time, I pull my hand back, and he frowns.

He doesn't get to touch me at will anymore. Me being shot doesn't change what happened between us.

"Tell me about it," Bree says. "I aged twenty years in five seconds when I heard your scream and then the line went dead."

"We need to talk before they get back," Mom says. "Ashley, that's a serious accusation to make against Julia. Especially without proof. I'm not saying I don't believe you, but why would she try to kill you?"

"Because she hates me, and she wants to permanently remove me as her competition."

"Competition for what? She has both your guys, or did I pick that up wrong?"

"Thanks for the compassion, Mom," I say with sarcasm underscoring my tone.

"She most definitely does not," Jase replies, growling at Mom before he turns to me. "I haven't touched her. You're still the only woman I love."

"Okay, enough. Honestly, your love life gives me a headache, Ashley."

It's official. My mother is an unsympathetic bitch.

"I agree Julia has motive, and she's vindictive enough to want to take you out, but—"

"She wouldn't fail." Jase completes Bree's train of thought.

"She wouldn't. This was amateur hour. A professional would not have missed the first shot."

"Maybe it was a warning? All I know is Anita was there for a reason."

"We need to pick that girl up," Mom says.

"I'll handle it." Jase sits down in the chair by my bed. "I'll get the truth out of her."

His meaning seems obvious, and I glare at him. "Really, Jase? You're going to seduce that bitch?"

"Who said anything about seduction? You couldn't pay me to touch that hag. Torture is more what I have in mind."

Relief seeps out of my pores. "Oh, very well then. You may proceed."

"The decision has been taken from our hands now anyway," Mom says, glancing at her cell. "Your uncle has arranged transportation for us to HQ. Their hospital facility is the best in the world, and he wants you checked out by our doctors. We're to be ready in twenty minutes."

"I don't want to go to HQ," I say over a yawn. "I want to stay here."

"Not an option. We can't ignore a Luminary directive."

"Of course, we can't," I mutter, fighting sleep.

"I'll explain to Doug and get rid of Chad and Ares," Jase says, standing. He leans down and kisses me before I can stop him. "I love you."

I don't say it back. He doesn't get a pardon just because I got shot. He has still been sleeping with other women behind my back, and there is no scenario where I could ever accept that.

Accepting I won't be returning the sentiment, Jase turns and exits the room.

Mom just shakes her head as she leaves to go sort out the discharge paperwork.

Bree sits down beside me. "Your boy drama is the best entertainment. We should pitch it for a reality show."

"No thanks. My current reality is not fit for public consumption."

"Truth." Bree glances at the door, chewing on the corner of her lip.

"Spit it out."

"I shouldn't burden you with this when you're lying in a hospital bed after getting shot."

"I'm not going to die, and my injuries aren't serious. No more secrets means no more secrets, Bree, so tell me."

"My guy found something on Hera and Ares. Chad was right all along."

Pain dances along my skull, and it's an effort to remain invested in this conversation when all I want to do is sleep. "In what way?"

"His dad was set up, Ash, and it was Hera and Ares who did it. They planted evidence of sex trafficking on him. Jasper Baldwin was sent down on bogus charges. That man died in prison for a crime he didn't commit."

Twenty minutes later, we are on our way in a souped-up black camper van that's like a luxury ambulance with ample guest space. A security vehicle travels behind us with four Luminary peeps wearing guns. I feel like a bona fide VIP. Mom and Dad are talking in hushed tones at the back of the vehicle while I'm drifting in and out of sleep as the pain meds start to take effect. A drip is attached to my hand, administering saline and morphine, and a nurse monitors the dosage and my vitals while Bree dozes and Jase just stares at me when he thinks I'm not noticing.

"You're like Creepy McCreep," I mumble, stifling a yawn as I squint at him through narrowed eyes. "Stop staring at me."

"I've missed looking at your beautiful face."

Touching the large white bandage now wrapped around my head, I shoot him a wry smile. "Pretty sure beautiful is the last thing I look right now."

"Pretty sure that's an impossibility." He dazzles me with a smile, and I return it until I remember.

"Why are you here, Jase? This doesn't change anything."

He glances over his shoulder, ensuring Bree is asleep and my parents are distracted in heated conversation. He leans in and whispers in my ear. "I haven't slept with anyone else. It was a setup to make you think I was having sex with Meredith, but I wasn't. She's actually one of us. She owed me a favor. I made sure Julia overheard my plans for the night, knowing she couldn't resist rubbing your nose in it. The other women you saw me disappearing with at parties were all for show. I didn't touch them. I swear."

"I don't understand."

"They forced me to toe the line, baby. They made me break things off with you." Pain is etched across his face. "They hurt Nix and Creed as a warning, and they have implemented a new rule for children conceived by Luminaries outside of arranged marriage. They are establishing a new orphanage. They would have taken our child, and nothing would have changed. We are still being forced to marry other people."

"I don't have the brainpower to comprehend all this right now," I say in a sleepy voice as I'm slowly dragged back under.

"It's okay. Sleep, baby. We can talk later. I just need you to know I have remained faithful to you."

I want to ask how this is possible when it's his Lust and Envy responsibility. And what about those thirteen women he said he slept with? But I don't get the chance before my eyelids droop, and I fall asleep.

I'm trapped in the middle of a nightmare. Screaming and crying rings out around me as I'm forcibly yanked from my bed. A stinging pain rips across the back of my hand, and my limbs feel like Jell-O as I'm lifted over a shoulder. Bree screams. Jase roars at someone, and Mom is crying.

My eyes blink open for a few seconds. The back of the van is wide-open, the doors busted like force was used to get inside. The kind nurse lies in a pool of blood on the floor amid overturned furniture and medical equipment.

My eyes shutter again, and everything is fading. I'm jostled from side to side, and it drags me from slumber. A groan slips from my mouth as my eyes pop open again.

It's not a nightmare.

Just another horrific development in my reality.

"No," I whimper, tears filling my eyes as I watch a man in a black cloak force my father to his knees and shoot him in the skull. "No!" I shout, my voice hoarse and dry as Dad slumps sideways to the ground, blood leaking from the round hole in his head.

Mom screams and then goes silent. I try to lift my head, but it feels too heavy.

I'm placed in a new van and thrown down on a cot, and cold fingers take my hand. There's a sharp pinch and then I feel the cool liquid entering my veins. I try to fight slumber as it creeps up on me, my eyes opening and closing as I watch them load Mom, Bree, and Jase into seats in the back. They strap them in. They are all unconscious, their heads lolling forward.

As the doors slowly close, I spot more commotion outside, and my heart pounds against my rib cage as I watch other men in black cloaks overpower Chad and Ares. They must have followed us. Someone stabs them in the neck with a needle, and they both crumple within seconds.

Pain tightens my chest as I watch them get shoved into a black SUV before the doors on our van are closed, and the vehicle moves forward.

"That's it, sweetie," an unfamiliar woman says, patting my hand with her cold fingers as my eyes shutter. "Go to sleep."

Chapter Fifty

Ashley

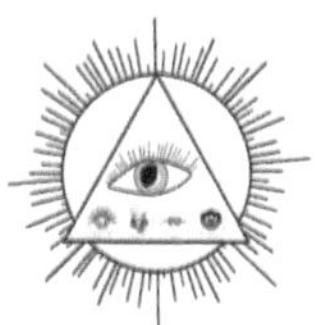

When I come to the next time, I'm in the place that haunts my dreams.

The crypt.

"Ah, finally." A man walks toward me through my blurry vision, leaning down to stare into my face. I'm disorientated from the drugs, so I don't place him at first. "How are you feeling, darling?" he asks, brushing knotty pink hair back from my face.

"Do you have to fuss over her?" Julia says from somewhere in the background. "I don't see the point when she's—"

"Quiet," the man barks, lifting a straw to my mouth. He holds it there while I take a few sips, and gradually my vision becomes clearer.

I take note of my surroundings as I drink the ice-cold water. I'm in a leather recliner that fully supports my sore, bandaged head. A blanket is draped over my lap, and it covers my legs. I don't appear to be restrained, but why would I be when I'm pretty sure I could barely stand if I tried. "Why am I here?" I ask, hating how raspy my throat sounds.

"I am sorry for the ambush, but it was necessary." He dangles the cup with the straw in front of my face. "Would you like some more?"

"No." The pain in my head is more of a fuzzy, dull ache now, thanks to the meds, but I'm still groggy. I glance to my right, and my blood pressure skyrockets. Mom, Bree, and Jase are all tied to wooden chairs. Their hands and feet are restrained with zip ties, and their mouths are covered with industrial duct tape. Jase looks at me with obvious concern flickering in his eyes. Mom's head is lolling forward, and she's moaning behind her mouth covering. Blood coats her pretty face, and splatters of it have dripped down onto the front of her white blouse.

"What is going on?" Blood pounds in my ears, and adrenaline surges through my veins. "Why is my mom all bloody and bruised?"

"Your mother has had that coming for a long time," the man says, his jaw tensing. "And that is only the start of her punishment if she refuses to cooperate."

There's a sadistic sheen behind his eyes as he talks about her, and fear ricochets up my spine. The events back on the road return, and I'm struggling to breathe. Tears prick my eyes. "Dad!" I cry out, praying the memory replaying in my brain was just a bad nightmare, but he's not here. Ignoring the pain, I angle my head and look around. I don't see Ares or Chad either. Did I imagine that, or was it real?

"Yes, darling?" The man in front of me looks pleased as he stares into my eyes.

Why is he looking at me like that? Now I can see his features more clearly, I recognize him. I know who he is, and it does nothing to ease my anxiety. "You're Rhett Carter," I whisper, working hard to curtail my panic. "The Greed & Gluttony Luminary."

"I am." He beams at me before leaning in and kissing my brow.

He's staring at me so strangely, and it's creeping me out. I squirm in my chair, wondering if I'm suffering from hallucinations. My limbs are heavy, my head is foggy, and I'm struggling to separate reality from fiction. "Where are my dad, Ares, and Chad?"

He doesn't like my question, his lips pulling tight as he straightens up. "If you mean Douglas Shaw, he's dead, but he's not your father. I am."

"What?" I blurt through my tears, hurting and confused.

"Douglas Shaw's blood doesn't flow through your veins. Mine does."

My gaze automatically seeks Jase's, and I'm sure the shock mirrored on his face is replicated on mine.

"You're lying."

"No, my sweet child. I'm not." Opening up a laptop, he places it on my lap over the blanket. Pulling up a report, he enlarges the screen and taps at the details. "This is a blood test result from the blood taken the night before your initiation ceremony." Walking over to Mom, he grips her chin and arches her head back. "Your mother was still trying to deny me the truth, swapping out the vials when she thought I wouldn't notice. But I have suspected for some time that she tricked me when you were born, and I was right." He fixes her with a venomous look. "I have actually known the truth for a while, but it was nice to get it officially verified."

One of Mom's eyes is swollen and sealed shut, congealed with blood, and it looks nasty. Her other eye is fine, and she glares at Rhett Carter like he's the devil incarnate.

He may very well be.

Mom tries to speak over the tape covering her mouth, but it comes out muffled.

"I don't understand." I lift a heavy arm to brush the tears from my cheeks as he sets the laptop down on a small table.

"Your tramp of a mother has lied to everyone for years," Julia says, coming up behind Rhett Carter and wrapping her arms around his middle. "She was supposed to marry Rhett, but instead she and my father concocted a plan to pass her unborn child off as Doug Shaw's child. All to avoid fulfilling her duties. She made my love a laughingstock, and now it's time you all pay the price."

Bree shouts something behind the tape. We can't hear her, but the hostility she feels for Julia is clear.

Rhett looks aggravated as he removes Julia's arms from around his torso and levels her with a glare. "Did I give you permission to speak? This is not your story to share." He slaps her across the face. "Don't interrupt me again."

Hurt shuttles across Julia's face as she lifts her hand to her cheek. There's a noticeable handprint on her skin. "I'm sorry, *Daddy*. It won't happen again," she says in that fake whiny voice she is fond of. The way she calls him Daddy and the adoring expression on her face make me want to puke.

Rhett grabs her shoulders and viciously shakes her. Losing her balance, she falls flat on her ass. Thankfully, her dress doesn't ride up this time. Not sure I could handle that a second time. "Do not call me that," he instructs, looming over her with a dark look.

"But you like it." Julia pouts, and her lower lip wobbles.

"Time and place, child." I watch a veil shroud his angry face, replaced with a neutral expression. He helps her to her feet before forcing her into a chair. "Sit down and stay quiet, like a good little girl."

Bree and I exchange looks. Whatever fucked-up relationship they have, it's obviously not healthy or equal.

Rhett walks over to Mom and rips the tape off her mouth in

one fast yank. "Tell her. Tell our daughter what you did." He turns her chair around so she's facing me. "Ashley deserves to know the truth."

"Fuck you, Rhett." Mom holds her head up high even as he raises his hand to slap her.

Her head whips back, and blood flies from her mouth as I cry out. "Please don't hurt her!"

Rhett's jaw clenches as he removes a gun from behind his back. "I have never wanted to hurt your mother, but she makes it so hard to be nice to her."

"That's because you're a monster," Mom says. "You beat me and raped me. I didn't want my child anywhere near a cruel bastard like you."

He puts the gun in her mouth, and I scream.

Julia laughs.

"I know you brought us here for a reason," I say, and it takes effort to sound calm. "Whatever it is you want of me, it won't happen if you kill my mother."

It won't happen, period, because this psycho has already killed my father. Pain stabs me through the heart, and tears flood my eyes again. But I purposely push all thoughts of Dad aside for now because I need to keep my wits about me. Something that is already challenging in my injured, drugged-up state.

"I don't want to kill her, Ashley." He strokes the gun along my mother's cheek. "But I won't tolerate her insubordination or her disrespect. She has disrespected me enough."

"Mom." I turn beseeching eyes on her. "Think of Emilie and Richard. They need you. I do too. Please just tell the truth."

"Explain to our daughter how you denied her her birthright," Rhett says, calmly rubbing the gun back and forth across Mom's face.

Mom lifts her head and looks at me with a glazed expression. "I was betrothed to Rhett from age four. By the time I started Lowell U, I was already madly in love with Richard, but he was promised to another." She glances between me and Jase. "A lot like you two."

Julia scoffs. "I'm sick of hearing about Ash and Jase." She inspects her fingernails. "It's tiring."

Rhett drills a look at her, and Julia lifts her chin and smiles at him like a lovesick puppy. "Continue, Pamela," he says, keeping his gaze focused on my cousin. "My whore won't interrupt you again, isn't that right, Julia?"

"Yes, *Daddy*." She smiles sweetly at him while parting her legs.

Jase and I lock gazes, and I know he's thinking the same thing I am. We were damn fools not to follow Julia. If we had, we might have discovered she was fucking Carter and realized they were playing some angle.

Rhett ignores her, turning back to Mom. "Keep going."

Mom shoots him a poisonous look before returning her focus to me. "When Rhett found out I was seeing Richard behind his back, he beat and raped me." She visibly gulps. "I tried to report it, but his father, who was the Greed & Gluttony Luminary back then, got wind of it, and he threatened to kill me. It's against the rules to rape any woman from a Luminary family even if that woman is your fiancée. Rhett would have most likely been stripped of his heir title." Her tongue darts out, sliding over her split lip. "When I discovered I was pregnant, I knew it was his child because Richard and I always used protection and the dates aligned." She gulps anxiously. "His father kidnapped me before I could tell anyone."

"What?" Shock splays across Rhett's face, and it's evident this is news to him.

"He violated me for days in a room where my mother's

corpse lay rotting on the floor. He had murdered her as a threat." Emotion splays across her face. "It wasn't necessary. I would have agreed to complete secrecy to keep you protected and to avoid marrying his son."

Rhett barks out a laugh, sounding more and more psychotic. "That crazy bastard. He's lucky he's dead."

"He was protecting you," Mom snaps. "He knew the baby I was carrying would prove your treachery, so he ensured my silence. It was his suggestion I find another man to claim ownership of my child, and he helped me and James to doctor the medical reports when Ashley was born."

"He still should have told me." Grabbing Mom's face, he leans down and kisses her blood-tinged lips. "All this time I blamed you." He slaps her across the face. "You're still not blameless, but this helps, Pamela." He kisses her again as she stares straight ahead. "Good girl for telling the truth."

"You got what you wanted. Now let us go." I know he won't, but I've got to try.

"You are very beautiful, Ashley," he says, ignoring my request. He brushes his fingers across my face. "Intelligent too. It pleases me."

This guy is seriously insane.

He smiles in a creepy way as he continues caressing my cheek, and I want to tell him to fuck off, but he's unhinged, and I don't want to set him off. "You look just like my younger daughter. She's going to be so excited to meet her new sister."

"Wait." Julia bolts upright in her chair. "What?"

"Julia." Rhett turns his gun in her direction. "What did I tell you!" he roars. "You are getting on my very last nerve. Just shut the fuck up. Finger your cunt. It'll help to distract you."

"As you wish, my love." Julia hikes her dress up to her hips, exposing her bare pussy, because she doesn't seem to believe in underwear, moaning as she runs a finger up and down her slit.

"You foolish girl." Mom shakes her head as she looks at her niece. "What have you done?"

"What have I done?" Julia screeches. She stops fingering herself and sits forward in her chair, glowering at Mom. "I have done what I needed to do to be a person of importance in our world. You were too stupid to see the opportunity you were granted." She casts a sneering look in my direction. "You should have just aborted the bitch and married Rhett, but your loss is my gain."

"You are clearly delusional if you truly believe that, and your father will not tolerate this betrayal."

"My father means nothing to me!" she yells. "Nothing is ever good enough for him—no matter how hard I try. Rhett has nurtured what my father was too blind to see." She tilts her head and smirks at me. "James is going down for the part he played in this subterfuge. When the Board discovers how you all conspired to hide Rhett's child from him, you will die."

"He raped me," Mom says. "Or didn't you listen to that part?"

"It will be your word against his, and who do you think they'll believe? There is nothing wrong with a man knocking his fiancée up. There was no reason for you to do what you did, and you're going down for it. You should have just married him." She leans back, her fingers returning to her pussy as she grins. "When my love is Lord of The Luminaries, I will rule as the Sloth Luminary in my own right." She shoots Jase a venomous look. "I will never bow at your feet or play second fiddle to you. I will be in charge, and you will do as you're told."

"You're even more crazy than I realized," I say. "No powerful man will ever put you in charge. I don't know what you were promised, but it's obvious to anyone with more than two brain cells between their ears that you have been played."

"You don't know what you're talking about! *Daddy* loves me, don't you, Rhetty baby?"

Rhetty baby looks close to strangling his love.

I wouldn't object if he did.

"You're such a dumb bitch, Ashley. I've been spying on you for years. As soon as Rhett realized the uncanny resemblance between you and Paisley, he knew for sure Pamela had lied to him. I took your hairbrush so he could prove it with a DNA test, and then we waited patiently until the time was ready to strike. Now you will die, just like poor Doug and soon-to-be unalived Pamela and James."

"You stupid girl." Mom shakes her head. "He has no intention of killing Ashley or telling anyone she is his daughter. If that were the case, he would have done it the moment he made the discovery." She eyeballs Rhett. "He can't claim her as his without the truth coming out. It's too risky, so what is this about?"

"All in good time, Pamela." He pats her on the head like she's a dog.

"You were the reason behind the initiation and how fast it was pushed through," I surmise.

"He needs you to be official for whatever he has planned," Mom says, musing aloud.

"Don't be ridiculous," Julia shouts, growing aggravated. "Rhett doesn't need her, and he's not going to claim her because she's filius nullius, and she's less than useless. Killing her in front of you will be the ultimate punishment. Then he'll let you live, bringing you to the brink of death over and over until you're begging him to murder you." She rubs her hands with glee.

Jase's chair rattles as he moves around in it, trying to get free, shouting behind his tape as he stares at me with mounting horror.

"Relax, son." Rhett plants a hand on his shoulder. "I brought you all here for a reason, and it wasn't to kill you, your sister, my daughter, or her mother."

"What?" Julia hops up, practically spitting blood. "What do you mean? You said she had to die. That they all had to die for betraying you."

"I lied," Rhett says. "And you've outlived your usefulness." Raising the gun, he pulls the trigger and shoots her.

Julia stumbles back, clutching her stomach as blood oozes out between her fingers. "What are you doing?" Horror sweeps over her features. "I love you. We were going to rule together."

"I was using you, Julia. That was never going to happen. You're way too weak and annoying. I certainly wasn't going to do it after you shot at my daughter and almost killed her."

Julia's eyes pop wide.

"You're a fool if you think I didn't realize you set that up. I have listened to your jealous rantings for years. It's why I fed you a steady dose of lies and told you what you wanted to hear. I would never kill my beautiful daughter." He cups my face, and I feel like hurling. "You were smart enough to know you couldn't kill her. I know you did it to accelerate this process because you were tired of waiting. You wanted me to believe she's in danger and force me to push the button before I was ready. Nevertheless, you may have done me a favor, so I won't prolong this."

Pointing the gun, he pumps bullets into her body, showing no remorse or emotion of any kind. Her body violently jerks before she falls to the floor. Rhett empties the chamber in her skull, destroying her face, as we all stare at him in shock.

"You can't kill an heir," I blurt, knowing it's one of their most sacred rules because it was drummed into me at HQ.

"You can when she tries to kill a first daughter. Though I can't admit that yet, unfortunately. We need to time your reveal for the perfect moment." He grins and waggles his brows while continuing to cup my face and stare at me like a creep. "She has always been unhinged and extremely jealous of you. When her shooting attempt failed, she orchestrated that ambush on the road. She was behind the killing of your precious father and a few unfortunate innocents. She came here today to kill all of you. Luckily, I was here, praying in our ancestors' room, and I was able to stop her. Her killing was purely self-defense. I know you'll all relay the same facts."

My God, he's as crazy as she was.

"Why would we verify your version of events?" Mom says, looking hugely troubled.

"You will do that and more," he calmly replies, finally releasing my face. "You were all brought here today because you are important to my plan. Cooperate and you'll get to live the life you want to lead. Ashley, you can marry Jase. Pamela, I'll let your lying, scheming ass live a long and happy life with Richard and your cute baby daughter, and you, Breanna, you get to kill that prick Salinger. I have a much better husband in mind for you."

"You murdered my father in cold blood right in front of me." I narrow my eyes at him. "Why would I do anything for you?"

He grips my chin as a muscle clenches in his jaw. "*I'm* your father, Ashley. That man had to die. It was the consequence of the part he played in deceiving me. As for why you will cooperate, I will give you back the birthright you were denied. Together, you and Jase will control the Sloth Luminary after I have James Manford removed for his duplicity. You will rule under my supervision, of course."

So, it's a hostile takeover of the Sloth Luminary, and Jase and I are to be his puppets. Julia's Lord of The Luminaries statement is making more sense now. This is a power play. Rhett Carter wants to hold the ultimate control.

He tips my chin up higher, and his dead eyes pin mine in place. "In return for your cooperation, I promise I will not kill your mother or your little sister, and I will guarantee my wife doesn't kill her new pet."

"New pet?" I whisper, wondering what fresh hell is about to be unleashed.

"He will be kept alive so long as you all cooperate." He lets his gaze roam the room before grabbing the laptop again. "Refuse and I'll give the order to kill him. Not before my wife has had her fun with him though." His devilish grin sends ice shooting through my veins as he turns the screen around so we can all see.

All the blood drains from my face when the screen loads, showing a dark-haired woman dressed in bondage leather with a long whip in her hand. She blows kisses at the screen toward her husband before the camera pans out, displaying the large windowless room.

On either side of the drab green walls are a number of large cages. Inside each one is a naked man wearing a collar. The camera moves slowly throughout the room, and I grow sicker with each passing second.

Some of the men are emaciated and so thin you can see their ribs protruding through flesh. Others have cuts, bruises, and various marks all over their bodies. A few are asleep, curled up on the floor, their limbs cramped in the small space. One man is lapping spilled water from the soiled floor of his cage, and another has his hands tied behind his back while his face is buried in a bowl of sludge that looks like it might be dog food.

A strangled gasp escapes my throat when the camera swings to the end cage and the newest prisoner. Chad is naked and unconscious, his body crammed behind the bars at an awkward angle. Rhett's wife slides her hand into the cage to caress Chad's thigh before her fingers wrap around his flaccid cock and she starts stroking him.

Bile swims up my throat at the violation and the realization of the hell he's about to endure. I squeeze my eyes shut, unable to bear witness to his assault.

"Seen enough?" Rhett asks, and I nod.

When I open my eyes, the last thing I see is Chad's terrified gaze staring back at me before the feed shuts down.

I clasp a trembling hand over my mouth as angry tears form in Bree's eyes. Mom just looks numb. Jase's expression is murderous, but I spot fear for his friend too.

"Now, do I have your attention?" Rhett asks.

"Yes." The word emerges in an anguished whisper.

"Are you going to cooperate?"

It doesn't matter how things are between us. Chad got caught up in this mess because of his association with me. This psycho has some twisted plan he needs us for. I don't have all the facts, but it doesn't matter. I'll do what I can to protect Chad, and Ares too because I know Rhett took him as well. My stepbrother's fate also lies in our hands.

There is no hesitation because there is only one answer. "Yes," I say. "I will do whatever you want."

"That's my girl," he says, petting my hair. "Now, let me tell you my plan."

TO BE CONTINUED

Dirty Crazy Bad Book Two is available now in e-book, paperback and audiobook.

Type this link into your browser to download the bonus chapter - https://bit.ly/DCB1BS

In the secret society of The Luminaries, no sin will go unpunished...

The Greed & Gluttony Luminary has trapped us into executing his evil plans, and it seems we have little option but to agree. Carter has orchestrated Chad's kidnapping, and he holds my mom's life in his hands.

Then he drops a game-changer

We must play our parts—or at least look like we are—because the fate of our loved ones, and the world at large, depends upon it. There is no choice.

It's a delicate balancing act, with many obstacles and no guarantee of success. Carter has spent years planning his takeover and knowing who to trust is impossible.

Teamwork is the only way we can defeat him. But that is challenging when relationships are fractured, the guys are sworn enemies, and loyalties have been pushed to their limits.

It's up to me to make this work, so I will push my grief aside to be there for Ares, Jase, and Chad.

Rhett Carter cannot become Lord of the Luminaries and we're the only ones that can stop him.

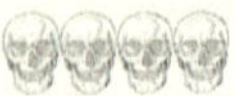

Available now in e-book, paperback and audiobook.

CLAIM YOUR FREE EBOOK – ONLY AVAILABLE TO NEWSLETTER SUBSCRIBERS!

The boy who broke my heart is now the man who wants to mend it.

Jared was my everything until an ocean separated us and he abandoned me when I needed him most.

He forgot the promises he made.

Forgot the love he swore was eternal.

It was over before it began.

Now, he's a hot commodity, universally adored, and I'm the woman no one wants.

Pining for a boy who no longer exists is pathetic. Years pass, men come and go, but I cannot move on.

Tell it To My Heart

I didn't believe my fractured heart and broken soul could endure any more pain. Until Jared rocks up to the art gallery where I work, with his fiancée in tow, and I'm drowning again.

Seeing him brings everything to the surface, so I flee. Placing distance between us again, I'm determined to put him behind me once and for all.

Then he reappears at my door, begging me for another chance.

I know I should turn him away.

Try telling that to my heart.

This angsty, new adult romance is a FREE full-length ebook, exclusively available to newsletter subscribers. Type this link into your browser to claim your free copy: https://dl.bookfunnel.com/521dpwbcnl

About the Author

Siobhan Davis is a *USA Today, Wall Street Journal*, and Amazon Top 5 bestselling romance author. **Siobhan** writes emotionally intense stories with swoon-worthy romance, complex characters, and tons of unexpected plot twists and turns that will have you flipping the pages beyond bedtime! She has sold over 2 million books, and her titles are translated into several languages.

Prior to becoming a full-time writer, Siobhan forged a successful corporate career in human resource management.

She lives in the Garden County of Ireland with her husband and two sons.

You can connect with Siobhan in the following ways:

Website: www.siobhandavis.com
Facebook: AuthorSiobhanDavis
Instagram: @siobhandavisauthor
Tiktok: @siobhandavisauthor
Email: siobhan@siobhandavis.com

Books by Siobhan Davis

KENNEDY BOYS SERIES

Upper Young Adult/New Adult Contemporary Romance

Finding Kyler

Losing Kyler

Keeping Kyler

The Irish Getaway

Loving Kalvin

Saving Brad

Seducing Kaden

Forgiving Keven

Summer in Nantucket

Releasing Keanu

Adoring Keaton

Reforming Kent

Moonlight in Massachusetts

****

STAND-ALONES

New Adult Contemporary Romance

Inseparable

Incognito

When Forever Changes

No Feelings Involved

Still Falling for You

Second Chances Box Set

Holding on to Forever

Always Meant to Be

Tell It to My Heart

The One I Want

Reverse Harem Romance

Surviving Amber Springs

Dark Mafia Romance

Vengeance of a Mafia Queen

***

RYDEVILLE ELITE SERIES

Dark High School Romance

Cruel Intentions

Twisted Betrayal

Sweet Retribution

Charlie

Jackson

Sawyer

*The Hate I Feel^*

Drew

MAZZONE MAFIA SERIES

Dark Mafia Romance

Condemned to Love

Forbidden to Love

Scared to Love

Mazzone Mafia: The Complete Series

***

THE ACCARDI TWINS

Dark Mafia Romance

*CKONY #1^*

*CKONY #2^*

***

THE SAINTHOOD (BOYS OF LOWELL HIGH)

Dark HS Reverse Harem Romance

Resurrection

Rebellion

Reign

Revere

The Sainthood: The Complete Series

DIRTY CRAZY BAD DUET

Dark College Reverse Harem Romance

Dirty Crazy Bad - A Prequel Short Story

Dirty Crazy Bad # 1

Dirty Crazy Bad #2

****

ALL OF ME DUET

Angsty New Adult Romance

Say I'm The One

Let Me Love You

Hold Me Close

All of Me: The Complete Series

****

ALINTHIA SERIES

Upper YA/NA Paranormal Romance/Reverse Harem

The Lost Savior

The Secret Heir

The Warrior Princess

The Chosen One

*The Rightful Queen^*

SAVEN SERIES

Young Adult Science Fiction/Paranormal Romance

Saven Deception

Logan

Saven Disclosure

Saven Denial

Saven Defiance

Axton

Saven Deliverance

Saven: The Complete Series

^Release date to be confirmed

www.ingramcontent.com/pod-product-compliance
Lightning Source LLC
Chambersburg PA
CBHW030341310726
48979CB00001B/138

* 9 7 8 1 9 5 9 1 9 4 2 8 6 *